Where on Earth

THE UNREAL AND THE REAL

Selected Stories of Ursula K. Le Guin

VOLUME 1
Where on Earth

The right of Ursula K. Le Guin to be identified as the author
of this work has been asserted by her in accordance with
the Copyright, Designs and Patents Act 1988.

First published in Great Britain in 2014
by Gollancz
An imprint of the Orion Publishing Group
Orion House, 5 Upper St Martin's Lane,
London WC2H 9EA
An Hachette UK Company

This edition published in Great Britain in 2014
by Gollancz

5 7 9 10 8 6

A CIP catalogue record for this book
is available from the British Library

ISBN 978 1 473 20283 2

Printed and bound in Great Britain by Clays Ltd, Elcograf S.p.A.

The Orion Publishing Group's policy is to use papers that
are natural, renewable and recyclable products and made
from wood grown in sustainable forests. The logging and
manufacturing processes are expected to conform to the
environmental regulations of the country of origin.

www.ursulakleguin.com
www.orionbooks.co.uk
www.gollancz.co.uk

Contents

Introduction	vii
Brothers and Sisters	1
A Week in the Country	37
Unlocking the Air	59
Imaginary Countries	73
The Diary of the Rose	83
Direction of the Road	107
The White Donkey	115
Gwilan's Harp	119
May's Lion	127
Buffalo Gals, Won't You Come Out Tonight	135
Horse Camp	165
The Water Is Wide	171
The Lost Children	183
Texts	185
Sleepwalkers	189
Hand, Cup, Shell	199
Ether, Or	233
Half Past Four	249

Introduction

I begged people—editors, friends, third cousins once removed—to help me select stories for this collection, but nobody would. So all the credit for good choices and all the blame for bad ones is mine. If something you rightfully expected to find here isn't here, I'm sorry. I had to leave out a lot of stories, because I've written a lot of them.

The first way I found to reduce the mob to a manageable size was: limit it to short stories. No novellas—even though the novella is my favorite story-form, a lovely length, in which you can do just about what a novel does without using all those words. But each novella would crowd out three, four, five short stories. So they all had to be shut out, tearfully.

There were still way too many stories, so I had to make arbitrary restrictions. I mostly avoided stories closely tied to novels, set on Gethen or on Anarres, etc.—and stories forming an integral part of story-suites, where the pieces are linked by characters, setting, and chronology, forming an almost-novelistic whole. But "May's Lion" is closely tied to *Always Coming Home*, and three of the stories from *Orsinian Tales* form a loose, many-decade sort of suite. . . . Oh well. Consistency is a virtue until it gets annoying.

So there I was with enough stories, still, to make a book about the size of the *Shorter Oxford Dictionary*. I therefore developed extremely scientific and methodical criteria for my choices.

The first criterion was: Do I like the story?

The answer was almost invariably Yes, so it wasn't much of a criterion. I refined it to: Do I really like the story a lot? That worked better. It resulted in a very large pile of stories I liked a lot.

I then exercised the next criterion: How well would this story work with all the others? which was very difficult to put into operation, but did eliminate some. And by then a further principle of selection had appeared as a question: Should I put a story in this collection because I think it has been overshadowed, has received less attention than it maybe deserved?

That's a tricky call. Luck, fashion, literary awards, and other uncontrollable factors play a part in when and whether a story gets noticed. The only near certainty is that the more often it's reprinted, the more often it will be reprinted. Familiarity sells. "Nine Lives" was republished more often than any of my other stories for years, until "The Ones Who Walk Away from Omelas" (after a slowish start despite winning the Hugo Award) took a handy lead and is still galloping happily along like Seabiscuit.

I did decide to include some stories partly because I wanted to bring them back into the light. Most of them, but not all, are in this first volume.

And here we arrive at the next choice I had to make, once I had chosen all the stories I wanted in the collection. They were to go in two volumes. How should I divide them?

At first I thought I should simply put them in chronological order as written. I tried it, and didn't like the effect. I ended up sorting them into the two parts I call *Where on Earth* and *Outer Space, Inner Lands*.

I think the two titles are sufficiently descriptive and need no further explanation. Some people will identify the first volume as "mundane" and the second as "science fiction," but they will be wrong. All the science-fiction stories are in the second volume, but not all the stories in the second volume are science fiction by any definition. I'll talk more about all that in the introduction to the second volume. Let's now find out where on earth we're going.

The Stories In This Volume

When I was a sophomore in college, I came upon or discovered or invented a country in central Europe called Orsinia. Orsinia gave me an entry to fiction. It gave me the ground, the room I needed. I had been writing realistic stories (bourgeois-U.S.A.-1948) because realism was what a serious writer was supposed to write under the rule of modernism, which had decreed that non-realistic fiction, if not mere kiddilit, was trash.

I was a very serious young writer. I never had anything against realistic novels, and loved many of them. I am not theory-minded, and did not yet try to question or argue with this arbitrary impoverishment of literature. But I was soon aware that the ground it offered my particular talent was small and stony. I had to find my own way elsewhere.

Orsinia was the way, lying between actuality, which was supposed to be the sole subject of fiction, and the limitless realms of the imagination. I found the country, drew the map, wrote stories about it, wrote two novels about it, one of which was published later as *Malafrena*, and revisited it happily now and then for many years. The first four stories in this volume are Orsinian tales, and the first of them, "Brothers and Sisters," was the first story I wrote that I knew was good, was right, was as close as I could come. I was in my mid-twenties by then.

Since the story "Unlocking the Air," written in 1990, I have had no word from Orsinia. I miss hearing from my people there.

I don't think "The Diary of the Rose" takes place in Orsinia, it seems more like South America to me, but the protagonist has an Orsinian name.

By the early Sixties, when I finally began getting stories published, I was quite certain that reality is often best represented slantwise, backwards, or as if it were an imaginary country, and also that I could write about anywhere and anything I liked, with a hope though no expectation that somebody, somewhere, would publish it.

I could even write realism, if I wanted to.

The stories "Texts," "Sleepwalkers," and "Hand, Cup, Shell," all from the collection *Searoad*, take place in present-day Oregon, in a semi-disguised beach-town I call Klatsand. The protagonist of "The Direction of the Road" still lives beside Highway 18, near McMinnville, in Oregon. "Buffalo Gals" is set in the high desert of Eastern Oregon. "Ether, OR" moves between the dry East side and the green West side of the state in a peaceful, improbable, taken-for-granted way that I think is something I learned from living in Oregon for fifty years.

"The White Donkey" seems to be in a dreamed India, and "Gwilan's Harp" somewhere along the borders of a fantasy-Wales. Spatial location of stories like "The Water is Wide" or "The Lost Children" is irrelevant, other than that they are in America—reflections of a moment in American time. "May's Lion" is set in the Napa Valley of California, where I spent the timeless summers of my childhood, and "Half Past Four" is mostly in Berkeley, where I grew up.

"Half Past Four" is pure realism, but in a somewhat unusual form. In a one-day writing workshop in San Jose, the poetry teacher and I traded classes after lunch: he got my fiction-writers and made them write poems, and I got his poets, to whom I was supposed to teach story-writing. They put up a huge fuss—poets always do. No, no, I am a Poet and cannot possibly tell stories! I said yes you can. I'll give you the names of four people and tell you their relative status; and you'll put them together in a specific place, and look at them for a while, and see that their relationship gives you the beginning of a story. (I made this all up on the spot.) The four character names I gave them were: Stephen, an older man in a position of relative power or authority; Ann, young, without authority; Ella, older, without much authority; and Todd, young or very young, without any authority.

One brave poet went home and did the assignment; she sent me her story, and it was good. I went home and did the assignment eight times, using those same four names (plus a few extras, such as Marie and Bill). I sent it to *The New Yorker.* They were game and published the piece. The feedback I got showed that many readers tried hard to make the eight Stephens into one Stephen, the eight Ellas into one Ella. It can't be done. The eight brief stories in "Half Past Four" are about thirty-two different people, thirty-two different characters, plus Marie and Bill sometimes. All eight stories have to do with power, identity, and relationship; certain themes and images recur in them and interweave; and they all take place at about four-thirty in the afternoon. I'm still pleased with my assignment.

—Ursula K. Le Guin. August 2012.

Brothers and Sisters

The injured quarrier lay on a high hospital bed. He had not recovered consciousness. His silence was grand and oppressive; his body under the sheet that dropped in stiff folds, his face were as indifferent as stone. The mother, as if challenged by that silence and indifference, spoke loudly: "What did you do it for? Do you want to die before I do? Look at him, look at him, my beauty, my hawk, my river, my son!" Her sorrow boasted of itself. She rose to the occasion like a lark to the morning. His silence and her outcry meant the same thing: the unendurable made welcome. The younger son stood listening. They bore him down with their grief as large as life. Unconscious, heedless, broken like a piece of chalk, that body, his brother, bore him down with the weight of the flesh, and he wanted to run away, to save himself.

The man who had been saved stood beside him, a little stooped fellow, middle-aged, limestone dust white in his knuckles. He too was borne down. "He saved my life," he said to Stefan, gaping, wanting an explanation. His voice was the flat toneless voice of the deaf.

"He would," Stefan said. "That's what he'd do."

He left the hospital to get his lunch. Everybody asked him about his brother. "He'll live," Stefan said. He went to the White Lion for lunch, drank too much. "Crippled? Him? Kostant? So he got a couple of tons of rock in the face, it won't hurt him, he's made of the stuff. He wasn't born, he was quarried out." They laughed at him as usual. "Quarried out," he said. "Like all the rest of you." He left the White Lion, went down Ardure Street four blocks straight out of town, and kept on straight, walking northeast, parallel with the railroad tracks a quarter mile away. The May sun was small and greyish overhead. Underfoot there were dust and small weeds. The Karst, the limestone plain, jigged tinily about him with heatwaves like the transparent vibrating wings of flies. Remote and small, rigid beyond that vibrant greyish haze, the mountains stood. He had known the mountains from far off all his life, and twice had seen them close, when he took the Brailava train, once going, once coming back. He knew they were clothed in trees, fir trees with roots clutching the banks of running streams and with branches dark in the mist that closed and parted in the mountain gullies in the light of dawn as the train clanked by, its smoke dropping down the green slopes like a dropping veil. In the mountains the streams ran noisy in the sunlight; there were waterfalls. Here on the karst the rivers ran underground, silent in dark veins of stone. You could ride a horse all day from Sfaroy Kampe and still not reach the mountains, still be in the limestone dust; but late on the second day you would come under the shade of trees, by running streams. Stefan Fabbre sat down by the side of the straight unreal road he had been walking on, and put his head in his arms. Alone, a mile from town, a quarter mile from the tracks, sixty miles from the mountains, he sat and cried for his brother. The plain of dust and stone quivered and grimaced about him in the heat like the face of a man in pain.

He got back an hour late from lunch to the office of the Chorin Company where he worked as an accountant. His boss came to his desk: "Fabbre, you needn't stay this afternoon."

"Why not?"

"Well, if you want to go to the hospital . . ."

"What can I do there? I can't sew him back up, can I?"

"As you like," the boss said, turning away.

"Not me that got a ton of rocks in the face, is it?" Nobody answered him.

When Kostant Fabbre was hurt in the rockslide in the quarry he was twenty-six years old; his brother was twenty-three; their sister Rosana was thirteen. She was beginning to grow tall and sullen, to weigh upon the earth. Instead of running, now, she walked, ungainly and somewhat hunched, as if at each step she crossed, unwilling, a threshold. She talked loudly, and laughed aloud. She struck back at whatever touched her, a voice, a wind, a word she did not understand, the evening star. She had not learned indifference, she knew only defiance. Usually she and Stefan quarrelled, touching each other where each was raw, unfinished. This night when he got home the mother had not come back from the hospital, and Rosana was silent in the silent house. She had been thinking all afternoon about pain, about pain and death; defiance had failed her.

"Don't look so down," Stefan told her as she served out beans for supper. "He'll be all right."

"Do you think . . . Somebody was saying he might be, you know. . . ."

"Crippled? No, he'll be all right."

"Why do you think he, you know, ran to push that fellow out of the way?"

"No why to it, Ros. He just did it."

He was touched that she asked these questions of him, and surprised at the certainty of his answers. He had not thought that he had any answers.

"It's queer," she said.

"What is?"

"I don't know. Kostant . . ."

"Knocked the keystone out of your arch, didn't it? Wham! One rock falls, they all go." She did not understand him; she did not recognise the place where she had come today, a place where she was like other people, sharing with them the singular catastrophe of being alive. Stefan was not the one to guide her. "Here we all are," he went on, "lying around each of us under our private pile of rocks. At least they got Kostant out from under his and filled him up with morphine. . . . D'you remember once when you were little you said 'I'm going to marry Kostant when I grow up.'"

Rosana nodded. "Sure. And he got real mad."

"Because mother laughed."

"It was you and dad that laughed."

Neither of them was eating. The room was close and dark around the kerosene lamp.

"What was it like when dad died?"

"You were there," Stefan said.

"I was nine. But I can't remember it. Except it was hot like now, and there were a lot of big moths knocking their heads on the glass. Was that the night he died?"

"I guess so."

"What was it like?" She was trying to explore the new land.

"I don't know. He just died. It isn't like anything else."

The father had died of pneumonia at forty-six, after thirty years in the quarries. Stefan did not remember his death much more clearly than Rosana did. He had not been the keystone of the arch.

"Have we got any fruit to eat?"

The girl did not answer. She was gazing at the air above the place at the table where the elder brother usually sat. Her forehead and dark eyebrows were like his, were his: likeness between kin is identity, the brother and sister were, by so much or so little, the curve of brow and temple, the same person; so that, for a moment, Kostant sat across the table mutely contemplating his own absence.

"Is there any?"

"I think there's some apples in the pantry," she answered, coming back to herself, but so quietly that in her brother's eyes she seemed briefly a woman, a quiet woman speaking out of her thoughts; and he said with tenderness to that woman, "Come on, let's go over to the hospital. They must be through messing with him by now."

The deaf man had come back to the hospital. His daughter was with him. Stefan knew she clerked at the butcher's shop. The deaf man, not allowed into the ward, kept Stefan half an hour in the hot, pine-floored waiting room that smelled of disinfectant and resin. He talked, walking about, sitting down, jumping up, arguing in the loud even monotone of his deafness. "I'm not going back to the pit. No sir. What if I'd said last night I'm not going into the pit tomorrow? Then how'd it be now, see? I wouldn't be here now, nor you wouldn't, nor he wouldn't, him in there, your brother. We'd all be home. Home safe and sound, see? I'm not going back to the pit. No, by God. I'm going out to the farm, that's where I'm going. I grew up there, see, out west in the foothills there, my brother's there. I'm going back and work the farm with him. I'm not going back to the pit again."

The daughter sat on the wooden bench, erect and still. Her face was narrow, her black hair was pulled back in a knot. "Aren't you hot?" Stefan asked her, and she answered gravely, "No, I'm all right." Her voice was clear. She was used to speaking to her deaf father. When Stefan said nothing more she looked down again and sat with her hands in her lap. The father was still talking. Stefan rubbed his hands through his sweaty hair and tried to interrupt. "Good, sounds like a good plan, Sachik. Why waste the rest of your life in the pits." The deaf man talked right on.

"He doesn't hear you."

"Can't you take him home?"

"I couldn't make him leave here even for dinner. He won't stop talking."

Her voice was much lower saying this, perhaps from embarrassment, and the sound of it caught at Stefan. He rubbed his sweaty hair again and stared at her, thinking for some reason of smoke, waterfalls, the mountains.

"You go on home." He heard in his own voice the qualities of hers, softness and clarity. "I'll get him over to the Lion for an hour."

"Then you won't see your brother."

"He won't run away. Go on home."

At the White Lion both men drank heavily. Sachik talked on about the farm in the foothills, Stefan talked about the mountains and his year at college in the city. Neither heard the other. Drunk, Stefan walked Sachik home to one of the rows of party-walled houses that the Chorin Company had put up in '95 when they opened the new quarry. The houses were on the west edge of town, and behind them the karst stretched in the light of the half-moon away on and on, pocked, pitted, level, answering the moonlight with its own pallor taken at third-hand from the sun. The moon, second-hand, worn at the edges, was hung up in the sky like something a housewife leaves out to remind her it needs mending. "Tell your daughter everything is all right," Stefan said, swaying at the door. "Everything is all right," Sachik repeated with enthusiasm, "aa-all right."

Stefan went home drunk, and so the day of the accident blurred in his memory into the rest of the days of the year, and the fragments that stayed with him, his brother's closed eyes, the dark girl looking at him, the moon looking at nothing, did not recur to his mind together as parts of a whole, but separately with long intervals between.

On the karst there are no springs; the water they drink in Sfaroy Kampe comes from deep wells and is pure, without taste. Ekata Sachik tasted the strange spring-water of the farm still on her lips as she scrubbed an iron skillet at the sink. She scrubbed with a stiff brush, using more energy than was needed, absorbed in the work deep below the level of conscious pleasure. Food had been burned in the skillet, the water she poured in fled brown from the bristles of the brush, glittering in the lamplight. They none of them knew how to cook here at the farm. Sooner or later she would take over the cooking and they could eat properly. She liked housework, she liked to clean, to bend hot-faced to the oven of a woodburning range, to call people in to supper; lively, complex work, not a bore like clerking at the butcher's shop, making change, saying "Good day" and "Good day" all day. She had left town with her family because she was sick of that. The farm family had taken the four of them in without comment, as a natural disaster, more mouths to feed, but also more hands to work. It was a big, poor farm. Ekata's mother, who was ailing, crept about behind the bustling aunt and cousin; the men, Ekata's uncle, father, and brother, tromped in and out in dusty boots; there were long discussions about buying another pig. "It's better here than in the town, there's nothing in the town," Ekata's widowed cousin said; Ekata did not answer her. She had no answer. "I think Martin will be going back," she said finally, "he never thought to be a farmer." And in fact her brother, who was sixteen, went back to Sfaroy Kampe in August to work in the quarries.

He took a room in a boarding house. His window looked down on the Fabbres' back yard, a fenced square of dust and weeds with a sad-looking fir tree at one corner. The landlady, a quarrier's widow, was dark, straight-backed, calm, like Martin's sister Ekata. With her the boy felt manly and easy. When she was out, her daughter and the other boarders, four single men in their twenties, took over; they laughed and slapped one another on the back; the railway clerk from Brailava would take out his guitar and play music-hall songs, rolling his eyes like raisins set in lard. The daughter, thirty and unmarried, would laugh and move about a great deal, her shirtwaist would come out of her belt in back and she would not tuck it in. Why did they make so much fuss? Why did they laugh, punch one another's shoulders, play the guitar and sing? They would begin to make fun of Martin. He would shrug and reply gruffly. Once he replied in the language used in the quarry pits. The guitar player took him aside and spoke to him seriously about how one must behave in front of ladies. Martin listened with his red face bowed. He was a big, broad-shouldered boy. He thought he might pick up this clerk from Brailava and break his neck. He did not do it. He had no right to. The clerk and the others were men; there was something they understood which he did not understand, the reason why they made a fuss, rolled their eyes, played and sang. Until he understood that, they were justified in telling him how to speak to ladies. He went up to his room and leaned out the window to smoke a cigarette. The smoke hung in the motionless evening air which enclosed the fir tree, the roofs, the world in a large dome of hard, dark-blue crystal. Rosana Fabbre came out into the fenced yard next door, dumped out a pan of dishwater with a short, fine swing of her arms, then stood still to look up at the sky, foreshortened, a dark head over a white blouse, caught in the blue crystal. Nothing moved for sixty miles in all directions except the last drops of water in the dishpan, which one by one fell to the ground, and the smoke of Martin's cigarette curling and dropping away from his fingers. Slowly he drew in his hand so that her eye would not be caught by the tiny curl of smoke. She sighed, whacked the dishpan on the jamb of the door to shake out the last drops, which had already run out, turned, went in; the door slammed. The blue air rejoined without a flaw where she had stood. Martin murmured to that flawless air the word he had been advised not to say in front of ladies, and in a moment, as if in answer, the evening star shone out northwestwards high and clear.

Kostant Fabbre was home, and alone all day now that he was able to get across a room on crutches. How he spent these vast silent days no one considered, probably least of all himself. An active man, the strongest and most intelligent worker in the quarries, a crew foreman since he was twenty-three, he had had no practice at all at idleness, or solitude. He had always used his time to the full in work. Now time must use him. He watched it at work upon him without dismay or impatience, carefully, like an apprentice watching a master. He employed all his strength to learn his new trade, that of weakness. The silence in which he passed the days clung to him now as the limestone dust had used to cling to his skin.

The mother worked in the dry-goods shop till six; Stefan got off work at five. There was an hour in the evening when the brothers were together alone. Stefan had used to spend this hour out in the back yard under the fir tree, stupid, sighing, watching swallows dart after invisible insects in the interminably darkening air, or else he had gone to the White Lion. Now he came home promptly, bringing Kostant the *Brailava Messenger.* They both read it, exchanging sheets. Stefan planned to speak, but did not. The dust lay on his lips. Nothing happened. Over and over the same hour passed. The older brother sat still, his handsome, quiet face bowed over the newspaper. He read slowly; Stefan had to wait to exchange sheets; he could see Kostant's eyes move from word to word. Then Rosana would come in yelling good-bye to schoolmates in the street, the mother would come in, doors would bang, voices ring from room to room, the kitchen would smoke and clatter, plates clash, the hour was gone.

One evening Kostant, having barely begun to read, laid the newspaper down. There was a long pause which contained no events and which Stefan, reading, pretended not to notice.

"Stefan, my pipe's there by you."

"Oh, sure," Stefan mumbled, took him his pipe. Kostant filled and lit it, drew on it a few times, set it down. His right hand lay on the arm of the chair, hard and relaxed, holding in it a knot of desolation too heavy to lift. Stefan hid behind his paper and the silence went on.

I'll read out this about the union coalition to him, Stefan thought, but he did not. His eyes insisted on finding another article, reading it. Why can't I talk to him?

"Ros is growing up," Kostant said.

"She's getting on," Stefan mumbled.

"She'll take some looking after. I've been thinking. This is no town for a girl growing up. Wild lads and hard men."

"You'll find them anywhere."

"Will you; no doubt," Kostant said, accepting Stefan's statement without question. Kostant had never been off the karst, never been out of Sfaroy Kampe. He knew nothing at all but limestone, Ardure Street and Chorin Street and Gulhelm Street, the mountains far off and the enormous sky.

"See," he said, picking up his pipe again, "she's a bit wilful, I think."

"Lads will think twice before they mess with Fabbre's sister," Stefan said. "Anyhow, she'll listen to you."

"And you."

"Me? What should she listen to me for?"

"For the same reasons," Kostant said, but Stefan had found his voice now—"What should she respect me for? She's got good enough sense. You and I didn't listen to anything dad said, did we? Same thing."

"You're not like him. If that's what you meant. You've had an education."

"An education, I'm a real professor, sure. Christ! One year at the Normal School!"

"Why did you fail there, Stefan?"

The question was not asked lightly; it came from the heart of Kostant's silence, from his austere, pondering ignorance. Unnerved at finding himself, like Rosana, included so deeply in the thoughts of this reserved and superb brother, Stefan said the first thing that came to mind—"I was afraid I'd fail. So I didn't work."

And there it was, plain as a glass of water, the truth, which he had never admitted to himself.

Kostant nodded, thinking over this idea of failure, which was surely not one familiar to him; then he said in his resonant, gentle voice, "You're wasting your time here in Kampe."

"I am? What about yourself?"

"I'm wasting nothing. I never won any scholarship." Kostant smiled, and the humor of his smile angered Stefan.

"No, you never tried, you went straight to the pit at fifteen. Listen, did you ever wonder, did you ever stop a minute to ask what am I doing here, why did I go into the quarries, what do I work there for, am I going to work there six days a week every week of the year every year of my life? For pay, sure, there's other ways to make a living. What's it *for?* Why does anybody stay here, in this Godforsaken town on this Godforsaken piece of rock where nothing grows? Why don't they get up and go somewhere? Talk about wasting your time! What in God's name is it all for—is this all there is to it?"

"I have thought that."

"I haven't thought anything else for years."

"Why not go, then?"

"Because I'm afraid to. It'd be like Brailava, like the college. But you—"

"I've got my work here. It's mine, I can do it. Anywhere you go, you can still ask what it's all for."

"I know." Stefan got up, a slight man moving and talking restlessly, half finishing his gestures and words. "I know. You take yourself with yourself. But that means one thing for me and something else again for you. You're wasting yourself here, Kostant. It's the same as this business, this hero business, smashing yourself up for that Sachik, a fool who can't even see a rockslide coming at him—"

"He couldn't *hear* it," Kostant put in, but Stefan could not stop now. "That's not the point; the point is, let that kind of man look after himself, what's he to you, what's his life to you? Why did you go in after him when you saw the slide coming? For the same reason as you went into the pit, for the same reason as you keep working in the pit. For no reason. Because it just came up. It just happened. You let things happen to you, you take what's handed you, when you could take it all in your hands and do what you wanted with it!"

It was not what he had meant to say, not what he had wanted to say. He had wanted Kostant to talk. But words fell out of his own mouth and bounced around him like hailstones. Kostant sat quiet, his strong hand closed not to open; finally he answered: "You're making something of me I'm not." That was not humility. There was none in him. His patience was that of pride. He understood Stefan's yearning but could not share it, for he lacked nothing; he was intact. He would go forward in the same, splendid, vulnerable integrity of body and mind towards whatever came to meet him on his road, like a king in exile on a land of stone, bearing all his kingdom—cities, trees, people, mountains, fields and flights of birds in spring—in his closed hand, a seed for the sowing; and, because there was no one of his language to speak to, silent.

"But listen, you said you've thought the same thing, what's it all for, is this all there is to life—If you've thought that, you must have looked for the answer!"

After a long pause Kostant said, "I nearly found it. Last May."

Stefan stopped fidgeting, looked out the front window in silence. He was frightened. "That—that's not an answer," he mumbled.

"Seems like there ought to be a better one," Kostant agreed.

"You get morbid sitting here. . . . What you need's a woman," Stefan said, fidgeting, slurring his words, staring out at the early-autumn evening rising from stone pavements unobscured by tree branches or smoke, even, clear, and empty. Behind him, his brother laughed. "It's the truth," Stefan said bitterly, not turning.

"Could be. How about yourself?"

"They're sitting out on the steps there at widow Katalny's. She must be night nursing at the hospital again. Hear the guitar? That's the fellow from Brailava, works at the railway office, goes after anything in skirts. Even goes after Nona Katalny. Sachik's kid lives there now. Works in the New Pit, somebody said. Maybe in your crew."

"What kid?"

"Sachik's."

"Thought he'd left town."

"He did, went to some farm in the west hills. This is his kid, must have stayed behind to work."

"Where's the girl?"

"Went with her father as far as I know."

The pause this time lengthened out, stretched around them like a pool in which their last words floated, desultory, vague, fading. The room was full of dusk. Kostant stretched and sighed. Stefan felt peace come into him, as intangible and real as the coming of the darkness. They had talked, and got nowhere; it was not a last step; the next step would come in its time. But for a moment he was at peace with his brother, and with himself.

"Evenings getting shorter," Kostant said softly.

"I've seen her once or twice. Saturdays. Comes in with a farm wagon."

"Where's the farm at?"

"West, in the hills, was all old Sachik said."

"Might ride out there, if I could," Kostant said. He struck a match for his pipe. The flare of the match in the clear dusk of the room was also a peaceful thing; when Stefan looked back at the window the evening seemed darker. The guitar had stopped and they were laughing out on the steps next door.

"If I see her Saturday I'll ask her to come by."

Kostant said nothing. Stefan wanted no answer. It was the first time in his life that his brother had asked his help.

The mother came in, tall, loud-voiced, tired. Floors cracked and cried under her step, the kitchen clashed and steamed, everything was noisy in her presence except her two sons, Stefan who eluded her, Kostant who was her master.

Stefan got off work Saturdays at noon. He sauntered down Ardure Street looking out for the farm wagon and roan horse. They were not in town, and he went to the White Lion, relieved and bored. Another Saturday came and a third. It was October, the afternoons were shorter. Martin Sachik was walking down Gulhelm Street ahead of him; he caught up and said, "Evening, Sachik." The boy looked at him with blank grey eyes; his face, hands, and clothes were grey with stone-dust and he walked as slowly and steadily as a man of fifty.

"Which crew are you in?"

"Five." He spoke distinctly, like his sister.

"That's my brother's."

"I know." They went on pace for pace. "They said he might be back in the pit next month."

Stefan shook his head.

"Your family still out there on that farm?" he asked.

Martin nodded, as they stopped in front of the Katalny house. He revived, now that he was home and very near dinner. He was flattered by Stefan Fabbre's speaking to him, but not shy of him. Stefan was clever, but he was spoken of as a moody, unsteady fellow, half a man where his brother was a man and a half. "Near Verre," Martin said. "A hell of a place. I couldn't take it."

"Can your sister?"

"Figures she has to stay with Ma. She ought to come back. It's a hell of a place."

"This isn't heaven," Stefan said.

"Work your head off there and never get any money for it, they're all loony on those farms. Right where Dad belongs." Martin felt virile, speaking disrespectfully of his father. Stefan Fabbre looked at him, not with respect, and said, "Maybe. Evening to you, Sachik." Martin went into the house defeated. When was he going to become a man, not subject to other men's reproof? Why did it matter if Stefan Fabbre looked at him and turned away? The next day he met Rosana Fabbre on the street. She was with a girl friend, he with a fellow quarrier; they had all been in school together last year. "How you doing, Ros?" Martin said loudly, nudging his friend. The girls walked by haughty as cranes. "There's a hot one," Martin said. "Her? She's just a kid," the friend said. "You'd be surprised," Martin told him with a thick laugh, then looked up and saw Stefan Fabbre crossing the street. For a moment he realised that he was surrounded, there was no escape.

Stefan was on the way to the White Lion, but passing the town hotel and livery stable he saw the roan horse in the yard. He went in, and sat in the brown parlour of the hotel in the smell of harness grease and dried spiders. He sat there two hours. She came in, erect, a black kerchief on her hair, so long awaited and so fully herself that he watched her go by with simple pleasure, and only woke as she started up the stairs. "Miss Sachik," he said.

She stopped, startled, on the stairs.

"Wanted to ask you a favor." Stefan's voice was thick after the strange timeless waiting. "You're staying here over tonight?"

"Yes."

"Kostant was asking about you. Wanted to ask about your father. He's still stuck indoors, can't walk much."

"Father's fine."

"Well, I wondered if—"

"I could look in. I was going to see Martin. It's next door, isn't it?"

"Oh, fine. That's—I'll wait."

Ekata ran up to her room, washed her dusty face and hands, and put on, to decorate her grey dress, a lace collar that she had brought to wear to church tomorrow. Then she took it off again. She retied the black kerchief over her black hair, went down, and walked with Stefan six blocks through the pale October sunlight to his house. When she saw Kostant Fabbre she was staggered. She had never seen him close to except in the hospital where he had been effaced by casts, bandages, heat, pain, her father's chatter. She saw him now.

They fell to talking quite easily. She would have felt wholly at ease with him if it had not been for his extraordinary beauty, which distracted her. His voice and what he said was grave, plain, and reassuring. It was the other way round with the younger brother, who was nothing at all to look at, but with whom she felt ill at ease, at a loss. Kostant was quiet and quieting; Stefan blew in gusts like autumn wind, bitter and fitful; you didn't know where you were with him.

"How is it for you out there?" Kostant was asking, and she replied, "All right. A bit dreary."

"Farming's the hardest work, they say."

"I don't mind the hard, it's the muck I mind."

"Is there a village near?"

"Well, it's halfway between Verre and Lotima. But there's neighbors, everybody within twenty miles knows each other."

"We're still your neighbors, by that reckoning," Stefan put in. His voice slurred off in midsentence. He felt irrelevant to these two. Kostant sat relaxed, his lame leg stretched out, his hands clasped round the other knee; Ekata faced him, upright, her hands lying easy in her lap. They did not look alike but might have been brother and sister. Stefan got up with a mumbled excuse and went out back. The north wind blew. Sparrows hopped in the sour dirt under the fir tree and the scurf of weedy grass.

Shirts, underclothes, a pair of sheets snapped, relaxed, jounced on the clothesline between two iron posts. The air smelt of ozone. Stefan vaulted the fence, cut across the Katalny yard to the street, and walked westward. After a couple of blocks the street petered out. A track led on to a quarry, abandoned twenty years ago when they struck water; there was twenty feet of water in it now. Boys swam there, summers. Stefan had swum there, in terror, for he had never learned to swim well and there was no foothold, it was all deep and bitter cold. A boy had drowned there years ago, last year a man had drowned himself, a quarrier going blind from stone-splinters in his eyes. It was still called the West Pit. Stefan's father had worked in it as a boy. Stefan sat down by the lip of it and watched the wind, caught down in the four walls, eddy in tremors over the water that reflected nothing.

"I have to go meet Martin," Ekata said. As she stood up Kostant put a hand out to his crutches, then gave it up: "Takes me too long to get afoot," he said.

"How much can you get about on those?"

"From here to there," he said, pointing to the kitchen. "Leg's all right. It's the back's slow."

"You'll be off them—?"

"Doctor says by Easter. I'll run out and throw 'em in the West Pit. . . ." They both smiled. She felt tenderness for him, and a pride in knowing him.

"Will you be coming in to Kampe, I wonder, when bad weather comes?"

"I don't know how the roads will be."

"If you do, come by," he said. "If you like."

"I will."

They noticed then that Stefan was gone.

"I don't know where he went to," Kostant said. "He comes and he goes, Stefan does. Your brother, Martin, they tell me he's a good lad in our crew."

"He's young," Ekata said.

"It's hard at first. I went in at fifteen. But then when you've got your strength, you know the work, and it goes easy. Good wishes to your family, then." She shook his big, hard, warm hand, and let herself out. On the doorstep she met Stefan face to face. He turned red. It shocked her to see a man blush. He spoke, as usual leaping straight into the subject—"You were the year behind me in school, weren't you?"

"Yes."

"You went around with Rosa Bayenin. She won the scholarship I did, the next year."

"She's teaching school now, in the Valone."

"She did more with it than I would have done.—I was thinking, see, it's queer how you grow up in a place like this, you know everybody, then you meet one and find out you don't know them."

She did not know what to answer. He said good-bye and went into the house; she went on, retying her kerchief against the rising wind.

Rosana and the mother came into the house a minute after Stefan. "Who was that on the doorstep you were talking to?" the mother said sharply. "That wasn't Nona Katalny, I'll be bound."

"You're right," Stefan said.

"All right, but you watch out for that one, you're just the kind she'd like to get her claws into, and wouldn't that be fine, you could walk her puppydog whilst she entertains her ma's gentlemen boarders." She and Rosana both began to laugh their loud, dark laughter. "Who was it you were talking to, then?"

"What's it to you?" he shouted back. Their laughter enraged him; it was like a pelting with hard clattering rocks, too thick to dodge.

"What is it to me who's standing on my own doorstep, you want to know, I'll let you know what it is to me—" Words leapt to meet her anger as they did to all her passions. "You so high and mighty all the time with all your going off to college, but you came sneaking back quick enough to this house, didn't you, and I'll let you know I want to know who comes into this house—" Rosana was shouting, "I know who it was, it was Martin Sachik's sister!" Kostant loomed up suddenly beside the three of them, stooped and tall on his crutches: "Cut it out," he said, and they fell silent.

Nothing was said, then or later, to the mother or between the two brothers, about Ekata Sachik's having been in the house.

Martin took his sister to dine at the Bell, the café where officials of the Chorin Company and visitors from out of town went to dine. He was proud of himself for having thought of treating her, proud of the white tableclothes and the forks and soupspoons, terrified of the waiter. He in his outgrown Sunday coat and his sister in her grey dress, how admirably they were behaving, how adult they were. Ekata looked at the menu so calmly, and her face did not change expression in the slightest as she murmured to him, "But there's two kinds of soup."

"Yes," he said, with sophistication.

"Do you choose which kind?"

"I guess so."

"You must, you'd bloat up before you ever got to the meat—" They snickered. Ekata's shoulders shook; she hid her face in her napkin; the napkin was enormous—"Martin, look, they've given me a bedsheet—" They both sat snorting, shaking, in torment, while the waiter, with another bedsheet on his shoulder, inexorably approached.

Dinner was ordered inaudibly, eaten with etiquette, elbows pressed close to the sides. The dessert was a chestnut-flour pudding, and Ekata, her elbows relaxing a little with enjoyment, said, "Rosa Bayenin said when she wrote the town she's in is right next to a whole forest of chestnut trees, everybody goes and picks them up in autumn, the trees grow thick as night, she said, right down to the river bank." Town after six weeks on the farm, the talk with Kostant and Stefan, dining at the restaurant had excited her. "This is awfully good," she said, but she could not say what she saw, which was sunlight striking golden down a river between endless dark-foliaged trees, a wind running upriver among shadows and the scent of leaves, of water, and of chestnut-flour pudding, a world of forests, of rivers, of strangers, the sunlight shining on the world.

"Saw you talking with Stefan Fabbre," Martin said.

"I was at their house."

"What for?"

"They asked me."

"What for?"

"Just to find out how we're getting on."

"They never asked me."

"You're not on the farm, stupid. You're in his crew, aren't you? You could look in sometime, you know. He's a grand man, you'd like him."

Martin grunted. He resented Ekata's visit to the Fabbres without knowing why. It seemed somehow to complicate things. Rosana had probably been there. He did not want his sister knowing about Rosana. Knowing what about Rosana? He gave it up, scowling.

"The younger brother, Stefan, he works at the Chorin office, doesn't he?"

"Keeps books or something. He was supposed to be a genius and go to college, but they kicked him out."

"I know." She finished her pudding, lovingly. "Everybody knows that," she said.

"I don't like him," Martin said.

"Why not?"

"Just don't." He was relieved, having dumped his ill humor onto Stefan. "You want coffee?"

"Oh, no."

"Come on. I do." Masterful, he ordered coffee for both. Ekata admired him, and enjoyed the coffee. "What luck, to have a brother," she said. The next morning, Sunday, Martin met her at the hotel and they went to church; singing the Lutheran hymns each heard the other's strong clear voice and each was pleased and wanted to laugh. Stefan Fabbre was at the service. "Does he usually come?" Ekata asked Martin as they left the church.

"No," Martin said, though he had no idea, having not been to church himself since May. He felt dull and fierce after the long sermon. "He's following you around."

She said nothing.

"He waited for you at the hotel, you said. Takes you out to see his brother, he says. Talks to you on the street. Shows up in church." Self-defense furnished him these items one after another, and the speaking of them convinced him.

"Martin," Ekata said, "if there's one kind of man I hate it's a meddler."

"If you weren't my sister—"

"If I wasn't your sister I'd be spared your stupidness. Will you go ask the man to put the horse in?" So they parted with mild rancor between them, soon lost in distance and the days.

In late November when Ekata drove in again to Sfaroy Kampe she went to the Fabbre house. She wanted to go, and had told Kostant she would, yet she had to force herself; and when she found that Kostant and Rosana were home, but Stefan was not, she felt much easier. Martin had troubled her with his stupid meddling. It was Kostant she wanted to see, anyhow.

But Kostant wanted to talk about Stefan.

"He's always out roaming, or at the Lion. Restless. Wastes his time. He said to me, one day we talked, he's afraid to leave Kampe. I've thought about what he meant. What is it he's afraid of?"

"Well, he hasn't any friends but here."

"Few enough here. He acts the clerk among the quarrymen, and the quarryman among the clerks. I've seen him, here, when my mates come in. Why don't he be what he is?"

"Maybe he isn't sure what he is."

"He won't learn it from mooning around and drinking at the Lion," said Kostant, hard and sure in his own intactness. "And rubbing up quarrels. He's had three fights this month. Lost 'em all, poor devil," and he laughed. She never expected the innocence of laughter on his grave face. And he was kind; his concern for Stefan was deep, his laughter without a sneer, the laughter of a good nature. Like Stefan, she wondered at him, at his beauty and his strength, but she did not think of him as wasted. The Lord keeps the house and knows his servants. If he had sent this innocent and splendid man to live obscure on the plain of stone, it was part of his housekeeping, of the strange economy of the stone and the rose, the rivers that run and do not run dry, the tiger, the ocean, the maggot, and the not eternal stars.

Rosana, by the hearth, listened to them talk. She sat silent, heavy and her shoulders stooped, though of late she had been learning again to hold herself erect as she had when she was a child, a year ago. They say one gets used to being a millionaire; so after a year or two a human being begins to get used to being a woman. Rosana was learning to wear the rich and heavy garment of her inheritance. Just now she was listening, something she had rarely done. She had never heard adults talk as these two were talking. She had never heard a conversation. At the end of twenty minutes she slipped quietly out. She had learned enough, too much, she needed time to absorb and practice. She began practicing at once. She went down the street erect, not slow and not fast, her face composed, like Ekata Sachik.

"Daydreaming, Ros?" jeered Martin Sachik from the Katalny yard.

She smiled at him and said, "Hello, Martin." He stood staring.

"Where you going?" he asked with caution.

"Nowhere; I'm just walking. Your sister's at our house."

"She is?" Martin sounded unusually stupid and belligerent, but she stuck to her practicing: "Yes," she said politely. "She came to see my brother."

"Which brother?"

"Kostant, why would she have come to see Stefan?" she said, forgetting her new self a moment and grinning widely.

"How come you're barging around all by yourself?"

"Why not?" she said, stung by "barging" and so reverting to an extreme mildness of tone.

"I'll go with you."

"Why not?"

They walked down Gulhelm Street till it became a track between weeds.

"Want to go on to the West Pit?"

"Why not?" Rosana liked the phrase; it sounded experienced.

They walked on the thin stony dirt between miles of dead grass too short to bow to the northwest wind. Enormous masses of cloud travelled backward over their heads so that they seemed to be walking very fast, the grey plain sliding along with them. "Clouds make you dizzy," Martin said, "like looking up a flagpole." They walked with faces upturned, seeing nothing but the motion of the wind. Rosana realised that though their feet were on the earth they themselves stuck up into the sky, it was the sky they were walking through, just as birds flew through it. She looked over at Martin walking through the sky.

They came to the abandoned quarry and stood looking down at the water, dulled by flurries of trapped wind.

"Want to go swimming?"

"Why not?"

"There's the mule trail. Looks funny, don't it, going right down into the water."

"It's cold here."

"Come on down the trail. There's no wind inside the walls hardly. That's where Penik jumped off from, they grappled him up from right under here."

Rosana stood on the lip of the pit. The grey wind blew by her. "Do you think he meant to? I mean, he was blind, maybe he fell in—"

"He could see some. They were going to send him to Brailava and operate on him. Come on." She followed him to the beginning of the path down. It looked very steep from above. She had become timorous the last year. She followed him slowly down the effaced, boulder-smashed track into the quarry. "Here, hold on," he said, pausing at a rough drop; he took her hand and brought her down after him. They separated at once and he led on to where the water cut across the path, which plunged on down to the hidden floor of the quarry. The water was lead-dark, uneasy, its surface broken into thousands of tiny pleatings, circles, counter-circles by the faint trapped wind jarring it ceaselessly against the walls. "Shall I go on?" Martin whispered, loud in the silence.

"Why not?"

He walked on. She cried, "Stop!" He had walked into the water up to his knees; he turned, lost his balance, careened back onto the path with a plunge that showered her with water and sent clapping echoes round the walls of rock. "You're crazy, what did you do that for?" Martin sat down, took off his big shoes to dump water out of them, and laughed, a soundless laugh mixed with shivering. "What did you do that for?"

"Felt like it," he said. He caught at her arm, pulled her down kneeling by him, and kissed her. The kiss went on. She began to struggle, and pulled away from him. He hardly knew it. He lay there on the rocks at the water's edge laughing; he was as strong as the earth and could not lift his hand. . . . He sat up, mouth open, eyes unfocussed. After a while he put on his wet, heavy shoes and started up the path. She stood at the top, a windblown stroke of darkness against the huge moving sky. "Come on!" she shouted, and wind thinned her voice to a knife's edge. "Come on, you can't catch me!" As he neared the top of the path, she ran. He ran, weighed down by his wet shoes and trousers. A hundred yards from the quarry he caught her and tried to capture both her arms. Her wild face was next to his for a moment. She twisted free, ran off again, and he followed her into town, trotting since he could not run any more. Where Gulhelm Street began she stopped and waited for him. They walked down the pavement side by side. "You look like a drowned cat," she jeered in a panting whisper. "Who's talking," he answered the same way, "look at the mud on your skirt." In front of the boarding house they stopped and looked at each other, and he laughed. "Good night, Ros!" he said. She wanted to bite him. "Good night!" she said, and walked the few yards to her own front door, not slow and not fast, feeling his gaze on her back like a hand on her flesh.

Not finding her brother at the boarding house, Ekata had gone back to the hotel to wait for him; they were to dine at the Bell again. She told the desk clerk to send her brother up when he came. In a few minutes there was a knock; she opened the door. It was Stefan Fabbre. He was the color of oatmeal and looked dingy, like an unmade bed.

"I wanted to ask you . . ." His voice slurred off. "Have some dinner," he muttered, looking past her at the room.

"My brother's coming for me. That's him now." But it was the hotel manager coming up the stairs. "Sorry, miss," he said loudly. "There's a parlour downstairs." Ekata stared at him blankly. "Now look, miss, you said to send up your brother, and the clerk he don't know your brother by sight, but I do. That's my business. There's a nice parlour downstairs for entertaining. All right? You want to come to a respectable hotel, I want to keep it respectable for you, see?"

Stefan pushed past him and blundered down the stairs. "He's drunk, miss," said the manager.

"Go away," Ekata said, and shut the door on him. She sat down on the bed with clenched hands, but she could not sit still. She jumped up, took up her coat and kerchief, and without putting them on ran downstairs and out, hurling the key onto the desk behind which the manager stood staring. Ardure Street was dark between pools of lamplight, and the winter wind blew down it. She walked the two blocks west, came back down the other side of the street the length of it, eight blocks; she passed the White Lion, but the winter door was up and she could not see in. It was cold, the wind ran through the streets like a river running. She went to Gulhelm Street and met Martin coming out of the boarding house. They went to the Bell for supper. Both were thoughtful and uneasy. They spoke little and gently, grateful for companionship.

Alone in church next morning, when she had made sure that Stefan was not there, she lowered her eyes in relief. The stone walls of the church and the stark words of the service stood strong around her. She rested like a ship in haven. Then as the pastor gave his text, "I will lift up mine eyes unto the hills, whence cometh my help," she shivered, and once again looked all about the church, moving her head and eyes slowly, surreptitiously, seeking him. She heard nothing of the sermon. But when the service was over she did not want to leave the church. She went out among the last of the congregation. The pastor detained her, asking about her mother. She saw Stefan waiting at the foot of the steps.

She went to him.

"Wanted to apologise for last night," he brought out all in one piece, "It's all right."

He was bareheaded and the wind blew his light, dusty-looking hair across his eyes; he winced and tried to smooth it back. "I was drunk," he said.

"I know."

They set off together.

"I was worried about you," Ekata said.

"What for? I wasn't that drunk."

"I don't know."

They crossed the street in silence.

"Kostant likes talking with you. Told me so." His tone was unpleasant. Ekata said drily, "I like talking with him."

"Everybody does. It's a great favor he does them."

She did not reply.

"I mean that."

She knew what he meant, but still did not say anything. They were near the hotel. He stopped. "I won't finish ruining your reputation."

"You don't have to grin about it."

"I'm not. I mean I won't go on to the hotel with you, in case it embarrassed you."

"I have nothing to be embarrassed about."

"I do, and I am. I am sorry, Ekata."

"I didn't mean you had to apologise again." Her voice turned husky so that he thought again of mist, dusk, the forests.

"I won't." He laughed. "Are you leaving right away?"

"I have to. It gets dark so early now."

They both hesitated.

"You could do me a favor," she said.

"I'd do that."

"If you'd see to having my horse put in, last time I had to stop after a mile and tighten everything. If you did that I could be getting ready."

When she came out of the hotel the wagon was out front and he was in the seat. "I'll drive you a mile or two, all right?" She nodded, he gave her a hand up; they drove down Ardure Street westward to the plain.

"That damned hotel manager," Ekata said. "Grinning and scraping this morning . . ."

Stefan laughed, but said nothing. He was cautious, absorbed; the cold wind blew, the old roan clopped along; he explained presently, "I've never driven before."

"I've never driven any horse but this one. He's never any trouble."

The wind whistled in miles of dead grass, tugged at her black kerchief, whipped Stefan's hair across his eyes.

"Look at it," he said softly. "A couple of inches of dirt, and under it rock. Drive all day, any direction, and you'll find rock, with a couple of inches of dirt on it. You know how many trees there are in Kampe? Fifty-four. I counted 'em. And not another, not one, all the way to the mountains." His voice as he talked as if to himself was dry and musical. "When I went to Brailava on the train I looked out for the first new tree. The fifty-fifth tree. It was a big oak by a farmhouse in the hills. Then all of a sudden there were trees everywhere, in all the valleys in the hills. You could never count 'em. But I'd like to try."

"You're sick of it here."

"I don't know. Sick of something. I feel like I was an ant, something smaller, so small you can hardly see it, crawling along on this huge floor. Getting nowhere because where is there to get. Look at us now, crawling across the floor, there's the ceiling. . . . Looks like snow, there in the north."

"Not before dark, I hope."

"What's it like on the farm?"

She considered some while before answering, and then said softly, "Closed in."

"Your father happy with it?"

"He never did feel easy in Kampe, I think."

"There's people made out of dirt, earth," he said in his voice that slurred away so easily into unheard monologue, "and then there's some made out of stone. The fellows who get on in Kampe are made out of stone." "Like my brother," he did not say, and she heard it.

"Why don't you leave?"

"That's what Kostant said. It sounds so easy. But see, if he left, he'd be taking himself with him. I'd be taking myself. . . . Does it matter where you go? All you have is what you are. Or what you meet."

He checked the horse. "I'd better hop off, we must have come a couple of miles. Look, there's the ant-heap." From the high wagon seat looking back they saw a darkness on the pale plain, a pinpoint spire, a glitter where the winter sun struck windows or roof-slates; and far behind the town, distinct under high, heavy, dark-grey clouds, the mountains.

He handed the traces to her. "Thanks for the lift," he said, and swung down from the seat.

"Thanks for the company, Stefan."

He raised his hand; she drove on. It seemed a cruel thing to do, to leave him on foot there on the plain. When she looked back she saw him far behind already, walking away from her between the narrowing wheel-ruts under the enormous sky.

Before she reached the farm that evening there was a dry flurry of snow, the first of an early winter. From the kitchen window all that

25

month she looked up at hills blurred with rain. In December from her bedroom, on days of sun after snow, she saw eastward across the plain a glittering pallor: the mountains. There were no more trips to Sfaroy Kampe. When they needed market goods her uncle drove to Verre or Lotima, bleak villages foundering like cardboard in the rain. It was too easy to stray off the wheel-ruts crossing the karst in snow or heavy rain, he said, "and then where are ye?"

"Where are ye in the first place?" Ekata answered in Stefan's soft dry voice. The uncle paid no heed.

Martin rode out on a livery-stable horse for Christmas day. After a few hours he got sullen and stuck to Ekata. "What's that thing Aunt's got hanging round her neck?"

"A nail through an onion. To keep off rheumatism."

"Christ Almighty!"

Ekata laughed.

"The whole place stinks of onion and flannel, can't you air it out?"

"No. Cold days they even close the chimney flues. Rather have the smoke than the cold."

"You ought to come back to town with me, Ekata."

"Ma's not well."

"You can't help that."

"No. But I'd feel mean to leave her without good reason. First things first." Ekata had lost weight; her cheekbones stood out and her eyes looked darker. "How's it going with you?" she asked presently.

"All right. We've been laid off a good bit, the snow."

"You've been growing up," Ekata said.

"I know."

He sat on the stiff farm-parlour sofa with a man's weight, a man's quietness.

"You walking out with anybody?"

"No." They both laughed. "Listen, I saw Fabbre, and he said to wish you joy of the season. He's better. Gets outside now, with a cane."

Their cousin came through the room. She wore a man's old boots stuffed with straw for warmth getting about in the ice and mud of the farmyard. Martin looked after her with disgust. "I had a talk with him.

Couple of weeks ago. I hope he's back in the pits by Easter like they say. He's my foreman, you know." Looking at him, Ekata saw who it was he was in love with.

"I'm glad you like him."

"There isn't a man in Kampe comes up to his shoulder. You liked him, didn't you?"

"Of course I did."

"See, when he asked about you, I thought—"

"You thought wrong," Ekata said. "Will you quit meddling, Martin?"

"I didn't say anything," he defended himself feebly; his sister could still overawe him. He also recalled that Rosana Fabbre had laughed at him when he had said something to her about Kostant and Ekata. She had been hanging out sheets in the back yard on a whipping-bright winter morning a few days ago, he had hung over the back fence talking to her. "Oh Lord, are you crazy?" she had jeered, while the damp sheets on the line billowed at her face and the wind tangled her hair. "Those two? Not on your life!" He had tried to argue; she would not listen. "He's not going to marry anybody from here. There's going to be some woman from far off, from Krasnoy maybe, a manager's wife, a queen, a beauty, with servants and all. And one day she'll be coming down Ardure Street with her nose in the air and she'll see Kostant coming with his nose in the air, and crack! that's it."

"That's what?" said he, fascinated by her fortune-teller's conviction.

"I don't know!" she said, and hoisted up another sheet. "Maybe they'll run off together. Maybe something else. All I know is Kostant knows what's coming to him, and he's going to wait for it."

"All right, if you know so much, what's coming your way?"

She opened her mouth wide in a big grin, her dark eyes under long dark brows flashed at him. "Men," she said like a cat hissing, and the sheets and shirts snapped and billowed around her, white in the flashing sunlight.

January passed, covering the surly plain with snow, February with a grey sky moving slowly over the plain from north to south day after day: a hard winter and a long one. Kostant Fabbre got a lift sometimes on a cart to the Chorin quarries north of town, and would stand watching the work, the teams of men and lines of wagons, the shunting boxcars, the white of snow and the dull white of new-cut limestone. Men would come up to the tall man leaning on his cane to ask him how he did, when he was coming back to work. "A few weeks yet," he would say. The company was keeping him laid off till April as their insurers requested. He felt fit, he could walk back to town without using his cane, it fretted him bitterly to be idle. He would go back, to the White Lion, and sit there in the smoky dark and warmth till the quarrymen came in, off work at four because of snow and darkness, big heavy men making the place steam with the heat of their bodies and buzz with the mutter of their voices. At five Stefan would come in, slight, with white shirt and light shoes, a queer figure among the quarriers. He usually came to Kostant's table, but they were not on good terms. Each was waiting and impatient.

"Evening," Martin Sachik said passing the table, a tired burly lad, smiling. "Evening, Stefan."

"I'm Fabbre and Mr to you, laddie," Stefan said in his soft voice that yet stood out against the comfortable hive-mutter. Martin, already past, chose to pay no attention.

"Why are you down on that one?"

"Because I don't choose to be on first names with every man's brat that goes down in the pits. Nor every man either. D'you take me for the town idiot?"

"You act like it, times," Kostant said, draining his beermug.

"I've had enough of your advice."

"I've had enough of your conceit. Go to the Bell if the company here don't suit you."

Stefan got up, slapped money on the table, and went out.

It was the first of March; the north half of the sky over the streets was heavy, without light; its edge was silvery blue, and from it south to the horizon the air was blue and empty except for a fingernail moon over the western hills and, near it, the evening star. Stefan went silent through the streets, a silent wind at his back. Indoors, the walls of the house enclosed his rage; it became a square, dark, musty thing full of the angles of tables and chairs, and flared up yellow with the kerosene lamp. The chimney of the lamp slithered out of his hand like a live animal, smashed itself shrilly against the corner of the table. He was on all fours picking up bits of glass when his brother came in.

"What did you follow me for?"

"I came to my own house."

"Do I have to go back to the Lion then?"

"Go where you damned well like." Kostant sat down and picked up yesterday's newspaper. Stefan, kneeling, broken glass on the palm of his hand, spoke: "Listen. I know why you want me patting young Sachik on the head. For one thing he thinks you're God Almighty, and that's agreeable. For another thing he's got a sister. And you want 'em all eating out of your hand, don't you? Like they all do? Well by God here's one that won't, and you might find your game spoiled, too." He got up and went to the kitchen, to the trash basket that stood by the week's heap of dirty clothes, and dropped the glass of the broken lamp into the basket. He stood looking at his hand: a sliver of glass bristled from the inner joint of his second finger. He had clenched his hand on the glass as he spoke to Kostant. He pulled out the sliver and put the bleeding finger to his mouth. Kostant came in. "What game, Stefan?" he said.

"You know what I mean."

"Say what you mean."

"I mean her. Ekata. What do you want her for anyhow? You don't need her. You don't need anything. You're the big tin god."

"You shut your mouth."

"Don't give me orders! By God I can give orders too. You just stay away from her. I'll get her and you won't, I'll get her under your nose, under your eyes—" Kostant's big hands took hold of his shoulders and shook him till his head snapped back and forth on his neck. He broke free and drove his fist straight at Kostant's face, but as he did so he felt a jolt as when a train-car is coupled to the train. He fell down backwards across the heap of dirty clothes. His head hit the floor with a dead sound like a dropped melon.

Kostant stood with his back against the stove. He looked at his right-hand knuckles, then at Stefan's face, which was dead white and curiously serene. Kostant took a pillowcase from the pile of clothes, wet it at the sink, and knelt down by Stefan. It was hard for him to kneel, the right leg was still stiff. He mopped away the thin dark line of blood that had run from Stefan's mouth. Stefan's face twitched, he sighed and blinked, and looked up at Kostant, gazing with vague, sliding recognition, like a young infant.

"That's better," Kostant said. His own face was white.

Stefan propped himself up on one arm. "I fell down," he said in a faint, surprised voice. Then he looked at Kostant again and his face began to change and tighten.

"Stefan—"

Stefan got up on all fours, then onto his feet; Kostant tried to take his arm, but he stumbled to the door, struggled with the catch, and plunged out. At the door, Kostant watched him vault the fence, cut across the Katalny yard, and run down Gulhelm Street with long, jolting strides. For several minutes the elder brother stood in the doorway, his face rigid and sorrowful. Then he turned, went to the front door and out, and made off down Gulhelm Street as fast as he could. The black cloud-front had covered all the sky but a thin band of blue-green to the south; the moon and stars were gone. Kostant followed the track over the plain to the West Pit. No one was ahead of him. He reached the lip of the quarry and saw the water quiet, dim, reflecting snow that had yet to fall. He called out once, "Stefan!" His lungs were raw and his throat dry from the effort he had made to run. There was no answer. It was not his brother's name that need be called there at the lip of the ruined quarry. It was the wrong name, and the wrong time. Kostant turned and started back towards Gulhelm Street, walking slowly and a little lame.

"I've got to ride to Kolle," Stefan said. The livery-stable keeper stared at his blood-smeared chin.

"It's dark. There's ice on the roads."

"You must have a sharp-shod horse. I'll pay double."

"Well . . ."

Stefan rode out of the stable yard, and turned right down Ardure Street towards Verre instead of left towards Kolle. The keeper shouted after him. Stefan kicked the horse, which fell into a trot and then, where the pavement ceased, into a heavy run. The band of blue-green light in the southwest veered and slid away, Stefan thought he was falling sideways, he clung to the pommel but did not pull the reins. When the horse ran itself out and slowed to a walk it was full night, earth and sky all dark. The horse snorted, the saddle creaked, the wind hissed in frozen grass. Stefan dismounted and searched the ground as best he could. The horse had kept to the wagon road and stood not four feet from the ruts. They went on, horse and man; mounted, the man could not see the ruts; he let the horse follow the track across the plain, himself following no road.

After a long time in the rocking dark something touched his face once, lightly.

He felt his cheek. The right side of his jaw was swollen and stiff, and his right hand holding the reins was locked by the cold, so that when he tried to change his grip he did not know if his fingers moved or not. He had no gloves, though he wore the winter coat he had never taken off when he came into the house, when the lamp broke, a long time ago. He got the reins in his left hand and put the right inside his coat to warm it. The horse jogged on patiently, head low. Again something touched Stefan's face very lightly, brushing his cheek, his hot sore lip. He could not see the flakes. They were soft and did not feel cold. He waited for the gentle, random touch of the snow. He changed hands on the reins again, and put the left hand under the horse's coarse, damp mane, on the warm hide. They both took comfort in the touch. Trying to see ahead, Stefan knew where sky and horizon met, or thought he did, but the plain was gone. The ceiling of sky was gone. The horse walked on darkness, under darkness, through darkness.

Once the word "lost" lit itself like a match in the darkness, and Stefan tried to stop the horse so he could get off and search for the wheel-ruts, but the horse kept walking on. Stefan let his numb hand holding the reins rest on the pommel, let himself be borne.

The horse's head came up, its gait changed for a few steps. Stefan clutched at the wet mane, raised his own head dizzily, blinked at a spiderweb of light tangled in his eyes. Through the splintery blur of ice on his lashes the light grew square and yellowish: a window. What house stood out alone here on the endless plain? Dim blocks of pallor rose up on both sides of him—storefronts, a street. He had come to Verre. The horse stopped and sighed so that the girths creaked loudly. Stefan did not remember leaving Sfaroy Kampe. He sat astride a sweating horse in a dark street somewhere. One window was alight in a second storey. Snow fell in sparse clumps, as if hurled down in handfuls. There was little on the ground, it melted as it touched, a spring snow. He rode to the house with the lighted window and called aloud, "Where's the road to Lotima?"

The door opened, snow flickered whirling in the shaft of light. "Are ye the doctor?"

"No. How do I get on to Lotima?"

"Next turn right. If ye meet the doctor tell him hurry on!"

The horse left the village unwillingly, lame on one leg and then the other. Stefan kept his head raised looking for the dawn, which surely must be near. He rode north now, the snow blowing in his face, blinding him even to the darkness. The road climbed, went down, climbed again. The horse stopped, and when Stefan did nothing, turned left, made a couple of stumbling steps, stopped again shuddering and neighed. Stefan dismounted, falling to hands and knees because his legs were too stiff at first to hold him. There was a cattle-guard of poles laid across a side-road. He let the horse stand and felt his way up the side-road to a sudden house lifting a dark wall and snowy roof above him. He found the door, knocked, waited, knocked; a window rattled, a woman said frightened to death over his head, "Who's that?"

"Is this the Sachik farm?"

"No! Who's that?"

"Have I passed the Sachiks'?"

"Are ye the doctor?"

"Yes."

"It's the next but one on the left side. Want a lantern, doctor?"

She came downstairs and gave him a lantern and matches; she held a candle, which dazzled his eyes so that he never saw her face.

He went at the horse's head now, the lantern in his left hand and the reins in his right, held close to the bridle. The horse's docile, patient, stumbling walk, the liquid darkness of its eye in the gleam of the lantern, grieved Stefan sorely. They walked ahead very slowly and he looked for the dawn.

A farmhouse flickered to his left when he was almost past it; snow, windplastered on its north wall, caught the light of the lantern. He led the horse back. The hinges of the gate squealed. Dark outbuildings crowded round. He knocked, waited, knocked. A light moved inside the house, the door opened, again a candle held at eye-level dazzled him.

"Who is that?"

"That's you, Ekata," he said.

"Who is that? Stefan?"

"I must have missed the other farm, the one in between."

"Come in—"

"The horse. Is that the stable?"

"There, to the left—"

He was all right while he found a stall for the horse, robbed the Sachiks' roan of some hay and water, found a sack and rubbed the horse down a bit; he did all that very well, he thought, but when he got back to the house his knees went weak and he could scarcely see the room or Ekata who took his hand to bring him in. She had on a coat over something white, a nightgown. "Oh lad," she said, "you rode from Kampe tonight?"

"Poor old horse," he said, and smiled. His voice said the words some while after he thought he had said them. He sat down on the sofa.

"Wait there," she said. It seemed she left the room for a while, then she was putting a cup of something in his hands. He drank; it was hot; the sting of brandy woke him long enough to watch her stir up the buried coals and put wood on the fire. "I wanted to talk to you, see," he said, and then he fell asleep.

She took off his shoes, put his legs up on the sofa, got a blanket and put it over him, tended the reluctant fire. He never stirred. She turned out the lamp and slipped back upstairs in the dark. Her bed was by the window of her attic room, and she could see or feel that it was now snowing soft and thick in the dark outside.

She roused to a knock and sat up seeing the even light of snow on walls and ceiling. Her uncle peered in. He was wearing yellowish-white woollen underwear and his hair stuck up like fine wire around his bald spot. The whites of his eyes were the same color as his underwear. "Who's that downstairs?"

Ekata explained to Stefan, somewhat later in the morning, that he was on his way to Lotima on business for the Chorin Company, that he had started from Kampe at noon and been held up by a stone in his horse's shoe and then by the snow.

"Why?" he said, evidently confused, his face looking rather childish with fatigue and sleep.

"I had to tell them something."

He scratched his head. "What time did I get here?"

"About two in the morning."

He remembered how he had looked for the dawn, hours away.

"What did you come for?" Ekata said. She was clearing the breakfast table; her face was stern, though she spoke softly.

"I had a fight," Stefan said. "With Kostant."

She stopped, holding two plates, and looked at him.

"You don't think I hurt him?" He laughed. He was lightheaded, tired out, serene. "He knocked me cold. You don't think I could have beat him?"

"I don't know," Ekata said with distress.

"I always lose fights," Stefan said. "And run away."

The deaf man came through, dressed to go outside in heavy boots, an old coat made of blanketing; it was still snowing. "Ye'll not get on to Lotima today, Mr Stefan," he said in his loud even voice, with satisfaction. "Tomas says the nag's lame on four legs." This had been discussed at breakfast, but the deaf man had not heard. He had not asked how Kostant was getting on, and when he did so later in the day it was with the same satisfied malice: "And your brother, he's down in the pits again, no doubt?" He did not try to hear the answer.

Stefan spent most of the day by the fire sleeping. Only Ekata's cousin was curious about him. She said to Ekata as they were cooking supper, "They say his brother is a handsome man."

"Kostant? The handsomest man I ever saw." Ekata smiled, chopping onions.

"I don't know as I'd call this one handsome," the cousin said tentatively.

The onions were making Ekata cry; she laughed, blew her nose, shook her head. "Oh no," she said.

After supper Stefan met Ekata as she came into the kitchen from dumping out peelings and swill for the pigs. She wore her father's coat, clogs on her shoes, her black kerchief. The freezing wind swept in with her till she wrestled the door shut. "It's clearing," she said, "the wind's from the south."

"Ekata, do you know what I came here for—"

"Do you know yourself?" she said, looking up at him as she set the bucket down.

"Yes, I do."

"Then I do, I suppose."

"There isn't anywhere," he said in rage as the uncle's clumping boots approached the kitchen.

"There's my room," she said impatiently. But the walls were thin, and the cousin slept in the next attic and her parents across the stairwell; she frowned angrily and said, "No. Wait till the morning."

In the morning, early, the cousin went off alone down the road. She was back in half an hour, her straw-stuffed boots smacking in the thawing snow and mud. The neighbor's wife at the next house but one had said, "He said he was the doctor, I asked who it was was sick with you. I gave him the lantern, it was so dark I didn't see his face, I thought it was the doctor, he said so." The cousin was munching the words sweetly, deciding whether to accost Stefan with them, or Ekata, or both before witnesses, when around a bend and down the snow-clotted, sun-bright grade of the road two horses came at a long trot: the livery-stable horse and the farm's old roan. Stefan and Ekata rode; they were both laughing. "Where ye going?" the cousin shouted, trembling. "Running away," the young man called back, and they went past her, splashing the puddles into diamond-slivers in the sunlight of March, and were gone.

A Week in the Country

On a sunny morning of 1962 in Cleveland, Ohio, it was raining in Krasnoy and the streets between grey walls were full of men. "It's raining down my neck in here," Kasimir complained, but his friend in the adjoining stall of the streetcorner W.C. did not hear him because he was also talking: "Historical necessity is a solecism, what is history except what had to happen? But you can't extend that. What happens next? God knows!" Kasimir followed him out, still buttoning his trousers, and looked at the small boy looking at the nine-foot-long black coffin leaning against the W.C. "What's in it?" the boy asked. "My great-aunt's body," Kasimir explained. He picked up the coffin, hurried on with Stefan Fabbre through the rain. "A farce, determinism's a farce. Anything to avoid awe. Show me a seed," Stefan Fabbre said stopping and pointing at Kasimir, "yes, I can tell you what it is, it's an apple seed. But can I tell you that an apple tree will grow from it? No! Because there's no freedom, we think there's a law. But there is no law. There's growth and death, delight and terror, an abyss, the rest we invent. We're going to miss the train." They jostled on up Tiypontiy Street, the rain fell harder. Stefan Fabbre strode swinging his briefcase, his mouth firmly closed, his white face shining wet. "Why didn't you take up the piccolo? Give me that awhile," he said as Kasimir tangled with an office-worker running for a bus. "Science bearing the burden of Art," Kasimir said, "heavy, isn't it?" as his friend hoisted the case and lugged it on, frowning and by the time they reached West Station gasping. On the platform in rain and steam they ran as others ran, heard whistles shriek and urgent Sanskrit blare from loudspeakers, and lurched exhausted into the first car. The compartments were all empty. It was the other train that was pulling out, jammed, a suburban train. Theirs sat still for ten minutes. "Nobody on this train but us?" Stefan Fabbre asked, morose, standing at the window. Then with one high peep the walls slid away. Raindrops shook and merged on the pane, tracks interwove on a viaduct, the two young men stared into bedroom windows and at brick walls painted with enormous letters. Abruptly nothing was left in the rain-dark evening sliding backwards to the east but a line of hills, black against a colorless clearing sky.

"The country," Stefan Fabbre said.

He got out a biochemical journal from amongst socks and undershirts in his briefcase, put on dark-rimmed glasses, read. Kasimir pushed back wet hair that had fallen all over his forehead, read the sign on the windowsill that said DO NOT LEAN OUT, stared at the shaking walls and the rain shuddering on the window, dozed. He dreamed that walls were falling down around him. He woke scared as they pulled out of Okats. His friend sat looking out the window, white-faced and black-haired, confirming the isolation and disaster of Kasimir's dream. "Can't see anything," he said. "Night. Country's the only place where they have night left." He stared through the reflection of his own face into the night that filled his eyes with blessed darkness.

"So here we are on a train going to Aisnar," Kasimir said, "but we don't know that it's going to Aisnar. It might go to Peking."

"It might derail and we'll all be killed. And if we do come to Aisnar? What's Aisnar? Mere hearsay."—"That's morbid," Kasimir said, glimpsing again the walls collapsing.—"No, exhilarating," his friend answered. "Takes a lot of work to hold the world together, when you look at it that way. But it's worthwhile. Building up cities, holding up the roofs by an act of fidelity. Not faith. Fidelity." He gazed out the window through his reflected eyes. Kasimir shared a bar of mud-like chocolate with him. They came to Aisnar.

Rain fell in the gold-paved, ill-lit streets while the autobus to Vermare and Prevne waited for its passengers in South Square under dripping sycamores. The case rode in the back seat. A chicken with a string round its neck scratched the aisle for grain, a bushy-haired woman held the other end of the string, a drunk farm-worker talked loudly to the driver as the bus groaned out of Aisnar southward into the country night, the same night, the blessed darkness.

"So I says to him, I says, you don't know what'll happen tomorrow—"

"Listen," said Kasimir, "if the universe is infinite, does that mean that everything that could possibly happen, is happening, somewhere, at some time?"

"Saturday, he says, Saturday."

"I don't know. It would. But we don't know what's possible. Thank God. If we did, I'd shoot myself, eh?"

"Come back Saturday, he says, and I says, Saturday be damned, I says."

In Vermare rain fell on the ruins of the Tower Keep, and the drunk got off leaving silence behind him. Stefan Fabbre looked glum, said he had a sore throat, and fell into a quick, weary sleep. His head jiggled to the ruts and bumps of the foothill road as the bus ran westward clearing a tunnel through solid black with its headlights. A tree, a great oak, bent down suddenly to shelter it. The doors opened admitting clean air, flashlights, boots and caps. Brushing back his fair hair Kasimir said softly, "Always happens. Only six miles from the border here." They felt in their breast-pockets, handed over. "Fabbre Stefan, domicile 136 Tome Street, Krasnoy, student, MR 64100282A. Augeskar Kasimir, domicile 4 Sorden Street, Krasnoy, student, MR 80104944A. Where are you going?"—"Prevne."—"Both of you? Business?"—"Vacation. A week in the country."—"What's that?"—"A bass-viol case."—"What's in it?"—"A bass viol." It was stood up, opened, closed again, lugged out, laid on the ground, opened again, and the huge viol stood fragile and magnificent among flashlights over the mud, boots, belt-buckles, caps. "Keep it off the ground!" Kasimir said in a sharp voice, and Stefan pushed in front of him. They fingered it, shook it. "Here, Kasi, does this unscrew?—No, there's no way to take it apart." The fat one slapped the great shining curve of wood saying something about his wife so that Stefan laughed, but the viol tilted in another's hands, a tuning-peg squawked, and on the patter of rain and mutter of the bus-engine idling, a booming twang uncurled, broken off short like the viol-string. Stefan took hold of Kasimir's arm. After the bus had started again they sat side by side in the warm stinking darkness. Kasimir said, "Sorry, Stefan. Thanks."

"Can you fix it?"

"Yes, just the peg snapped. I can fix it."

"Damn sore throat." Stefan rubbed his head and left his hands over his eyes. "Taking cold. Damn rain."

"We're near Prevne now."

In Prevne very fine rain drifted down one street between two streetlamps. Behind the roofs something loomed—treetops, hills? No one met them since Kasimir had forgotten to write which night they were coming. Returning from the one public telephone, he joined Stefan and the bass-viol case at a table of the Post-Telephone Bar. "Father has the car out on a call. We can walk or wait here. Sorry." His long fair face was discouraged; contrite. "It's a couple of miles." They set off. They walked in silence up a dirt road in rain and darkness between fields. The air smelt of wet earth. Kasimir began to whistle but the rain wet his lips, he stopped. It was so dark that they walked slowly, not able to see where each step took them, whether the road was rough or plain. It was so still that they heard the multitudinous whisper of the rain on fields to left and right. They were climbing. The hill loomed ahead of them, solider darkness. Stefan stopped to turn up his wet coatcollar and because he was dizzy. As he went forward again in the chill whispering country silence he heard a soft clear sound, a girl laughing behind the hill. Lights sprang up at the hillcrest, sparkling, waving. "What's that?" he said stopping unnerved in the broken dark. A child shouted, "There they are!" The lights above them danced and descended, they were encircled by lanterns, flashlights, voices calling, faces and arms lit by flashes and vanishing again into night; clearly once more, right at his side, the sweet laugh rang out. "Father didn't come back and you didn't come, so we all came to meet you."—"Did you bring your friend, where is he?"—"Hello, Kasi!" Kasimir's fair head bent to another in the gleam of a lantern. "Where's your fiddle, didn't you bring it?"—"It's been raining like this all week."—"Left it with Mr Praspayets at the Post-Telephone."—"Let's go on and get it, it's lovely walking."—"I'm

Bendika, are you Stefan?" She laughed as they sought each other's hands to shake in darkness; she turned her lantern round and was dark-haired, as tall as her brother, the only one of them he saw clearly before they all went back down the road talking, laughing, flashing lightbeams over the road and roadside weeds or up into the rain-thick air. He saw them all for a moment in the bar as Kasimir got his bull-fiddle: two boys, a man, tall Bendika, the young blonde one who had kissed Kasimir, another still younger, all of them he saw all at once and then they were off up the road again and he must wonder which of the three girls, or was it four, had laughed before they met. The chill rain picked at his hot face. Beside him, beaming a flashlight so they could see the road, the man said, "I'm Joachim Bret."—"Enzymes," Stefan replied hoarsely.—"Yes, what's your field?"—"Molecular genetics."—"No! too good! you work with Metor, then? Catch me up, will you? Do you see the American journals?" They talked helices for half a mile, Bret voluble, Stefan laconic as he was still dizzy and still listened for the laugh; but all of them laughed, he could not be sure. They all fell silent a moment, only the two boys ran far ahead, calling. "There's the house," tall Bendika said beside him; pointing to a yellow gleam. "Still with us, Stefan?" Kasimir called from somewhere in the dark. He growled yes, resenting the silly good cheer, the running and calling and laughing, the enthusiastic jerky Bret, the yellow windows that to all of them were home but to him not. Inside the house they shed wet coats, spread, multiplied, regathered around a table in a high dark room shot through with noise and lamplight, for coffee and coffeecake borne in by Kasimir's mother. She walked hurried and tranquil under a grey and dark-brown coronet of braids. Bass-viol-shaped, mother of seven, she merged Stefan with all the other young people whom she distinguished one from another only by name. They were named Valeria, Bendika, Antony, Bruna, Kasimir, Joachim, Paul. They joked and chattered, the little dark girl screamed with laughter, Kasimir's fair hair fell over his eyes, the two boys of eleven squabbled, the gaunt smiling man sat with a guitar and presently played, his face beaked like a crow's over the instrument. His right hand plucking the strings was slightly crippled or deformed. They sang, all but Stefan who did not know the songs, had a sore throat, would not sing, sat rancorous amid the singers. Dr Augeskar came in. He shook Kasimir's hand, welcoming and effacing him, a tall king with a slender and unlikely heir. "Where's your friend? Sorry I couldn't meet you, had an emergency up the road. Appendectomy on the dining table. Like carving the Christmas goose. Get to bed, Antony. Bendika, get me a glass. Joachim? You, Fabbre?" He poured out red wine and sat down with them at the great round table. They sang again. Augeskar suggested the songs, his voice led the others; he filled the room. The fair daughter flirted with him, the little dark one screeched with laughter, Bendika teased Kasimir, Bret sang a love-song in Swedish; it was only eleven o'clock. Dr Augeskar had grey eyes, clear under blond brows. Stefan met their stare. "You've got a cold?"—"Yes."—"Then go to bed. Diana! where does Fabbre sleep?" Kasimir jumped up contrite, led Stefan upstairs and through corridors and rooms all smelling of hay and rain. "When's breakfast?"—"Oh, anytime," for Kasimir never knew the time of any event. "Good night, Stefan." But it was a bad night, miserable, and all through it Bret's crippled hand snapped off one great coiling string after another with a booming twang while he explained, "This is how you go after them the latest," grinning. In the morning Stefan could not get up. Sunlit walls leaned inward over the bed and the sky came stretching in the windows, a huge blue balloon. He lay there. He hid his pin-stiff aching black hair under his hands and moaned. The tall golden-grey man came in and said to him with perfect certainty, "My boy, you're sick." It was balm. Sick, he was sick, the walls and sky were all right. "A very respectable fever you're running," said the doctor and Stefan smiled, near tears, feeling himself respectable, lapped in the broad indifferent tenderness of the big man who was kingly, certain, uncaring as sunlight in the sky. But in the forests and caves and small crowded rooms of his fever no sunlight came, and after a time no water.

The house stood quiet in the September sunlight and dark.

That night Mrs Augeskar, yarn, needle, sock poised one moment in her hands, lifted her braid-crowned head, listening as she had listened years ago to her first son, Kasimir, crying out in sleep in his crib upstairs. "Poor child," she whispered. And Bruna raised her fair head listening too, for the first time, hearing the solitary cry from the forests where she had never been. The house stood still around them. On the second day the boys played outdoors till rain fell and night fell. Kasimir stood in the kitchen sawing on his bull-fiddle, his face by the shining neck of the instrument quiet and closed, keeping right on when others came in to perch on stools and lean against the sink and talk, for after all there were seven young people there on vacation, they could not stay silent. But under their voices the deep, weak, singing voice of Kasimir's fiddle went on wordless, like a cry from the depths of the forest; so that Bruna suddenly past patience and dependence, solitary, not the third daughter and fourth child and one of the young people, slipped away and went upstairs to see what it was like, this grave sickness, this mortality.

It was not like anything. The young man slept. His face was white, his hair black on white linen: clear as printed words, but in a foreign language.

She came down and told her mother she had looked in, he was sleeping quietly; true enough, but not the truth. What she had confirmed up there was that she was now ready to learn the way through the forest; she had come of age, and was now capable of dying.

He was her guide, the young man who had come in out of the rain with a case of pneumonia. On the afternoon of the fifth day she went up to his room again. He was lying there getting well, weak and content, thinking about a morning ten years ago when he had walked out with his father and grandfather past the quarries, an April morning on a dry plain awash with sunlight and blue flowers. After they had passed the Chorin Company quarries they suddenly began to talk politics, and he understood that they had come out of town onto the empty plain in order to say things aloud, in order to let him hear what his father said: "There'll always be enough ants to fill up all the ant-hills—worker ants, army ants." And the grandfather, the dry, bitter, fitful man, in his seventies angrier and gentler than his son, vulnerable as his thirteen-year-old grandson: "Get out, Kosta, why don't you get out?" That was only a taunt. None of them would run away, or get away. A man, he walked with men across a barren plain blue with flowers in brief April; they shared with him their anger, their barren helpless obduracy and the brief blue fire of their anger. Talking aloud under the open sky, they gave him the key to the house of manhood, the prison where they lived and he would live. But they had known other houses. He had not. Once his grandfather, Stefan Fabbre, put his hand on young Stefan's shoulder while he spoke. "What would we do with freedom if we had it, Kosta? What has the West done with it? Eaten it. Put it in its belly. A great wondrous belly, that's the West. With a wise head on top of it, a man's head, with a man's mind and eyes—but the rest all belly. He can't walk any more. He sits at table eating, eating, thinking up machines to bring him more food, more food. Throwing food to the black and yellow rats under the table so they won't gnaw down the walls around him. There he sits, and here we are, with nothing in our bellies but air, air and cancer, air and rage. We can still walk. So we're yoked. Yoked to the foreign plow. When we smell food we bray and kick. —Are we men, though, Kosta? I doubt it." All the time his hand lay on the boy's shoulder, tender, almost deferent, because the boy had never seen his inheritance at all but had been born in jail, where nothing is any good, no anger, understanding, or pride, nothing is any good except obduracy, except fidelity. Those remain, said the weight of the old man's hand on his shoulder. So when a blonde girl came into his room where he lay weak and content, he looked at her from that sunwashed barren April plain with trust and welcome, it being irrelevant to this moment that his grandfather had died in a deportation train and his father had been shot along with forty-two other men on the plain outside town in the reprisals of 1956. "How do you feel?" she said, and he said, "Fine."

"Can I bring you anything?"

He shook his head, the same black-and-white head she had seen clear and unintelligible as Greek words on a white page, but now his eyes were open and he spoke her language. It was the same voice that had called faintly from the black woods of fever, the neighborhood of death, a few nights ago, which now said, "I can't remember your name." He was very nice, he was a nice fellow, this Stefan Fabbre, embarrassed by lying there sick, glad to see her. "I'm Bruna, I come next after Kasi. Would you like some books? Are you getting bored yet?"—"Bored? No. You don't know how good it is to lie here doing nothing, I've never done that. Your parents are so kind, and this big house, and the fields outside there—I lie here thinking, Jesus, is this me? In all this peace, in all this space, in a room to myself doing nothing?" She laughed, by which he knew her: the one who had laughed in rain and darkness before lights broke over the hill. Her fair hair was parted in the middle and waved on each side down nearly to the light, thick eyebrows; her eyes were an indeterminate color, unclear, grey-brown or grey. He heard it now indoors in daylight, the tender and exultant laugh. "Oh you beauty, you fine proud filly-foal never broken to harness, you scared and restive, gentle girl laughing. . . ."

Wanting to keep her he asked, "Have you always lived here?" and she said, "Yes, summers," glancing at him from her indeterminate, shining eyes in the shadow of fair hair. "Where did you grow up?"

"In Sfaroy Kampe, up north."

"Your family's still there?"

"My sister lives there." She still asked about families. She must be very innocent, more elusive and intact even than Kasimir, who placed his reality beyond the touch of any hands or asking of identity. Still to keep her with him, he said, "I lie here thinking. I've thought more already today than in the last three years."

"What do you think of?"

"Of the Hungarian nobleman, do you know that story? The one that was taken prisoner by the Turks, and sold as a slave. It was in the sixteenth century. Well, a Turk bought him, and yoked him to a plow, like an ox, and he plowed the fields, driven with a whip. His family finally managed to buy him back. And he went home, and got his sword, and went back to the battlefields. And there he took prisoner the Turk that had bought him, owned him. Took the Turk back to his manor. Took the chains off him, had him brought outside. And the poor Turk looked around for the impaling stake, you know, or the pitch they'd rub on him and set fire to, or the dogs, or at least the whip. But there was nothing. Only the Hungarian, the man he'd bought and sold. And the Hungarian said, "Go on back home. . . ."

"Did he go?"

"No, he stayed and turned Christian. But that's not why I think of it."

"Why do you?"

"I'd like to be a nobleman," Stefan Fabbre said, grinning. He was a tough, hard fellow, lying there nearly defeated but not defeated. He

grinned, his eyes had a black flicker to them; at twenty-five he had no
innocence, no confidence, no hope at all of profit. The lack of that was
the black flicker, the coldness in his eyes. Yet he lay there taking what
came, a small man but hard, possessing weight, a man of substance. The
girl looked at his strong, blunt hands on the blanket and then up at the
sunlit windows, thinking of his being a nobleman, thinking of the one
fact she knew of him from Kasimir, who seldom mentioned facts: that
he shared a tenement room in Krasnoy with five other students, three
beds were all they could fit into it. The room, with three high windows,
curtains pulled back, hummed with the silence of September afternoon
in the country. A boy's voice rang out from fields far away. "Not much
chance of it these days," she said in a dull soft voice, looking down,
meaning nothing, for once wholly cast down, tired, without tenderness
or exultation. He would get well, would go back a week late to the city, to
the three bedsteads and five roommates, shoes on the floor and rust and
hairs in the washbasin, classrooms, laboratories, after that employment
as an inspector of sanitation on State farms in the north and northeast, a
two-room flat in State housing on the outskirts of a town near the State
foundries, a black-haired wife who taught the third grade from State-
approved textbooks, one child, two legal abortions, and the hydrogen
bomb. Oh was there no way out, no way? "Are you very clever?"

"I'm very good at my work."

"It's science, isn't it?"

"Biology. Research."

Then the laboratories would persist; the flat became perhaps a four-
room flat in the Krasnoy suburbs; two children, no abortions, two-week
vacations in summer in the mountains, then the hydrogen bomb. Or no
hydrogen bomb. It made no difference.

"What do you do research on?"

"Certain molecules. The molecular structure of life."

That was strange, the structure of life. Of course he was talking
down to her; things are not briefly described, her father had said, when
one is talking of life. So he was good at finding out the molecular
structure of life, this fellow whose wordless cry she had heard faintly
from congested lungs, from the dark neighborhood and approaches of

his death; he had called out and "Poor child," her mother had whispered, but it was she who had answered, had followed him. And now he brought her back to life.

"Ah," she said, still not lifting her head, "I don't understand all that. I'm stupid."

"Why did they name you Bruna, when you're blonde?"

She looked up startled, laughed. "I was bald till I was ten months old." She looked at him, seeing him again, and the future be damned, since all possible futures ever envisaged are—rusty sinks, two-week vacations and bombs or collective fraternity or harps and houris— endlessly, sordidly dreary, all delight being in the present and its past, all truth too, and all fidelity in the word, the flesh, the present moment: for the future, however you look at it, contains only one sure thing and that is death. But the moment is unpredictable. There is simply no telling what will happen. Kasimir came in with a bunch of red and blue flowers and said, "Mother wants to know if you'd like milk-toast for supper."

"Oatbread, oatbread," Bruna sang arranging the cornflowers and poppies in Stefan's water-glass. They ate oats three times a day here, some poultry, turnips, potatoes; the little brother Antony raised lettuce, the mother cooked, the daughters swept the big house; there was no wheat-flour, no beef, no milk, no housemaid, not any more, not since before Bruna was born. They camped here in their big old country house, they lived like gypsies, said the mother: a professor's daughter born in the middle class, nurtured and married in the middle class, giving up order, plenty, and leisure without complaint but not giving up the least scruple of the discriminations she had been privileged to learn. So Kasimir for all his gentleness could still hold himself untouched. So Bruna still thought of herself as coming next after Kasimir, and asked about one's family. So Stefan knew himself here in a fortress, in a family, at home. He and Kasimir and Bruna were laughing aloud together when the father came in. "Out," Dr Augeskar said, standing heroic and absolute in the doorway, the sun-king or a solar myth; his son and daughter, laughing and signalling child-like to Stefan behind his back, went out. "Enough is enough," Augeskar said, ausculting, and Stefan lay guilty, smiling, child-like.

The seventh day, when Stefan and Kasimir should have taken bus and train back to Krasnoy where the University was now open, was hot. Warm darkness followed, windows open, the whole house open to choruses of frogs by the river, choruses of crickets in the furrows, a southwest wind bearing odors of the forest over dry autumn hills. Between the curtains billowing and going slack burned six stars, so bright in the dry dark sky that they might set fire to the curtains. Bruna sat on the floor by Stefan's bed, Kasimir lay like a huge wheatstalk across the foot of it, Bendika, whose husband was in Krasnoy, nursed her five-month-old firstborn in a chair by the empty fireplace. Joachim Bret sat on the windowsill, his shirtsleeves rolled up so that the bluish figures OA46992 were visible on his lean arm, playing his guitar to accompany an English lute-song:

Yet be just and constant still,
  Love may beget a wonder,
Not unlike a summer's frost or
    winter's fatal thunder:
He that holds his sweetheart dear
    until his day of dying
Lives of all that ever lived
    most worthy the envying.

Then, since he liked to sing praise and blame of love in all the languages he knew and did not know, he began to strum out "Plaisir d'Amour," but came to grief on the shift of key, while the baby was sat up to belch loudly causing merriment. The baby was flung aloft by Kasimir while Bendika protested softly, "He's full, Kasi, he'll spill."—"I am your uncle. I am Uncle Kasimir, my pockets are full of peppermints and papal indulgences. Look at me, whelp! You don't dare vomit on your uncle. You don't dare. Go vomit on your aunt." The baby stared unwinking at Bruna and waved its hands; its fat, silky belly showed between shirt and diaper. The girl returned its gaze as silently, as steadily. "Who are you?" said the baby. "Who are you?" said the maiden, without words, in wonder, while Stefan watched and faint chords in A sobbed joyously on Bret's guitar between the lighted room and the dark dry night of autumn. The tall young mother carried the baby off to bed, Kasimir turned off the light. Now the autumn night was in the room, and their voices spoke among the choruses of crickets and frogs on the fields, by the streams. "It was clever of you to get sick, Stefan," said Kasimir, lying again across the foot of the bed, long arms white in the dusk. "Stay sick, and we can stay here all winter."

"All year. For years. Did you get your fiddle fixed?"

"Oh yes. Been practicing the Schubert. Pa, pa, poum *pah.*"

"When's the concert?"

"Sometime in October. Plenty of time. Poum, poum—swim, swim, little trout. Ah!" The long white arms sawed vaguely a viol of dusk. "Why did you choose the bass viol, Kasimir?" asked Bret's voice among frogs and crickets, across marshbottoms and furrows, from the windowsill. "Because he's shy," said Bruna's voice like a country wind. "Because he's an enemy of the feasible," said Stefan's dark dry voice. Silence. "Because I showed extraordinary promise as a student of the cello," said Kasimir's voice, "and so I was forced to consider, did I want to perform the Dvorak Concerto to cheering audiences and win a People's Artist award, or did I not? I chose to be a low buzz in the background. Poum, pa poum. And when I die, I want you to put my corpse in the fiddle case, and ship it rapid express deep-freeze to Pablo Casals with a label saying 'Corpse of Great Central European Cellist.'" The hot wind blew through the dark. Kasimir was done, Bruna and Stefan were ready to pass on, but Joachim Bret was not able to. He spoke of a man who had been helping people get across the border; here in the southwest rumors of him were thick now; a young man, Bret said, who had been jailed, had escaped, got to England, and come back; set up an escape route, got over a hundred people out in ten months, and only now had been spotted and was being hunted by the secret police. "Quixotic? Traitorous? Heroic?" Bret asked. "He's hiding in the attic now," Kasimir said, and Stefan added, "Sick of milk-toast." They evaded and would not judge; betrayal and fidelity were immediate to them, could not be weighed any more than a pound of flesh, their own flesh. Only Bret, who had been born outside prison, was excited, insistent. Prevne was crawling with agents, he went, even if you went to buy a newspaper your identification was checked. "Easier to have it tattooed on, like you," said Kasimir. "Move your foot, Stefan."—

"Move your fat rump, then."—"Oh, mine are German numbers, out of date. A few more wars and I'll run out of skin."—"Shed it, then, like a snake."—"No, they go right down to the bone."—"Shed your bones, then," Stefan said, "be a jellyfish. Be an amoeba. When they pin me down, I bud off. Two little spineless Stefans where they thought they had one MR 64100282A. Four of them, eight, sixteen thirty-two sixty-four a hundred and twenty-eight. I would entirely cover the surface of the globe were it not for my natural enemies." The bed shook, Bruna laughed in darkness. "Play the English song again, Joachim," she said.

Yet be just and constant still,
Love may beget a wonder . . .

"Stefan," she said in the afternoon light of the fourteenth day as she sat, and he lay with his head on her lap, on a green bank above the river-marshes south of the house. He opened his eyes: "Must we go?"

"No."

He closed his eyes again, saying, "Bruna." He sat up and sat beside her, staring at her. "Bruna, oh God! I wish you weren't a virgin." She laughed and watched him, wary, curious, defenseless. "If only—here, now—I've got to go away day after tomorrow!"—"But not right under the kitchen windows," she said tenderly. The house stood thirty yards from them. He collapsed by her burying his head in the angle of her arm, against her side, his lips on the very soft skin of her forearm. She stroked his hair and the nape of his neck.

"Can we get married? Do you want to get married?"

"Yes, I want to marry you, Stefan."

He lay still awhile longer, then sat up again, slowly this time, and looked across the reeds and choked, sunlit river to the hills and the mountains behind them.

"I'll have my degree next year."

"I'll have my teaching certificate in a year and a half."

They were silent awhile.

"I could quit school and work. We'll have to apply for a place . . ." The walls of the one rented room facing a courtyard strung with sooty washing rose up around them, indestructible. "All right," he said. "Only I hate to waste this." He looked from the sunlit water up to the mountains. The warm wind of evening blew past them. "All right. But Bruna, do you understand . . ." that all this is new to me, that I have never waked before at dawn in a high-windowed room and lain hearing the perfect silence, never walked out over fields in a bright October morning, never sat down at table with fair, laughing brothers and sisters, never spoken in early evening by a river with a girl who loved me, that I have known that order, peace, and tenderness must exist but never hoped even to witness them, let alone possess them? And day after tomorrow I must go back. No, she did not understand. She was only the country silence and the blessed dark, the bright stream, the wind, the hills, the cool house; all that was hers and her; she could not understand. But she took him in, the stranger in the rainy night, who would destroy her. She sat beside him and said softly, "I think it's worth it, Stefan, it's worthwhile."

"It is. We'll borrow. We'll beg, we'll steal, we'll filch. I'll be a great scientist, you know. I'll create life in a test-tube. After a squalid early career Fabbre rose to sudden prominence. We'll go to meetings in Vienna. In Paris. The hell with life in a test-tube! I'll do better than that, I'll get you pregnant within five minutes, oh you beauty, laugh, do you? I'll show you, you filly, you little trout, oh you darling—" There under the windows of the house and under the mountains still in sunlight, while the boys shouted playing tennis up beside the house, she lay soft, fair, heavy in his arms under his weight, absolutely pure, flesh and spirit one pure will: to let him come in, let him come in.

Not now, not here. His will was mixed, and obdurate. He rolled away and lay face up in the grass, a black flicker in his eyes looking at the sky. She sat with her hand on his hand. Peace had never left her. When he sat up she looked at him as she had looked at Bendika's baby, steadily, with pondering recognition. She had no praise for him, no reservation, no judgment. Here he is; this is he.

"It'll be meager, Bruna. Meager and unprofitable."

"I expect so," she said, watching him.

He stood up and brushed grass off his trousers. "I love Bruna!" he shouted, lifting his hand; and from the sunlit slopes across the river-marshes where dusk was rising came a vague short sound, not her name, not his voice. "You see?" he said standing over her, smiling. "Echoes, even. Get up, the sun's going, do you want me to get pneumonia again?" She reached out her hand, he took it and pulled her up to him. "I'll be very loyal, Bruna," he said. He was a small man and when they stood together she did not look up to him but straight at him at eye level. "That's what I have to give," he said, "that's all I have to give. You may get sick of it, you know." Her eyes, grey-brown or grey, unclear, watched him steadily. In silence he raised his hand to touch for a moment, with reserve and tenderness, her fair parted hair. They went back up to the house, past the tennis court where Kasimir on one side of the net and the two boys on the other swung, missed, leapt and shouted. Under the oaks Bret sat practicing a guitar-tune. "What language is that one?" Bruna asked, standing light in the shadow, utterly happy. Bret cocked his head to answer, his misshapen right hand lying across the strings. "Greek; I got it from a book; it means, 'O young lovers who pass beneath my window, can't you see it's raining?'" She laughed aloud, standing by Stefan who had turned to watch the three run and poise on the tennis court in rising shadow, the ball soar up from moment to moment into the level gold light.

He walked into Prevne next day to buy their tickets with Kasimir, who wanted to see the weekly market there; Kasimir took joy in markets, fairs, auctions, the noise of people getting and selling, the barrows of white and purple turnips, racks of old shoes, mounds of print cotton, stacks of bluecoated cheese, the smell of onions, fresh lavender, sweat, dust. The road that had been long the night they came was brief in the warm morning. "Still looking for that get-em-out-alive fellow, Bret says," said Kasimir. Tall, frail, calm, he moseyed along beside his friend, his bare head bright in the sunlight. "Bruna and I want to get married," Stefan said.

"You do?"

"Yes."

Kasimir hesitated a moment in his longlegged amble, went on, hands in his pockets. Slowly on his face appeared a smile. "Do you really?"

"Yes."

Kasimir stopped, took his right hand out of his pocket, shook Stefan's. "Good work," he said, "well done." He was blushing a little. "Now that's something real," he said, going on, hands in his pockets; Stefan glanced at his long, quiet young face. "That's absolute," Kasimir said, "that's real." After a while he said, "That beats Schubert."

"Main problem is finding a place to live, of course, but if I can borrow something to get started on, Metor still wants me for that project— we'd like to do it straight off—if it's all right with your parents, of course." Kasimir listened fascinated to these chances and circumstances confirming the central fact, just as he watched fascinated the buyers and sellers, shoes and turnips, racks and carts of a market-fair that confirmed men's need of food and of communion. "It'll work out," he said. "You'll find a place."—"I expect so," said Stefan never doubting it. He picked up a rock, tossed it up and caught it, hurled it white through sunlight far into the furrows to their left. "If you knew how happy I am, Kasimir—" His friend answered, "I have some notion. Here, shake hands again." They stopped again to shake hands. "Move in with us, eh, Kasi?"—"All right, get me a truckle-bed." They were coming into town. A khaki-colored truck crawled down Prevne's main street between flyblown shops, old houses painted with garlands long faded; over the roofs rose high yellow hills. Under lindens the market square was dusty and sun-dappled: a few racks, a few stands and carts, a noseless man selling sugarcandy, three dogs cringingly, unwearyingly following a white bitch, old women in black shawls, old men in black vests, the lanky keeper of the Post-Telephone Bar leaning in his doorway and spitting, two fat men dickering in a mumble over a pack of cigarettes. "Used to be more to it," Kasimir said. "When I was a kid here. Lots of cheese from Portacheyka, vegetables, mounds of 'em. Everybody turned out for it." They wandered between the stalls, content, aware of brotherhood. Stefan wanted to buy Bruna something, anything, a scarf; there were buttonless mud-colored overalls, cracked shoes. "Buy her a cabbage," Kasimir said, and Stefan bought a large red cabbage. They went into the Post-Telephone Bar to buy their tickets to Aisnar. "Two on the S.W. to Aisnar, Mr Praspayets."—"Back to work, eh?"—"Right." Three men came up to the counter, two on Kasimir's side one on Stefan's. They handed over. "Fabbre Stefan, domicile 136

Tome Street, Krasnoy, student, MR 64100282A. Augeskar Kasimir, domicile 4 Sorden Street, Krasnoy, student, MR 80104944A. Business in Aisnar?"—"Catching the train to Krasnoy." The men returned to a table. "In here all day, past ten days," the innkeeper said in a thready mumble, "kills my business. I need another hundred kroner, Mr Kasimir; trying to short-change me?" Two of the men, one thickset, the other slim and wearing an army gunbelt under his jacket, were by them again. The smiling innkeeper went blank like a television set clicked off. He watched the agents go through the young men's pockets and feel up and down their bodies; when they had gone back to the table he handed Kasimir his change, silent. They went out in silence. Kasimir stopped and stood looking at the golden lindens, the golden light dappling dust where three dogs still trotted abased and eager after the white bitch, a fat housewife laughed with an old cackling man, two boys dodged yelling among the carts, a donkey hung his grey head and twitched one ear. "Oh well," Stefan said. Kasimir said nothing. "I've budded off," Stefan said, "come on, Kasi." They set off slowly. "Right," Kasimir said straightening up a little. "It's not relevant, you know," said Stefan. "Is the innkeeper really named Praspayets?"—"Evander Praspayets. Has a brother runs the winery here, Belisarius Praspayets." Stefan grinned, Kasimir smiled a little vaguely. They were at the edge of the market-place about to cross the street. "Damn, I forgot my cabbage in the bar," Stefan said, turning, and saw some men running across the market-place between the carts and stalls. There was a loud clapping noise. Kasimir grabbed at Stefan's shoulder for some reason, but missed, and stood there with his arms spread out, making a coughing, retching sound in his throat. His arms jerked wider and he fell down, backwards, and lay at Stefan's feet, his eyes open, his mouth open and full of blood. Stefan stood there. He looked around. He dropped on his knees by Kasimir who did not look at him. Then he was pulled up and held by the arm; there were men around him and one of them was waving something, a paper, saying loudly, "This is him, the traitor, this is what happens to traitors. These are his forged papers. This is him." Stefan wanted to get to Kasimir, but was held back; he saw men's backs, a dog, a woman's red staring face in the background under golden trees. He thought they were helping him to stand, for his knees had given under him, but as they forced him to turn and walk he tried to pull free, crying out, "Kasimir!"

He was lying on his face on a bed, which was not the bed in the high-windowed room in the Augeskar house. He knew it was not but kept thinking it was, hearing the boys calling down on the tennis court. Then understanding that it was his room in Krasnoy and his roommates were asleep he lay still for a long time, despite a fierce headache. Finally he sat up and looked around at the pine-plank walls, the grating in the door, the stone floor with cigarette butts and dried urine on it. The guard who brought his breakfast was the thickset agent from the Post-Telephone Bar, and did not speak. There were pine splinters in the quicks of his nails on both his hands; he spent a long time getting them out.

On the third day a different guard came, a fat dark-jowled fellow reeking of sweat and onions like the market under the lindens. "What town am I in?"—"Prevne." The guard locked the door, offered a cigarette through the grating, held a lighted match through. "Is my friend dead? Why did they shoot him?"—"Man they wanted got away," said the guard. "Need anything in there? You'll be out tomorrow."—"Did they kill him?" The guard grunted yes and went off. After a while a half-full pack of cigarettes and a box of matches dropped in through the grating near Stefan's feet where he sat on the cot. He was released next day, seeing no one but the dark-jowled guard who led him to the door of the village lock-up. He stood on the main street of Prevne half a block down from the market-place. Sunset was over, it was cold, the sky clear and dark above the lindens, the roofs, the hills.

His ticket to Aisnar was still in his pocket. He walked slowly and carefully to the market-place and across it under dark trees to the Post-Telephone Bar. No bus was waiting. He had no idea when they ran. He went in and sat down, hunched over, shaking with cold, at one of the three tables. Presently the owner came out from a back room.

"When's the next bus?" He could not think of the man's name, Praspets, Prayespets, something like that. "Aisnar, eight-twenty in the morning," the man said.—"To Portacheyka?" Stefan asked after a pause.—"Local to Portacheyka at ten."—"Tonight?"—"Ten tonight."— "Can you change this for a . . . ticket to Portacheyka?" He held out his ticket for Aisnar. The man took it and after a moment said, "Wait, I'll see." He went off again to the back. Stefan got change ready for a cup of coffee, and sat hunched over. It was seven-ten by the white-faced alarm clock on the bar. At seven-thirty when three big townsmen came in for a beer he moved as far back as he could, by the pool table, and sat there facing the wall, only glancing round quickly now and then to check the time on the alarm clock. He was still shaking, and so cold that after a while he put his head down on his arms and shut his eyes. Bruna said, "Stefan."

She had sat down at the table with him. Her hair looked pale as cotton round her face. His head still hunched forward, his arms on the table, he looked at her and then looked down.

"Mr Praspayets telephoned us. Where were you going?"

He did not answer.

"Did they tell you to get out of town?"

He shook his head.

"They just let you go? Come on. I brought your coat, here, you must be cold. Come on home." She rose, and at this he sat up; he took his coat from her and said, "No. I can't."

"Why not?"

"Dangerous for you. Can't face it, anyway."

"Can't face us? Come on. I want to get out of here. We're driving back to Krasnoy tomorrow, we were waiting for you. Come on, Stefan." He got up and followed her out. It was night now. They set off across the street and up the country road, Bruna holding a flashlight beamed before them. She took his arm; they walked in silence. Around them were dark fields, stars.

"Do you know what they did with . . ."

"They took him off in the truck, we were told."

"I don't—When everybody in the town knew who he was—" He felt her shrug. They kept walking. The road was long again as when he and Kasimir had walked it the first time without light. They came to the hill where the lights had appeared, the laughter and calling all round them in the rain. "Come faster, Stefan," the girl beside him said timidly, "you're cold." He had to stop soon, and breaking away from her went blind to the roadside seeking anything, a fencepost or tree, anything to lean against till he could stop crying; but there was nothing. He stood there in the darkness and she stood near him. At last he turned and they went on together. Rocks and weeds showed white in the ragged circle of light from her flashlight. As they crossed the hillcrest she said with the same timidity and stubbornness, "I told mother we want to marry. When we heard they had you in jail here I told her. Not father, yet. This was—this was what he couldn't stand, he can't take it. But mother's all right, and so I told her. I'd like to be married quite soon, if you would, Stefan." He walked beside her, silent. "Right," he said finally. "No good letting go, is there." The lights of the house below them were yellow through the trees; above them stars and a few thin clouds drifted through the sky. "No good at all."

Unlocking the Air

This is a fairy tale. People stand in the lightly falling snow. Something is shining, trembling, making a silvery sound. Eyes are shining. Voices sing. People laugh and weep, clasp one another's hands, embrace. Something shines and trembles. They live happily ever after. The snow falls on the roofs and blows across the parks, the squares, the river.

This is history. Once upon a time a good king lived in his palace in a kingdom far away. But an evil enchantment fell upon that land. The wheat withered in the ear, the leaves dropped from the trees of the forest, and no thing thrived.

This is a stone. It's a paving stone of a square that slants downhill in front of an old, reddish, almost windowless fortress called the Roukh Palace. The square was paved nearly three hundred years ago, so a lot of feet have walked on this stone, bare feet and shod, children's little pads, horses' iron shoes, soldiers' boots; and wheels have gone over and over it, cart wheels, carriage wheels, car tires, tank treads. Dogs' paws every now and then. There's been dogshit on it, there's been blood, both soon washed away by water sloshed from buckets or run from hoses or dropped from the clouds. You can't get blood from a stone, they say, nor can you give it to a stone; it takes no stain. Some of the pavement, down near that street that leads out of Roukh Square through the old Jewish quarter to the river, got dug up once or twice and piled into a barricade, and some of the stones even found themselves flying through the air, but not for long. They were soon put back in their place, or replaced by others. It made no difference to them. The man hit by the flying stone dropped down like a stone beside the stone that killed him. The man shot through the brain fell down and his blood ran out on this stone, or another one maybe, it makes no difference to them. The soldiers washed his blood away with water sloshed from buckets, the buckets their horses drank from. The rain fell after a while. The snow fell. Bells rang the hours, the Christmases, the New Years. A tank stopped with its treads on this stone. You'd think that that would leave a mark, a huge heavy thing like a tank, but the stone shows nothing. Only all the feet bare and shod over the centuries have worn a quality into it, not a smoothness exactly but a kind of softness like leather or like skin. Unstained, unmarked, indifferent, it does have that quality of having been worn for a long time by life. So it is a stone of power, and who sets foot on it may be transformed.

This is a story. She let herself in with her key and called, "Mama? It's me, Fana," and her mother in the kitchen of the apartment called, "I'm in here," and they met and hugged in the doorway of the kitchen.

"Come on, come on!"

"Come where?"

"It's Thursday, Mama!"

"Oh," said Bruna Fabbre, retreating towards the stove, making vague protective gestures at the saucepans, the dishcloths, the spoons.

"You said."

"But it's nearly four already—"

"We can be back by six-thirty."

"I have all the papers to read for the advancement tests."

"You have to come, Mama. You do. You'll see!"

A heart of stone might resist the shining eyes, the coaxing, the bossiness. "Come on!" she said again, and the mother came.

But grumbling. "This is for you," she said on the stairs.

On the bus she said it again. "This is for you. Not me."

"What makes you think that?"

Bruna did not reply for a while, looking out the bus window at the grey city lurching by, the dead November sky behind the roofs.

"Well, you see," she said, "before Kasi, my brother Kasimir, before he was killed, that was the time that would have been for me. But I was too young. Too stupid. And then they killed Kasi."

"By mistake."

"It wasn't a mistake. They were hunting for a man who'd been getting people out across the border, and they'd missed him. So it was to . . ."

"To have something to report to the Central Office."

Bruna nodded. "He was about the age you are now," she said. The bus stopped, people climbed on, crowding the aisle. "Since then, twenty-seven years, always since then it's been too late. For me. First too stupid, then too late. This time is for you. I missed mine."

"You'll see," Stefana said. "There's enough time to go round."

This is history. Soldiers stand in a row before the reddish, almost windowless palace; their muskets are at the ready. Young men walk across the stones towards them, singing,

Beyond this darkness is the light,
O Liberty, of thine eternal day!

The soldiers fire their guns. The young men live happily ever after.

This is biology.

"Where the hell is everybody?"

"It's Thursday," Stefan Fabbre said, adding, "Damn!" as the figures on the computer screen jumped and flickered. He was wearing his topcoat over sweater and scarf, since the biology laboratory was heated only by a spaceheater which shorted out the computer circuit if they were on at the same time. "There are programs that could do this in two seconds," he said, jabbing morosely at the keyboard.

Avelin came up and glanced at the screen. "What is it?"

"The RNA comparison count. I could do it faster on my fingers."

Avelin, a bald, spruce, pale, dark-eyed man of forty, roamed the laboratory, looked restlessly through a folder of reports. "Can't run a university with this going on," he said. "I'd have thought you'd be down there."

Fabbre entered a new set of figures and said, "Why?"

"You're an idealist."

"Am I?" Fabbre leaned back, stretched, rolled his head to get the cricks out. "I try hard not to be," he said.

"Realists are born, not made." The younger man sat down on a lab stool and stared at the scarred, stained counter. "It's coming apart," he said.

"You think so? Seriously?"

Avelin nodded. "You heard that report from Prague."

Fabbre nodded.

"Last week . . . This week . . . Next year—Yes. An earthquake. The stones come apart—it falls apart—there was a building, now there's not. History is made. So I don't understand why you're here, not there."

"Seriously, you don't understand that?"

Avelin smiled and said, "Seriously."

"All right." Fabbre stood up and began walking up and down the long room as he spoke. He was a slight, grey-haired man with youthfully intense, controlled movements. "Science or political activity, either/or: choose. Right? Choice is responsibility, right? So I chose my responsibility responsibly. I chose science and abjured all action but the acts of science. The acts of a responsible science. Out there they can change the rules; in here they can't change the rules; when they try to I resist. This is my resistance." He slapped the laboratory bench as he turned round. "I'm lecturing. I walk up and down like this when I lecture. So. Background of the choice. I'm from the northeast. '56, in the northeast, do you remember? My grandfather, my father—reprisals. So, in '60, I come here, to the university. '62, my best friend, my wife's brother. We were walking through a village market, talking, then he stopped, he stopped talking, they had shot him. A kind of mistake. Right? He was a musician. A realist. I felt that I owed it to him, that I owed it to them, you see, to live carefully, with responsibility, to do the best I could do. The best I could do was this," and he gestured around the laboratory. "I'm good at it. So I go on trying to be a realist. As far as possible under the circumstances, which have less and less to do with reality. But they are only circumstances. The circumstances in which I do my work as carefully as I can."

Avelin sat on the lab stool, his head bowed. When Fabbre was done, he nodded. After a while he said, "But I have to ask you if it's realistic to separate the circumstances, as you put it, from the work."

"About as realistic as separating the body from the mind," Fabbre said. He stretched again and reseated himself at the computer. "I want to get this series in," he said, and his hands went to the keyboard and his gaze to the notes he was copying. After five or six minutes he started the printer and spoke without turning. "You're serious, Givan, you think it's coming apart as a whole?"

"Yes. I think the experiment is over."

The printer scraped and screeched, and they raised their voices to be heard over it.

"Here, you mean."

"Here and everywhere. They know it, down at Roukh Square. Go down there. You'll see. There could be such jubilation only at the death of a tyrant or the failure of a great hope."

"Or both."

"Or both," Avelin agreed.

The paper jammed in the printer, and Fabbre opened the machine to free it. His hands were shaking. Avelin, spruce and cool, hands behind his back, strolled over, looked, reached in, disengaged the corner that was jamming the feed.

"Soon," he said, "we'll have an IBM. A Mactoshin. Our hearts' desire."

"Macintosh," Fabbre said.

"Everything can be done in two seconds."

Fabbre restarted the printer and looked around. "Listen, the principles—"

Avelin's eyes shone strangely, as if full of tears; he shook his head. "So much depends on the circumstances," he said.

This is a key. It locks and unlocks a door, the door to Apartment 2–I of the building at 43 Pradinestrade in the Old North Quarter of the city of Krasnoy. The apartment is enviable, having a kitchen with saucepans, dishcloths, spoons, and all that is necessary, and two bedrooms, one of which is now used as a sitting room with chairs, books, papers, and all that is necessary, as well as a view from the window between other buildings of a short section of the Molsen River. The river at this moment is lead-colored and the trees above it are bare and black. The apartment is unlighted and empty. When they left, Bruna Fabbre locked the door and dropped the key, which is on a steel ring along with the key to her desk at the Lyceum and the key to her sister Bendika's apartment in the Trasfiuve, into her small imitation leather handbag, which is getting shabby at the corners, and snapped the handbag shut. Bruna's daughter Stefana has a copy of the key in her jeans pocket, tied on a bit of braided cord along with the key to the closet in her room in Dormitory G of the University of Krasnoy, where she is a graduate student in the department of Orsinian and Slavic Literature working for a degree in the field of Early Romantic Poetry. She never locks the closet. The two women walk down Pradinestrade three blocks and wait a few minutes at the corner for the number 18 bus, which runs on Bulvard Settentre from North Krasnoy to the center of the city.

Pressed in the crowded interior of the handbag and the tight warmth of the jeans pocket, the key and its copy are inert, silent, forgotten. All a key can do is lock and unlock its door; that's all the function it has, all the meaning; it has a responsibility but no rights. It can lock or unlock. It can be found or thrown away.

This is history. Once upon a time in 1830, in 1848, in 1866, in 1918, in 1947, in 1956, stones flew. Stones flew through the air like pigeons, and hearts, too, hearts had wings. Those were the years when the stones flew, the hearts took wing, the young voices sang. The soldiers raised their muskets to the ready, the soldiers aimed their rifles, the soldiers poised their machine guns. They were young, the soldiers. They fired. The stones lay down, the pigeons fell. There's a kind of red stone called pigeon's blood, a ruby. The red stones of Roukh Square were never rubies; slosh a bucket of water over them or let the rain fall and they're grey again, lead grey, common stones. Only now and then in certain years they have flown, and turned to rubies.

This is a bus. Nothing to do with fairy tales and not romantic; certainly realistic; though in a way, in principle, in fact, it is highly idealistic. A city bus crowded with people in a city street in Central Europe on a November afternoon, and it's stalled. What else? Oh, dear. Oh, damn. But no, it hasn't stalled; the engine, for a wonder, hasn't broken down; it's just that it can't go any farther. Why not? Because there's a bus stopped in front of it, and another one stopped in front of that one at the cross street, and it looks like everything's stopped. Nobody on this bus has yet heard the word "gridlock," the name of an exotic disease of the mysterious West. There aren't enough private cars in Krasnoy to bring about a gridlock even if they knew what it was. There are cars, and a lot of wheezing idealistic busses, but all there is enough of to stop the flow of traffic in Krasnoy is people. It is a kind of equation, proved by experiments conducted over many years, perhaps not in a wholly scientific or objective spirit but nonetheless presenting a well-documented result confirmed by repetition: there are not enough people in this city to stop a tank. Even in much larger cities it has been authoritatively demonstrated as recently as last spring that there are not enough people to stop a tank. But there are enough people in this city to stop a bus, and they are doing so. Not by throwing themselves in front of it, waving banners, or singing songs about Liberty's eternal day, but merely by being in the street getting in the way of the bus, on the supposition that the bus driver has not been trained in either homicide or suicide; and on the same supposition—upon which all cities stand or fall—they are also getting in the way of all the other busses and all the cars and in one another's way, too, so that nobody is going much of anywhere, in a physical sense.

"We're going to have to walk from here," Stefana said, and her mother clutched her imitation leather handbag. "Oh, but we can't, Fana. Look at that crowd! What are they—Are they—?"

"It's Thursday, ma'am," said a large, red-faced, smiling man just behind them in the aisle. Everybody was getting off the bus, pushing and talking. "Yesterday I got four blocks closer than this," a woman said crossly, and the red-faced man said, "Ah, but this is Thursday."

"Fifteen thousand last time," said somebody, and somebody else said, "Fifty, fifty thousand today!"

"We can never get anywhere near the Square, I don't think we should try," Bruna told her daughter as they squeezed into the crowd outside the bus door.

"You stay with me, don't let go, and don't worry," said the student of Early Romantic Poetry, a tall, resolute young woman, and she took her mother's hand in a firm grasp. "It doesn't really matter where we get, but it would be fun if you could see the Square. Let's try. Let's go round behind the post office."

Everybody was trying to go the same direction. Stefana and Bruna got across one street by dodging and stopping and pushing gently; then turning against the flow they trotted down a nearly empty alley, cut across the cobbled court back of the Central Post Office, and rejoined an even thicker crowd moving slowly down a wide street and out from between the buildings. "There, there's the palace, see!" said Stefana, who could see it, being taller. "This is as far as we'll get except by osmosis." They practised osmosis, which necessitated letting go of each other's hands, and made Bruna unhappy. "This is far enough, this is fine here," she kept saying. "I can see everything. There's the roof of the palace. Nothing's going to happen, is it? I mean, will anybody speak?" It was not what she meant, but she did not want to shame her daughter with her fear, her daughter who had not been alive when the stones turned to rubies. And she spoke quietly because although there were so many people pressed and pressing into Roukh Square, they were not noisy. They talked to one another in ordinary, quiet voices. Only now and then somebody down nearer the palace shouted out a name, and then many, many other voices would repeat it with a roll and crash like a wave breaking. Then they would be quiet again, murmuring vastly, like the sea between big waves.

The street lights had come on. Roukh Square was sparsely lighted by tall, old, cast-iron standards with double globes that shed a soft light high in the air. Through that serene light, which seemed to darken the sky, came drifting small, dry flecks of snow.

The flecks melted to droplets on Stefana's dark, short hair and on the scarf Bruna had tied over her fair, short hair to keep her ears warm.

When Stefana stopped at last, Bruna stood up as tall as she could, and because they were standing on the highest edge of the Square, in front of the old Dispensary, by craning she could see the great crowd, the faces like snowflakes, countless. She saw the evening darkening, the snow falling, and no way out, and no way home. She was lost in the forest. The palace, whose few lighted windows shone dully above the crowd, was silent. No one came out, no one went in. It was the seat of government; it held the power. It was the powerhouse, the powder magazine, the bomb. Power had been compressed, jammed into those old reddish walls, packed and forced into them over years, over centuries, till if it exploded it would burst with horrible violence, hurling pointed shards of stone. And out here in the twilight in the open there was nothing but soft faces with shining eyes, soft little breasts and stomachs and thighs protected only by bits of cloth.

She looked down at her feet on the pavement. They were cold. She would have worn her boots if she had thought it was going to snow, if Fana hadn't hurried her so. She felt cold, lost, lonely to the point of tears. She set her jaw and set her lips and stood firm on her cold feet on the cold stone.

There was a sound, sparse, sparkling, faint, like the snow crystals. The crowd had gone quite silent, swept by low laughing murmurs, and through the silence ran that small, discontinuous, silvery sound.

"What is that?" asked Bruna, beginning to smile. "Why are they doing that?"

This is a committee meeting. Surely you don't want me to describe a committee meeting? It meets as usual on Friday at eleven in the morning in the basement of the Economics Building. At eleven on Friday night, however, it is still meeting, and there are a good many onlookers, several million in fact, thanks to the foreigner with the camera, a television camera with a long snout, a one-eyed snout that peers and sucks up what it sees. The cameraman focusses for a long time on the tall, dark-haired girl who speaks so eloquently in favor of a certain decision concerning bringing a certain man back to the capital. But the millions of onlookers will not understand her argument, which is spoken in her obscure language and is not translated for them. All they will know is how the eye-snout of the camera lingered on her young face, sucking it.

This is a love story. Two hours later the cameraman was long gone but the committee was still meeting.

"No, listen," she said, "seriously, this is the moment when the betrayal is always made. Free elections, yes, but if we don't look past that now, when will we? And who'll do it? Are we a country or a client state changing patrons?"

"You have to go one step at a time, consolidating—"

"When the dam breaks? You have to shoot the rapids! All at once!"

"It's a matter of choosing direction—"

"Exactly, direction. Not being carried senselessly by events."

"But all the events are sweeping in one direction."

"They always do. Back! You'll see!"

"Sweeping to what, to dependence on the West instead of the East, like Fana said?"

"Dependence is inevitable—realignment, but not occupation—"

"The hell it won't be occupation! Occupation by money, materialism, their markets, their values, you don't think we can hold out against them, do you? What's social justice to a color TV set? That battle's lost before it's fought. Where do we stand?"

"Where we always stood. In an absolutely untenable position."

"He's right. Seriously, we are exactly where we always were. Nobody else is. We are. They have caught up with us, for a moment, for this moment, and so we can act. The untenable position is the center of power. Now. We can act *now*."

"To prevent color-TV-zation? How? The dam's broken! The goodies come flooding in. And we drown in them."

"Not if we establish the direction, the true direction, right now——"

"But will Rege listen to us? Why are we turning back when we should be going forward? If we——"

"We have to establish——"

"No! We have to act! Freedom can be established only in the moment of freedom——"

They were all shouting at once in their hoarse, worn-out voices. They had all been talking and listening and drinking bad coffee and living for days, for weeks, on love. Yes, on love; these are lovers' quarrels. It is for love that he pleads, it is for love that she rages. It was always for love. That's why the camera snout came poking and sucking into this dirty basement room where the lovers meet. It craves love, the sight of love; for if you can't have the real thing you can watch it on TV, and soon you don't know the real thing from the images on the little screen where everything, as he said, can be done in two seconds. But the lovers know the difference.

This is a fairy tale, and you know that in the fairy tale, after it says that they lived happily ever after, there is no after. The evil enchantment was broken; the good servant received half the kingdom as his reward; the king ruled long and well. Remember the moment when the betrayal is made, and ask no questions. Do not ask if the poisoned fields grew white again with grain. Do not ask if the leaves of the forests grew green that spring. Do not ask what the maiden received as her reward. Remember the tale of Koshchey the Deathless, whose life was in a needle, and the needle was in an egg, and the egg was in a swan, and the swan was in an eagle, and the eagle was in a wolf, and the wolf was in the palace whose walls were built of the stones of power. Enchantment within enchantment! We are a long way yet from the egg that holds the needle that must be broken so that Koshchey the Deathless can die. And so the tale ends. Thousands and thousands and thousands of people stood on the slanting pavement before the palace. Snow sparkled in the air, and the people sang. You know the song, that old song with words like "land," "love," "free," in the language you have known the longest. Its words make stone part from stone, its words prevent tanks, its words transform the world, when it is sung at the right time by the right people, after enough people have died for singing it.

A thousand doors opened in the walls of the palace. The soldiers laid down their arms and sang. The evil enchantment was broken. The good king returned to his kingdom, and the people danced for joy on the stones of the city streets.

And we do not ask what happened after. But we can tell the story over, we can tell the story till we get it right.

"My daughter's on the Committee of the Student Action Council," said Stefan Fabbre to his neighbor Florens Aske as they stood in a line outside the bakery on Pradinestrade. His tone of voice was complicated.

"I know. Erreskar saw her on the television," Aske said.

"She says they've decided that bringing Rege here is the only way to provide an immediate, credible transition. They think the army will accept him."

They shuffled forward a step.

Aske, an old man with a hard brown face and narrow eyes, stuck his lips out, thinking it over.

"You were in the Rege Government," Fabbre said.

Aske nodded. "Minister of Education for a week," he said, and gave a bark like a sea lion, owp!—a cough or a laugh.

"Do you think he can pull it off?"

Aske pulled his grubby muffler closer round his neck and said, "Well, Rege is not stupid. But he's old. What about that scientist, that physicist fellow?"

"Rochoy. She says their idea is that Rege's brought in first, for the transition, for the symbolism, the link to '56, right? And if he survives, Rochoy would be the one they'd run in an election."

"The dream of the election . . ."

They shuffled forward again. They were now in front of the bakery window, only eight or ten people away from the door.

"Why do they put up the old men?" asked the old man. "These boys and girls, these young people. What the devil do they want us for again?"

"I don't know," Fabbre said. "I keep thinking they know what they're doing. She had me down there, you know, made me come to one of their meetings. She came to the lab—Come on, leave that, follow me! I did. No questions. She's in charge. All of them, twenty-two, twenty-three, they're in charge. In power. Seeking structure, order, but very definite: violence is defeat, to them, violence is the loss of options. They're absolutely certain and completely ignorant. Like spring—like the lambs in spring. They have never done anything and they know exactly what to do."

"Stefan," said his wife, Bruna, who had been standing at his elbow for several sentences, "you're lecturing. Hello, dear. Hello, Florens, I just saw Margarita at the market, we were queueing for cabbages. I'm on my way downtown, Stefan. I'll be back, I don't know, sometime after seven, maybe."

"Again?" he said, and Aske said, "Downtown?"

"It's Thursday," Bruna said, and bringing up the keys from her handbag, the two apartment keys and the desk key, she shook them in the air before the men's faces, making a silvery jingle; and she smiled.

"I'll come," said Stefan Fabbre.

"Owp! owp!" went Aske. "Oh, hell, I'll come too. Does man live by bread alone?"

"Will Margarita worry where you are?" Bruna asked as they left the bakery line and set off towards the bus stop.

"That's the problem with the women, you see," said the old man, "they worry that she'll worry. Yes. She will. And you worry about your daughter, eh, your Fana."

"Yes," Stefan said, "I do."

"No," Bruna said, "I don't. I fear her, I fear for her, I honor her. She gave me the keys." She clutched her imitation leather handbag tight between her arm and side as they walked.

This is the truth. They stood on the stones in the lightly falling snow and listened to the silvery, trembling sound of thousands of keys being shaken, unlocking the air, once upon a time.

Imaginary Countries

"We can't drive to the river on Sunday," the baron said, "because we're leaving on Friday." The two little ones gazed at him across the breakfast table. Zida said, "Marmalade, please," but Paul, a year older, found in a remote, disused part of his memory a darker dining-room from the windows of which one saw rain falling. "Back to the city?" he asked. His father nodded. And at the nod the sunlit hill outside these windows changed entirely, facing north now instead of south. That day red and yellow ran through the woods like fire, grapes swelled fat on the heavy vines, and the clear, fierce, fenced fields of August stretched themselves out, patient and unboundaried, into the haze of September. Next day Paul knew the moment he woke that it was autumn, and Wednesday. "This is Wednesday," he told Zida, "tomorrow's Thursday, and then Friday when we leave."

"I'm not going to," she replied with indifference, and went off to the Little Woods to work on her unicorn trap. It was made of an eggcrate and many little bits of cloth, with various kinds of bait. She had been making it ever since they found the tracks, and Paul doubted if she would catch even a squirrel in it. He, aware of time and season, ran full speed to the High Cliff to finish the tunnel there before they had to go back to the city.

Inside the house the baroness's voice dipped like a swallow down the attic stairs. "O Rosa! Where is the blue trunk then?" And Rosa not answering, she followed her voice, pursuing it and Rosa and the lost trunk down stairs and ever farther hallways to a joyful reunion at the cellar door. Then from his study the baron heard Tomas and the trunk come grunting upward step by step, while Rosa and the baroness began to empty the children's closets, carrying off little loads of shirts and dresses like delicate, methodical thieves. "What are you doing?" Zida asked sternly, having come back for a coat-hanger in which the unicorn might entangle his hoof. "Packing," said the maid. "Not my things," Zida ordered, and departed. Rosa continued rifling her closet. In his study the baron read on undisturbed except by a sense of regret which rose perhaps from the sound of his wife's sweet, distant voice, perhaps from the quality of the sunlight falling across his desk from the uncurtained window.

In another room his older son Stanislas put a microscope, a tennis racket, and a box full of rocks with their labels coming unstuck into his suitcase, then gave it up. A notebook in his pocket, he went down the cool red halls and stairs, out the door into the vast and sudden sunlight of the yard. Josef, reading under the Four Elms, said, "Where are you off to? It's hot." There was no time for stopping and talking. "Back soon," Stanislas replied politely and went on, up the road in dust and sunlight, past the High Cliff where his half-brother Paul was digging. He stopped to survey the engineering. Roads metalled with white clay zigzagged over the cliff-face. The Citroen and the Rolls were parked near a bridge spanning an erosion-gully. A tunnel had been pierced and was in process of enlargement. "Good tunnel," Stanislas said. Radiant and filthy, the engineer replied, "It'll be ready to drive through this evening, you want to come to the ceremony?" Stanislas nodded, and went on. His road led up a long, high hillslope, but he soon turned from it and, leaping the ditch, entered his kingdom and the kingdom of the trees. Within a few steps all dust and bright light were gone. Leaves overhead and underfoot; an air like green water through which birds swam and the dark trunks rose lifting their burdens, their crowns, towards the other element, the sky. Stanislas went first to the Oak and stretched his arms out, straining to reach a quarter of the way around the trunk. His chest and cheek were pressed against the harsh, scored bark; the smell of it and its shelf-fungi and moss was in his nostrils and the darkness of it in his eyes. It was a bigger thing than he could ever hold. It was very old, and alive, and did not know that he was there. Smiling, he went on quietly, a notebook full of maps in his pocket, among the trees towards yet-uncharted regions of his land.

Josef Brone, who had spent the summer assisting his professor with documentation of the history of the Ten Provinces in the Early Middle Ages, sat uneasily reading in the shade of elms. Country wind blew across the pages, across his lips. He looked up from the Latin chronicle of a battle lost nine hundred years ago to the roofs of the house called Asgard. Square as a box, with a sediment of porches, sheds, and stables, and square to the compass, the house stood in its flat yard; after a while in all directions the fields rose up slowly, turning into hills, and behind them were higher hills, and behind them sky. It was like a white box in a blue and yellow bowl, and Josef, fresh from college and intent upon the Jesuit seminary he would enter in the fall, ready to read documents and make abstracts and copy references, had been embarrassed to find that the baron's family called the place after the home of the northern gods. But this no longer troubled him. So much had happened here that he had not expected, and so little seemed to have been finished. The history was years from completion. In three months he had never found out where Stanislas went, alone, up the road. They were leaving on Friday. Now or never. He got up and followed the boy. The road passed a ten-foot bank, halfway up which clung the little boy Paul, digging in the dirt with his fingers, making a noise in his throat: rrrm, rrrrm. A couple of toy cars lay at the foot of the bank. Josef followed the road on up the hill and presently began expecting to reach the top, from which he would see where Stanislas had gone. A farm came into sight and went out of sight, the road climbed, a lark went up singing as if very near the sun; but there was no top. The only way to go downhill on this road was to turn around. He did so. As he neared the woods above Asgard a boy leapt out onto the road, quick as a hawk's shadow. Josef called his name, and they met in the white glare of dust. "Where have you been?" asked Josef, sweating.—"In the Great Woods," Stanislas answered, "that grove there." Behind him the trees gathered thick and dark. "Is it cool in there?" Josef asked wistfully. "What do you do in there?"—"Oh, I map trails. Just for the fun of it. It's bigger than it looks." Stanislas hesitated, then added, "You haven't been in it? You might like to see the Oak." Josef followed him over the ditch and through the close green air to the Oak. It was the biggest tree he had ever seen; he had not seen very many. "I suppose it's very old," he said, looking up puzzled at the reach of branches, galaxy after galaxy of green leaves without end. "Oh, a century or two or three or six," said the boy, "see if you can reach around it!" Josef spread out his arms and strained, trying vainly to keep his cheek off the rough bark. "It takes four men to reach around it," Stanislas said. "I call it Yggdrasil. You know. Only of course Yggdrasil was an ash, not an oak. Want to see Loki's Grove?" The road and the hot white sunlight were gone entirely. The young man followed his guide farther into the maze and game of names which was also a real forest: trees, still air, earth. Under tall grey alders above a dry streambed they discussed the tale of the death of Baldur, and Stanislas pointed out to Josef the dark clots, high in the boughs of lesser oaks, of mistletoe. They left the woods and went down the road towards Asgard. Josef walked along stiffly in the dark suit he had bought for his last year at the University, in his pocket a book in a dead language. Sweat ran down his face, he felt very happy. Though he had no maps and was rather late arriving, at least he had walked once through the forest. They passed Paul still burrowing, ignoring the clang of the iron triangle down at the house, which signalled meals, fires, lost children, and other noteworthy events. "Come on, lunch!" Stanislas ordered. Paul slid down the bank and they proceeded, seven, fourteen and twenty-one, sedately to the house.

That afternoon Josef helped the professor pack books, two trunks full of books, a small library of medieval history. Josef liked to read books, not pack them. The professor had asked him, not Tomas, "Lend me a hand with the books, will you?" It was not the kind of work he had expected to do here. He sorted and lifted and stowed away load after load of resentment in insatiable iron trunks, while the professor worked with energy and interest, swaddling incunabula like babies, handling each volume with affection and despatch. Kneeling with keys he said, "Thanks, Josef! That's that," and lowering the brass catchbars locked away their summer's work, done with, that's that. Josef had done so much here that he had not expected to do, and now nothing was left to do. Disconsolate, he wandered back to the shade of the elms; but the professor's wife, with whom he had not expected to fall in love, was sitting there. "I stole your chair," she said amiably, "sit on the grass." It was more dirt than grass, but they called it grass, and he obeyed. "Rosa and I are worn out," she said, "and I can't bear to think of tomorrow. It's the worst, the next-to-last day—linens and silver and turning dishes upside down and putting out mousetraps and there's always a doll lost and found after everybody's searched for hours under a pile of laundry— and then sweeping the house and locking it all up. And I hate every bit of it, I hate to close this house." Her voice was light and plaintive as a bird's calling in the woods, careless whether anybody heard its plaintiveness, careless of its plaintiveness. "I hope you've liked it here," she said.

"Very much, baroness."

"I hope so. I know Severin has worked you very hard. And we're so disorganised. We and the children and the visitors, we always seem to scatter so, and only meet in passing. . . . I hope it hasn't been distracting." It was true; all summer in tides and cycles the house had been full or half full of visitors, friends of the children, friends of the baroness, friends, colleagues and neighbors of the baron, duck-hunters who slept in the disused stable since the spare bedrooms were full of Polish medieval historians, ladies with broods of children the smallest of whom fell inevitably into the pond about this time of the afternoon. No wonder it was so still, so autumnal now: the rooms vacant, the pond smooth, the hills empty of dispersing laughter.

"I have enjoyed knowing the children," Josef said, "particularly Stanislas." Then he went red as a beet, for Stanislas alone was not her child. She smiled and said with timidity, "Stanislas is very nice. And fourteen—fourteen is such a fearful age, when you find out so fast what you're capable of being, but also what a toll the world expects. . . . He handles it very gracefully. Paul and Zida now, when they get that age they'll lump through it and be tiresome. But Stanislas learned loss so young. . . . When will you enter the seminary?" she asked, moving from the boy to him in one reach of thought. "Next month," he answered looking down, and she asked, "Then you're quite certain it's the life you want to lead?" After a pause and still not looking at her face, though the white of her dress and the green and gold of leaves above her filled his eyes, he said, "Why do you ask, baroness?"

"Because the idea of celibacy terrifies me," she replied, and he wanted to stretch out on the ground flecked with elm leaves like thin oval coins of gold, and die.

"Sterility," she said, "you see, sterility is what I fear, I dread. It is my enemy. I know we have other enemies, but I hate it most, because it makes life less than death. And its allies are horrible: hunger, sickness, deformation, and perversion, and ambition, and the wish to be secure. What on earth are the children doing down there?" Paul had asked Stanislas at lunch if they could play Ragnarok once more. Stanislas had consented, and so was now a Frost Giant storming with roars the ramparts of Asgard represented by a drainage ditch behind the pond. Odin hurled lightning from the walls, and Thor—"Stanislas!" called the mother rising slender and in white from her chair beside the young man, "don't let Zida use the hammer, please."

"I'm Thor, I'm Thor, I got to have a hammer!" Zida screamed. Stanislas intervened briefly, then made ready to storm the ramparts again, with Zida now at his side, on all fours. "She's Fenris the Wolf now," he called up to the mother, his voice ringing through the hot afternoon with the faintest edge of laughter. Grim and stern, one eye shut, Paul gripped his staff and faced the advancing armies of Hel and the Frozen Lands.

"I'm going to find some lemonade for everybody," the baroness said, and left Josef to sink at last face down on the earth, surrendering to the awful sweetness and anguish she had awakened in him, and would it ever sleep again? while down by the pond Odin strove with the icy army on the sunlit battlements of heaven.

Next day only the walls of the house were left standing. Inside it was only a litter of boxes and open drawers and hurrying people carrying things. Tomas and Zida escaped, he, being slow-witted amid turmoil and the only year-round occupant of Asgard, to clean up the yard out of harm's way, and she to the Little Woods all afternoon. At five Paul shrilled from his window, "The car! The car! It's coming!" An enormous black taxi built in 1923 groaned into the yard, feeling its way, its blind, protruding headlamps flashing in the western sun. Boxes, valises, the blue trunk and the two iron trunks were loaded into it by Tomas, Stanislas, Josef, and the taxi-driver from the village, under the agile and efficient supervision of Baron Severin Egideskar, holder of the Follen Chair of Medieval Studies at the University of Krasnoy. "And you'll get us back together with all this at the station tomorrow at eight—right?" The taxi-driver, who had done so each September for seven years, nodded. The taxi laden with the material impediments of seven people lumbered away, changing gears down the road in the weary, sunny stillness of late afternoon, in which the house stood intact once more room after empty room.

The baron now also escaped. Lighting a pipe he strolled slowly but softly, like one escaping, past the pond and past Tomas's chickencoops, along a fence overgrown with ripe wild grasses bowing their heavy, sunlit heads, down to the grove of weeping birch called the Little Woods. "Zida?" he said, pausing in the faint, hot shade shaken by the ceaseless trilling of crickets in the fields around the grove. No answer. In a cloud of blue pipe-smoke he paused again beside an egg-crate decorated with many little bits of figured cloth and colored paper. On the mossy, much-trodden ground in front of it lay a wooden coat hanger. In one of the compartments of the crate was an eggshell painted gold, in another a bit of quartz, in another a breadcrust. Nearby, a small girl lay sound asleep with her shoes off, her rump higher than her head. The baron sat down on the moss near her, relit his pipe, and contemplated the egg-crate. Presently he tickled the soles of the child's feet. She snorted. When she began to wake, he took her onto his lap.

"What is that?"

"A trap for catching a unicorn." She brushed hair and leafmold off her face and arranged herself more comfortably on him.

"Caught any?"

"No."

"Seen any?"

"Paul and I found some tracks."

"Split-hoofed ones, eh?"

She nodded. Delicately through twilight in the baron's imagination walked their neighbor's young white pig, silver between birch trunks.

"Only young girls can catch them, they say," he murmured, and then they sat still for a long time.

"Time for dinner," he said. "All the tablecloths and knives and forks are packed. How shall we eat?"

"With our fingers!" She leapt up, sprang away. "Shoes," he ordered, and laboriously she fitted her small, cool, dirty feet into leather sandals, and then, shouting "Come on, papa!" was off. Quick and yet reluctant, seeming not to follow and yet never far behind her, he came on between the long vague shadows of the birch trees, along the fence, past the chickencoops and the shining pond, into captivity.

They all sat on the ground under the Four Elms. There was cold ham, pickles, cold fried eggplant with salt, hard bread and hard red wine. Elm leaves like thin coins stuck to the bread. The pure, void, windy sky of after-sunset reflected in the pond and in the wine. Stanislas and Paul had a wrestling match and dirt flew over the remains of the ham; the baroness and Rosa, lamenting, dusted the ham. The boys went off to run cars through the tunnel in High Cliff, and discuss what ruin the winter rains might cause. For it would rain. All the nine months they were gone from Asgard rain would beat on the roads and hills, and the tunnel would collapse. Stanislas lifted his head a moment thinking of the Oak in winter when he had never seen it, the roots of the tree that upheld the world drinking dark rain underground. Zida rode clear round the house twice on the shoulders of the unicorn, screaming loudly for pure joy, for eating outside on the ground with fingers, for the first star seen (only from the corner of the eye) over the high fields faint in twilight. Screaming louder with rage she was taken to bed by Rosa, and instantly fell asleep. One by one the stars came out, meeting the eye straight on. One by one the young people went to bed. Tomas with the last half-bottle sang long and hoarsely in the Dorian mode in his room above the stable. Only the baron and his wife remained out in the autumn darkness under leaves and stars.

"I don't want to leave," she murmured.

"Nor I."

"Let's send the books and clothes on back to town, and stay here without them. . . ."

"Forever," he said; but they could not. In the observance of season lies order, which was their realm. They sat on for a while longer, close side by side as lovers of twenty; then rising he said, "Come along, it's late, Freya." They went through darkness to the house, and entered.

In coats and hats, everyone ate bread and drank hot milk and coffee out on the porch in the brilliant early morning. "The car! It's coming!" Paul shouted, dropping his bread in the dirt. Grinding and changing gears, headlamps sightlessly flashing, the taxi came, it was there. Zida stared at it, the enemy within the walls, and began to cry. Faithful to the last to the lost cause of summer, she was carried into the taxi head first, screaming, "I won't go! I don't want to go!" Grinding and changing gears the taxi started. Stanislas's head stuck out of the right front window, the baroness's head out of the left rear, and Zida's red, desolate, and furious face was pressed against the oval back window, so that those three saw Tomas waving good-bye under the white walls of Asgard in the sunlight in the bowl of hills. Paul had no access to a window; but he was already thinking of the train. He saw, at the end of the smoke and the shining tracks, the light of candles in a high dark dining-room, the stare of a rockinghorse in an attic corner, leaves wet with rain overhead on the way to school, and a grey street shortened by a cold, foggy dusk through which shone, remote and festive, the first streetlight of December.

But all this happened a long time ago, nearly forty years ago; I do not know if it happens now, even in imaginary countries.

The Diary of the Rose

Dr. Nades recommends that I keep a diary of my work. She says that if you keep it carefully, when you reread it you can remind yourself of observations you made, notice errors and learn from them, and observe progress in or deviations from positive thinking, and so keep correcting the course of your work by a feedback process.

I promise to write in this notebook every night, and reread it at the end of each week.

I wish I had done it while I was an assistant, but it is even more important now that I have patients of my own.

As of yesterday I have six patients, a full load for a scopist, but four of them are the autistic children I have been working with all year for Dr. Nades's study for the Nat'l Psych. Bureau (my notes on them are in the cli psy files). The other two are new admissions:

Ana Jest, 46, bakery packager, md., no children, diag. depression, referral from city police (suicide attempt).

Flores Sorde, 36, engineer, unmd., no diag., referral from TRTU (Psychopathic behavior—Violent).

Dr. Nades says it is important that I write things down each night just as they occurred to me at work: it is the spontaneity that is most informative in self-examination (just as in autopsychoscopy). She says it is better to write it, not dictate onto tape, and keep it quite private, so that I won't be self-conscious. It is hard. I never wrote anything that was private before. I keep feeling as if I was really writing it for Dr. Nades! Perhaps if the diary is useful I can show her some of it, later, and get her advice.

My guess is that Ana Jest is in menopausal depression and hormone therapy will be sufficient. There! Now let's see how bad a prognostician I am.

Will work with both patients under scope tomorrow. It is exciting to have my own patients, I am impatient to begin. Though, of course, teamwork was very educational.

31 August

Half-hour scope session with Ana J. at 8:00. Analyzed scope material, 11:00–17:00. N.B.: Adjust right-brain pickup next session! Weak visual Concrete. Very little aural, weak sensory, erratic body image. Will get lab analyses tomorrow of hormone balance.

It is amazing how banal most people's minds are. Of course the poor woman is in severe depression. Input in the Con dimension was foggy and incoherent, and the Uncon dimension was deeply open, but obscure. But the things that came out of the obscurity were so trivial! A pair of old shoes, and the word "geography"! And the shoes were dim, a mere schema of a pair-of-shoes, maybe a man's maybe a woman's, maybe dark blue maybe brown. Although definitely a visual type, she does not see anything clearly. Not many people do. It is depressing. When I was a student in first year I used to think how wonderful other people's minds would be, how wonderful it was going to be to share in all the different worlds, the different colors of their passions and ideas. How naive I was!

I realised this first in Dr. Ramia's class when we studied a tape from a very famous successful person, and I noticed that the subject had never looked at a tree, never touched one, did not know any difference between an oak and a poplar, or even between a daisy and a rose. They were all just "trees" or "flowers" to him, apprehended schematically. It was the same with people's faces, though he had tricks for telling them apart: mostly he saw the name, like a label, not the face. That was an Abstract mind, of course, but it can be even worse with the Concretes, whose perceptions come in a kind of undifferentiated sludge—bean soup with a pair of shoes in it.

But aren't I "going native"? I've been studying a depressive's thoughts all day and have got depressed. Look, I wrote up there, "It is depressing." I see the value of this diary already. I know I am over-impressionable.

Of course, that is why I am a good psychoscopist. But it is dangerous.

No session with F. Sorde today, since sedation had not worn off. TRTU referrals are often so drugged that they cannot be scoped for days.

REM scoping session with Ana J. at 4:00 tomorrow. Better go to bed!

1 September

Dr. Nades says the kind of thing I wrote yesterday is pretty much what she had in mind, and invited me to show her this diary again whenever I am in doubt. Spontaneous thoughts—not the technical data, which are recorded in the files anyhow. Cross nothing out. Candor all-important.

Ana's dream was interesting but pathetic. The wolf who turned into a pancake! Such a disgusting, dim, hairy pancake, too. Her visuality is clearer in dream, but the feeling tone remains low (but remember: *you* contribute the affect—don't read it in). Started her on hormone therapy today.

F. Sorde awake, but too confused to take to scope room for session. Frightened. Refused to eat. Complained of pain in side. I thought he was unclear what kind of hospital this is, and told him there was nothing wrong with him physically. He said, "How the hell do you know?" which was fair enough, since he was in a straitjacket, due to the V notation on his chart. I examined and found bruising and contusion, and ordered X ray, which showed two ribs cracked. Explained to patient that he had been in a condition where forcible restraint had been necessary to prevent self-injury. He said, "Every time one of them asked a question the other one kicked me." He repeated this several times, with anger and confusion. Paranoid delusional system? If it does not weaken as the drugs wear off, I will proceed on that assumption. He responds fairly well to me, asked my name when I went to see him with the X-ray plate, and agreed to eat. I was forced to apologise to him, not a good beginning with a paranoid. The rib damage should have been marked on his chart by the referring agency or by the medic who admitted him. This kind of carelessness is distressing.

But there's good news too. Rina (Autism Study subject 4) saw a first-person sentence today. Saw it: in heavy, black, primer print, all at once in the high Con foreground: *I want to sleep in the big room.* (She sleeps alone because of the feces problem.) The sentence stayed clear for over 5 seconds. She was reading it in her mind just as I was reading it on the holoscreen. There was weak subverbalisation, but not subvocalisation, nothing on the audio. She has not yet spoken, even to herself, in the first person. I told Tio about it at once and he asked her after the session, "Rina, where do you want to sleep?"—"Rina sleep in the big room." No pronoun, no conative. But one of these days she will say *I want*—aloud. And on that build a personality, maybe, at last: on that foundation. I want, therefore I am.

There is so much fear. Why is there so much fear?

4 September

Went to town for my two-day holiday. Stayed with B. in her new flat on the north bank. Three rooms to herself!!! But I don't really like those old buildings, there are rats and roaches, and it feels so old and strange, as if somehow the famine years were still there, waiting. Was glad to get back to my little room here, all to myself but with others close by on the same floor, friends and colleagues. Anyway I missed writing in this book. I form habits very fast. Compulsive tendency.

Ana much improved: dressed, hair combed, was knitting. But session was dull. Asked her to think about pancakes, and there it came filling up the whole Uncon dimension, the hairy, dreary, flat wolf-pancake, while in the Con she was obediently trying to visualize a nice cheese blintz. Not too badly: colors and outlines already stronger. I am still willing to count on simple hormone treatment. Of course they will suggest ECT, and a co-analysis of the scope material would be perfectly possible, we'd start with the wolf-pancake, etc. But is there any real point to it? She has been a bakery packager for 24 years and her physical health is poor. She cannot change her life situation. At least with good hormone balance she may be able to endure it.

F. Sorde: rested but still suspicious. Extreme fear reaction when I said it was time for his first session. To allay this I sat down and talked about the nature and operation of the psychoscope. He listened intently and finally said, "Are you going to use only the psychoscope?"

I said Yes.

He said, "Not electroshock?"

I said No.

He said, "Will you promise me that?"

I explained that I am a psychoscopist and never operate the electroconvulsive therapy equipment, that is an entirely different department. I said my work with him at present would be diagnostic, not therapeutic. He listened carefully. He is an educated person and understands distinctions such as "diagnostic" and "therapeutic." It is interesting that he asked me to *promise.* That does not fit a paranoid pattern, you don't ask for promises from those you can't trust. He came with me docilely, but when we entered the scope room he stopped and turned white at sight of the apparatus. I made Dr. Aven's little joke about the dentist's chair, which she always used with nervous patients. F.S. said, "So long as it's not an electric chair!"

I believe that with intelligent subjects it is much better not to make mysteries and so impose a false authority and a feeling of helplessness on the subject (see T. R. Olma, *Psychoscopy Technique*). So I showed him the chair and electrode crown and explained its operation. He has a layman's hearsay knowledge of the psychoscope, and his questions also reflected his engineering education. He sat down in the chair when I asked him. While I fitted the crown and clasps he was sweating profusely from fear, and this evidently embarrassed him, the smell. If he knew how Rina smells after she's been doing shit paintings. He shut his eyes and gripped the chair arms so that his hands went white to the wrist. The screens were almost white too. After a while I said in a joking tone, "It doesn't really hurt, does it?"

"I don't know."

"Well, does it?"

"You mean it's on?"

"It's been on for ninety seconds."

He opened his eyes then and looked around, as well as he could for the head clamps. He asked, "Where's the screen?"

I explained that a subject never watches the screen live, because the objectification can be severely disturbing, and he said, "Like feedback from a microphone?" That is exactly the simile Dr. Aven used to use. F.S. is certainly an intelligent person. N.B.: Intelligent paranoids are dangerous!

He asked, "What do you see?" and I said, "Do be quiet, I don't want to see what you're saying, I want to see what you're thinking," and he said, "But that's none of your business, you know," quite gently, like a joke. Meanwhile the fear-white had gone into dark, intense, volitional convolutions, and then, a few seconds after he stopped speaking, a rose appeared on the whole Con dimension: a full-blown pink rose, beautifully sensed and visualised, clear and steady, whole.

He said presently, "What am I thinking about, Dr. Sobel?" and I said, "Bears in the Zoo." I wonder now why I said that. Self-defense? Against what? He gave a laugh and the Uncon went crystal-dark, relief, and the rose darkened and wavered. I said, "I was joking. Can you bring the rose back?" That brought back the fear-white. I said, "Listen, it's really very bad for us to talk like this during a first session, you have to learn a great deal before you can co-analyse, and I have a great deal to learn about you, so no more jokes, please? Just relax physically, and think about anything you please."

There was flurry and subverbalisation on the Con dimension, and the Uncon faded into grey, suppression. The rose came back weakly a few times. He was trying to concentrate on it, but couldn't. I saw several quick visuals: myself, my uniform, TRTU uniforms, a grey car, a kitchen, the violent ward (strong aural images—screaming), a desk, the papers on the desk. He stuck to those. They were the plans for a machine. He began going through them. It was a deliberate effort at suppression, and quite effective. Finally I said, "What kind of machine is that?" and he began to answer aloud but stopped and let me get the answer subvocally in the earphone: "Plans for a rotary engine assembly for traction," or something like that, of course the exact words are on the tape. I repeated it aloud and said, "They aren't classified plans, are they?" He said, "No," aloud, and added, "I don't know any secrets." His reaction to a question is intense and complex, each sentence is like a shower of pebbles thrown into a pool, the interlocking rings spread out quick and wide over the Con and into the Uncon, responses rising on all levels. Within a few seconds all that was hidden by a big signboard that appeared in the high Con foreground, deliberately visualised like the rose and the plans, with auditory reinforcement as he read it over and over: KEEP OUT! KEEP OUT! KEEP OUT!

It began to blur and flicker, and somatic signals took over, and soon he said aloud, "I'm tired," and I closed the session (12.5 min.).

After I took off the crown and clamps I brought him a cup of tea from the staff stand in the hall. When I offered it to him he looked startled and then tears came into his eyes. His hands were so cramped from gripping the armrests that he had trouble taking hold of the cup. I told him he must not be so tense and afraid, we are trying to help him not to hurt him.

He looked up at me. Eyes are like the scope screen and yet you can't read them. I wished the crown was still on him, but it seems you never catch the moments you most want on the scope. He said, "Doctor, why am I in this hospital?"

I said, "For diagnosis and therapy."

He said, "Diagnosis and therapy of *what?*"

I said he perhaps could not now recall the episode, but he had behaved strangely. He asked how and when, and I said that it would all come clear to him as therapy took effect. Even if I had known what his psychotic episode was, I would have said the same. It was correct procedure. But I felt in a false position. If the TRTU report was not classified, I would be speaking from knowledge and the facts. Then I could make a better response to what he said next:

"I was waked up at two in the morning, jailed, interrogated, beaten up, and drugged. I suppose I did behave a little oddly during that. Wouldn't you?"

"Sometimes a person under stress misinterprets other people's actions," I said. "Drink up your tea and I'll take you back to the ward. You're running a temperature."

"The ward," he said, with a kind of shrinking movement, and then he said almost desperately, "Can you really not know why I'm here?"

That was strange, as if he has included me in his delusional system, *on "his side."* Check this possibility in Rheingeld. I should think it would involve some transference and there has not been time for that.

Spent pm analysing Jest and Sorde holos. I have never seen any psychoscopic realisation, not even a drug-induced hallucination, so fine and vivid as that rose. The shadows of one petal on another, the velvety damp texture of the petals, the pink color full of sunlight, the yellow central crown—I am sure the scent was there if the apparatus had olfactory pickup—it wasn't like a mentifact but a real thing rooted in the earth, alive and growing, the strong thorny stem beneath it.

Very tired, must go to bed.

Just reread this entry. Am I keeping this diary right? All I have written is what happened and what was said. Is that spontaneous? But it was *important* to me.

5 September

Discussed the problem of conscious resistance with Dr. Nades at lunch today. Explained that I have worked with unconscious blocks (the children, and depressives such as Ana J.) and have some skill at reading through, but have not before met a conscious block such as F.S.'s KEEP OUT sign, or the device he used today, which was effective for a full 20-minute session: a concentration on his breathing, bodily rhythms, pain in ribs, and visual input from the scope room. She suggested that I use a blindfold for the latter trick, and keep my attention on the Uncon dimension, as he cannot prevent material from appearing there. It is surprising, though, how large the interplay area of his Con and Uncon fields is, and how much one resonates into the other. I believe his concentration on his breathing rhythm allowed him to achieve something like "trance" condition. Though, of course, most so-called "trance" is mere occultist fakirism, a primitive trait without interest for behavioral science.

Ana thought through "a day in my life" for me today. All so grey and dull, poor soul! She never thought even of food with pleasure, though she lives on minimum ration. The single thing that came bright for a moment was a child's face, clear dark eyes, a pink knitted cap, round cheeks. She told me in post-session discussion that she always walks by a school playground on the way to work because "she likes to see the little ones running and yelling." Her husband appears on the screen as a big bulky suit of work clothes and a peevish, threatening mumble. I wonder if she knows that she hasn't seen his face or heard a word he says for years? But no use telling her that. It may be just as well she doesn't.

The knitting she is doing, I noticed today, is a pink cap.

Reading De Cams's *Disaffection: A Study*, on Dr. Nades's recommendation.

6 September

In the middle of session (breathing again) I said loudly: "Flores!"

Both psy dimensions whited out but the soma realisation hardly changed. After 4 seconds he responded aloud, drowsily. It is not "trance," but autohypnosis.

I said, "Your breathing's monitored by the apparatus. I don't need to know that you're still breathing. It's boring."

He said, "I like to do my own monitoring, Doctor."

I came around and took the blindfold off him and looked at him. He has a pleasant face, the kind of man you often see running machinery, sensitive but patient, like a donkey. That is stupid. I will not cross it out. I am supposed to be spontaneous in this diary. Donkeys do have beautiful faces. They are supposed to be stupid and balky but they look wise and calm, as if they had endured a lot but held no grudges, as if they knew some reason why one should not hold grudges. And the white ring around their eyes makes them look defenseless.

"But the more you breathe," I said, "the less you think. I need your cooperation. I'm trying to find out what it is you're afraid of."

"But I know what I'm afraid of," he said.

"Why won't you tell me?"

"You never asked me."

"That's most unreasonable," I said, which is funny, now I think about it, being indignant with a mental patient because he's unreasonable. "Well, then, now I'm asking you."

He said, "I'm afraid of electroshock. Of having my mind destroyed. Being kept here. Or only being let out when I can't remember anything." He gasped while he was speaking.

I said, "All right, why won't you think about that while I'm watching the screens?"

"Why should I?"

"Why not? You've said it to me, why can't you think about it? I want to see the color of your thoughts!"

"It's none of your business, the color of my thoughts," he said angrily, but I was around to the screen while he spoke, and saw the unguarded activity. Of course it was being taped while we spoke, too, and I have studied it all afternoon. It is fascinating. There are two subverbal levels running aside from the spoken words. All sensory-emotive reactions and distortions are vigorous and complex. He "sees" me, for instance, in at least three different ways, probably more, analysis is impossibly difficult! And the Con-Uncon correspondences are so complicated, and the memory traces and current impressions inter-weave so rapidly, and yet the whole is unified in its complexity. It is like that machine he was studying, very intricate but all one thing in a mathematical harmony. Like the petals of the rose.

When he realised I was observing he shouted out, "Voyeur! Damned voyeur! Let me alone! Get out!" and he broke down and cried. There was a clear fantasy on the screen for several seconds of himself breaking the arm and head clamps and kicking the apparatus to pieces and rushing out of the building, and there, outside, there was a wide hilltop, covered with short dry grass, under the evening sky, and he stood there all alone. While he sat clamped in the chair sobbing.

I broke session and took off the crown, and asked him if he wanted some tea, but he refused to answer. So I freed his arms, and brought him a cup. There was sugar today, a whole box full. I told him that and told him I'd put in two lumps.

After he had drunk some tea he said, with an elaborate ironical tone, because he was ashamed of crying, "You know I like sugar? I suppose your psychoscope told you I liked sugar?"

"Don't be silly," I said, "everybody likes sugar if they can get it."

He said, "No, little doctor, they don't." He asked in the same tone how old I was and if I was married. He was spiteful. He said, "Don't want to marry? Wedded to your work? Helping the mentally unsound back to a constructive life of service to the Nation?"

"I like my work," I said, "because it's difficult, and interesting. Like yours. You like your work, don't you?"

"I did," he said. "Good-bye to all that."

"Why?"

He tapped his head and said, "*Zzzzzt!*—All gone. Right?"

"Why are you so convinced you're going to be prescribed electroshock? I haven't even diagnosed you yet."

"Diagnosed me?" he said. "Look, stop the playacting, please. My diagnosis was made. By the learned doctors of the TRTU. Severe case of disaffection. Prognosis: Evil! Therapy: Lock him up with a roomful of screaming thrashing wrecks, and then go through his mind the same way you went through his papers, and then burn it . . . burn it out. Right, Doctor? Why do you have to go through all this posing, diagnosis, cups of tea? Can't you just get on with it? Do you have to paw through everything I am before you burn it?"

"Flores," I said very patiently, "*you're* saying 'Destroy me'—don't you hear yourself? The psychoscope destroys nothing. And I'm not using it to get evidence, either. This isn't a court, you're not on trial. And I'm not a judge. I'm a doctor."

He interrupted—"If you're a doctor, can't you see that I'm not sick?"

"How can I see anything so long as you block me out with your stupid KEEP OUT signs?" I shouted. I did shout. My patience *was* a pose and it just fell to pieces. But I saw that I had reached him, so I went right on. "You look sick, you act sick—two cracked ribs, a temperature, no appetite, crying fits—is that good health? If you're not sick, then prove it to me! Let me see how you are inside, inside all that!"

He looked down into his cup and gave a kind of laugh and shrugged. "I can't win," he said. "Why do I talk to you? You *look* so honest, damn you!"

I walked away. It is shocking how a patient can hurt one. The trouble is, I am used to the children, whose rejection is absolute, like animals that freeze, or cower, or bite, in their terror. But with this man, intelligent and older than I am, first there is communication and trust and then the blow. It hurts more.

It is painful writing all this down. It hurts again. But it is useful. I do understand some things he said much better now. I think I will not show it to Dr. Nades until I have completed diagnosis. If there is any truth to what he said about being arrested on suspicion of disaffection (and he is certainly careless in the way he talks), Dr. Nades might feel that she should take over the case, due to my inexperience. I should regret that. I need the experience.

7 September

Stupid! That's why she gave you De Cams's book. Of course she knows. As Head of the Section she has access to the TRTU dossier on F.S. She gave me this case deliberately.

It is certainly educational.

Today's session: F.S. still angry and sulky. Intentionally fantasized a sex scene. It was memory, but when she was heaving around underneath him he suddenly stuck a caricature of my face on her. It was effective. I doubt a woman could have done it, women's recall of having sex is usually darker and grander and they and the other do not become meat-puppets like that, with switchable heads. After a while he got bored with the performance (for all its vividness there was little somatic participation, not even an erection) and his mind began to wander. For the first time. One of the drawings on the desk came back. He must be a designer, because he changed it, with a pencil. At the same time there was a tune going on the audio, in mental puretone; and in the Uncon lapping over into the interplay area, a large, dark room seen from a child's height, the windowsills very high, evening outside the windows, tree branches darkening, and inside the room a woman's voice, soft, maybe reading aloud, sometimes joining with the tune. Meanwhile the whore on the bed kept coming and going in volitional bursts, falling apart a little more each time, till there was nothing left but one nipple. This much I analysed out this afternoon, the first sequence of over 10 sec. that I have analysed clear and entire.

When I broke session he said, "What did you learn?" in the satirical voice.

I whistled a bit of the tune.

He looked scared.

"It's a lovely tune," I said, "I never heard it before. If it's yours, I won't whistle it anywhere else."

"It's from some quartet," he said, with his "donkey" face back, defenseless and patient. "I like classical music. Didn't you—"

"I saw the girl," I said. "And my face on her. Do you know what I'd like to see?"

He shook his head. Sulky, hangdog.

"Your childhood."

That surprised him. After a while he said, "All right. You can have my childhood. Why not? You're going to get all the rest anyhow. Listen. You tape it all, don't you? Could I see a playback? I want to see what you see."

"Sure," I said. "But it won't mean as much to you as you think it will. It took me eight years to learn to observe. You start with your own tapes. I watched mine for months before I recognised anything much."

I took him to my seat, put on the earphone, and ran him 30 sec. of the last sequence.

He was quite thoughtful and respectful after it. He asked, "What was all that running-up-and-down-scales motion in the, the background I guess you'd call it?"

"Visual scan—your eyes were closed—and subliminal proprioceptive input. The Unconscious dimension and the Body dimension overlap to a great extent all the time. We bring the three dimensions in separately, because they seldom coincide entirely anyway, except in babies. The bright triangular motion at the left of the holo was probably the pain in your ribs."

"I don't see it that way!"

"You don't see it; you weren't consciously feeling it, even, then. But we can't translate a pain in the rib onto a holoscreen, so we give it a visual symbol. The same with all sensations, affects, emotions."

"You watch all that at once?"

"I told you it took eight years. And you do realise that that's only a fragment? Nobody could put a whole psyche onto a four-foot screen. Nobody knows if there are any limits to the psyche. Except the limits of the universe."

He said after a while, "Maybe you aren't a fool, Doctor. Maybe you're just very absorbed in your work. That can be dangerous, you know, to be so absorbed in your work."

"I love my work, and I hope that it is of positive service," I said. I was alert for symptoms of disaffection.

He smiled a little and said, "Prig," in a sad voice.

Ana is coming along. Still some trouble eating. Entered her in George's mutual-therapy group. What she needs, at least one thing she needs, is companionship. After all why should she eat? Who needs her to be alive? What we call psychosis is sometimes simply realism. But human beings can't live on realism alone.

F.S.'s patterns do not fit any of the classical paranoid psychoscopic patterns in Rheingeld.

The De Cams book is hard for me to understand. The terminology of politics is so different from that of psychology. Everything seems backwards. I must be genuinely attentive at P.T. sessions Sunday nights from now on. I have been lazy-minded. Or, no, but as F.S. said, too absorbed in my work—and so inattentive to its context, he meant. Not thinking about what one is working *for.*

10 September

Have been so tired the last two nights I skipped writing this journal. All the data are on tape and in my analysis notes, of course. Have been working really hard on the F.S. analysis. It is very exciting. It is a truly unusual mind. Not brilliant, his intelligence tests are good average, he is not original or an artist, there are no schizophrenic insights, I can't say what it is, I feel honored to have shared in the childhood he remembered for me. I can't say what it is. There was pain and fear of course, his father's death from cancer, months and months of misery while F.S. was twelve, that was terrible, but it does not come out pain in the end, he has not forgotten or repressed it but it is all changed, by his love for his parents and his sister and for music and for the shape and weight and fit of things and his memory of the lights and weathers of days long past and his mind always working quietly, reaching out, reaching out to be whole.

There is no question yet of formal co-analysis, it is far too early, but he cooperates so intelligently that today I asked him if he was aware consciously of the Dark Brother figure that accompanied several Con memories in the Uncon dimension. When I described it as having a matted shock of hair he looked startled and said, "Dokkay, you mean?"

That word had been on the subverbal audio, though I hadn't connected it with the figure.

He explained that when he was five or six Dokkay had been his name for a "bear" he often dreamed or daydreamed about. He said, "I rode him. He was big, I was small. He smashed down walls, and destroyed things, bad things, you know, bullies, spies, people who scared my mother, prisons, dark alleys I was afraid to cross, policemen with guns, the pawnbroker. Just knocked them over. And then he walked over all the rubble on up to the hilltop. With me riding on his back. It was quiet up there. It was always evening, just before the stars come out. It's strange to remember it. Thirty years ago! Later on he turned into a kind of friend, a boy or man, with hair like a bear. He still smashed things, and I went with him. It was good fun."

I write this down from memory as it was not taped; session was interrupted by power outage. It is exasperating that the hospital comes so low on the list of Government priorities.

Attended the Pos. Thinking session tonight and took notes. Dr. K. spoke on the dangers and falsehoods of liberalism.

❦

11 September

F.S. tried to show me Dokkay this morning but failed. He laughed and said aloud, "I can't see him any more. I think at some point I turned into him."

"Show me when that happened," I said, and he said, "All right," and began at once to recall an episode from his early adolescence. It had nothing to do with Dokkay. He saw an arrest. He was told that the man had been passing out illegal printed matter. Later on he saw one of these pamphlets, the title was in his visual bank, "Is There Equal Justice?" He read it, but did not recall the text or managed to censor it from me. The arrest was terribly vivid. Details like the young man's blue shirt and the coughing noise he made and the sound of the hitting, the TRTU agents' uniforms, and the car driving away, a big grey car with blood on the door. It came back over and over, the car driving away down the street, driving away down the street. It was a traumatic incident for F.S. and may explain the exaggerated fear of the violence of national justice justified by national security which may have led him to behave irrationally when investigated and so appeared as a tendency to disaffection, falsely I believe.

I will show why I believe this. When the episode was done I said, "Flores, think about democracy for me, will you?"

He said, "Little doctor, you don't catch old dogs quite that easily."

"I am not catching you. Can you think about democracy or can't you?"

"I think about it a good deal," he said. And he shifted to right-brain activity, music. It was a chorus of the last part of the Ninth Symphony by Beethoven, I recognised it from the Arts term in high school. We sang it to some patriotic words. I yelled, "Don't censor!" and he said, "Don't shout, I can hear you." Of course the room was perfectly silent, but the pickup on the audio was tremendous, like thousands of people singing together. He went on aloud, "I'm not censoring. I'm thinking about democracy. That is democracy. Hope, brotherhood, no walls. All the walls unbuilt. You, we, I make the universe! Can't you hear it?" And it was the hilltop again, the short grass and the sense of being up high, and the wind, and the whole sky. The music was the sky.

When it was done and I released him from the crown I said, "Thank you."

I do not see why the doctor cannot thank the patient for a revelation of beauty and meaning. Of course the doctor's authority is important but it need not be domineering. I realise that in politics the authorities must lead and be followed but in psychological medicine it is a little different, a doctor cannot "cure" the patient, the patient "cures" himself with our help, this is not contradictory to Positive Thinking.

14 September

I am upset after the long conversation with F.S. today and will try to clarify my thinking.

Because the rib injury prevents him from attending work therapy, he is restless. The Violent ward disturbed him deeply so I used my authority to have the V removed from his chart and have him moved into Men's Ward B, three days ago. His bed is next to old Arca's, and when I came to get him for session they were talking, sitting on Arca's bed. F.S. said, "Dr. Sobel, do you know my neighbor, Professor Arca of the Faculty of Arts and Letters of the University?" Of course I know the old man, he has been here for years, far longer than I, but F.S. spoke so courteously and gravely that I said, "Yes, how do you do, Professor Arca?" and shook the old man's hand. He greeted me politely as a stranger—he often does not know people from one day to the next.

As we went to the scope room F.S. said, "Do you know how many electroshock treatments he had?" and when I said no he said, "Sixty. He tells me that every day. With pride." Then he said, "Did you know that he was an internationally famous scholar? He wrote a book, *The Idea of Liberty*, about twentieth-century ideas of freedom in politics and the arts and sciences. I read it when I was in engineering school. It existed then. On bookshelves. It doesn't exist any more. Anywhere. Ask Dr. Arca. He never heard of it."

"There is almost always some memory loss after electroconvulsive therapy," I said, "but the material lost can be relearned, and is often spontaneously regained."

"After sixty sessions?" he said.

F.S. is a tall man, rather stooped, even in the hospital pajamas he is an impressive figure. But I am also tall, and it is not because I am shorter than he that he calls me "little doctor." He did it first when he was angry at me and so now he says it when he is bitter but does not want what he says to hurt me, the me he knows. He said, "Little doctor, quit faking. You know the man's mind was deliberately destroyed."

Now I will try to write down exactly what I said, because it is important.

"I do not approve of the use of electroconvulsive therapy as a general instrument. I would not recommend its use on my patients except perhaps in certain specific cases of senile melancholia. I went into psychoscopy because it is an integrative rather than a destructive instrument."

That is all true, and yet I never said or consciously thought it before.

"What will you recommend for me?" he said.

I explained that once my diagnosis is complete my recommendation will be subject to the approval of the Head and Assistant Head of the Section. I said that so far nothing in his history or personality structure warranted the use of ECT but that after all we had not got very far yet.

"Let's take a long time about it," he said, shuffling along beside me with his shoulders hunched.

"Why? Do you like it?"

"No. Though I like you. But I'd like to delay the inevitable end."

"Why do you insist that it's inevitable, Flores? Can't you see that your thinking on that one point is quite irrational?"

"Rosa," he said, he has never used my first name before. "Rosa, you can't be reasonable about pure evil. There are faces reason cannot see. Of course I'm irrational, faced with the imminent destruction of my memory—my self. But I'm not inaccurate. You know they're not going to let me out of here un . . ." He hesitated a long time and finally said, "unchanged."

"One psychotic episode—"

"I had no psychotic episode. You must know that by now."

"Then why were you sent here?"

"I have some colleagues who prefer to consider themselves rivals, competitors. I gather they informed the TRTU that I was a subversive liberal."

"What was their evidence?"

"Evidence?" We were in the scope room by now. He put his hands over his face for a moment and laughed in a bewildered way. "Evidence? Well, once at a meeting of my section I talked a long time with a visiting foreigner, a fellow in my field, a designer. And I have friends, you know, unproductive people, bohemians. And this summer I showed our section head why a design he'd got approved by the Government wouldn't work. That was stupid. Maybe I'm here for, for imbecility. And I read. I've read Professor Arca's book."

"But none of that matters, you think positively, you love your country, you're not disaffected!"

He said, "I don't know. I love the idea of democracy, the hope, yes, I love that. I couldn't live without that. But the country? You mean the thing on the map, lines, everything inside the lines is good and nothing outside them matters? How can an adult love such a childish idea?"

"But you wouldn't betray the nation to an outside enemy."

He said, "Well, if it was a choice between the nation and humanity, or the nation and a friend, I might. If you call that betrayal. I call it morality."

He *is* a liberal. It is exactly what Dr. Katin was talking about on Sunday.

It is classic psychopathy: the absence of normal affect. He said that quite unemotionally—"I might."

No. That is not true. He said it with difficulty, with pain. It was I who was so shocked that I felt nothing—blank, cold.

How am I to treat this kind of psychosis, a *political* psychosis? I have read over De Cams's book twice and I believe I do understand it now, but still there is this gap between the political and the psychological, so that the book shows me how to think but does not show me how to *act* positively. I see how F.S. should think and feel, and the difference between that and his present state of mind, but I do not know how to educate him so that he can think positively. De Cams says that disaffection is a negative condition which must be filled with positive ideas and emotions, but this does not fit F.S. The gap is not in him. In fact that gap in De Cams between the political and the psychological is exactly where *his* ideas apply. But if they are wrong ideas how can this be?

I want advice badly, but I cannot get it from Dr. Nades. When she gave me the De Cams she said, "You'll find what you need in this." If I tell her that I haven't it is like a confession of helplessness and she will take the case away from me. Indeed I think it is a kind of test case, testing me. But I need this experience, I am learning, and besides, the patient trusts me and talks freely to me. He does so because he knows that I keep what he tells me in perfect confidence. Therefore I cannot show this journal or discuss these problems with anyone until the cure is under way and confidence is no longer essential.

But I cannot see when that could happen. It seems as if confidence will always be essential between us.

I have got to teach him to adjust his behavior to reality, or he will be sent for ECT when the Section reviews cases in November. He has been right about that all along.

9 October

I stopped writing in this notebook when the material from F.S. began to seem "dangerous" to him (or to myself). I just reread it all over tonight. I see now that I can never show it to Dr. N. So I am going to go ahead and write what I please in it. Which is what she said to do, but I think she always expected me to show it to her, she thought I would want to, which I did, at first, or that if she asked to see it I'd give it to her. She asked about it yesterday. I said that I had abandoned it, because it just repeated things I had already put into the analysis files. She was plainly disapproving but said nothing. Our dominance-submission relationship has changed these past few weeks. I do not feel so much in need of guidance, and after the Ana Jest discharge, the autism paper, and my successful analysis of the T. R. Vinha tapes she cannot insist upon my dependence. But she may resent my independence. I took the covers off the notebook and am keeping the loose pages in the split in the back cover of my copy of Rheingeld, it would take a very close search to find them there. While I was doing that I felt rather sick at the stomach and got a headache.

Allergy: A person can be exposed to pollen or bitten by fleas a thousand times without reaction. Then he gets a viral infection or a psychic trauma or a bee sting, and next time he meets up with ragweed or a flea he begins to sneeze, cough, itch, weep, etc. It is the same with certain other irritants. One has to be sensitized.

"Why is there so much fear?" I wrote. Well now I know. Why is there no privacy? It is unfair and sordid. I cannot read the "classified" files kept in her office, though I work with the patients and she does not. But I am not to have any "classified" material of my own. Only persons in authority can have secrets. Their secrets are all good, even when they are lies.

Listen. Listen Rosa Sobel. Doctor of Medicine, Deg. Psychotherapy, Deg. Psychoscopy. Have you gone native?

Whose thoughts are you thinking?

You have been working 2 to 5 hours a day for 6 weeks inside one person's mind. A generous, integrated, sane mind. You never worked with anything like that before. You have only worked with the crippled and the terrified. You never met an equal before.

Who is the therapist, you or he?

But if there is nothing wrong with him what am I supposed to cure? How can I help him? How can I save him?

By teaching him to lie?

(Undated)

I spent the last two nights till midnight reviewing the diagnostic scopes of Professor Arca, recorded when he was admitted, eleven years ago, before electroconvulsive treatment.

This morning Dr. N inquired why I had been "so far back in the files." (That means that Selena reports to her on what files are used. I know every square centimeter of the scope room but all the same I check it over daily now.) I replied that I was interested in studying the development of ideological disaffection in intellectuals. We agreed that intellectualism tends to foster negative thinking and may lead to psychosis, and those suffering from it should ideally be treated, as Prof. Arca was treated, and released if still competent. It was a very interesting and harmonious discussion.

I lied. I lied. I lied. I lied deliberately, knowingly, well. She lied. She is a liar. She is an intellectual too! She is a lie. And a coward, afraid.

I wanted to watch the Arca tapes to get perspective. To prove to myself that Flores is by no means unique or original. This is true. The differences are fascinating. Dr. Arca's Con dimension was splendid, architectural, but the Uncon material was less well integrated and less interesting. Dr. Arca knew very much more, and the power and beauty of the motions of his thought was far superior to Flores's. Flores is often extremely muddled. That is an element of his vitality. Dr. Arca is an, was an Abstract thinker, as I am, and so I enjoyed his tapes less. I missed the solidity, spatiotemporal realism, and intense sensory clarity of Flores's mind.

In the scope room this morning I told him what I had been doing. His reaction was (as usual) not what I expected. He is fond of the old man and I thought he would be pleased. He said, "You mean they saved the tapes, and destroyed the mind?" I told him that all tapes are kept for use in teaching, and asked him if that didn't cheer him, to know that a record of Arca's thoughts in his prime existed: wasn't it like his book, after all, the lasting part of a mind which sooner or later would, have to grow senile and die anyhow? He said, "No! Not so long as the book is banned and the tape is classified! Neither freedom nor privacy even in death? That is the worst of all!"

After session he asked if I would be able or willing to destroy his diagnostic tapes, if he is sent to ECT. I said such things could get misfiled and lost easily enough, but that it seemed a cruel waste. I had learned from him and others might, later, too. He said, "Don't you see that I will not serve the people with security passes? I will not be used, that's the whole point. You have never used me. We have worked together. Served our term together."

Prison has been much in his mind lately. Fantasies, daydreams of jails, labor camps. He dreams of prison as a man in prison dreams of freedom.

Indeed as I see the way narrowing in I would get him sent to prison if I could, but since he is *here* there is no chance. If I reported that he is, in fact, politically dangerous, they will simply put him back in the Violent ward and give him ECT. There is no judge here to give him a life sentence. Only doctors to give death sentences.

What I can do is stretch out the diagnosis as long as possible, and put in a request for full co-analysis, with a strong prognosis of complete cure. But I have drafted the report three times already and it is very hard to phrase it so that it's clear that I know the disease is ideological (so that they don't just override my diagnosis at once) but still making it sound mild and curable enough that they'd let me handle it with the psychoscope. And then, why, spend up to a year, using expensive equipment, when a cheap and simple instant cure is at hand? No matter what I say, they have that argument. There are two weeks left until Sectional Review. I have got to write the report so that it will be really impossible for them to override it. But what if Flores is right, all this is just playacting, lying about lying, and they have had orders right from the start from TRTU, "wipe this one out"—

(Undated)

Sectional Review today.

If I stay on here I have some power, I can do some good No no no but I don't I don't even in this one thing even in this what can I do now how can I stop

(Undated)

Last night I dreamed I rode on a bear's back up a deep gorge between steep mountainsides, slopes going steep up into a dark sky, it was winter, there was ice on the rocks

(Undated)

Tomorrow morning will tell Nades I am resigning and requesting transfer to Children's Hospital. But she must approve the transfer. If not

I am out in the cold. I am in the cold already. Door locked to write this. As soon as it is written will go down to furnace room and burn it all. There is no place any more.

We met in the hall. He was with an orderly.

I took his hand. It was big and bony and very cold. He said, "Is this it, now, Rosa—the electroshock?" in a low voice. I did not want him to lose hope before he walked up the stairs and down the corridor. It is a long way down the corridor. I said, "No. Just some more tests—EEG probably."

"Then I'll see you tomorrow?" he asked, and I said yes.

And he did. I went in this evening. He was awake. I said, "I am Dr. Sobel, Flores. I am Rosa."

He said, "I'm pleased to meet you," mumbling. There is a slight facial paralysis on the left. That will wear off.

I am Rosa. I am the rose. The rose, I am the rose. The rose with no flower, the rose all thorns, the mind he made, the hand he touched, the winter rose.

Direction of the Road

They did not use to be so demanding. They never hurried us into anything more than a gallop, and that was rare; most of the time it was just a jigjog foot-pace. And when one of them was on his own feet, it was a real pleasure to approach him. There was time to accomplish the entire act with style. There he'd be, working his legs and arms the way they do, usually looking at the road, but often aside at the fields, or straight at me: and I'd approach him steadily but quite slowly, growing larger all the time, synchronizing the rate of approach and the rate of growth perfectly, so that at the very moment that I'd finished enlarging from a tiny speck to my full size—sixty feet in those days—I was abreast of him and hung above him, loomed, towered, overshadowed him. Yet he would show no fear. Not even the children were afraid of me, though often they kept their eyes on me as I passed by and started to diminish.

Sometimes on a hot afternoon one of the adults would stop me right there at our meeting-place, and lie down with his back against mine for an hour or more. I didn't mind in the least. I have an excellent hill, good sun, good wind, good view; why should I mind standing still for an hour or an afternoon? It's only a relative stillness, after all. One need only look at the sun to realize how fast one is going; and then, one grows continually—especially in summer. In any case I was touched by the way they would entrust themselves to me, letting me lean against their little warm backs, and falling sound asleep there between my feet. I liked them. They have seldom lent us Grace as do the birds; but I really preferred them to squirrels.

In those days the horses used to work for them, and that too was enjoyable from my point of view. I particularly liked the canter, and got quite proficient at it. The surging and rhythmical motion accompanied shrinking and growing with a swaying and swooping, almost an illusion of flight. The gallop was less pleasant. It was jerky, pounding: one felt tossed about like a sapling in a gale. And then, the slow approach and growth, the moment of looming-over, and the slow retreat and diminishing, all that was lost during the gallop. One had to hurl oneself into it, cloppety-cloppety-cloppety! and the man usually too busy riding, and the horse too busy running, even to look up. But then, it didn't happen often. A horse is mortal, after all, and like all the loose creatures grows tired easily; so they didn't tire their horses unless there was urgent need. And they seemed not to have so many urgent needs, in those days.

It's been a long time since I had a gallop, and to tell the truth I shouldn't mind having one. There was something invigorating about it, after all.

I remember the first motorcar I saw. Like most of us, I took it for a mortal, some kind of loose creature new to me. I was a bit startled, for after a hundred and thirty-two years I thought I knew all the local fauna. But a new thing is always interesting, in its trivial fashion, so I observed this one with attention. I approached it at a fair speed, about the rate of a canter, but in a new gait, suitable to the ungainly looks of the thing: an uncomfortable, bouncing, rolling, choking, jerking gait. Within two minutes, before I'd grown a foot tall, I knew it was not mortal creature, bound or loose or free. It was a making, like the carts the horses got hitched to. I thought it so very ill-made that I didn't expect it to return, once it gasped over the West Hill, and I heartily hoped it never would, for I disliked that jerking bounce.

But the thing took to a regular schedule, and so, perforce, did I. Daily at four I had to approach it, twitching and stuttering out of the West, and enlarge, loom-over, and diminish. Then at five back I had to come, poppeting along like a young jackrabbit for all my sixty feet, jigging and jouncing out of the East, until at last I got clear out of sight of the wretched little monster and could relax and loosen my limbs to the evening wind. There were always two of them inside the machine: a young male holding the wheel, and behind him an old female wrapped in rugs, glowering. If they ever said anything to each other I never heard It. In those days I overheard a good many conversations on the road, but not from that machine. The top of it was open, but it made so much noise that it overrode all voices, even the voice of the song-sparrow I had with me that year. The noise was almost as vile as the jouncing.

I am of a family of rigid principle and considerable self-respect. The Quercian motto is "Break but bend not," and I have always tried to uphold it. It was not only personal vanity, but family pride, you see, that was offended when I was forced to jounce and bounce in this fashion by a mere making.

The apple trees in the orchard at the foot of the hill did not seem to mind; but then, apples are tame. Their genes have been tampered with for centuries. Besides, they are herd creatures; no orchard tree can really form an opinion of its own.

I kept my own opinion to myself.

But I was very pleased when the motorcar ceased to plague us. All month went by without it, and all month I walked at men and trotted at horses most willingly, and even bobbed for a baby on its mother's arm, trying hard though unsuccessfully to keep in focus.

Next month, however—September it was, for the swallows had left a few days earlier—another of the machines appeared, a new one, suddenly dragging me and the road and our hill, the orchard, the fields, the farmhouse roof, all jigging and jouncing and racketing along from East to West; I went faster than a gallop, faster than I had ever gone before. I had scarcely time to loom, before I had to shrink right down again.

And the next day there came a different one.

Yearly then, weekly, daily, they became commoner. They became a major feature of the local Order of Things. The road was dug up and re-metalled, widened, finished off very smooth and nasty, like a slug's trail, with no ruts, pools, rocks, flowers, or shadows on it. There used to be a lot of little loose creatures on the road, grasshoppers, ants, toads, mice, foxes, and so on, most of them too small to move for, since they couldn't really see one. Now the wise creatures took to avoiding the road, and the unwise ones got squashed. I have seen all too many rabbits die in that fashion, right at my feet. I am thankful that I am an oak, and that though I may be wind-broken or uprooted, hewn or sawn, at least I cannot, under any circumstances, be squashed.

With the presence of many motorcars on the road at once, a new level of skill was required of me. As a mere seedling, as soon as I got my head above the weeds, I had learned the basic trick of going two directions at once. I learned it without thinking about it, under the simple pressure of circumstances on the first occasion that I was a walker in the East and a horseman facing him in the West. I had to go two directions at once, and I did so. It's something we trees master without real effort, I suppose. I was nervous, but I succeeded in passing the rider and then shrinking away from him while at the same time I was still jigjogging towards the walker, and indeed passed him (no looming, back in those days!) only when I had got quite out of sight of the rider. I was proud of myself, being very young, that at first time I did it; but it sounds more difficult than it really is. Since those days of course I had done it innumerable times, and thought nothing about it; I could do it in my sleep. But have you ever considered the feat accomplished, the skill involved, when a tree enlarges, simultaneously yet at slightly different rates and in slightly different manners, for each one of forty motorcar drivers facing two opposite directions, while at the same time diminishing for forty more who have got their backs to it, meanwhile remembering to loom over each single one at the right moment: and to do this minute after minute, hour after hour, from daybreak till nightfall or long after?

For my road had become a busy one; it worked all day long under almost continual traffic. It worked, and I worked. I did not jounce and bounce so much any more, but I had to run faster and faster: to grow enormously, to loom in a split second, to shrink to nothing, all in a hurry, without time to enjoy the action, and without rest: over and over and over.

Very few of the drivers bothered to look at me, not even a seeing glance. They seemed, indeed, not to see any more. They merely stared ahead. They seemed to believe that they were "going somewhere." Little mirrors were affixed to the front of their cars, at which they glanced to see where they had been; then they stared ahead again. I had thought that only beetles had this delusion of Progress. Beetles are always rushing about, and never looking up. I had always had a pretty low opinion of beetles. But at least they let me be.

I confess that sometimes, in the blessed nights of darkness with no moon to silver my crown and no stars occluding with my branches, when I could rest, I would think seriously of escaping my obligation to the general Order of Things: of *failing to move.* No, not seriously. Half-seriously. It was mere weariness. If even a silly, three-year-old, female pussy willow at the foot of the hill accepted her responsibility, and jounced and rolled and accelerated and grew and shrank for each motorcar on the road, was I, an oak, to shirk? Noblesse oblige, and I trust I have never dropped an acorn that did not know its duty.

For fifty or sixty years, then, I have upheld the Order of Things, and have done my share in supporting the human creatures' illusion that they are "going somewhere." And I am not unwilling to do so. But a truly terrible thing has occurred, which I wish to protest.

I do not mind going two directions at once; I do not mind growing and shrinking simultaneously; I do not mind moving, even at the disagreeable rate of sixty or seventy miles an hour. I am ready to go on doing all these things until I am felled or bulldozed. They're my job. But I do object, passionately, to being made eternal.

Eternity is none of my business. I am an oak, no more, no less. I have my duty, and I do it; I have my pleasures, and enjoy them, though they are fewer, since the birds are fewer, and the wind's foul. But, long-lived though I may be, impermanence is my right. Mortality is my privilege. And it has been taken from me.

It was taken from me on a rainy evening in March last year.

Fits and bursts of cars, as usual, filled the rapidly moving road in both directions. I was so busy hurtling along, enlarging, looming, diminishing, and the light was failing so fast, that I scarcely noticed what was happening until it happened. One of the drivers of one of the cars evidently felt that his need to "go somewhere" was exceptionally urgent, and so attempted to place his car in front of the car in front of it. This maneuver involves a temporary slanting of the Direction of the Road and a displacement onto the far side, the side which normally runs the other direction (and may I say that I admire the road very highly for its skill in executing such maneuvers, which must be difficult for an unliving creature, a mere making). Another car, however, happened to be quite near the urgent one, and facing it, as it changed sides; and the road could not do anything about it, being already overcrowded. To avoid impact with the facing car, the urgent car totally violated the Direction of the Road, swinging it round to North-South in its own terms, and so forcing me to leap directly at it. I had no choice. I had to move, and move fast—eighty-five miles an hour. I leapt: I loomed enormous, larger than I have ever loomed before. And then I hit the car.

I lost a considerable piece of bark, and, what's more serious, a fair bit of cambium layer; but as I was seventy-two feet tall and about nine feet in girth at the point of impact, no real harm was done. My branches trembled with the shock enough that a last-year's robin's nest was dislodged and fell; and I was so shaken that I groaned. It is the only time in my life that I have ever said anything out loud.

The motorcar screamed horribly. It was smashed by my blow, squashed, in fact. Its hinder parts were not much affected, but the forequarters knotted up and knurled together like an old root, and little bright bits of it flew all about and lay like brittle rain.

The driver had no time to say anything; I killed him instantly.

It is not this that I protest. I had to kill him, I had no choice, and therefore have no regret. What I protest, what I cannot endure, is this: as I leapt at him, he saw me. He looked up at last. He saw me as I have never been seen before, not even by a child, not even in the days when the people looked at things. He saw me whole, and saw nothing else—then, or ever.

He saw me under the aspect of eternity. He confused me with eternity. And because he died in that moment of false vision, because it can never change, I am caught in it, eternally.

This is unendurable. I cannot uphold such an illusion. If the human creatures will not understand Relativity, very well; but they must understand Relatedness.

If it is necessary to the Order of Things, I will kill drivers of cars, though killing is not a duty usually required of oaks. But it is unjust to require me to play the part, not of the killer only, but of death. For I am not death. I am life: I am mortal.

If they wish to see death visibly in the world, that is their business, not mine. I will not act Eternity for them. Let them not turn to the trees for death. If that is what they want to see, let them look into one another's eyes and see it there.

The White Donkey

There were snakes in the old stone place, but the grass grew so green and rank there that she brought the goats back every day. "The goats are looking fat," Nana said. "Where are you grazing them, Sita?" And when Sita said, "At the old stone place, in the forest," Nana said, "It's a long way to take them," and Uncle Hira said, "Look out for snakes in that place," but they were thinking of the goats, not of her, so she did not ask them, after all, about the white donkey.

She had seen the donkey first when she was putting flowers on the red stone under the pipal tree at the edge of the forest. She liked that stone. It was the Goddess, very old, round, sitting comfortably among the roots of the tree. Everybody who passed by there left the Goddess some flowers or poured a bit of water on her, and every spring her red paint was renewed. Sita was giving the Goddess a rhododendron flower when she looked round, thinking one of the goats was straying off into the forest; but it wasn't a goat. It was a white animal that had caught her eye, whiter than a Brahminee bull. Sita followed it to see what it was. When she saw the neat round rump and the tail like a rope with a tassel, she knew it was a donkey; but such a beautiful donkey! And whose? There were three donkeys in the village, and Chandra Bose owned two, all of them grey, bony, mournful, laborious beasts. This was a tall, sleek, delicate donkey, a wonderful donkey. It could not belong to Chandra Bose, or to anybody in the village, or to anybody in the other village. It wore no halter or harness. It must be wild; it must live in the forest alone.

Sure enough, when she brought the goats along by whistling to clever Kala, and followed where the white donkey had gone into the forest, first there was a path, and then they came to the place where the old stones were, blocks of stone as big as houses all half buried and overgrown with grass and kerala vines; and there the white donkey was standing looking back at her from the darkness under the trees.

She thought then that the donkey was a god, because it had a third eye in the middle of its forehead like Shiva. But when it turned she saw that that was not an eye, but a horn—not curved like a cow's or a goat's horns, a straight spike like a deer's—just the one horn, between the eyes, like Shiva's eye. So it might be a kind of god donkey; and in case it was, she picked a yellow flower off the kerala vine and offered it, stretching out her open palm.

The white donkey stood a while considering her and the goats and the flower; then it came slowly back among the big stones towards her. It had split hooves like the goats, and walked even more neatly than they did. It accepted the flower. Its nose was pinkish-white, and very soft where it snuffled on Sita's palm. She quickly picked another flower, and the donkey accepted it too. But when she wanted to stroke its face around the short, white, twisted horn and the white, nervous ears, it moved away, looking sidelong at her from its long dark eyes.

Sita was a little afraid of it, and thought it might be a little afraid of her, so she sat down on one of the half-buried rocks and pretended to be watching the goats, who were all busy grazing on the best grass they had had for months. Presently the donkey came close again, and standing beside Sita, rested its curly-bearded chin on her lap. The breath from its nostrils moved the thin glass bangles on her wrist. Slowly and very gently she stroked the base of the white, nervous ears, the fine, harsh hair at the base of the horn, the silken muzzle; and the white donkey stood beside her, breathing long, warm breaths.

Every day since then she brought the goats there, walking carefully because of snakes; and the goats were getting fat; and her friend the donkey came out of the forest every day, and accepted her offering, and kept her company.

"One bullock and one hundred rupees cash," said Uncle Hira, "you're crazy if you think we can marry her for less!"

"Moti Lal is a lazy man," Nana said. "Dirty and lazy."

"So he wants a wife to work and clean for him! And he'll take her for only one bullock and one hundred rupees cash!"

"Maybe he'll settle down when he's married," Nana said.

So Sita was betrothed to Moti Lal from the other village, who had watched her driving the goats home at evening. She had seen him watching her across the road, but had never looked at him. She did not want to look at him.

"This is the last day," she said to the white donkey, while the goats cropped the grass among the big, carved, fallen stones, and the forest stood all about them in the singing stillness. "Tomorrow I'll come with Uma's little brother to show him the way here. He'll be the village goatherd now. The day after tomorrow is my wedding day."

The white donkey stood still, its curly, silky beard resting against her hand.

"Nana is giving me her gold bangle," Sita said to the donkey. "I get to wear a red sari, and have henna on my feet and hands."

The donkey stood still, listening.

"There'll be sweet rice to eat at the wedding," Sita said; then she began to cry.

"Good-bye, white donkey," she said. The white donkey looked at her sidelong, and slowly, not looking back, moved away from her and walked into the darkness under the trees.

Gwilan's Harp

The harp had come to Gwilan from her mother, and so had her mastery of it, people said. "Ah," they said when Gwilan played, "you can tell, that's Diera's touch," just as their parents had said when Diera played, "Ah, that's the true Penlin touch!" Gwilan's mother had had the harp from Penlin, a musician's dying gift to the worthiest of pupils. From a musician's hands Penlin, too, had received it; never had it been sold or bartered for, nor any value put upon it that can be said in numbers. A princely and most incredible instrument it was for a poor harper to own. The shape of it was perfection, and every part was strong and fine: the wood as hard and smooth as bronze, the fittings of ivory and silver. The grand curves of the frame bore silver mountings chased with long intertwining lines that became waves and the waves became leaves, and the eyes of gods and stags looked out from among the leaves that became waves and the waves became lines again. It was the work of great craftsmen, you could see that at a glance, and the longer you looked the clearer you saw it. But all this beauty was practical, obedient, shaped to the service of sound. The sound of Gwilan's harp was water running and rain and sunlight on the water, waves breaking and the foam on the brown sands, forests, the leaves and branches of the forest and the shining eyes of gods and stags among the leaves when the wind blows in the valleys. It was all that and none of that. When Gwilan played, the harp made music; and what is music but a little wrinkling of the air?

Play she did, wherever they wanted her. Her singing voice was true but had no sweetness, so when songs and ballads were wanted she accompanied the singers. Weak voices were borne up by her playing, fine voices gained a glory from it; the loudest, proudest singers might keep still a verse to hear her play alone. She played along with the flute and reed flute and tambour, and the music made for the harp to play alone, and the music that sprang up of itself when her fingers touched the strings. At weddings and festivals it was, "Gwilan will be here to play," and at music-day competitions, "When will Gwilan play?"

She was young; her hands were iron and her touch was silk; she could play all night and the next day too. She travelled from valley to valley, from town to town, stopping here and staying there and moving on again with other musicians on their wanderings. They walked, or a wagon was sent for them, or they got a lift on a farmer's cart. However they went, Gwilan carried her harp in its silk and leather case at her back or in her hands. When she rode she rode with the harp and when she walked she walked with the harp and when she slept, no, she didn't sleep with the harp, but it was there where she could reach out and touch it. She was not jealous of it, and would change instruments with another harper gladly; it was a great pleasure to her when at last they gave her back her own, saying with sober envy, "I never played so fine an instrument." She kept it clean, the mountings polished, and strung it with the harp strings made by old Uliad, which cost as much apiece as a whole set of common harp strings. In the heat of summer she carried it in the shade of her body, in the bitter winter it shared her cloak. In a firelit hall she did not sit with it very near the fire, nor yet too far away, for changes of heat and cold would change the voice of it, and perhaps harm the frame. She did not look after herself with half the care. Indeed she saw no need to. She knew there were other harpers, and would be other harpers; most not as good, some better. But the harp was the best. There had not been and there would not be a better. Delight and service were due and fitting to it. She was not its owner but its player. It was her music, her joy, her life, the noble instrument.

She was young; she travelled from town to town; she played "A Fine Long Life" at weddings, and "The Green Leaves" at festivals. There were funerals, with the burial feast, the singing of elegies, and Gwilan to play the Lament of Orioth, the music that crashes and cries out like the sea and the seabirds, bringing relief and a burst of tears to the grief-dried heart. There were music days, with a rivalry of harpers and a shrilling of fiddlers and a mighty outshouting of tenors. She went from town to town in sun and rain, the harp on her back or in her hands. So she was going one day to the yearly music day at Comin, and the landowner of Torm Vale was giving her a lift, a man who so loved music that he had traded a good cow for a bad horse, since the cow would not take him where he could hear music played. It was he and Gwilan in a rickety cart, and the lean-necked roan stepping out down the steep, sunlit road from Torm.

A bear in the forest by the road, or a bear's ghost, or the shadow of a hawk: the horse shied half across the road. Torm had been discussing music deeply with Gwilan, waving his hands to conduct a choir of voices, and the reins went flipping out of those startled hands. The horse jumped like a cat, and ran. At the sharp curve of the road the cart swung round and smashed against the rocky cutting. A wheel leapt free and rolled, rocking like a top, for a few yards. The roan went plunging and sliding down the road with half the wrecked cart dragging behind, and was gone, and the road lay silent in the sunlight between the forest trees.

Torm had been thrown from the cart, and lay stunned for a minute or two.

Gwilan had clutched the harp to her when the horse shied, but had lost hold of it in the smash. The cart had tipped over and dragged on it. It was in its case of leather and embroidered silk, but when, one-handed, she got the case out from under the wheel and opened it, she did not take out a harp, but a piece of wood, and another piece, and a tangle of strings, and a sliver of ivory, and a twisted shell of silver chased with lines and leaves and eyes, held by a silver nail to a fragment of the frame.

It was six months without playing after that, since her arm had broken at the wrist. The wrist healed well enough, but there was no mending the harp; and by then the landowner of Torm had asked her if she would marry him, and she had said yes. Sometimes she wondered why she had said yes, having never thought much of marriage before, but if she looked steadily into her own mind she saw the reason why. She saw Torm on the road in the sunlight kneeling by the broken, harp, his face all blood and dust, and he was weeping. When she looked at that she saw that the time for rambling and roving was over and gone. One day is the day for moving on, and overnight, the next day, there is no more good in moving on, because you have come where you were going to.

Gwilan brought to the marriage a gold piece, which had been the prize last year at Four Valleys music day; she had sewn it to her bodice as a brooch, because where on earth could you spend a gold piece. She also had two silver pieces, five coppers, and a good winter cloak. Torm contributed house and household, fields and forests, four tenant farmers even poorer than himself, twenty hens, five cows, and forty sheep.

They married in the old way, by themselves, over the spring where the stream began, and came back and told the household. Torm had never suggested a wedding, with singing and harp-playing, never a word of all that. He was a man you could trust, Torm was.

What began in pain, in tears, was never free from the fear of pain. The two of them were gentle to each other. Not that they lived together thirty years without some quarrelling. Two rocks sitting side by side would get sick of each other in thirty years, and who knows what they say now and then when nobody is listening. But if people trust each other they can grumble, and a good bit of grumbling takes the fuel from wrath. Their quarrels went up and burnt out like bits of paper, leaving nothing but a feather of ash, a laugh in bed in the dark. Torm's land never gave more than enough, and there was no money saved. But it was a good house, and the sunlight was sweet on those high stony fields. There were two sons, who grew up into cheerful sensible men. One had a taste for roving, and the other was a farmer born; but neither had any gift of music.

Gwilan never spoke of wanting another harp. But about the time her wrist was healed, old Uliad had a travelling musician bring her one on loan; when he had an offer to buy it at its worth, he sent for it back again.

At that time Torm would have it that there was money from selling three good heifers to the landowner of Comin High Farm, and the money should buy a harp, which it did. A year or two later an old friend, a flute player still on his travels and rambles, brought her a harp from the South as a present. The three-heifers harp was a common instrument, plain and heavy; the Southern harp was delicately carved and gilt, but cranky to tune and thin of voice. Gwilan could draw sweetness from the one and strength from the other. When she picked up a harp, or spoke to a child, it obeyed her.

She played at all festivities and funerals in the neighborhood, and with the musician's fees she bought good strings; not Uliad's strings, though, for Uliad was in his grave before her second child was born. If there was a music day nearby she went to it with Torm. She would not play in the competitions, not for fear of losing, but because she was not a harper now, and if they did not know it, she did. So they had her judge the competitions, which she did well and mercilessly. Often in the early years musicians would stop by on their travels and stay two or three nights at Torm; with them she would play the Hunts of Orioth, the Dances of Cail, the difficult and learned music of the North, and learn from them the new songs. Even in winter evenings there was music in the house of Torm: she playing the harp—usually the three-heifers one, sometimes the fretful Southerner—and Torm's good tenor voice, and the boys singing, first in sweet treble, later on in husky unreliable baritone; and one of the farm's men was a lively fiddler; and the shepherd Keth, when he was there, played on the pipes, though he never could tune them to anyone else's note. "It's our own music day tonight," Gwilan would say. "Put another log on the fire, Torm, and sing 'The Green Leaves' with me, and the boys will take the descant."

Her wrist that had been broken grew a little stiff as the years went on; then the arthritis came into her hands. The work she did in house and farm was not easy work. But then who, looking at a hand, would say it was made to do easy work? You can see from the look of it that it is meant to do difficult things, that it is the noble, willing servant of the heart and mind. But the best servants get clumsy as the years go on.

Gwilan could still play the harp, but not as well as she had played, and she did not much like half measures. So the two harps hung on the wall, though she kept them tuned. About that time the younger son went wandering off to see what things looked like in the North, and the elder married and brought his bride to Torm. Old Keth was found dead up on the mountain in the spring rain, his dog crouched silent by him and the sheep nearby. And the drouth came, and the good year, and the poor year, and there was food to eat and to be cooked and clothes to wear and to be washed, poor year or good year. In the depth of a winter Torm took ill. He went from a cough to a high fever to quietness, and died while Gwilan sat beside him.

Thirty years, how can you say how long that is, and yet no longer than the saying of it: thirty years. How can you say how heavy the weight of thirty years is, and yet you can hold all of them together in your hand lighter than a bit of ash, briefer than a laugh in the dark. The thirty years began in pain; they passed in peace, contentment. But they did not end there. They ended where they began.

Gwilan got up from her chair and went into the hearth room. The rest of the household were asleep. In the light of her candle she saw the two harps hung against the wall, the three-heifers harp and the gilded Southern harp, the dull music and the false music. She thought, "I'll take them down at last and smash them on the hearthstone, crush them till they're only bits of wood and tangles of wire, like my harp." But she did not. She could not play them at all any more, her hands were far too stiff. It is silly to smash an instrument you cannot even play.

"There is no instrument left that I can play," Gwilan thought, and the thought hung in her mind for a while like a long chord, till she knew the notes that made it. "I thought my harp was myself. But it was not. It was destroyed, I was not. I thought Torm's wife was myself, but she was not. He is dead, I am not. I have nothing left at all now but myself. The wind blows from the valley, and there's a voice on the wind, a bit of a tune. Then the wind falls, or changes. The work has to be done, and we did the work. It's their turn now for that, the children. There's nothing left for me to do but sing. I never could sing. But you play the instrument you have." So she stood by the cold hearth and sang the melody of Orioth's Lament. The people of the household wakened in their beds and heard her singing, all but Torm; but he knew that tune already. The untuned strings of the harps hung on the wall wakened and answered softly, voice to voice, like eyes that shine among the leaves when the wind is blowing.

May's Lion

Jim remembers it as a bobcat, and he was May's nephew, and ought to know. It probably was a bobcat. I don't think May would have changed her story, though you can't trust a good story-teller not to make the story suit herself, or get the facts to fit the story better. Anyhow she told it to us more than once, because my mother and I would ask for it; and the way I remember it, it was a mountain lion. And the way I remember May telling it is sitting on the edge of the irrigation tank we used to swim in, cement rough as a lava flow and hot in the sun, the long cracks tarred over. She was an old lady then with a long Irish upper lip, kind and wary and balky. She liked to come sit and talk with my mother while I swam; she didn't have all that many people to talk to. She always had chickens, in the chickenhouse very near the back door of the farmhouse, so the whole place smelled pretty strong of chickens, and as long as she could she kept a cow or two down in the old barn by the creek. The first of May's cows I remember was Pearl, a big, handsome Holstein who gave fourteen or twenty-four or forty gallons or quarts of milk at a milking, whichever is right for a prize milker. Pearl was beautiful in my eyes when I was four or five years old; I loved and admired her. I remember how excited I was, how I reached upward to them, when Pearl or the workhorse Prince, for whom my love amounted to worship, would put an immense and sensitive muzzle through the three-strand fence to whisk a cornhusk from my fearful hand; and then the munching; and the sweet breath and the big nose would be at the barbed wire again: the offering is acceptable. . . . After Pearl there was Rosie, a purebred Jersey. May got her either cheap or free because she was a runt calf, so tiny that

May brought her home on her lap in the back of the car, like a fawn. And Rosie always looked like she had some deer in her. She was a lovely, clever little cow and even more willful than old May. She often chose not to come in to be milked. We would hear May calling and then see her trudging across our lower pasture with the bucket, going to find Rosie wherever Rosie had decided to be milked today on the wild hills she had to roam in, a hundred acres of our and Old Jim's land. Then May had a fox terrier named Pinky, who yipped and nipped and turned me against fox terriers for life, but he was long gone when the mountain lion came; and the black cats who lived in the barn kept discreetly out of the story. As a matter of fact now I think of it the chickens weren't in it either. It might have been quite different if they had been. May had quit keeping chickens after old Mrs. Walter died. It was just her all alone there, and Rosie and the cats down in the barn, and nobody else within sight or sound of the old farm. We were in our house up the hill only in the summer, and Jim lived in town, those years. What time of year it was I don't know, but I imagine the grass still green or just turning gold. And May was in the house, in the kitchen, where she lived entirely unless she was asleep or outdoors, when she heard this noise.

Now you need May herself, sitting skinny on the edge of the irrigation tank, seventy or eighty or ninety years old, nobody knew how old May was and she had made sure they couldn't find out, opening her pleated lips and letting out this noise—a huge, awful yowl, starting soft with a nasal hum and rising slowly into a snarling gargle that sank away into a sobbing purr. . . . It got better every time she told the story.

"It was some meow," she said.

So she went to the kitchen door, opened it, and looked out. Then she shut the kitchen door and went to the kitchen window to look out, because there was a mountain lion under the fig tree.

Puma, cougar, catamount; *Felis concolor,* the shy, secret, shadowy lion of the New World, four or five feet long plus a yard of black-tipped tail, weighs about what a woman weighs, lives where the deer live from Canada to Chile, but always shyer, always fewer; the color of dry leaves, dry grass.

There were plenty of deer in the Valley in the forties, but no mountain lion had been seen for decades anywhere near where people lived. Maybe way back up in the canyons; but Jim, who hunted, and knew every deer-trail in the hills, had never seen a lion. Nobody had, except May, now, alone in her kitchen.

"I thought maybe it was sick," she told us. "It wasn't acting right. I don't think a lion would walk right into the yard like that if it was feeling well. If I'd still had the chickens it'd be a different story maybe! But it just walked around some, and then it lay down there," and she points between the fig tree and the decrepit garage. "And then after a while it kind of meowed again, and got up and come into the shade right there." The fig tree, planted when the house was built, about the time May was born, makes a great, green, sweet-smelling shade. "It just laid there looking around. It wasn't well," says May.

She had lived with and looked after animals all her life; she had also earned her living for years as a nurse.

"Well, I didn't know exactly what to do for it. So I put out some water for it. It didn't even get up when I come out the door. I put the water down there, not so close to it that we'd scare each other, see, and it kept watching me, but it didn't move. After I went back in it did get up and tried to drink some water. Then it made that kind of meowowow. I do believe it come here because it was looking for help. Or just for company, maybe."

The afternoon went on, May in the kitchen, the lion under the fig tree.

But down in the barnyard by the creek was Rosie the cow. Fortunately the gate was shut, so she could not come wandering up to the house and meet the lion; but she would be needing to be milked, come six or seven o'clock, and that got to worrying May. She also worried how long a sick mountain lion might hang around, keeping her shut in the house. May didn't like being shut in.

"I went out a time or two, and went shoo!"

Eyes shining amidst fine wrinkles, she flaps her thin arms at the lion. "Shoo! Go on home now!"

But the silent wild creature watches her with yellow eyes and does not stir.

"So when I was talking to Miss Macy on the telephone, she said it might have rabies, and I ought to call the sheriff. I was uneasy then. So finally I did that, and they come out, those county police, you know. Two carloads."

Her voice is dry and quiet.

"I guess there was nothing else they knew how to do. So they shot it."

She looks off across the field Old Jim, her brother, used to plow with Prince the horse and irrigate with the water from this tank. Now wild oats and blackberry grow there. In another thirty years it will be a rich man's vineyard, a tax write-off.

"He was seven feet long, all stretched out, before they took him off. And so thin! They all said, 'Well, Aunt May, I guess you were scared there! I guess you were some scared!' But I wasn't. I didn't want him shot. But I didn't know what to do for him. And I did need to get to Rosie."

I have told this true story which May gave to us as truly as I could, and now I want to tell it as fiction, yet without taking it from her: rather to give it back to her, if I can do so. It is a tiny part of the history of the Valley, and I want to make it part of the Valley outside history. Now the field that the poor man plowed and the rich man harvested lies on the edge of a little town, houses and workshops of timber and fieldstone standing among almond, oak, and eucalyptus trees; and now May is an old woman with a name that means the month of May: Rains End. An old woman with a long, wrinkled-pleated upper lip, she is living alone for the summer in her summer place, a meadow a mile or so up in the hills above the little town, Sinshan. She took her cow Rose with her, and since Rose tends to wander she keeps her on a long tether down by the tiny creek, and moves her into fresh grass now and then. The summerhouse is what they call a nine-pole house, a mere frame of poles stuck in the ground—one of them is a live digger-pine sapling—with stick and matting walls, and mat roof and floors. It doesn't rain in the dry season, and the roof is just for shade. But the house and its little front yard where Rains End has her camp stove and clay oven and matting loom are well shaded by a fig tree that was planted there a hundred years or so ago by her grandmother.

Rains End herself has no grandchildren; she never bore a child, and her one or two marriages were brief and very long ago. She has a nephew and two grandnieces, and feels herself an aunt to all children, even when they are afraid of her and rude to her because she has got so ugly with old age, smelling as musty as a chickenhouse. She considers it natural for children to shrink away from somebody partway dead, and knows that when they're a little older and have got used to her they'll ask her for stories. She was for sixty years a member of the Doctors Lodge, and though she doesn't do curing any more people still ask her to help with nursing sick children, and the children come to long for the kind, authoritative touch of her hands when she bathes them to bring a fever down, or changes a dressing, or combs out bed-tangled hair with witch hazel and great patience.

So Rains End was just waking up from an early afternoon nap in the heat of the day, under the matting roof, when she heard a noise, a huge, awful yowl that started soft with a nasal hum and rose slowly into a snarling gargle that sank away into a sobbing purr. . . . And she got up and looked out from the open side of the house of sticks and matting, and saw a mountain lion under the fig tree. She looked at him from her house; he looked at her from his.

And this part of the story is much the same: the old woman; the lion; and, down by the creek, the cow.

It was hot. Crickets sang shrill in the yellow grass on all the hills and canyons, in all the chaparral. Rains End filled a bowl with water from an unglazed jug and came slowly out of the house. Halfway between the house and the lion she set the bowl down on the dirt. She turned and went back to the house.

The lion got up after a while and came and sniffed at the water. He lay down again with a soft, querulous groan, almost like a sick child, and looked at Rains End with the yellow eyes that saw her in a different way than she had ever been seen before.

She sat on the matting in the shade of the open part of her house and did some mending. When she looked up at the lion she sang under her breath, tunelessly; she wanted to remember the Puma Dance Song but could only remember bits of it, so she made a song for the occasion:

> You are there, lion.
> You are there, lion. . . .

As the afternoon wore on she began to worry about going down to milk Rose. Unmilked, the cow would start tugging at her tether and making a commotion. That was likely to upset the lion. He lay so close to the house now that if she came out that too might upset him, and she did not want to frighten him or to become frightened of him. He had evidently come for some reason, and it behoved her to find out what the reason was. Probably he was sick; his coming so close to a human person was strange, and people who behave strangely are usually sick or in some kind of pain. Sometimes, though, they are spiritually moved to act strangely. The lion might be a messenger, or might have some message of his own for her or her townspeople. She was more used to seeing birds as messengers; the four-footed people go about their own business. But the lion, dweller in the Seventh House, comes from the place dreams come from. Maybe she did not understand. Maybe someone else would understand. She could go over and tell Valiant and her family, whose summerhouse was in Gahheya meadow, farther up the creek; or she could go over to Buck's, on Baldy Knoll. But there were four or five adolescents there, and one of them might come and shoot the lion, to boast that he'd saved old Rains End from getting clawed to bits and eaten.

Mooooo! said Rose, down by the creek, reproachfully.

The sun was still above the southwest ridge, but the branches of pines were across it and the heavy heat was out of it, and shadows were welling up in the low fields of wild oats and blackberry.

Mooooo! said Rose again, louder.

The lion lifted up his square, heavy head, the color of dry wild oats, and gazed down across the pastures. Rains End knew from that weary movement that he was very ill. He had come for company in dying, that was all.

"I'll come back, lion," Rains End sang tunelessly. "Lie still. Be quiet. I'll come back soon." Moving softly and easily, as she would move in a room with a sick child, she got her milking pail and stool, slung the stool on her back with a woven strap so as to leave a hand free, and came out of the house. The lion watched her at first very tense, the yellow eyes firing up for a moment, but then put his head down again with that little grudging, groaning sound. "I'll come back, lion," Rains End said. She went down to the creekside and milked a nervous and indignant cow. Rose could smell lion, and demanded in several ways, all eloquent, just what Rains End intended to *do?* Rains End ignored her questions and sang milking songs to her: "Su bonny, su bonny, be still my grand cow . . ." Once she had to slap her hard on the hip. "Quit that, you old fool! Get over! I am *not* going to untie you and have you walking into trouble! I won't let him come down this way."

She did not say how she planned to stop him.

She retethered Rose where she could stand down in the creek if she liked. When she came back up the rise with the pail of milk in hand, the lion had not moved. The sun was down, the air above the ridges turning clear gold. The yellow eyes watched her, no light in them. She came to pour milk into the lion's bowl. As she did so, he all at once half rose up. Rains End started, and spilled some of the milk she was pouring. "Shoo! Stop that!" she whispered fiercely, waving her skinny arm at the lion. "Lie down now! I'm afraid of you when you get up, can't you see that, stupid? Lie down now, lion. There you are. Here I am. It's all right. You know what you're doing." Talking softly as she went, she returned to her house of stick and matting. There she sat down as before, in the open porch, on the grass mats.

The mountain lion made the grumbling sound, ending with a long sigh, and let his head sink back down on his paws.

Rains End got some cornbread and a tomato from the pantry box while there was still daylight left to see by, and ate slowly and neatly. She did not offer the lion food. He had not touched the milk, and she thought he would eat no more in the House of Earth.

From time to time as the quiet evening darkened and stars gathered thicker overhead she sang to the lion. She sang the five songs of *Going Westward to the Sunrise,* which are sung to human beings dying. She did not know if it was proper and appropriate to sing these songs to a dying mountain lion, but she did not know his songs.

Twice he also sang: once a quavering moan, like a housecat challenging another tom to battle, and once a long, sighing purr.

Before the Scorpion had swung clear of Sinshan Mountain, Rains End had pulled her heavy shawl around herself in case the fog came in, and had gone sound asleep in the porch of her house.

She woke with the grey light before sunrise. The lion was a motionless shadow, a little farther from the trunk of the fig tree than he had been the night before. As the light grew, she saw that he had stretched himself out full length. She knew he had finished his dying, and sang the fifth song, the last song, in a whisper, for him:

The doors of the Four Houses
are open.
Surely they are open.

Near sunrise she went to milk Rose, and to wash in the creek. When she came back up to the house she went closer to the lion, though not so close as to crowd him, and stood for a long time looking at him stretched out in the long, tawny, delicate light "As thin as I am!" she said to Valiant, when she went up to Gahheya later in the morning to tell the story and to ask help carrying the body of the lion off where the buzzards and coyotes could clean it.

It's still your story, Aunt May; it was your lion. He came to you. He brought his death to you, a gift; but the men with the guns won't take gifts, they think they own death already. And so they took from you the honor he did you, and you felt that loss. I wanted to restore it. But you don't need it. You followed the lion where he went, years ago now.

Buffalo Gals, Won't You Come Out Tonight

i

"You fell out of the sky," the coyote said.

Still curled up tight, lying on her side, her back pressed against the overhanging rock, the child watched the coyote with one eye. Over the other eye she kept her hand cupped, its back on the dirt.

"There was a burned place in the sky, up there alongside the rimrock, and then you fell out of it," the coyote repeated, patiently, as if the news was getting a bit stale. "Are you hurt?"

She was all right. She was in the plane with Mr. Michaels, and the motor was so loud she couldn't understand what he said even when he shouted, and the way the wind rocked the wings was making her feel sick, but it was all right. They were flying to Canyonville. In the plane.

She looked. The coyote was still sitting there. It yawned. It was a big one, in good condition, its coat silvery and thick. The dark tearline from its long yellow eye was as clearly marked as a tabby cat's.

She sat up, slowly, still holding her right hand pressed to her right eye.

"Did you lose an eye?" the coyote asked, interested.

"I don't know," the child said. She caught her breath and shivered. "I'm cold."

"I'll help you look for it," the coyote said. "Come on! If you move around you won't have to shiver. The sun's up."

Cold lonely brightness lay across the falling land, a hundred miles of sagebrush. The coyote was trotting busily around, nosing under clumps of rabbit-brush and cheatgrass, pawing at a rock. "Aren't you going to look?" it said, suddenly sitting down on its haunches and abandoning the search. "I knew a trick once where I could throw my eyes way up into a tree and see everything from up there, and then whistle, and they'd come back into my head. But that goddam bluejay stole them, and when I whistled nothing came. I had to stick lumps of pine pitch into my head so I could see anything. You could try that. But you've got one eye that's OK, what do you need two for? Are you coming, or are you dying there?"

The child crouched, shivering.

"Well, come if you want to," said the coyote, yawned again, snapped at a flea, stood up, turned, and trotted away among the sparse clumps of rabbit-brush and sage, along the long slope that stretched on down and down into the plain streaked across by long shadows of sagebrush. The slender, grey-yellow animal was hard to keep in sight, vanishing as the child watched.

She struggled to her feet, and without a word, though she kept saying in her mind, "Wait, please wait," she hobbled after the coyote. She could not see it. She kept her hand pressed over the right eyesocket. Seeing with one eye there was no depth; it was like a huge, flat picture. The coyote suddenly sat in the middle of the picture, looking back at her, its mouth open, its eyes narrowed, grinning. Her legs began to steady and her head did not pound so hard, though the deep, black ache was always there. She had nearly caught up to the coyote when it trotted off again. This time she spoke. "Please wait!" she said.

"OK," said the coyote, but it trotted right on. She followed, walking downhill into the flat picture that at each step was deep.

Each step was different underfoot; each sage bush was different, and all the same. Following the coyote she came out from the shadow of the rimrock cliffs, and the sun at eyelevel dazzled her left eye. Its bright warmth soaked into her muscles and bones at once. The air, that all night had been so hard to breathe, came sweet and easy.

The sage bushes were pulling in their shadows and the sun was hot on the child's back when she followed the coyote along the rim of a gully. After a while the coyote slanted down the undercut slope and the child scrambled after, through scrub willows to the thin creek in its wide sandbed. Both drank.

The coyote crossed the creek, not with a careless charge and splashing like a dog, but singlefoot and quiet like a cat; always it carried its tail low. The child hesitated, knowing that wet shoes make blistered feet, and then waded across in as few steps as possible. Her right arm ached with the effort of holding her hand up over her eye. "I need a bandage," she said to the coyote. It cocked its head and said nothing. It stretched out its forelegs and lay watching the water, resting but alert. The child sat down nearby on the hot sand and tried to move her right hand. It was glued to the skin around her eye by dried blood. At the little tearing-away pain, she whimpered; though it was a small pain it frightened her. The coyote came over close and poked its long snout into her face. Its strong, sharp smell was in her nostrils. It began to lick the awful, aching blindness, cleaning and cleaning with its curled, precise, strong wet tongue, until the child was able to cry a little with relief, being comforted. Her head was bent close to the grey-yellow ribs, and she saw the hard nipples, the whitish belly-fur. She put her arm around the she-coyote, stroking the harsh coat over back and ribs.

"OK," the coyote said, "let's go!" And set off without a backward glance. The child scrambled to her feet and followed. "Where are we going?" she said, and the coyote, trotting on down along the creek, answered, "On down along the creek . . ."

There must have been a while she was asleep while she walked, because she felt like she was waking up, but she was walking along, only in a different place. She didn't know how she knew it was different. They were still following the creek, though the gully was flattened out to nothing much, and there was still sagebrush range as far as the eye could see. The eye—the good one—felt rested. The other one still ached, but not so sharply, and there was no use thinking about it. But where was the coyote?

She stopped. The pit of cold into which the plane had fallen reopened and she fell. She stood falling, a thin whimper making itself in her throat.

"Over here!"

The child turned. She saw a coyote gnawing at the half-dried-up carcass of a crow, black feathers sticking to the black lips and narrow jaw.

She saw a tawny-skinned woman kneeling by a campfire, sprinkling something into a conical pot. She heard the water boiling in the pot, though it was propped between rocks, off the fire. The woman's hair was yellow and grey, bound back with a string. Her feet were bare. The upturned soles looked as dark and hard as shoe soles, but the arch of the foot was high, and the toes made two neat curving rows. She wore bluejeans and an old white shirt. She looked over at the girl. "Come on, eat crow!" she said. The child slowly came toward the woman and the fire, and squatted down. She had stopped falling and felt very light and empty; and her tongue was like a piece of wood stuck in her mouth.

Coyote was now blowing into the pot or basket or whatever it was. She reached into it with two fingers, and pulled her hand away shaking it and shouting, "Ow! Shit! Why don't I ever have any spoons?" She broke off a dead twig of sagebrush, dipped it into the pot, and licked it. "Oh, boy," she said. "Come on!"

The child moved a little closer, broke off a twig, dipped. Lumpy pinkish mush clung to the twig. She licked. The taste was rich and delicate.

"What is it?" she asked after a long time of dipping and licking.

"Food. Dried salmon mush," Coyote said. "It's cooling down." She stuck two fingers into the mush again, this time getting a good load, which she ate very neatly. The child, when she tried, got mush all over her chin. It was like chopsticks, it took practice. She practiced. They ate turn and turn until nothing was left in the pot but three rocks. The child did not ask why there were rocks in the mush-pot. They licked the rocks clean. Coyote licked out the inside of the pot-basket, rinsed it once in the creek, and put it onto her head. It fit nicely, making a conical hat. She pulled off her bluejeans. "Piss on the fire!" she cried, and did so, standing straddling it. "Ah, steam between the legs!" she said. The child, embarrassed, thought she was supposed to do the same thing, but did not want to, and did not. Bareassed, Coyote danced around the dampened fire, kicking her long thin legs out and singing,

> "Buffalo gals, won't you come out tonight,
> Come out tonight, come out tonight,
> Buffalo gals, won't you come out tonight,
> And dance by the light of the moon?"

She pulled her jeans back on. The child was burying the remains of the fire in creek-sand, heaping it over, seriously, wanting to do right. Coyote watched her.

"Is that you?" she said. "A Buffalo Gal? What happened to the rest of you?"

"The rest of me?" The child looked at herself, alarmed.

"All your people."

"Oh. Well, Mom took Bobbie, he's my little brother, away with Uncle Norm. He isn't really my uncle, or anything. So Mr. Michaels was going there anyway so he was going to fly me over to my real father, in Canyonville. Linda, my stepmother, you know, she said it was OK for the summer anyhow if I was there, and then we could see. But the plane."

In the silence the girl's face became dark red, then greyish white. Coyote watched, fascinated. "Oh," the girl said, "Oh—Oh—Mr. Michaels—he must be—Did the—"

"Come on!" said Coyote, and set off walking.

The child cried, "I ought to go back—"

"What for?" said Coyote. She stopped to look round at the child, then went on faster. "Come on, Gal!" She said it as a name; maybe it was the child's name, Myra, as spoken by Coyote. The child, confused and despairing, protested again, but followed her. "Where are we going? Where *are* we?"

"This is my country," Coyote answered, with dignity, making a long, slow gesture all round the vast horizon. "I made it. Every goddam sage bush."

And they went on. Coyote's gait was easy, even a little shambling, but she covered the ground; the child struggled not to drop behind. Shadows were beginning to pull themselves out again from under the rocks and shrubs. Leaving the creek, they went up a long, low, uneven slope that ended away off against the sky in rimrock. Dark trees stood one here, another way over there; what people called a juniper forest, a desert forest, one with a lot more between the trees than trees. Each juniper they passed smelled sharply, cat-pee smell the kids at school called it, but the child liked it; it seemed to go into her mind and wake her up. She picked off a juniper berry and held it in her mouth, but after a while spat it out. The aching was coming back in huge black waves, and she kept stumbling. She found that she was sitting down on the ground. When she tried to get up her legs shook and would not go under her. She felt foolish and frightened, and began to cry.

"We're home!" Coyote called from way on up the hill.

The child looked with her one weeping eye, and saw sagebrush, juniper, cheatgrass, rimrock. She heard a coyote yip far off in the dry twilight

She saw a little town up under the rimrock, board houses, shacks, all unpainted. She heard Coyote call again, "Come on, pup! Come on, Gal, we're home!" She could not get up, so she tried to go on all fours, the long way up the slope to the houses under the rimrock. Long before she got there, several people came to meet her. They were all children, she thought at first, and then began to understand that most of them were grown people, but all were very short; they were broad-bodied, fat, with fine, delicate hands and feet. Their eyes were bright. Some of the women helped her stand up and walk, coaxing her, "It isn't much farther, you're doing fine." In the late dusk lights shone yellow-bright through doorways and through unchinked cracks between boards. Woodsmoke hung sweet in the quiet air. The short people talked and laughed all the time, softly. "Where's she going to stay?"—"Put her in with Robin, they're all asleep already!"—"Oh, she can stay with us."

The child asked hoarsely, "Where's Coyote?"

"Out hunting," the short people said.

A deeper voice spoke: "Somebody new has come into town?"

"Yes, a new person," one of the short men answered. Among these people the deep-voiced man bulked impressive; he was broad and tall, with powerful hands, a big head, a short neck. They made way for him respectfully. He moved very quietly, respectful of them also. His eyes when he stared down at the child were amazing. When he blinked, it was like the passing of a hand before a candleflame.

"It's only an owlet," he said. "What have you let happen to your eye, new person?"

"I was—We were flying—"

"You're too young to fly," the big man said in his deep, soft voice. "Who brought you here?"

"Coyote."

And one of the short people confirmed: "She came here with Coyote, Young Owl."

"Then maybe she should stay in Coyote's house tonight," the big man said.

"It's all bones and lonely in there," said a short woman with fat cheeks and a striped shirt. "She can come with us."

That seemed to decide it. The fat-cheeked woman patted the child's arm and took her past several shacks and shanties to a low, windowless house. The doorway was so low even the child had to duck down to enter. There were a lot of people inside, some already there and some crowding in after the fat-cheeked woman. Several babies were fast asleep in cradle-boxes in corners. There was a good fire, and a good smell, like toasted sesame seeds. The child was given food, and ate a little, but her head swam and the blackness in her right eye kept coming across her left eye so she could not see at all for a while. Nobody asked her name or told her what to call them. She heard the children call the fat-cheeked woman Chipmunk. She got up courage finally to say, "Is there somewhere I can go to sleep, Mrs. Chipmunk?"

"Sure, come on," one of the daughters said, "in here," and took the child into a back room, not completely partitioned off from the crowded front room, but dark and uncrowded. Big shelves with mattresses and blankets lined the walls. "Crawl in!" said Chipmunk's daughter, patting the child's arm in the comforting way they had. The child climbed onto a shelf, under a blanket. She laid down her head. She thought, "I didn't brush my teeth."

ii

She woke; she slept again. In Chipmunk's sleeping room it was always stuffy, warm, and half-dark, day and night. People came in and slept and got up and left, night and day. She dozed and slept, got down to drink from the bucket and dipper in the front room, and went back to sleep and doze.

She was sitting up on the shelf, her feet dangling, not feeling bad any more, but dreamy, weak. She felt in her jeans pockets. In the left front one was a pocket comb and a bubblegum wrapper, in the right front, two dollar bills and a quarter and a dime.

Chipmunk and another woman, a very pretty dark-eyed plump one, came in. "So you woke up for your dance!" Chipmunk greeted her, laughing, and sat down by her with an arm around her.

"Jay's giving you a dance," the dark woman said. "He's going to make you all right. Let's get you all ready!"

There was a spring up under the rimrock, that flattened out into a pool with slimy, reedy shores. A flock of noisy children splashing in it ran off and left the child and the two women to bathe. The water was warm on the surface, cold down on the feet and legs. All naked, the two soft-voiced laughing women, their round bellies and breasts, broad hips and buttocks gleaming warm in the late afternoon light, sluiced the child down, washed and stroked her limbs and hands and hair, cleaned around the cheekbone and eyebrow of her right eye with infinite softness, admired her, sudsed her, rinsed her, splashed her out of the water, dried her off, dried each other off, got dressed, dressed her, braided her hair, braided each other's hair, tied feathers on the braid-ends, admired her and each other again, and brought her back down into the little straggling town and to a kind of playing field or dirt parking lot in among the houses. There were no streets, just paths and dirt, no lawns and gardens, just sagebrush and dirt. Quite a few people were gathering or wandering around the open place, looking dressed up, wearing colorful shirts, print dresses, strings of beads, earrings. "Hey there, Chipmunk, Whitefoot!" they greeted the women.

A man in new jeans, with a bright blue velveteen vest over a clean, faded blue workshirt, came forward to meet them, very handsome, tense, and important. "All right, Gal!" he said in a harsh, loud voice, which startled among all these soft-speaking people. "We're going to get that eye fixed right up tonight! You just sit down here and don't worry about a thing." He took her wrist, gently despite his bossy, brassy manner, and led her to a woven mat that lay on the dirt near the middle of the open place. There, feeling very foolish, she had to sit down, and was told to stay still. She soon got over feeling that everybody was looking at her, since nobody paid her more attention than a checking glance or, from Chipmunk or Whitefoot and their families, a reassuring wink. Every now and then Jay rushed over to her and said something like, "Going to be as good as new!" and went off again to organize people, waving his long blue arms and shouting.

Coming up the hill to the open place, a lean, loose, tawny figure— and the child started to jump up, remembered she was to sit still, and sat still, calling out softly, "Coyote! Coyote!"

Coyote came lounging by. She grinned. She stood looking down at the child. "Don't let that Bluejay fuck you up, Gal," she said, and lounged on.

The child's gaze followed her, yearning.

People were sitting down now over on one side of the open place, making an uneven half-circle that kept getting added to at the ends until there was nearly a circle of people sitting on the dirt around the child, ten or fifteen paces from her. All the people wore the kind of clothes the child was used to, jeans and jeans-jackets, shirts, vests, cotton dresses, but they were all barefoot; and she thought they were more beautiful than the people she knew, each in a different way, as if each one had invented beauty. Yet some of them were also very strange: thin black shining people with whispery voices, a long-legged woman with eyes like jewels. The big man called Young Owl was there, sleepy-looking and dignified, like Judge McCown who owned a sixty-thousand acre ranch; and beside him was a woman the child thought might be his sister, for like him she had a hook nose and big, strong hands; but she was lean and dark, and there was a crazy look in her fierce eyes. Yellow eyes, but round, not long and slanted like Coyote's. There was Coyote sitting yawning, scratching her armpit, bored. Now somebody was entering the circle: a man, wearing only a kind of kilt and a cloak painted or beaded with diamond shapes, dancing to the rhythm of the rattle he carried and shook with a buzzing fast beat. His limbs and body were thick yet supple, his movements smooth and pouring. The child kept her gaze on him as he danced past her, around her, past again. The rattle in his hand shook almost too fast to see, in the other hand was something thin and sharp. People were singing around the circle now, a few notes repeated in time to the rattle, soft and tuneless. It was exciting and boring, strange and familiar. The Rattler wove his dancing closer and closer to her, darting at her. The first time she flinched away, frightened by the lunging movement and by his flat, cold face with narrow eyes, but after that she sat still, knowing her part. The dancing went on, the singing went on, till they carried her past boredom into a floating that could go on forever.

Jay had come strutting into the circle, and was standing beside her. He couldn't sing, but he called out, "Hey! Hey! Hey! Hey!" in his big, harsh voice, and everybody answered from all round, and the echo came down from the rimrock on the second beat. Jay was holding up a stick with a ball on it in one hand, and something like a marble in the other. The stick was a pipe: he got smoke into his mouth from it and blew it in four directions and up and down and then over the marble, a puff each time. Then the rattle stopped suddenly, and everything was silent for several breaths. Jay squatted down and looked intently into the child's face, his head cocked to one side. He reached forward, muttering something in time to the rattle and the singing that had started up again louder than before; he touched the child's right eye in the black center of the pain. She flinched and endured. His touch was not gentle. She saw the marble, a dull yellow ball like beeswax, in his hand; then she shut her seeing eye and set her teeth.

"There!" Jay shouted. "Open up. Come on! Let's see!"

Her jaw clenched like a vise, she opened both eyes. The lid of the right one stuck and dragged with such a searing white pain that she nearly threw up as she sat there in the middle of everybody watching

"Hey, can you see? How's it work? It looks great!" Jay was shaking her arm, railing at her. "How's it feel? Is it working?"

What she saw was confused, hazy, yellowish. She began to discover, as everybody came crowding around peering at her, smiling, stroking and patting her arms and shoulders, that if she shut the hurting eye and looked with the other, everything was clear and flat; if she used them both, things were blurry and yellowish, but deep.

There, right close, was Coyote's long nose and narrow eyes and grin. "What is it, Jay?" she was asking, peering at the new eye. "One of mine you stole that time?"

"It's pine pitch," Jay shouted furiously. "You think I'd use some stupid secondhand coyote eye? I'm a doctor."

"Ooooh, Ooooh, a doctor," Coyote said. "Boy, that is one ugly eye. Why didn't you ask Rabbit for a rabbit-dropping? That eye looks like shit." She put her lean face yet closer, till the child thought she was going to kiss her; instead, the thin, firm tongue once more licked accurate across the pain, cooling, clearing. When the child opened both eyes again the world looked pretty good.

"It works fine," she said.

"Hey!" Jay yelled. "She says it works fine! It works fine, she says so! I told you! What'd I tell you?" He went off waving his arms and yelling. Coyote had disappeared. Everybody was wandering off.

The child stood up, stiff from long sitting. It was nearly dark; only the long west held a great depth of pale radiance. Eastward the plains ran down into night.

Lights were on in some of the shanties. Off at the edge of town somebody was playing a creaky fiddle, a lonesome chirping tune.

A person came beside her and spoke quietly: "Where will you stay?"

"I don't know," the child said. She was feeling extremely hungry. "Can I stay with Coyote?"

"She isn't home much," the soft-voiced woman said. "You were staying with Chipmunk, weren't you? Or there's Rabbit, or Jackrabbit, they have families . . ."

"Do you have a family?" the girl asked, looking at the delicate, soft-eyed woman.

"Two fawns," the woman answered, smiling. "But I just came into town for the dance."

"I'd really like to stay with Coyote," the child said after a little pause, timid, but obstinate.

145

"OK, that's fine. Her house is over here." Doe walked along beside the child to a ramshackle cabin on the high edge of town. No light shone from inside. A lot of junk was scattered around the front. There was no step up to the half-open door. Over the door a battered pine board, nailed up crooked, said BIDE-A-WEE.

"Hey, Coyote? Visitors," Doe said. Nothing happened.

Doe pushed the door farther open and peered in. "She's out hunting, I guess. I better be getting back to the fawns. You going to be OK? Anybody else here will give you something to eat—you know . . . OK?"

"Yeah. I'm fine. Thank you," the child said.

She watched Doe walk away through the clear twilight, a severely elegant walk, small steps, like a woman in high heels, quick, precise, very light.

Inside Bide-A-Wee it was too dark to see anything and so cluttered that she fell over something at every step. She could not figure out where or how to light a fire. There was something that felt like a bed, but when she lay down on it, it felt more like a dirty-clothes pile, and smelt like one. Things bit her legs, arms, neck, and back. She was terribly hungry. By smell she found her way to what had to be a dead fish hanging from the ceiling in one corner. By feel she broke off a greasy flake and tasted it. It was smoked dried salmon. She ate one succulent piece after another until she was satisfied, and licked her fingers clean. Near the open door starlight shone on water in a pot of some kind; the child smelled it cautiously, tasted it cautiously, and drank just enough to quench her thirst, for it tasted of mud and was warm and stale. Then she went back to the bed of dirty clothes and fleas, and lay down. She could have gone to Chipmunk's house, or other friendly households; she thought of that as she lay forlorn in Coyote's dirty bed. But she did not go. She slapped at fleas until she fell asleep.

Along in the deep night somebody said, "Move over, pup," and was warm beside her.

Breakfast, eaten sitting in the sun in the doorway, was dried-salmon-powder mush. Coyote hunted, mornings and evenings, but what they ate was not fresh game but salmon, and dried stuff, and any berries in season. The child did not ask about this. It made sense to her. She was going to ask Coyote why she slept at night and waked in the day like humans, instead of the other way round like coyotes, but when she framed the question in her mind she saw at once that night is when you sleep and day when you're awake; that made sense too. But one question she did ask, one hot day when they were lying around slapping fleas.

"I don't understand why you all look like people," she said.

"We are people."

"I mean, people like me, humans."

"Resemblance is in the eye," Coyote said. "How is that lousy eye, by the way?"

"It's fine. But—like you wear clothes—and live in houses—with fires and stuff—"

"That's what you think . . . If that loudmouth Jay hadn't horned in, I could have done a really good job."

The child was quite used to Coyote's disinclination to stick to any one subject, and to her boasting. Coyote was like a lot of kids she knew, in some respects. Not in others.

"You mean what I'm seeing isn't true? Isn't real—like on TV, or something?"

"No," Coyote said. "Hey, that's a tick on your collar." She reached over, flicked the tick off, picked it up on one finger, bit it, and spat out the bits.

"Yecch!" the child said. "So?"

"So, to me you're basically greyish yellow and run on four legs. To that lot—" she waved disdainfully at the warren of little houses next down the hill—"you hop around twitching your nose all the time. To Hawk, you're an egg, or maybe getting pinfeathers. See? It just depends on how you look at things. There are only two kinds of people."

"Humans and animals?"

"No. The kind of people who say, 'There are two kinds of people' and the kind of people who don't." Coyote cracked up, pounding her thigh and yelling with delight at her joke. The child didn't get it, and waited.

"OK," Coyote said. "There's the first people, and then the others. That's the two kinds."

"The first people are—?"

"Us, the animals . . . and things. All the old ones. You know. And you pups, kids, fledglings. All first people."

"And the—others?"

"Them," Coyote said. "You know. The others. The new people. The ones who came." Her fine, hard face had gone serious, rather formidable. She glanced directly, as she seldom did, at the child, a brief gold sharpness. "We were here," she said. "We were always here. We are always here. Where we are is here. But it's their country now. They're running it . . . Shit, even I did better!"

The child pondered and offered a word she had used to hear a good deal: "They're illegal immigrants."

"Illegal!" Coyote said, mocking, sneering. "Illegal is a sick bird. What the fuck's illegal mean? You want a code of justice from a coyote? Grow up, kid!"

"I don't want to."

"You don't want to grow up?"

"I'll be the other kind if I do."

"Yeah. So," Coyote said, and shrugged. "That's life." She got up and went around the house, and the child heard her pissing in the back yard.

A lot of things were hard to take about Coyote as a mother. When her boyfriends came to visit, the child learned to go stay with Chipmunk or the Rabbits for the night, because Coyote and her friend wouldn't even wait to get on the bed but would start doing that right on the floor or even out in the yard. A couple of times Coyote came back late from hunting with a friend, and the child had to lie up against the wall in the same bed and hear and feel them doing that right next to her. It was something like fighting and something like dancing, with a beat to it, and she didn't mind too much except that it made it hard to stay asleep.

Once she woke up and one of Coyote's friends was stroking her stomach in a creepy way. She didn't know what to do, but Coyote woke up and realized what he was doing, bit him hard, and kicked him out of bed. He spent the night on the floor, and apologized next morning— "Aw, hell, Ki, I forgot the kid was there, I thought it was you—"

Coyote, unappeased, yelled, "You think I don't got any standards? You think I'd let some coyote rape a kid in my bed?" She kicked him out of the house, and grumbled about him all day. But a while later he spent the night again, and he and Coyote did that three or four times.

Another thing that was embarrassing was the way Coyote peed anywhere, taking her pants down in public. But most people here didn't seem to care. The thing that worried the child most, maybe, was when Coyote did number two anywhere and then turned around and talked to it. That seemed so awful. As if Coyote was—the way she often seemed, but really wasn't—crazy.

The child gathered up all the old dry turds from around the house one day while Coyote was having a nap, and buried them in a sandy place near where she and Bobcat and some of the other people generally went and did and buried their number twos.

Coyote woke up, came lounging out of Bide-A-Wee, rubbing her hands through her thick, fair, greyish hair and yawning, looked all around once with those narrow eyes, and said, "Hey! Where are they?" Then she shouted, "Where are you? Where are you?"

And a faint, muffled chorus came from over in the sandy draw, "Mommy! Mommy! We're here!"

Coyote trotted over, squatted down, raked out every turd, and talked with them for a long time. When she came back she said nothing, but the child, redfaced and heart pounding, said, "I'm sorry I did that."

"It's just easier when they're all around close by," Coyote said, washing her hands (despite the filth of her house, she kept herself quite clean, in her own fashion).

"I kept stepping on them," the child said, trying to justify her deed.

"Poor little shits," said Coyote, practicing dance steps.

"Coyote," the child said timidly. "Did you ever have any children? I mean real pups?"

"Did I? Did I have children? Litters! That one that tried feeling you up, you know? that was my son. Pick of the litter . . . Listen, Gal. Have daughters. When you have anything, have daughters. At least they clear out."

❧

The child thought of herself as Gal, but also sometimes as Myra. So far as she knew, she was the only person in town who had two names. She had to think about that, and about what Coyote had said about the two kinds of people; she had to think about where she belonged. Some persons in town made it clear that as far as they were concerned she didn't and never would belong there. Hawk's furious stare burned through her; the Skunk children made audible remarks about what she smelled like. And though Whitefoot and Chipmunk and their families were kind, it was the generosity of big families, where one more or less simply doesn't count. If one of them, or Cottontail, or Jackrabbit, had come upon her in the desert lying lost and half-blind, would they have stayed with her, like Coyote? That was Coyote's craziness, what they called her craziness. She wasn't afraid. She went between the two kinds of people, she crossed over. Buck and Doe and their beautiful children weren't really afraid, because they lived so constantly in danger. The Rattler wasn't afraid, because he was so dangerous. And yet maybe he was afraid of her, for he never spoke, and never came close to her. None of them treated her the way Coyote did. Even among the children, her only constant playmate was one younger than herself, a preposterous and fearless little boy called Horned Toad Child. They dug and built together, out among the sagebrush, and played at hunting and gathering and keeping house and holding dances, all the great games. A pale, squatty child with fringed eyebrows, he was a self-contained but loyal friend; and he knew a good deal for his age.

"There isn't anybody else like me here," she said, as they sat by the pool in the morning sunlight

"There isn't anybody much like me anywhere," said Horned Toad Child.

"Well, you know what I mean."

"Yeah . . . There used to be people like you around, I guess."

"What were they called?"

"Oh—people. Like everybody . . ."

"But where do my people live? They have towns. I used to live in one. I don't know where they are, is all. I ought to find out. I don't know where my mother is now, but my daddy's in Canyonville. I was going there when."

"Ask Horse," said Horned Toad Child, sagaciously. He had moved away from the water, which he did not like and never drank, and was plaiting rushes.

"I don't know Horse."

"He hangs around the butte down there a lot of the time. He's waiting till his uncle gets old and he can kick him out and be the big honcho. The old man and the women don't want him around till then. Horses are weird. Anyway, he's the one to ask. He gets around a lot. And his people came here with the new people, that's what they say, anyhow."

Illegal immigrants, the girl thought. She took Homed Toad's advice, and one long day when Coyote was gone on one of her unannounced and unexplained trips, she took a pouchful of dried salmon and salmonberries and went off alone to the flat-topped butte miles away in the southwest.

There was a beautiful spring at the foot of the butte, and a trail to it with a lot of footprints on it. She waited there under willows by the clear pool, and after a while Horse came running, splendid, with copper-red skin and long, strong legs, deep chest, dark eyes, his black hair whipping his back as he ran. He stopped, not at all winded, and gave a snort as he looked at her. "Who are you?"

Nobody in town asked that—ever. She saw it was true: Horse had come here with her people, people who had to ask each other who they were.

"I live with Coyote," she said, cautiously.

"Oh, sure, I heard about you," Horse said. He knelt to drink from the pool, long deep drafts, his hands plunged in the cool water. When he had drunk he wiped his mouth, sat back on his heels, and announced, "I'm going to be king."

"King of the Horses?"

"Right! Pretty soon now. I could lick the old man already, but I can wait. Let him have his day," said Horse, vain-glorious, magnanimous. The child gazed at him, in love already, forever.

"I can comb your hair, if you like," she said.

"Great!" said Horse, and sat still while she stood behind him, tugging her pocket comb through his coarse, black, shining, yard-long hair. It took a long time to get it smooth. She tied it in a massive ponytail with willowbark when she was done. Horse bent over the pool to admire himself. "That's great," he said. "That's really beautiful!"

"Do you ever go . . . where the other people are?" she asked in a low voice.

He did not reply for long enough that she thought he wasn't going to; then he said, "You mean the metal places, the glass places? The holes? I go around them. There are all the walls now. There didn't used to be so many. Grandmother said there didn't used to be any walls. Do you know Grandmother?" he asked naively, looking at her with his great, dark eyes.

"Your grandmother?"

"Well, yes—Grandmother—You know. Who makes the web. Well, anyhow. I know there's some of my people, horses, there. I've seen them across the walls. They act really crazy. You know, we brought the new people here. They couldn't have got here without us, they only have two legs, and they have those metal shells. I can tell you that whole story. The King has to know the stories."

"I like stories a lot."

"It takes three nights to tell it. What do you want to know about them?"

"I was thinking that maybe I ought to go there. Where they are."

"It's dangerous. Really dangerous. You can't go through—they'd catch you."

"I'd just like to know the way."

"I know the way," Horse said, sounding for the first time entirely adult and reliable; she knew he did know the way. "It's a long run for a colt." He looked at her again. "I've got a cousin with different-color eyes," he said, looking from her right to her left eye. "One brown and one blue. But she's an Appaloosa."

"Bluejay made the yellow one," the child explained. "I lost my own one. In the . . . when . . . You don't think I could get to those places?"

"Why do you want to?"

"I sort of feel like I have to."

Horse nodded. He got up. She stood still.

"I could take you, I guess," he said.

"Would you? When?"

"Oh, now, I guess. Once I'm King I won't be able to leave, you know. Have to protect the women. And I sure wouldn't let my people get anywhere near those places!" A shudder ran right down his magnificent body, yet he said, with a toss of his head, "They couldn't catch me, of course, but the others can't run like I do . . ."

"How long would it take us?"

Horse thought a while. "Well, the nearest place like that is over by the red rocks. If we left now we'd be back here around tomorrow noon. It's just a little hole."

She did not know what he meant by "a hole," but did not ask.

"You want to go?" Horse said, flipping back his ponytail.

"OK," the girl said, feeling the ground go out from under her.

"Can you run?"

She shook her head. "I walked here, though."

Horse laughed, a large, cheerful laugh. "Come on," he said, and knelt and held his hands backturned like stirrups for her to mount to his shoulders. "What do they call you?" he teased, rising easily, setting right off at a jogtrot. "Gnat? Fly? Flea?"

"Tick, because I stick!" the child cried, gripping the willowbark tie of the black mane, laughing with delight at being suddenly eight feet tall and traveling across the desert without even trying, like the tumbleweed, as fast as the wind.

Moon, a night past full, rose to light the plains for them. Horse jogged easily on and on. Somewhere deep in the night they stopped at a Pygmy Owl camp, ate a little, and rested. Most of the owls were out hunting, but an old lady entertained them at her campfire, telling them tales about the ghost of a cricket, about the great invisible people, tales that the child heard interwoven with her own dreams as she dozed and half-woke and dozed again. Then Horse put her up on his shoulders and on they went at a tireless slow lope. Moon went down behind them, and before them the sky paled into rose and gold. The soft nightwind was gone; the air was sharp, cold, still. On it, in it, there was a faint, sour smell of burning. The child felt Horse's gait change, grow tighter, uneasy.

"Hey, Prince!"

A small, slightly scolding voice: the child knew it, and placed it as soon as she saw the person sitting by a juniper tree, neatly dressed, wearing an old black cap.

"Hey, Chickadee!" Horse said, coming round and stopping. The child had observed, back in Coyote's town, that everybody treated Chickadee with respect. She didn't see why. Chickadee seemed an ordinary person, busy and talkative like most of the small birds, nothing like so endearing as Quail or so impressive as Hawk or Great Owl.

"You're going on that way?" Chickadee asked Horse.

"The little one wants to see if her people are living there," Horse said, surprising the child. Was that what she wanted?

Chickadee looked disapproving as she often did. She whistled a few notes thoughtfully, another of her habits, and then got up. "I'll come along."

"That's great," Horse said, thankfully.

"I'll scout," Chickadee said, and off she went, surprisingly fast, ahead of them, while Horse took up his steady long lope.

The sour smell was stronger in the air.

Chickadee halted, way ahead of them on a slight rise, and stood still. Horse dropped to a walk, and then stopped. "There," he said in a low voice.

The child stared. In the strange light and slight mist before sunrise she could not see clearly, and when she strained and peered she felt as if her left eye were not seeing at all. "What is it?" she whispered.

"One of the holes. Across the wall—see?"

It did seem there was a line, a straight, jerky line drawn across the sagebrush plain, and on the far side of it—nothing? Was it mist? Something moved there—"It's cattle!" she said. Horse stood silent, uneasy. Chickadee was coming back towards them.

"It's a ranch," the child said. "That's a fence. There's a lot of Herefords." The words tasted like iron, like salt in her mouth. The things she named wavered in her sight and faded, leaving nothing—a hole in the world, a burned place like a cigarette burn. "Go closer!" she urged Horse. "I want to see."

And as if he owed her obedience, he went forward, tense but unquestioning.

Chickadee came up to them. "Nobody around," she said in her small, dry voice, "but there's one of those fast turtle things coming."

Horse nodded, but kept going forward.

Gripping his broad shoulders, the child stared into the blank, and as if Chickadee's words had focused her eyes, she saw again: the scattered whitefaces, a few of them looking up with bluish, rolling eyes—the fences—over the rise a chimneyed house-roof and a high barn—and then in the distance something moving fast, too fast, burning across the ground straight at them at terrible speed. "Run!" she yelled to Horse, "run away! Run!" As if released from bonds he wheeled and ran, flat out, in great reaching strides, away from sunrise, the fiery burning chariot, the smell of acid, iron, death. And Chickadee flew before them like a cinder on the air of dawn.

iv

"Horse?" Coyote said. "That prick? Catfood!"

Coyote had been there when the child got home to Bide-A-Wee, but she clearly hadn't been worrying about where Gal was, and maybe hadn't even noticed she was gone. She was in a vile mood, and took it all wrong when the child tried to tell her where she had been.

"If you're going to do damn fool things, next time do 'em with me, at least I'm an expert," she said, morose, and slouched out the door. The child saw her squatting down, poking an old, white turd with a stick, trying to get it to answer some question she kept asking it. The turd lay obstinately silent. Later in the day the child saw two coyote men, a young one and a mangy-looking older one, loitering around near the spring, looking over at Bide-A-Wee. She decided it would be a good night to spend somewhere else.

The thought of the crowded rooms of Chipmunk's house was not attractive. It was going to be a warm night again tonight, and moonlit.

Maybe she would sleep outside. If she could feel sure some people wouldn't come around, like the Rattler . . . She was standing indecisive halfway through town when a dry voice said, "Hey, Gal."

"Hey, Chickadee."

The trim, black-capped woman was standing on her doorstep shaking out a rug. She kept her house neat, trim like herself. Having come back across the desert with her the child now knew, though she still could not have said, why Chickadee was a respected person.

"I thought maybe I'd sleep out tonight," the child said, tentative.

"Unhealthy," said Chickadee. "What are nests for?"

"Mom's kind of busy," the child said.

"Tsk!" went Chickadee, and snapped the rug with disapproving vigor. "What about your little friend? At least they're decent people."

"Horny-toad? His parents are so shy . . ."

"Well. Come in and have something to eat, anyhow," said Chickadee.

The child helped her cook dinner. She knew now why there were rocks in the mush-pot

"Chickadee," she said, "I still don't understand, can I ask you? Mom said it depends who's seeing it, but still, I mean if I see you wearing clothes and everything like humans, then how come you cook this way, in baskets, you know, and there aren't any—any of the things like they have—there where we were with Horse this morning?"

"I don't know," Chickadee said. Her voice indoors was quite soft and pleasant. "I guess we do things the way they always were done. When your people and my people lived together, you know. And together with everything else here. The rocks, you know. The plants and everything." She looked at the basket of willowbark, fernroot, and pitch, at the blackened rocks that were heating in the fire. "You see how it all goes together . . . ?"

"But you have fire—That's different—"

"Ah!" said Chickadee, impatient, "you people! Do you think you invented the sun?"

She took up the wooden tongs, plopped the heated rocks into the water-filled basket with a terrific hiss and steam and loud bubblings. The child sprinkled in the pounded seeds, and stirred.

Chickadee brought out a basket of fine blackberries. They sat on the newly-shaken-out rug, and ate. The child's two-finger scoop technique with mush was now highly refined.

"Maybe I didn't cause the world," Chickadee said, "but I'm a better cook than Coyote."

The child nodded, stuffing.

"I don't know why I made Horse go there," she said, after she had stuffed. "I got just as scared as him when I saw it. But now I feel again like I have to go back there. But I want to stay here. With my, with Coyote. I don't understand."

"When we lived together it was all one place," Chickadee said in her slow, soft home-voice. "But now the others, the new people, they live apart. And their places are so heavy. They weigh down on our place, they press on it, draw it, suck it, eat it, eat holes in it, crowd it out . . . Maybe after a while longer there'll only be one place again, their place. And none of us here. I knew Bison, out over the mountains. I knew Antelope right here. I knew Grizzly and Grey-wolf, up west there. Gone. All gone. And the salmon you eat at Coyote's house, those are the dream salmon, those are the true food; but in the rivers, how many salmon now? The rivers that were red with them in spring? Who dances, now, when the First Salmon offers himself? Who dances by the river? Oh, you should ask Coyote about all this. She knows more than I do! But she forgets . . . She's hopeless, worse than Raven, she has to piss on every post, she's a terrible housekeeper . . ." Chickadee's voice had sharpened. She whistled a note or two, and said no more.

After a while the child asked very softly, "Who is Grandmother?"

"Grandmother," Chickadee said. She looked at the child, and ate several blackberries thoughtfully. She stroked the rug they sat on.

"If I built the fire on the rug, it would burn a hole in it," she said. "Right? So we build the fire on sand, on dirt . . . Things are woven together. So we call the weaver the Grandmother." She whistled four notes, looking up the smokehole. "After all," she added, "maybe all this place, the other places too, maybe they're all only one side of the weaving. I don't know. I can only look with one eye at a time, how can I tell how deep it goes?"

Lying that night rolled up in a blanket in Chickadee's back yard, the child heard the wind soughing and storming in the cottonwoods down in the draw, and then slept deeply, weary from the long night before. Just at sunrise she woke. The eastern mountains were a cloudy dark red as if the level light shone through them as through a hand held before the fire. In the tobacco patch—the only farming anybody in this town did was to raise a little wild tobacco—Lizard and Beetle were singing some kind of growing song or blessing song, soft and desultory, huh-huh-huh-huh, huh-huh-huh-huh, and as she lay warm-curled on the ground the song made her feel rooted in the ground, cradled on it and in it, so where her fingers ended and the dirt began she did not know, as if she were dead, but she was wholly alive, she was the earth's life. She got up dancing, left the blanket folded neatly on Chickadee's neat and already empty bed, and danced up the hill to Bide-A-Wee. At the half-open door she sang

> "Danced with a gal with a hole in her stocking
> And her knees kept a knocking and her toes kept a rocking
> Danced with a gal with a hole in her stocking,
> Danced by the light of the moon!"

Coyote emerged, tousled and lurching, and eyed her narrowly. "Sheeeoot," she said. She sucked her teeth and then went to splash water all over her head from the gourd by the door. She shook her head and the water-drops flew. "Let's get out of here," she said. "I have had it. I don't know what got into me. If I'm pregnant again, at my age, oh, shit. Let's get out of town. I need a change of air."

In the foggy dark of the house, the child could see at least two coyote men sprawled snoring away on the bed and floor. Coyote walked over to the old white turd and kicked it. "Why didn't you stop me?" she shouted.

"I *told* you," the turd muttered sulkily.

"Dumb shit," Coyote said. "Come on, Gal. Let's go. Where to?" She didn't wait for an answer. "I know. Come on!"

And she set off through town at that lazy-looking rangy walk that was so hard to keep up with. But the child was full of pep, and came dancing, so that Coyote began dancing too, skipping and pirouetting and fooling around all the way down the long slope to the level plains. There she slanted their way off north-eastward. Horse Butte was at their backs, getting smaller in the distance.

Along near noon the child said, "I didn't bring anything to eat."

"Something will turn up," Coyote said, "sure to." And pretty soon she turned aside, going straight to a tiny grey shack hidden by a couple of half-dead junipers and a stand of rabbit-brush. The place smelled terrible. A sign on the door said: FOX. PRIVATE. NO TRESPASSING!—but Coyote pushed it open, and trotted right back out with half a small smoked salmon. "Nobody home but us chickens," she said, grinning sweetly.

"Isn't that stealing?" the child asked, worried.

"Yes," Coyote answered, trotting on.

They ate the fox-scented salmon by a dried-up creek, slept a while, and went on.

Before long the child smelled the sour burning smell, and stopped. It was as if a huge, heavy hand had begun pushing her chest, pushing her away, and yet at the same time as if she had stepped into a strong current that drew her forward, helpless.

"Hey, getting close!" Coyote said, and stopped to piss by a juniper stump.

"Close to what?"

"Their town. See?" She pointed to a pair of sage-spotted hills. Between them was an area of greyish blank.

"I don't want to go there."

"We won't go all the way in. No way! We'll just get a little closer and look. It's fun," Coyote said, putting her head on one side, coaxing. "They do all these weird things in the air."

The child hung back.

Coyote became business-like, responsible. "We're going to be very careful," she announced. "And look out for big dogs, OK? Little dogs I can handle. Make a good lunch. Big dogs, it goes the other way. Right? Let's go, then."

Seemingly as casual and lounging as ever, but with a tense alertness in the carriage of her head and the yellow glance of her eyes, Coyote led off again, not looking back; and the child followed.

All around them the pressures increased. It was if the air itself was pressing on them, as if time was going too fast, too hard, not flowing but pounding, pounding, pounding faster and harder till it buzzed like Rattler's rattle. Hurry, you have to hurry! everything said, there isn't time! everything said. Things rushed past screaming and shuddering. Things turned, flashed, roared, stank, vanished. There was a boy—he came into focus all at once, but not on the ground: he was going along a couple of inches above the ground, moving very fast, bending his legs from side to side in a kind of frenzied swaying dance, and was gone. Twenty children sat in rows in the air all singing shrilly and then the walls closed over them. A basket no a pot no a can, a garbage can, full of salmon smelling wonderful no full of stinking deerhides and rotten cabbage stalks, keep out of it, Coyote! Where was she?

"Mom!" the child called. "Mother!"—standing a moment at the end of an ordinary small-town street near the gas station, and the next moment in a terror of blanknesses, invisible walls, terrible smells and pressures and the overwhelming rush of Time straight forward rolling her helpless as a twig in the race above a waterfall. She clung, held on trying not to fall—"Mother!"

Coyote was over by the big basket of salmon, approaching it, wary, but out in the open, in the full sunlight, in the full current. And a boy and a man borne by the same current were coming down the long, sage-spotted hill behind the gas station, each with a gun, red hats, hunters, it was killing season. "Hell, will you look at that damn coyote in broad daylight big as my wife's ass," the man said, and cocked aimed shot all as Myra screamed and ran against the enormous drowning torrent. Coyote fled past her yelling "Get out of here!" She turned and was borne away.

Far out of sight of that place, in a little draw among low hills, they sat and breathed air in searing gasps until after a long time it came easy again.

"Mom, that was *stupid*," the child said furiously.

"Sure was," Coyote said. "But did you see all that food!"

"I'm not hungry," the child said sullenly. "Not till we get all the way away from here."

"But they're your folks," Coyote said. "All yours. Your kith and kin and cousins and kind. Bang! Pow! There's Coyote! Bang! There's my wife's ass! Pow! There's anything—BOOOOM! Blow it away, man! BOOOOOOM!"

"I want to go home," the child said.

"Not yet," said Coyote. "I got to take a shit." She did so, then turned to the fresh turd, leaning over it. "It says I have to stay," she reported, smiling.

"It didn't say anything! I was listening!"

"You know how to understand? You hear everything Miss Big Ears? Hears all—Sees all with her crummy gummy eye—"

"You have pine-pitch eyes too! You told me so!"

"That's a story," Coyote snarled. "You don't even know a story when you hear one! Look, do what you like, it's a free country. I'm hanging around here tonight. I like the action." She sat down and began patting her hands on the dirt in a soft four-four rhythm and singing under her breath, one of the endless tuneless songs that kept time from running too fast, that wove the roots of trees and bushes and ferns and grass in the web that held the stream in the streambed and the rock in the rock's place and the earth together. And the child lay listening.

"I love you," she said.

Coyote went on singing.

Sun went down the last slope of the west and left a pale green clarity over the desert hills.

Coyote had stopped singing. She sniffed. "Hey," she said. "Dinner." She got up and moseyed along the little draw. "Yeah," she called back softly. "Come on!"

Stiffly, for the fear-crystals had not yet melted out of her joints, the child got up and went to Coyote. Off to one side along the hill was one of the lines, a fence. She didn't look at it. It was OK. They were outside it.

"Look at that!"

A smoked salmon, a whole chinook, lay on a little cedar-bark mat. "An offering! Well, I'll be darned!" Coyote was so impressed she didn't even swear. "I haven't seen one of these for years! I thought they'd forgotten!"

"Offering to who?"

"Me! Who else? Boy, *look* at that!"

The child looked dubiously at the salmon.

"It smells funny."

"How funny?"

"Like burned."

"It's smoked, stupid! Come on."

"I'm not hungry."

"OK. It's not your salmon anyhow. It's mine. My offering, for me. Hey, you people! You people over there! Coyote thanks you! Keep it up like this and maybe I'll do some good things for you too!"

"Don't, don't yell, Mom! They're not that far away—"

"They're all my people," said Coyote with a great gesture, and then sat down crosslegged, broke off a big piece of salmon, and ate.

Evening Star burned like a deep, bright pool of water in the clear sky. Down over the twin hills was a dim suffusion of light, like a fog. The child looked away from it, back at the star.

"Oh," Coyote said. "Oh, shit."

"What's wrong?"

"That wasn't so smart, eating that," Coyote said, and then held herself and began to shiver, to scream, to choke—her eyes rolled up, her long arms and legs flew out jerking and dancing, foam spurted out between her clenched teeth. Her body arched tremendously backwards, and the child, trying to hold her, was thrown violently off by the spasms of her limbs. The child scrambled back and held the body as it spasmed again, twitched, quivered, went still.

By moonrise Coyote was cold. Till then there had been so much warmth under the tawny coat that the child kept thinking maybe she was alive, maybe if she just kept holding her, keeping her warm, she would recover, she would be all right. She held her close, not looking at the black lips drawn back from the teeth, the white balls of the eyes. But when the cold came through the fur as the presence of death, the child let the slight, stiff corpse lie down on the dirt.

She went nearby and dug a hole in the stony sand of the draw, a shallow pit. Coyote's people did not bury their dead, she knew that. But her people did. She carried the small corpse to the pit, laid it down, and covered it with her blue and white bandanna. It was not large enough; the four stiff paws stuck out. The child heaped the body over with sand and rocks and a scurf of sagebrush and tumbleweed held down with more rocks. She also went to where the salmon had lain on the cedar mat, and finding the carcass of a lamb heaped dirt and rocks over the poisoned thing. Then she stood up and walked away without looking back.

At the top of the hill she stood and looked across the draw toward the misty glow of the lights of the town lying in the pass between the twin hills.

"I hope you all die in pain," she said aloud. She turned away and walked down into the desert.

v

It was Chickadee who met her, on the second evening north of Horse Butte.

"I didn't cry," the child said.

"None of us do," said Chickadee. "Come with me this way now. Come into Grandmother's house."

It was underground, but very large, dark and large, and the Grandmother was there at the center, at her loom. She was making a rug or blanket of the hills and the black rain and the white rain, weaving in the lightning. As they spoke she wove.

"Hello, Chickadee. Hello, New Person."

"Grandmother," Chickadee greeted her.

The child said, "I'm not one of them."

Grandmother's eyes were small and dim. She smiled and wove. The shuttle thrummed through the warp.

"Old Person, then," said Grandmother. "You'd better go back there now, Granddaughter. That's where you live."

"I lived with Coyote. She's dead. They killed her."

"Oh, don't worry about Coyote!" Grandmother said, with a little huff of laughter. "She gets killed all the time."

The child stood still. She saw the endless weaving.

"Then I—Could I go back home—to her house—?"

"I don't think it would work," Grandmother said. "Do you, Chickadee?"

Chickadee shook her head once, silent.

"It would be dark there now, and empty, and fleas . . . You got outside your people's time, into our place; but I think that Coyote was taking you back, see. Her way. If you go back now, you can still live with them. Isn't your father there?"

The child nodded.

"They've been looking for you."

"They have?"

"Oh, yes, ever since you fell out of the sky. The man was dead, but you weren't there—they kept looking."

"Serves him right. Serves them all right," the child said. She put her hands up over her face and began to cry terribly, without tears.

"Go on, little one, Granddaughter," Spider said. "Don't be afraid. You can live well there. I'll be there too, you know. In your dreams, in your ideas, in dark corners in the basement. Don't kill me, or I'll make it rain . . ."

"I'll come around," Chickadee said. "Make gardens for me."

The child held her breath and clenched her hands until her sobs stopped and let her speak.

"Will I ever see Coyote?"

"I don't know," the Grandmother replied.

The child accepted this. She said, after another silence, "Can I keep my eye?"

"Yes. You can keep your eye."

"Thank you, Grandmother," the child said. She turned away then and started up the night slope towards the next day. Ahead of her in the air of dawn for a long way a little bird flew, black-capped, light-winged.

Horse Camp

All the other seniors were over at the street side of the parking lot, but Sal stayed with Norah while they waited for the bus drivers. "Maybe you'll be in the creek cabin," Sal said, quiet and serious. "I had it second year. It's the best one. Number Five."

"How do they, when do you, like find out, what cabin?"

"They better remember we're in the same cabin," Ev said, sounding shrill. Norah did not look at her. She and Ev had planned for months and known for weeks that they were to be cabin-mates, but what good was that if they never found their cabin, and also Sal was not looking at Ev, only at Norah. Sal was cool, a tower of ivory. "They show you around, as soon as you get there," she said, her quiet voice speaking directly to Norah's lastnight dream of never finding the room where she had to take a test she was late for and looking among endless thatched barracks in a forest of thin black trees growing very close together like hair under a hand-lens. Norah had told no one the dream and now remembered and forgot it. "Then you have dinner, and First Campfire," Sal said. "Kimmy's going to be a counselor again. She's really neat. Listen, you tell old Meredy . . ."

Norah drew breath. In all the histories of Horse Camp which she had asked for and heard over and over for three years—the thunderstorm story, the horsethief story, the wonderful Stevens Mountain stories—in all of them Meredy the handler had been, Meredy said, Meredy did, Meredy knew.

"Tell him I said hi," Sal said, with a shadowy smile, looking across the parking lot at the far, insubstantial towers of downtown. Behind them the doors of the Junior Girls bus gasped open. One after another the engines of the four busses roared and spewed. Across the asphalt in the hot morning light small figures were lining up and climbing into the Junior Boys bus. High, rough, faint voices bawled. "OK, hey, have fun," Sal said. She hugged Norah and then, keeping a hand on her arm, looked down at her intently for a moment from the tower of ivory. She turned away. Norah watched her walk lightfoot and buxom across the black gap to the others of her kind who enclosed her, greeting her, "Sal! Hey, Sal!"

Ev was twitching and nickering, "Come on, Nor, come on, we'll have to sit way at the back, come on!" Side by side they pressed into the line below the gaping doorway of the bus.

In Number Five cabin four iron cots, thin-mattressed, grey-blanketed, stood strewn with bottles of insect repellent and styling mousse, T-shirts lettered UCSD and I ♥ Teddy Bears, a flashlight, an apple, a comb with hair caught in it, a paperback book open face down: *The Black Colt of Pirate Island*. Over the shingle roof huge second-growth redwoods cast deep shade, and a few feet below the porch the creek ran out into sunlight over brown stones streaming bright green weed. Behind the cabin Jim Meredith the horse-handler, a short man of fifty who had ridden as a jockey in his teens, walked along the well-beaten path, quick and a bit bowlegged. Meredith's lips were pressed firmly together. His eyes, narrow and darting, glanced from cabin to cabin, from side to side. Far through the trees high voices cried.

The Counselors know what is to be known. Red Ginger, blonde Kimmy, and beautiful black Sue: they know the vices of Pal, and how to keep Trigger from putting her head down and drinking for ten minutes from every creek. They strike the great shoulders smartly, "Aw, get over, you big lunk!" They know how to swim underwater, how to sing in harmony, how to get seconds, and when a shoe is loose. They know where they are. They know where the rest of Horse Camp is. "Home Creek runs into Little River here," Kimmy says, drawing lines in the soft dust with a redwood twig that breaks. "Senior Girls here, Senior Boys across there, Junior Birdmen about here."—"Who needs 'em?" says Sue, yawning. "Come on, who's going to help me walk the mares?"

They were all around the campfire on Quartz Meadow after the long first day of the First Overnight. The counselors were still singing, but very soft, so soft you almost couldn't hear them, lying in the sleeping bag listening to One Spot stamp and Trigger snort and the shifting at the pickets, standing in the fine, cool alpine grass listening to the soft voices and the sleepers shifting and later one coyote down the mountain singing all alone.

"Nothing wrong with you. Get up!" said Meredy, and slapped her hip. Turning her long, delicate head to him with a deprecating gaze, Philly got to her feet. She stood a moment, shuddering the reddish silk of her flank as if to dislodge flies, tested her left foreleg with caution, and then walked on, step by step. Step by step, watching, Norah went with her. Inside her body there was still a deep trembling. As she passed him, the handler just nodded. "You're all right," he meant. She was all right.

Freedom, the freedom to run, freedom is to run. Freedom is galloping. What else can it be? Only other ways to run, imitations of galloping across great highlands with the wind. Oh Philly sweet Philly my love! If Ev and Trigger couldn't keep up she'd slow down and come round in a while, after a while, over there, across the long, long field of grass, once she had learned this by heart and knew it forever, the purity, the pure joy.

"Right leg, Nor," said Meredy. And passed on to Cass and Tammy.

You have to start with the right fore. Everything else is all right. Freedom depends on this, that you start with the right fore, that long leg well balanced on its elegant pastern, that you set down that tiptoe middle-fingernail so hard and round, and spurn the dirt. Highstepping, trot past old Meredy, who always hides his smile.

Shoulder to shoulder, she and Ev, in the long heat of afternoon, in a trance of light, across the home creek in the dry wild oats and cow parsley of the Long Pasture. "I was afraid before I came here," thinks Norah, incredulous, remembering childhood. She leans her head against Ev's firm and silken side. The sting of small flies awakens, the swish of long tails sends to sleep. Down by the creek in a patch of coarse grass Philly grazes and dozes. Sue comes striding by, winks wordless, beautiful as a burning coal, lazy and purposeful, bound for the shade of the willows. Is it worth getting up to go down to get your feet in the cool water? Next year Sal will be too old for a camper, but can come back as a counselor, come back here. Norah will come back a second-year camper, Sal a counselor. They will be here. This is what freedom is, what goes on, the sun in summer, the wild grass, coming back each year.

Coming back from the Long Pack Trip to Stevens Mountain weary and dirty, thirsty and in bliss, coming down from the high places, in line, Sue jogging just in front of her and Ev half asleep behind her, some sound or motion caught and turned Norah's head to look across the alpine field. On the far side under dark firs a line of horses, mounted and with packs—"Look!"

Ev snorted, Sue flicked her ears and stopped. Norah halted in line behind her, stretching her neck to see. She saw her sister going first in the distant line, the small head proudly borne. She was walking lightfoot and easy, fresh, just starting up to the high passes of the mountain. On her back a young man sat erect, his fine, fair head turned a little aside, to the forest. One hand was on his thigh, the other on the reins, guiding her. Norah called out and then broke from the line, going to Sal, calling out to her. "No, no, no, no!" she called. Behind her Ev and then Sue called to her, "Nor! Nor!"

Sal did not hear or heed. Going straight ahead, the color of ivory, distant in the clear, dry light, she stepped into the shadow of the trees. The others and their riders followed, jogging one after the other till the last was gone.

Norah had stopped in the middle of the meadow, and stood in grass in sunlight. Flies hummed.

She tossed her head, turned, and trotted back to the line. She went along it from one to the next, teasing, chivying, Kimmy yelling at her to get back in line, till Sue broke out of line to chase her and she ran, and then Ev began to run, whinnying shrill, and then Cass, and Philly, and all the rest, the whole bunch, cantering first and then running flat out, running wild, racing, heading for Horse Camp and the Long Pasture, for Meredy and the long evening standing in the fenced field, in the sweet dry grass, in the fetlock-shallow water of the home creek.

The Water Is Wide

"You here?"

"To see you."

After a while he said, "Where's here?" He was lying flat, so could not have much in view but ceiling and the top third of Anna; in any case his eyes looked unfocussed.

"Hospital."

Another pause. He said something like, "Is it me that's here?" The words were slurred. He added clearly enough, "It's not you. You look all right."

"I am. You're here. And I'm here. To see you."

This made him smile. The smile of an adult lying flat on his back resembles the smile of an infant, in that gravity works with it, not against it.

"Can I be told," he said, "or will the knowledge kill me?"

"If knowledge could kill you, you'd have been dead for years."

"Am I sick?"

"Do you feel well?"

He turned his head away, the first bodily movement he had made. "I feel ill." The words were slurred. "Full of drugs, some kind drugs." The head moved again, restless. "Don't like it," he said. He looked straight at her now. "I don't feel well," he said. "Anna, I'm cold. I feel cold." Tears filled the eyes and ran down from them into the greying hair. This happens in cases of human suffering, when the sufferer is lying face up and is middleaged.

Anna said his name and took his hand. Her hand was somewhat smaller than his, several degrees warmer, and very similar in structure and texture; even the shape of the nails was similar. She held his hand. He held her hand. After some time his hand began to relax.

"Kind drugs," he said. The eyes were shut now.

He spoke once more; he said either "Wait," or "Weight." Anna answered the first, saying, "I will." Then she thought he had spoken of a weight that lay upon him. She could see the weight in the way he breathed, asleep.

"It's the drugs," she said, "he's asked every time if you could stop giving him the drugs. Could you decrease the dose?"

The doctor said, "Chemotherapy," and other words, some of which were the names of drugs, ending in zil and ine.

"He says that he can't sleep, but he can't wake up either. I think he needs to sleep. And to wake up."

The doctor said many other words. He said them in so rapid, distinct, and fluent a manner, and with such assurance, that Anna believed them all for at least three hours.

"Is this a loony bin?" Gideon inquired with perfect clarity.

"Mhm." Anna knitted.

"Thought wards."

"Oh, it's all private rooms here. It's a nice private sort of place. Rest home. Polite. Expensive."

"Senile, incont . . . incontinent. Can't talk. Anna."

"Mhm?"

"Stroke?"

"No, no." She put her knitting down on her knee. "You got overtired."

"Tumor?"

"No. You're sound as a bell. Only a little cracked. You got tired. You acted funny."

"What'd I do?" he asked, his eyes brightening.

"Made an awful fool of yourself."

"Did?"

"Well, you washed all the blackboards. At the Institute. With soap and water."

"That all?"

"You said it was time to start all over. You made the Dean fetch the soap and buckets." They both jolted softly with laughter at the same time. "Never mind the rest. You had them all quite busy, believe me."

They all understood now that his much publicised New Year's Day letter to the *Times*, which he had defended with uncharacteristic vehemence, had been a symptom. This was a relief to many people, who had uncomfortably been thinking of the letter as a moral statement. Looking back, everyone at the Institute could now see that Gideon had not been himself for some months. Indeed the change could be traced back three years, to the death of his wife Dorothea of leukemia. He had borne his loss well, of course, but had he not remained somewhat withdrawn—increasingly withdrawn? Only no one had noticed it, because he had been so busy. He had ceased to take vacations at the family cabin up at the lake, and had done a good deal of public speaking in connection with the peace organisation of which he was co-chairman. He had been working much too hard. It was all clear now. Unfortunately it had not become clear until the evening in April when he began a public lecture on the Question of Ethics in Science by gazing at the audience in silence for 35 seconds (approx.: one of the mathematical philosophers present in the audience had begun to time the silence at the point when it became painful, though not yet unendurable), and then, in a slow, soft, rough voice which no one who heard it could forget, announced, "The quantification of Death is now the major problem facing theoretical physicists in the latter half of the Western Hemisphere." He had then closed his mouth and stood gazing at them.

Hansen, who had introduced his talk and sat on the speakers' platform, was a large man and a quick-witted one. He had without much trouble induced Gideon to come backstage with him, to one of the seminar rooms. It was there that Gideon had insisted that they wash all the blackboards perfectly clean. He had not become violent, though his behavior had been what Hansen termed "extraordinarily wilful." Later on, in private, Hansen wondered whether Gideon's behavior had not always been wilful, in that it had always been self-directed, and whether he should not have used, instead, the word "irrational." That would have been the expectable word. But its expectability led him to wonder if Gideon's behavior (as a theoretical physicist) had ever been rational; and, in fact, if his own behavior (as a theoretical physicist, or otherwise) had ever been adequately describable by the term "rational." He said nothing, however, of these speculations, and worked very hard for several weekends at building a rock garden at the side of his house.

Though he offered no violence to others or himself, Gideon had attempted escape. At a certain moment he appeared to understand suddenly that medical aid had been summoned. He acted with decision. He told the Dean, Dr. Hansen, Dr. Mehta, and the student Mr. Chew, all of whom were with him (several other members of the audience or of the Institute were busy keeping busybodies and reporters out), "You finish the blackboards in here, I'll do Room 40," and taking up a bucket and a sponge went rapidly across the hall into a vacant classroom, where Chew and Hansen, following him at once, prevented him from opening a window. The room was on the ground floor, and his intention was made clear by his saying, "Let me get out, please, help me get out." Chew and Hansen were compelled to restrain his arms by force. He struggled briefly to free himself; failing, he became silent and apparently thoughtful. Shortly before the medical personnel arrived he suggested in a low voice to Chew, "If we sat down on the floor here they might not see us." When the medical personnel entered the room and came close to him he said loudly, "All right, have it your way," and at once began to yell wordlessly, or scream. The graduate student Chew, a brilliant young biophysicist who had not had much experience of human suffering, let go of his arm and broke into tears. The medical personnel, having had perhaps excessive experience of human suffering, promptly administered a quick-acting sedative or tranquilliser by hypodermic. Within 35 seconds (approx.) the patient fell silent and became tractable, accepting the straitjacket without resistance, and with only a slight expression (facial, not verbal) of bewilderment, or, possibly, curiosity.

"I have to get out of here."

"Oh, Gid, not yet, you need to rest. It's a decent place. They've eased up on the drugs. I can see the difference."

"I have to get out, Anna."

"You're not well yet."

"I am not a patient. I am impatient. Help me get out. Please."

"Why, Gid? What for?"

"They won't let me go where I have to go."

"Where do you have to go?"

"Mad."

Dear Lin,

They continue to let me visit Gideon every afternoon from five to six, because I am his only relative, the widower's widowed sister, and I just sort of barge in. I don't think the doctor approves of my visits, I think he thinks I leave the patient disturbed, but he hasn't the authority to keep me out, I guess, until Gideon is committed. I guess he doesn't really have any authority, in a private rest home like this, but he makes me feel guilty. I never did understand when to obey people. He is supposed to be the best man here for nervous breakdowns. He has been disapproving lately and says Gideon is deteriorating, ceasing to respond, but all he gives him to respond to is drugs. What is he supposed to say to them? He hasn't eaten for four days. He responds to me, when nobody else is there, or anyhow he talks, and I respond. He asked me about you kids yesterday. I told him about Kate's divorce. It made him sad. "Everybody is divorcing everybody else," he said. I was sad, too, and I said, "Well, we didn't. You and Dorothea, me and Louis. Death us did part. Which is preferable, I wonder?" He said, "It comes out much the same. Fission, fusion. The human race is one great Nuclear Family." I wondered if the doctor would think that's the way an insane person talks. Maybe he would think that's the way two insane people talk

Later on Gideon told me what the weight is. It is all the people who are dying. A lot of them are children, little, hollow, empty children. Some of them are old people, very light, hollow, old men and women. They don't weigh much separately, but there are so many of them. The old people lie across his legs. The children are in a great heap on his chest, across his breastbone. It makes it hard for him to breathe.

Today he only asked me to help him get out and go where he has to go. When he speaks of that he cries. I always hated for him to cry when we were children, it made me cry, too, even when I was thirteen or fourteen. He only cried for real griefs. The doctor says that what he has is an acute depression, and it should be cured with chemicals. But Gideon is not depressed. I think what he has is grief. Why can't he be allowed to grieve? Would it destroy the rest of us, his grief? It's the people who don't grieve who are destroying us, it seems to me.

"Here's your clothes. You'll have to get up and get dressed, Gideon. If you want to come away with me. I didn't get permission. I just can't get through to that doctor, he wants to cure you. If you want to go, you'll have to get up and walk."

"Shall I take up my bed?"

"Don't be silly."

"Bible."

"For God's sake don't go religious now. If you do I'll bring you right back here. Hurry up. Here's your pants."

"Please get off me just for a minute," he said to the dying children and old men and women.

"Oof, how thin you are. Let me button that. All right. Can you manage? Hang on. No! hang onto me. You haven't been eating, you're dizzy."

"Dizzy Giddy."

"Do shut up! Try to look ordinary."

"We are ordinary."

They walked out of the room and down the hall arm in arm, an ordinary middle-aged couple. They walked past the old woman in the wheel-chair nursing her doll, and past the room of the young man who stared. They walked past the receptionist's desk. Anna smiled and said in a peculiar voice at the receptionist, "Going out for a walk in the garden." The receptionist smiled and said, "Lovely weather." They walked out onto the brick front path of the rest home, and down it, between lawns, to the iron gate. They walked through the gate and turned left. Anna's car was parked halfway down the block, under elm trees.

"Oh, oh, if I have a heart attack it's all your fault. Wait. I'm so shaky I can't get the key in. You all right?"

"Sure. Where are we going?"

"To the lake."

"He went out with his sister, doctor. For a walk. About half an hour ago."

"A walk, my God," the doctor said. "Where to?"

I am Anna. I am Gideon. I am Gideanna. I am sister's brother, brother's sister. I am Gideon who am dying, but it is your death I die, not mine. I am Anna who am not mad, but I am your brother, who is mad. Take my hand, brother, from the dark! Reich' mir das Hand, mein Leben, komm' in mein Schloss mit mir. O, but that castle I do not want to enter, brother mine; that is the castle I do not want to enter. It has a dark tower. Who do you think I am, Childe Roland? A Roland to your Oliver? No, look, we know this place, this is the old place, where we were children. Let's dance here, on the lakeshore, by the water. You be the tower, I will be the lake. You will dance in me reflected, I will be full of you, of the wave-broken shimmering stones. Lie lightly on me, tower, brother, see, if you lie lightly we are one. But we have always been one, sisterbrother. We have always danced alone. I am Gideon who dances in your soul, and I am dying. I can't dance any longer. I am borne down, borne down, borne down. I cannot lie, I cannot dance. All the reflections are dissolved. I cannot dance. I cannot breathe. They lie on me, they lie in me. How can the starving be so heavy, Anna?

Gideon, is it our fault? It can't be your fault. You never harmed a living soul.

But I am the fault, you know, The fault in my soul and yours, the fault itself. The line on which the ground moves. So the earthquake comes, and the people die, the little puzzled children, and the young men with guns, and the women pausing shopping bag in hand in the dissolving supermarket, and the old people who crouch down and reach out with wrinkled fingers to the faltering earth. I have betrayed them all. I did not give them enough food to eat.

How could you have? You're not God!

Oh yes I am. We are.

We are?

Yes, we are. Indeed we are. If I weren't God how should I be dying now? God is what dies. God is bereavement. We all die for each other.

If I am God I am the Woman-God, and I shall be reborn. Out of my own body I shall bear my birth.

Surely you will, but only if I die; and I am you. Or do you deny me, at the grave's edge, after fifty years?

No, no, no. I don't deny you, though I've often wanted to. But that's not a grave's edge, my young darkness, my terror, my little brother soul. It's only a lakeshore, see?

There is no other shore.

There must be.

No; all seas have one shore only. How could they have more?

Well, there's only one way to find out.

I'm cold. It's cold, the water's cold.

Look: there they are. So many of them, so many. The children float because they're hollow, swollen up with air. The older people swim, for a while. Look how that old man holds a clod of earth in his hand, the piece of the world he held to when the earthquake came. A little island, not quite big enough. Look how she holds her baby up above the water. I must help her, I must go to her!

If I touch one, they will take hold of me. They will clutch me with the grip of the drowning and drag me down with them. I'm not that good a swimmer. If I touch them, I'll drown.

Look there, I know that face. Isn't that Hansen? He's holding onto a rock, poor soul, a plank would serve him better.

There's Kate. There's Kate's ex-husband. And there's Lin. Lin's a good swimmer, always was, I'm not worried about Lin. But Kate's in trouble. She needs help. Kate! Don't wear yourself out, honey, don't kick so hard. The water's very wide. Save your strength, swim slowly, sweetheart, Kate my child!

There's young Chew. And look there, there's the doctor, in right over his head. And the receptionist. And the old woman with the doll. But there are so many more, so many. If I reach out my hand to one, a hundred will reach for it, a thousand, a thousand million, and pull me down and drown me. I can't save one child, one single child. I can't save myself.

Then let it be so. Take my hand, child! stranger in the darkness, in the deep waters, take my hand. Swim with me, while we can. Let us be drowned together, for it's certain we shall not be saved alone.

It's silent, out here in the deep waters. I can't see the faces any more.

Dorothea, there's someone following us. Don't look back.

I'm not Lot's wife, Louis, I'm Gideon's wife. I can look back, and still not turn to salt. Besides, my blood was never salt enough. It's you who shouldn't look back.

Do you take me for Orpheus? I was a good pianist, but not that good. But I admit, it scares me to look back. I don't really want to.

I just did. There's two of them. A woman and a man.

I was afraid of that.

Do you think it's them?

Who else would follow us?

Yes, it's them, our husband and our wife. Go back! Go back! This is no place for you!

This is the place for everyone, Dorothea.

Yes, but not yet, not yet. O Gideon, go back! He doesn't hear me. I can't speak clearly any more. Louis, you call to them.

Go back! Don't follow us! They can't hear us, Dorothea. Look how they come, as if the sand were water. Don't they know there's no water here?

I don't know what they know, Louis. I have forgotten. Gideon, O Gideon, take my hand!

Anna, take my hand!

Can they hear us? Can they touch us?

I don't know. I have forgotten.

It's cold, I'm cold. It's too deep, too far to go. I have reached out my hand, and reached out my hand into the darkness, but I couldn't tell what good it did; if I held up some child for a while, or if some shadow hand reached back to me, I don't know. I can't tell the way. Back on the dry land they were right. They told me not to grieve. They told me not to look. They told me to forget. They told me eat my lunch and take my pills that end in zil and ine. And they were right. They told me to be quiet, not to shout, not to cry out aloud. Be quiet now, be good. And they were right. What's the good in shouting? What's the good in shouting Help me, help, I'm drowning! when all the rest of them are drowning too? I heard them crying Help me, help me, please. But now I hear nothing. I hear the sound of the deep waters only. O take my hand, my love, I'm cold, cold, cold.

> *The water is wide, I cannot get over,*
> *And neither have I wings to fly.*
> *Give me a boat that will carry two,*
> *And both shall row, my love and I.*

There is, oh, there is another shore! Look at the light, the light of morning on the rocks, the light on the shores of morning. I am light. The weight's gone. I am light.

But it is the same shore, Gideanna.

Then we have come home. We rowed all night in darkness, in the cold, and we came home: the home where we have never been before, the home we never left. Take my hand, and step ashore with me, my sister life, my brother death. Look: it is the beginning place. Here we begin, here by the flood that parts us.

The Lost Children

He lifted the silver pipe to his lips and played. In his patchwork jacket and multistripe pants and two-tone shoes, he walked the city streets piping a tune. What tune? They turned and listened, passersby, businessmen, shoppers, secretaries, smokers, tourists, bag ladies, beggars. As the piper went past they cocked their heads, straining their ears, with an inward look in their eyes. Did they hear the tune? Yes—No—? Some of them followed him a little way, trying to hear what he was playing on his pipe. A bag lady shook her shopping cart in rage and shouted obscenities after him. A Japanese visitor ran to get ahead of him to take his photograph, but lost him in the crowds. A lawyer fell into step beside him, trying to hear the sound of the pipe, which surely was very high and sweet; but he could catch only the faintest sound on the very edge of hearing, and he turned off at Broadway. Three boys ran shoving and yelling past the piper through the crowds, their canvas and plastic shoes gaudier than his jacket. A woman coming out of a clothing store stopped, her back stooped, her lips parted, and gazed after him. Her little daughter tugged at her hand, impatient. "Mama, I want to go home, let's go to the bus stop, mama!" Inside the mother, inside each of the women and the men he passed, a child jumped up crying in a high voice, "I hear it! I hear it! Listen!" But she could not hear, and her daughter paid no attention, did not listen, tugged at her hand, and she followed, obedient. Children shot past running or on skateboards or rollerblades. Men and women strolled or hurried on, turned to their business with a shrug or a comment about street musicians, continued their conversation about municipal bonds, the football game, the price of halibut, the trial, the election, the breakdown. Some of the men, some of the women felt a little flutter of the breath, a kind of gasp or a slight pang at the breastbone, and others felt nothing at all, when the child inside them broke out, broke free, and ran invisibly after the piper, inaudibly crying, "Wait! Wait for me!" as the gaudy, nimble figure passed on through the throngs, threading the traffic at the crossings, always playing his silver pipe. Among the crowds these escaped children passed quick and slight as dust motes or wisps of steam, more and more of them, a cloud, a comet-tail of immaterial children following the piper, skipping, capering, dancing to the tune he played, dancing right out of the city, through the suburbs, across the superhighways, till they came at last to the malls and the fast food strip. Did the piper go on past the malls towards the hidden country or did he slip away from the children among the endless aisles of the vast, windowless buildings? Did the children catch up to him or did they lose him, distracted by the signs and the goods, the toy stores, the candy stores? They dispersed quite suddenly, all the escaped children, wandering off into the shops and theaters and arcades to enter into electronic games, jumping and shooting and destroying one another in puffs of sparks, to enter into videos of isneyland and whizneyland and busineyland, running through towers and castles of smiling machinery and tunnels and orbits of machinery screaming. There the lost children are. When they are hungry they feed on the sweet greasy smoke from the grills where hamburger meat is fried forever, while the loudspeakers forever play the piper's tune.

Texts

Messages came, Johanna thought, usually years too late, or years before one could crack their code or had even learned the language they were in. Yet they came increasingly often and were so urgent, so compelling in their demand that she read them, that she do something, as to force her at last to take refuge from them. She rented, for the month of January, a little house with no telephone in a seaside town that had no mail delivery. She had stayed in Klatsand several times in summer; winter, as she had hoped, was even quieter than summer. A whole day would go by without her hearing or speaking a word. She did not buy the paper or turn on the television, and the one morning she thought she ought to find some news on the radio she got a program in Finnish from Astoria. But the messages still came. Words were everywhere.

Literate clothing was no real problem. She remembered the first print dress she had ever seen, years ago, a genuine *print* dress with typography involved in the design—green on white, suitcases and hibiscus and the names *Riviera* and *Capri* and *Paris* occurring rather blobbily from shoulder seam to hem, sometimes right side up, sometimes upside down. Then it had been, as the saleswoman said, very unusual. Now it was hard to find a T-shirt that did not urge political action, or quote lengthily from a dead physicist, or at least mention the town it was for sale in. All this she had coped with, she had even worn.

But too many things were becoming legible.

She had noticed in earlier years that the lines of foam left by waves on the sand after stormy weather lay sometimes in curves that looked like handwriting, cursive lines broken by spaces, as if in words; but it was not until she had been alone for over a fortnight and had walked many times down to Wreck Point and back that she found she could read the writing. It was a mild day, nearly windless, so that she did not have to march briskly but could mosey along between the foam-lines and the water's edge where the sand reflected the sky. Every now and then a quiet winter breaker driving up and up the beach would drive her and a few gulls ahead of it onto the drier sand; then as the wave receded she and the gulls would follow it back. There was not another soul on the long beach. The sand lay as firm and even as a pad of pale brown paper, and on it a recent wave at its high mark had left a complicated series of curves and bits of foam. The ribbons and loops and lengths of white looked so much like handwriting in chalk that she stopped, the way she would stop, half willingly, to read what people scratched in the sand in summer. Usually it was "Jason + Karen" or paired initials in a heart; once, mysteriously and memorably, three initials and the dates 1973–1984, the only such inscription that spoke of a promise not made but broken. Whatever those eleven years had been, the length of a marriage? a child's life? they were gone, and the letters and numbers also were gone when she came back by where they had been, with the tide rising. She had wondered then if the person who wrote them, had written them to be erased. But these foam words lying on the brown sand now had been written by the erasing sea itself. If she could read them they might tell her a wisdom a good deal deeper and bitterer than she could possibly swallow. Do I want to know what the sea writes? she thought, but at the same time she was already reading the foam, which though in vaguely cuneiform blobs rather than letters of any alphabet was perfectly legible as she walked along beside it. "Yes," it read, "esse hes hetu tokye to' ossusess ekyes. Seham hute' u." (When she wrote it down later she used the apostrophe to represent a kind of stop or click like the last sound in "Yep!") As she read it over, backing up some yards to do so, it continued to say the same thing, so she walked up and down it several times and memorized it. Presently, as bubbles burst and the blobs began to shrink, it changed here and there to read, "Yes, e hes etu kye to' ossusess kye. ham te u." She felt that this was not significant change but mere loss, and kept the original text in mind. The water of the foam sank into the sand and the bubbles dried away till the marks and lines lessened into a faint lacework of dots and scraps, half legible. It looked enough like delicate bits of fancywork that she wondered if one could also read lace or crochet.

When she got home she wrote down the foam words so that she would not have to keep repeating them to remember them, and then she looked at the machine-made Quaker lace tablecloth on the little round dining table. It was not hard to read but was, as one might expect, rather dull. She made out the first line inside the border as "pith wot pith wot pith wot" interminably, with a "dub" every thirty stitches where the border pattern interrupted.

But the lace collar she had picked up at a secondhand clothing store in Portland was a different matter entirely. It was handmade, handwritten. The script was small and very even. Like the Spencerian hand she had been taught fifty years ago in the first grade, it was ornate but surprisingly easy to read. "My soul must go," was the border, repeated many times, "my soul must go, my soul must go," and the fragile webs leading inward read, "sister, sister, sister, light the light." And she did not know what she was to do, or how she was to do it.

Sleepwalkers

John Felburne

I told the maid not to come to clean the cabin before four o'clock, when I go running. I explained that I'm a night person and write late and sleep in, mornings. Somehow it came out that I'm writing a play. She said, "A stage play?" I said yes, and she said, "I saw one of those once." What a wonderful line. It was some high school production, it turned out some musical. I told her mine was a rather different kind of play, but she didn't ask about it. And actually there would be no way to explain to that sort of woman what I write about. Her life experience is so incredibly limited. Living out here, cleaning rooms, going home and watching TV—*Jeopardy* probably. I thought of trying to put her in my characters notebook and got as far as "Ava: the Maid," and then there was nothing to write. It would be like trying to describe a glass of water. She's what people who say "nice" mean when they say, "She's nice." She'd be completely impossible in a play, because she never does or says anything but what everybody else does and says. She talks in clichés. She *is* a cliché. Forty or so, middle-sized, heavy around the hips, pale, not very good complexion, blondish—half the white women in America look like that. Pressed out of a mold, made with a cookie cutter. I run for an hour, hour and a half, while she's cleaning the cabin, and I was thinking, she'd never do anything like running, probably doesn't do any exercise at all. People like that don't take any control over their lives. People like her in a town like this live a mass-produced existence, stereotypes, getting their ideas from the TV. Sleepwalkers. That would make a good title, *Sleepwalkers*. But how could you write meaningfully about a person who's totally predictable? Even the sex would be boring.

There's a woman in the creekside cabin this week. When I jog down to the beach, afternoons, she watches me. I asked Ava about her. She said she's Mrs. McAn, comes every summer for a month. Ava said, "She's very nice," of course. McAn has rather good legs. But old.

Katharine McAn

If I had an air gun I could hide on my deck and pop that young man one on the buttock when he comes pumping past in his little purple stretchies. He eyes me.

I saw Virginia Herne in Hambleton's today. Told her the place was turning into a goddamn writers colony, with her collecting all these Pulitzers or whatever they are, and that young man in the shingled cabin sitting at his computer till four in the morning. It's so quiet at the Hideaway that I can hear the thing clicking and peeping all night. "Maybe he's a very diligent accountant," Virginia said. "Not in shiny purple stretch shorts," I said, She said, "Oh, that's John" Somebody, "yes, he's had a play produced, in the East somewhere, he told me." I said, "What's he doing here, sitting at your feet?" and she said, "No, he told me he needed to escape the pressures of culture, so he's spending a summer in the West." Virginia looks very well. She has that dark, sidelong flash in her eye. A dangerous woman, mild as milk. "How's Ava?" she asked. Ava house-sat her place up on Breton Head last summer when she and Jaye were traveling, and she takes an interest in her, though she doesn't know the story Ava told me. I said Ava was doing all right.

I think she is, in fact. She still walks carefully, though. Maybe that's what Virginia saw. Ava walks like a tai ji walker, like a woman on a high wire. One foot directly in front of the other, and never any sudden movements.

I had tea ready when she knocked, my first morning here. We sat at the table in the kitchen nook, just like the other summers, and talked. Mostly about Jason. He's in tenth grade now, plays baseball, skateboards, surfboards, crazy to get one of those windsail things and go up to Hood River—"Guess the ocean isn't enough for him," Ava said. Her voice is without color, speaking of him. My guess is that the boy is like his father, physically at least, and that troubles or repels her, though she clings to him loyally, cleaves to him. And there might be a jealousy of him as the survivor: *Why you, and not her?* I don't know what Jason knows or feels about all that. The little I've seen of him when he comes by here, he seems a sweet boy, caught up in these sports boys spend themselves on, I suppose because at least they involve doing something well.

Ava and I always have to re-agree on what work she's to do when I'm here. She claims if she doesn't vacuum twice a week and take out the trash, Mr. Shoto will "get after" her. I doubt he would, but it's her job and her conscience. So she's to do that, and look in every day or so to see if I need anything. Or to have a cup of tea with me. She likes Earl Grey.

Ken Shoto

She's reliable. I told Deb at breakfast, you don't know how lucky we are. The Brinnesis have to hire anything they can pick up, high school girls that don't know how to make a bed and won't learn, ethnics that can't talk the language and move on just when you've got them trained. After all, who wants a job cleaning motel rooms? Only somebody who hasn't enough education or self-respect to find something better. Ava wouldn't have kept at it if I treated her the way the Brinnesis treat their maids, either. I knew right away we were in luck with this one. She knows how to clean and she'll work for a dollar over minimum wage. So why shouldn't I treat her like one of us? After four years? If she wants to clean one cabin at seven in the morning and another one at four in the afternoon, that's her business. She works it out with the customers. I don't interfere. I don't push her. "Get off Ava's case, Deb," I told her this morning. "She's reliable, she's honest, and she's permanent—she's got that boy in the high school here. What more do you want? I tell you, she takes half the load off my back!"

"I suppose you think *I* ought to be running after her supervising her," Deb says. God, she can drive me crazy sometimes. What did she say that for? I wasn't blaming her for anything.

"She doesn't need supervising," I said.

"So you think," Deb said.

"Well, what's she done wrong?"

"Done? Oh, nothing. She couldn't do anything wrong!"

I don't know why she has to talk like that. She couldn't be jealous, not of Ava, my God. Ava's all right looking, got all her parts, but hell, she doesn't let you see her that way. Some women just don't. They just don't give the signals. I can't even think about thinking about her that way. Can't Deb see that? So what the hell does she have against Ava? I always thought she liked her OK.

"She's sneaky," is all she'd say. "Creepy."

I told her, "Aw, come on, Deb. She's quiet. Maybe not extra bright. I don't know. She isn't talkative. Some people aren't."

"I'd like to have a woman around who could say more than two words. Stuck in the woods out here."

"Seems like you spend all day in town anyhow," I said, not meaning it to be a criticism. It's just the fact. And why shouldn't she? I didn't take on this place to work my wife to death, or tie her down to it. I manage it and keep it up, and Ava Evans cleans the cabins, and Deb's free to do just what she wants to do. That's how I meant it to be. But it's like it's not enough, or she doesn't believe it, or something. "Well," she said, "if *I* had any responsibility, I wonder if you'd find *me* reliable." It is terrible how she cuts herself down. I wish I knew how to stop her from cutting herself down.

Deb Shoto

It's the demon that speaks. Ken doesn't know how it got into me. How can I tell him? If I tell him, it will kill me from inside.

But it knows that woman, Ava. She looks so mild and quiet, *yes Mrs. Shoto, sure Mrs. Shoto,* pussyfooting it around here with her buckets and mops and brooms and wastebaskets. She's hiding. I know when a woman is hiding. The demon knows it. It found me. It'll find her.

There isn't any use trying to get away. I have thought I ought to tell her that. Once they put the demon inside you, it never goes away. It's instead of being pregnant.

She has that son, so it must have happened to her later, it must have been her husband.

I wouldn't have married Ken if I'd known it was in me. But it only began speaking last year. When I had the cysts and the doctor thought they were cancer. Then I knew they had been put inside me. Then when they weren't cancerous, and Ken was so happy, it began moving inside me where they had been, and then it began saying things to me, and now it says things in my voice. Ken knows it's there, but he doesn't know how it got there. Ken knows so much, he knows how to live, he lives for me, he is my life. But I can't talk to him. I can't say anything before it comes into my mouth just like my own tongue and says things. And what it says hurts Ken. But I don't know what to do. So he leaves, with his heavy walk and his mouth pulled down, and goes to his work. He works all the time, but he's getting fat. He shouldn't eat so much cholesterol. But he says he always has. I don't know what to do.

I need to talk to somebody. It doesn't talk to women, so I can. I wish I could talk to Mrs. McAn. But she's snobbish. College people are snobbish. She talks so quick, and her eyebrows move. Nobody like that would understand. She'd think I was crazy. I'm not crazy. There is a demon in me. I didn't put it there.

I could talk to the girl in the A-frame cabin. But she is so young. And they drive away every day in their pickup truck. And they are college people, too.

There is a woman comes into Hambleton's, a grandmother. Mrs. Inman. She looks kind. I wish I could talk to her.

Linsey Hartz

The people here in Hannah's Hideaway are so weird, I can't believe them. The Shotos. Wow. He's really sweet, but he goes around this place all day digging in the little channel he's cut from the creek to run through the grounds, a sort of toy creek, and weeding, and pruning, and raking, and the other afternoon when we came home he was picking up spruce needles off the path, like a housewife would pick threads off a carpet.

And there's the little bridges over the little toy creek, and the rocks along the edges of the little paths between the cabins. He rearranges the rocks every day. Getting them lined up even, getting the sizes matched.

Mrs. Shoto watches him out her kitchen window. Or she gets in her car and drives one quarter mile into town and shops for five hours and comes back with a quart of milk. With her tight, sour mouth closed. She hates to smile. Smiling is a big production for her, she works hard at it, probably has to rest for an hour afterwards.

Then there's Mrs. McAn, who comes every summer and knows everybody and goes to bed at nine P.M. and gets up at five A.M. and does Chinese exercises on her porch and meditates on her roof. She gets onto the roof from the roof of her deck. She gets onto the roof of the deck from the window of the cabin.

And then there's Mr. Preppie, who goes to bed at five A.M. and gets up at three P.M. and doesn't mingle with the aborigines. He communicates only with his computer, and his modems, no doubt, and probably he has a fax in there. He runs on the beach every day at four, when the most people are on the beach, so that they can all see his purple spandex and his muscley legs and his hundred-and-forty-dollar running shoes.

And then there's me and George going off every day to secretly map where the Forest Service and the lumber companies are secretly cutting old growth stands illegally in the Coast Range so that we can write an article about it that nobody will publish even secretly.

Three obsessive-compulsives, one egomaniac, and two paranoids.

The only normal person at Hannah's Hideaway is the maid, Ava. She just comes and says "Hi," and "Do you need towels?" and she vacuums while we're out logger-stalking, and generally acts like a regular human being. I asked her if she was from around here. She said she'd lived here several years. Her son's in the high school. "It's a nice town," she said. There's something very clear about her face, something pure and innocent, like water. This is the kind of person we paranoids would be saving the forests for, if we were. Anyhow, thank goodness there are still some people who aren't totally fucked up.

Katharine McAn

I asked Ava if she thought she'd stay on here at the Hideaway. She said she guessed so.

"You could get a better job," I said.

"Yeah, I guess so," she said.

"Pleasanter work."

"Mr. Shoto is a really nice man."

"But Mrs. Shoto—"

"She's all right," Ava said earnestly. "She can be hard on him sometimes, but she never takes it out on me. I think she's a really nice person, but—"

"But?"

She made a slow, dignified gesture with her open hand: I don't know, who knows, it's not her fault, we're all in the same boat. "I get on OK with her," she said.

"You get on OK with anybody. You could get a better job, Ava."

"I got no skills, Mrs. McAn. I was brought up to be a wife. Where I lived in Utah, women are wifes." She pronounced it with the *f*, wifes. "So I know how to do this kind of job, cleaning and stuff. Anyhow."

I felt I had been disrespectful of her work. "I guess I just wish you could get better pay," I said.

"I'm going to ask Mr. Shoto for a raise at Thanksgiving," she said, her eyes bright. Obviously it was a long-thought-out plan. "He'll give it to me." Her smile is brief, never lingering on her mouth.

"Do you want Jason to go on to college?"

"If he wants to," she said vaguely. The idea troubled her. She winced away from it. Any idea of leaving Klatsand, of even Jason's going out into a larger world, scares her, probably will always scare her.

"There's no danger, Ava," I said very gently. It is painful to me to see her fear, and I always try to avoid pain. I want her to realize that she is free.

"I know," she said with a quick, deep breath, and again the wincing movement.

"Nobody's after you. They never were. It was a suicide. You showed me the clipping."

"I burned that," she said.

LOCAL MAN SHOOTS, KILLS DAUGHTER, SELF

She had showed the newspaper clipping to me summer before last. I could see it in my mind's eye with extreme clarity.

"It was the most natural thing in the world for you to move away. It wasn't 'suspicious.' You don't have to hide, Ava. There's nothing to hide from."

"I know," she said.

She believes I know what I'm talking about. She accepts what I say, she believes me, as well as she can. And I believe her. All she told me I accepted as the truth. How do I know it's true? Simply on her word, and a newspaper clipping that might have been nothing but the seed of a fantasy? Certainly I have never known any truth in my life like it.

Weeding the vegetable garden behind their house in Indo, Utah, she heard a shot, and came in the back door and through the kitchen to the front room. Her husband was sitting in his armchair. Their twelve-year-old daughter Dawn was lying on the rug in front of the TV set. Ava stood in the doorway and asked a question, she doesn't remember what she asked, "What happened?" or "What's wrong?" Her husband said, "I punished her. She has polluted me." Ava went to her daughter and saw that she was naked and that her head had been beaten in and that she had been shot in the chest. The shotgun was on the coffee table. She picked it up. The stock was slimy. "I guess I was afraid of him," she said to me. "I don't know why I picked it up. Then he said, 'Put that down.' And I backed off towards the front door with it, and he got up. I cocked it, but he came towards me. I shot him. He fell down forwards, practically onto me. I put the gun down on the floor near his head, just inside the door. I went out and went down the road. I knew Jason would be coming home from baseball practice and I wanted to keep him out of the house. I met him on the road, and we went to Mrs.——" She halted herself, as if her neighbor's name must not be spoken—"to a neighbor's house, and they called the police and the ambulance." She recited the story quietly. "They all thought it was a murder and suicide. I didn't say anything."

"Of course not," I murmured, dry of tongue.

"I did shoot him," she said, looking up at me, as if to make certain that I understood. I nodded.

She never told me his name, or their married name. Evans was her middle name, she said.

Immediately after the double funeral, she asked a neighbor to drive her and Jason to the nearest town where there was an Amtrak station. She had taken all the cash her husband had kept buried in the cellar under their stockpile of supplies in case of nuclear war or a Communist takeover. She bought two coach seats on the next train west. It went to Portland. At first sight she knew Portland was "too big," she said. There was a Coast Counties bus waiting at the Greyhound station down the street from the train station. She asked the driver, 'Where does this bus go?" and he named off the little coast towns on his loop. "I picked the one that sounded fartherest," she said.

She and ten-year-old Jason arrived in Klatsand as the summer evening was growing dark. The White Gull Motel was full, and Mrs. Brinnesi sent her to Hannah's Hideaway.

"Mrs. Shoto was nice," Ava said. "She didn't say anything about us coming in on foot or anything. It was dark when we got here. I couldn't believe it was a motel. I couldn't see anything but the trees, like a forest. She just said, 'Well, that young man looks worn out,' and she put us in the A-frame, it was the only one empty. She helped me with the rollabed for Jason. She was really nice." She wanted to linger on these details of finding haven. "And next morning I went to the office and asked if they knew anyplace where I could find work, and Mr. Shoto said they needed a full-time maid. It was like they were waiting for me," she said in her earnest way, looking up at me.

Don't question the Providence that offers shelter. Was it also Providence that put the gun in her hand? Or in his?

She and Jason have a little apartment, an add-on to the Hanningers' house on Clark Street. I imagine that she keeps a photograph of her daughter Dawn in her room. A framed five-by-seven school picture, a smiling seventh-grader. Maybe not. I should not imagine anything about Ava Evans. This is not ground for imagination. I should not imagine the child's corpse on the rug between the coffee table and the TV set. I should not have to imagine it. Ava should not have to remember it. Why do I want her to get a better job, nicer work, higher wages—what am I talking about? The pursuit of happiness?

"I have to go clean Mr. Felburne's cabin," she said. "The tea was delicious."

"Now? But you're off at three, aren't you?"

"Oh, he keeps funny hours. He asked me not to come and clean till after four."

"So you have to wait around here an hour? The nerve!" I said. Indignation, the great middle-class luxury. "So he can go *running?* I'd tell him to go jump in the creek!" Would I? If I was the maid?

She thanked me again for the tea. "I really enjoy talking with you," she said. And she went down the neatly raked path that winds between the cabins, among the dark old spruce trees, walking carefully, one foot in front of the other. No sudden movements.

Hand, Cup, Shell

The last house on Searoad stood in the field behind the dunes. Its windows looked north to Breton Head, south to Wreck Rock, east to the marshes, and from the second story, across the dunes and the breakers, west to China. The house was empty more than it was full, but it was never silent.

The family arrived and dispersed. Having come to be together over the weekend, they fled one another without hesitation, one to the garden, one to the kitchen, one to the bookshelf, two north up the beach, one south to the rocks.

Thriving on salt and sand and storms, the rosebushes behind the house climbed all over the paling fence and shot up long autumn sprays, disheveled and magnificent. Roses may do best if you don't do anything for them at all except keep the sword fern and ivy from strangling them; bronze Peace grows wild as well as any wild rose. But the ivy, now. Loathsome stuff. Poisonous berries. Crawling out from hiding everywhere, stuffed full of horrors: spiders, centipedes, millipedes, billipedes, snakes, rats, broken glass, rusty knives, dog turds, dolls' eyes. I must cut the ivy right back to the fence, Rita thought, pulling up a long stem that led her back into the leafy mass to a parent vine as thick as a garden hose. I must come here oftener, and keep the ivy off the spruce trees. Look at that, it'll have the tree dead in another year. She tugged. The cable of ivy gave no more than a steel hawser would. She went back up the porch steps, calling, "Are there any pruning shears, do you think?"

"Hanging on the wall there, aren't they?" Mag called back from the kitchen. "Anyway, they ought to be." There ought to be flour in the canister, too, but it was empty. Either she had used it up in August and forgotten, or Phil and the boys had made pancakes when they were over last month. So where was the list pad to write *flour* on for when she walked up to Hambleton's? Nowhere to be found. She would have to buy a little pad to write *pad* on. She found a ballpoint pen in the things drawer. It was green and translucent, imprinted with the words HANK'S COAST HARDWARE AND AUTO SUPPLIES. She wrote *flour, bans, o.j., cereal, yog, list pad* on a paper towel, wiping blobs of excess green ink off the penpoint with a corner of the towel. Everything is circular, or anyhow spiral. It was no time at all, certainly not twelve months, since last October in this kitchen, and she was absolutely standing in her tracks. It wasn't *déjà vu* but *déjà vécu*, and all the Octobers before it, and still all the same this was now, and therefore different feet were standing in her tracks. A half size larger than last year, for one thing. Would they go on breaking down and spreading out forever, until she ended up wearing men's size 12 logging boots? Mother's feet hadn't done that. She'd always worn 7N, still wore 7N, always would wear 7N, but then she always wore the same kind of shoes, too, trim inch-heel pumps or penny loafers, never experimenting with Germanic clogs, Japanese athletics, or the latest toe-killer fad. It came of having had to dress a certain way, of course, as the Dean's wife, but also of being Daddy's girl, small-town princess, not experimenting just knowing.

"I'm going on down to Hambleton's, do you want anything?" Mag called out the kitchen door through the back-porch screen to her mother fighting ivy in the garden.

"I don't think so. Are you going to walk?"

"Yes."

They were right: it took a certain effort to say *yes* just flatly, to refrain from qualifying it, softening it: *Yes, I think so; Yes, I guess so; Yes I thought I would. . . .* Unqualified *yes* had a gruff sound to it, full of testosterone. If Rita had said *no* instead of *I don't think so*, it would have sounded rude or distressed, and she probably would have responded in some way to find out what was wrong, why her mother wasn't speaking in the mother tongue. "Going to Hambleton's," she said to Phil, who was kneeling at the bookcase in the dark little hall, and went out. She went down the four wooden steps of the front porch and through the front gate, latched the gate behind her, and turned right on Searoad to walk into town. These familiar movements gave her great pleasure. She walked on the dune side of the road, and between dunes saw the ocean, the breakers that took all speech away. She walked in silence, seeing glimpses between dune grass of the beach where her children had gone.

Gret had gone as far as the beach went. It ended in a tumble of rusty brown basalt under Wreck Point, but she knew the ways up through the rocks to the slopes and ledges of the Point, places where nobody came. Sitting there on the wind-bitten grass looking out over the waves bashing on Wreck Rock and the reef Dad called Rickrack and out to the horizon, you could keep going farther still. At least you ought to be able to, but there wasn't any way to be alone any more. There was a beer can in the grass, a tag of orange plastic ribbon tied to a stake up near the summit, a Coast Guard helicopter yammering and prying over the sea up to Breton Head and back south again. Nobody wanted anybody to be alone, ever. You had to do away with that, unmake it, all the junk, trash, crap, trivia, David, the midterms, Gran, what people thought, other people. You had to go away from them. All the way away. It used to be easy to do that, easy to go and hard to come back, but now it was harder and harder to go: and she never could go all the way. To sit up here and stare at the ocean and be thinking about stupid David, and what's that stake for, and why did Gran look at my fingernails that way, what's wrong with me? Am I going to be this way the rest of my life? Not even seeing the ocean? Seeing stupid beer cans? She stood, raging, backed up, aimed, and kicked the beer can in a low, fast arc off the cliff into the sea unseen below. She turned and scrambled up to the summit, braced her knees in soggy bracken, and wrenched the orange-ribboned stake out of the ground. She hurled it southward and saw it fall into bracken and salal scrub and be swallowed. She stood up, rubbing her hands where the raw wood had scraped the skin. The wind felt cold on her teeth. She had been baring them, an angry ape. The sea lay grey at eye level, taking her immediately now into its horizontality. Nothing cluttered. As she sucked the heel of her thumb and got her front teeth warm, she thought, My soul is ten thousand miles wide and extremely invisibly deep. It is the same size as the sea, it is bigger than the sea, it *holds* the sea, and you cannot, you cannot cram it into beer cans and fingernails and stake it out in lots and own it. It will drown you all and never even notice.

But how old I am, thought the grandmother, to come to the beach and not look at the sea! How horrible! Straight out into the backyard, as if all that mattered was grubbing ivy. As if the sea belonged to the children. To assert her right to the ocean, she carried ivy cuttings to the trash bin beside the house and after cramming them into the bin stood and looked at the dunes, across which it was. It wasn't going to go away, as Amory would have said. But she went on out the garden gate, crossed sandy-rutted Searoad, and in ten more steps saw the Pacific open out between the grass-crowned dunes. There you are, you old grey monster. You aren't going to go away, but I am. Her brown loafers, a bit loose on her bony feet, were already full of sand. Did she want to go on down, onto the beach? It was always so windy. As she hesitated, looking about, she saw a head bobbing along between the crests of dune grass. Mag coming back with the groceries. Slow black bobbing head like the old mule coming up the rise to the sagebrush ranch when? old Bill the mule—Mag the mule, trudging obstinate silent. She went down to the road and stood first on one foot then the other emptying sand out of her shoes, then walked to meet her daughter. "How are things at Hambleton's?"

"Peart," Mag said. "Right peart. When is whatsername coming?"

"By noon, I think she said." Rita sighed. "I got up at five. I think I'm going to go in and have a little lie-down before she comes. I hope she won't stay hours."

"Who is she, again?"

"Oh . . . damn . . ."

"I mean, what's she doing?"

Rita gave up the vain search for the lost name. "She's some sort of assistant research assistant I suppose to whatsisname at the University, you know, doing the book about Amory. I expect somebody suggested to him that maybe it would look odd if he did a whole biography without talking to the widow, but of course it's really only Amory's ideas that interest him, I believe he's very theoretical the way they are now. Probably bored stiff at the idea of actual *people*. So he's sending the young lady into the hencoop."

"So that you don't sue him."

"Oh you don't think so."

"Certainly. Co-optation. And you'll get thanked for your invaluable assistance, in the acknowledgments, just before he thanks his wife and his typist."

"What was that terrible thing you told me about Mrs. Tolstoy?"

"Copied *War and Peace* for him six times by hand. But you know, it would beat copying most books six times by hand."

"Shepard."

"What?"

"Her. The girl. Something Shepard."

"Whose invaluable assistance Professor Whozis gratefully . . . no, she's only a grad student, isn't she. Lucky if she gets mentioned at all. What a safety net they have, don't they? All the women the knots in the net."

But that cut a bit close to the bones of Amory Inman, and his widow did not answer his daughter as she helped her put away the flour, cornflakes, yogurt, cookies, bananas, grapes, lettuce, avocado, tomatoes, and vinegar Mag had bought (she had forgotten to buy a list pad). "Well, I'm off, shout when she comes," Rita said, and made her way past her son-in-law, who was sitting on the hall floor by the bookcase, to the stairs.

The upstairs of the house was simple, rational, and white: the stairs landing and a bathroom down the middle, a bedroom in each corner. Mag and Phil SW, Gran NW, Gret NE, boys SE. The old folks got the sunset, the kids got dawn. Rita was the first to listen and hear the sea in the house. She looked out over the dunes and saw the tide coming in and the wind combing the manes of the white horses. She lay down and looked with pleasure at the narrow, white-painted boards of the ceiling in the sea-light like no other light. She did not want to go to sleep but her eyes were tired and she had not brought a book upstairs. She heard the girl's voice below, the girls' voices, piercing soft, the sound of the sea.

"Where's Gran?"

"Upstairs."

"This woman's come."

Mag brought the dish towel on which she was drying her hands into the front room, a signal flag: I work in the kitchen and have nothing to do with interviews. Gret had left the girl standing out on the front deck. "Won't you come in?"

"Susan Shepard."

"Mag Rilow. That's Greta. Gret, go up and tell Gran, OK?"

"It's so lovely here! What a beautiful place!"

"Maybe you'd like to sit out on the deck to talk? It's so mild. Would you like some coffee? Beer, anything?"

"Oh, yes—coffee—"

"Tea?"

"That would be wonderful."

"Herbal?" Everybody there at the University in the Klamath Time Warp drank herbal tea. Sure enough, chamomile-peppermint would be wonderful. Mag got her sitting in the wicker chair on the deck and came back in past Phil, who was still on the floor in the hall by the bookcase, reading. "Take it into the *light*," she said, and he said, "Yeah, I will," smiling, and turned a page. Gret, coming down the stairs, said, "She'll be down in a minute."

"Go talk to the girl. She's at the U."

"What in?"

"I don't know. Find out."

Gret snarled and turned away. Edging past her father in the narrow hall, she said, "Why don't you get some *light*?" He smiled, turned a page, and said, "Yeah, I will." She strode out onto the deck and said, "My mother says you're at the U," at the same time as the woman said, "You're at the U, aren't you?"

Gret nodded.

"I'm in Ed. I'm Professor Nabe's research assistant for his book. It's really exciting to be interviewing your grandmother."

"It seems fairly weird to me," Gret said.

"The University?"

"No."

There was a little silence filled by the sound of the sea.

"Are you a freshman?"

"Freshwoman." She edged towards the steps.

"Will you major in Education, do you think?"

"Oh, God, no."

"I suppose having such a distinguished grandfather, people always just expect. Your mother's an educator, too, isn't she?"

"She teaches," Gret said. She had got as far as the steps and now went down them, because they were the shortest way to get away, though she had been coming into the house to go to her room when Sue Student drove up and she got caught.

Gran appeared in the open doorway, looking wary and rather bleary, but using her politically correct smile and voice: "Hello! I'm Rita Inman." While Sue Student was jumping up and being really excited, Gret got back up the steps, past Gran, and into the house.

Daddy was still sitting on the floor in the dark hall by the bookcase, reading. She unplugged the gooseneck lamp from the end table by the living-room couch, set it on the bookcase in the hall, and found the outlet was too far for the cord to reach. She brought the lamp as close to him as she could, setting it on the floor about three feet from him, and then plugged in the plug. The light glared across the pages of his book. "Oh, hey, great," he said, smiling, and turned a page. She went on upstairs to her room. Walls and ceiling were white, the bedspreads on the two narrow beds were blue. A picture of blue mountains she had painted in ninth-grade art class was pinned to the closet door, and she reconfirmed with a long look at it that it was beautiful. It was the only good picture she had ever painted, and she marveled at it, the gift that had given itself to her, undeserved, no strings attached. She opened the backpack she had dumped on one bed, got out a geology textbook and a highlighter, lay down on the other bed, and began to reread for the midterm examination. At the end of a section on subduction, she turned her head to look at the picture of blue mountains again, and thought, I wonder what would it be like?—or those are the words she might have used to express the feelings of curiosity, pleasure, and awe which accompanied the images in her mind of small figures scattered among great lava cliffs on the field trip in September, of journeys, of levels stretching to the horizon, high deserts under which lay fossils folded like tissue paper; of moraines; of long veins of ore and crystals in the darkness underground. Intent and careful, she turned the page and started the next section.

Sue Shepard fussed with her little computer thing. Her face was plump, pink, round-eyed, and Rita had to make the interpretation "intellectual" consciously. It would not arise of itself from the pink face, the high voice, the girlish manner, as it would from the pink face, high voice, and boyish manner of a male counterpart. She knew that she still so identified mind and masculinity that only women who imitated men were immediately recognizable to her as intellectuals, even after all these years, even after Mag. Also, Sue Shepard might be disguising her intellect, as Mag didn't. And the jargon of the Education Department was a pretty good disguise in itself. But she was keen, it was a keen mind, and perhaps Professor Whozis didn't like to be reminded of it, so young, so bright, so close behind. Probably he liked flutter and butter, as Amory used to call it, in his graduate-student women. But fluttery buttery little Sue had already set aside a whole sheaf of the professor's questions as time-wasting, and was asking, intently and apparently on her own hook, about Rita's girlhood.

"Well, when I was born we lived on a ranch out from Prineville, in the high country. The sagebrush, you know. But I don't remember much that's useful. I think Father must have been keeping books for the ranch. It was a big operation—huge—all the way to the John Day River, I think. When I was nine, he took over managing a mill in Ultimate, in the Coast Range. A lumber mill. Nothing left of all that now. There isn't even a gravel road in to Ultimate any more. Half the state's like that, you know. It's very strange. Easterners come and think it's this wild pristine wilderness and actually it's all Indian graveyards underfoot and old homesteads and second growth and towns nobody even remembers were there. It's just that the trees and the weeds grow back so fast. Like ivy. Where are you from?"

"Seattle," said Sue Shepard, friendly, but not to be misled as to who was interviewing whom.

"Well, I'm glad. I seem to have more and more trouble talking with Easterners."

Sue Shepard laughed, probably not understanding, and pursued; "So you went to school in Ultimate?"

"Yes, until high school. Then I came to live with Aunt Josie in Portland and went to old Lincoln High. The nearest high school to Ultimate was thirty miles on logging roads, and anyhow it wasn't good enough for Father. He was afraid I'd grow up to be a roughneck, or marry one. . . ." Sue Shepard clicketed on her little machine, and Rita thought, But what did Mother think? Did she want to send me away at age thirteen to live in the city with her sister-in-law? The question opened on a blank area that she gazed into, fascinated. I know what Father wanted, but why don't I know what she wanted? Did she cry? No, of course not. Did I? I don't think so. I can't even remember talking about it with Mother. We made my clothes that summer. That's when she taught me how to cut out a pattern. And then we came up to Portland the first time, and stayed at the old Multnomah Hotel, and we bought shoes for me for school—and the oyster silk ones for dressing up, the little undercut heel and one strap, I wish they still made them. I was already wearing Mother's size. And we ate lunch in that restaurant, the cut-glass water goblets, the two of us, where was Father? But I never even wondered what she thought, I never knew. I never know what Mag really thinks, either. They don't say. Rocks. Look at Mag's mouth, just like Mother's, like a seam in a rock. Why did Mag go into teaching, talk, talk, talk all day, when she really hates talking? Although she never was quite as gruff as Gret is, but that's because Amory wouldn't have stood for it. But why didn't Mother and I say anything to each other? She was so stoical. Rock. And then I was happy in Portland, and there she was in Ultimate. . . . "Oh, yes, I loved it," she answered Sue Shepard. "The twenties were a nice time to be a teen-ager, we really were very spoiled, not like now, poor things. It's terribly hard to be thirteen or fourteen now, isn't it? We went to dancing school, they've got AIDS and the atomic bomb. My granddaughter's twice as old as I was at eighteen. In some ways. She's amazingly young for her age in others. It's so complicated. After all, think of Juliet! It's never *really* simple, is it? But I think I had a very nice, innocent time in high school, and right on into college. Until the crash. The mill closed in '32, my second year. But actually we went right on having a good time. But it was terribly depressing for my parents and my brothers. The mill shut right down, and they all came up to Portland looking for work, everybody did. And then I left school after my junior year, because I'd got a summer job bookkeeping in the University accounting office, and they wanted me to stay on, and so I did, since everybody else in the family was out of work, except Mother finally got a job in a bakery, nights. It was terrible for men, the Depression, you know. It killed my father. He looked and looked for work and couldn't find anything, and there I was, doing what he was qualified to do, only of course at a very low level, and terrible pay—sixty dollars a month, can you imagine?"

"A week?"

"No, a month. But still, I was making it. And men of his generation were brought up to be depended on, which is a wonderful thing, but then they weren't allowed ever *not* to be depended on, when they had to depend on other people, which everybody actually does. It was terribly unrealistic, I think, a real whatdyoucallit. Double time?"

"Double bind," said young Sue, sharp as tacks, clicketing almost inaudibly away on her little lap computer, while the tape recorder tape went silently round and round, recording Rita's every maunder and meander. Rita sighed. "I'm sure that's why he died so young," she said. "He was only fifty."

But Mother hadn't died young, though her husband had, and her elder son had drifted off to Texas to be swallowed alive so far as his mother was concerned by a jealous wife, and her younger son had poured whiskey onto diabetes and died at thirty-one. Men did seem to be so fragile. But what had kept Margaret Jamison Holz going? Her independence? But she had been brought up to be dependent, hadn't she? Anyhow, nobody could keep going long on mere independence; when they tried to they ended up pushing shopping carts full of stuff and sleeping in doorways. Mother hadn't done that. She had sat here on the deck looking out at the dunes, a small, tough, old woman. No retirement pension, of course, and a tiny little dribble of insurance money, and she did let Amory pay the rent on her two-room apartment in Portland, but she was independent to the end, visiting them only once or twice a year at the University, and then always for a full month here, in summer. Gret's room now had been Mother's room then. How strange it was, how it changed! But recently Rita had wakened in the deep night or when it was just beginning to get light and had lain there in bed thinking, not with fear but with a kind of frightened, lively thrill, It is so strange, all of it is so *strange!*

"When were you able to go back to college?" Sue Shepard asked, and she answered, "In '35," resolving to stick to the point and stop babbling.

"And then you met Dr. Inman when you took his class."

"No. I never took a class in Education."

"Oh," Sue Shepard said, blank.

"I met him in the accounting office. I was still clerking there halftime, paying my way. And he came in because he hadn't been paid his salary for three months. People used to be just as good at mistakes like that as computers are now. It took days and days to find out how they'd managed to lose him from the faculty payroll. Did he tell somebody that I'd taken his class and that's how we met?" Sue Shepard wasn't going to admit it; she was discreet. "How funny. It was one of the other women he went out with, and he got his memories crossed. Students were always falling in love with him. He was *extremely* attractive—I used to think Charles Boyer without the French accent—"

Mag heard them laughing on the front deck as she came through the hall, edging around her husband. A gooseneck lamp standing on the floor near him glared in his eyes, but he was holding his book so that its pages were in shadow.

"Phil."

"*Mm.*"

"Get up and go read in the living room."

He smiled, reading. "Found this . . . "

"The interviewer's here. She'll be staying for lunch. You're in the way. You've been in the way for two hours. You're in the dark. There's daylight six feet away. Get up and go read in the living room."

"People . . ."

"Nobody's there! People come through *here*. Are you—" The wave of hatred and compassion set free by her words carried her on past him, though she had checked the words. In silence, she turned the corner and climbed the stairs. She went into the southwest bedroom and looked for a decent shirt in the crowded closet; the cotton sweater she had worn from Portland was too warm for this mild coastal weather. The search led her into a rummage-out of summer clothes. She sorted, rehung, folded her clothes, then Phil's. From the depths she pulled out paint-stiff, knee-frayed blue jeans, a madras shirt with four buttons gone which had been stuffed into the closet unwashed. Even here at the beach house, her father's clothes had always been clean, smelled clean, smelled of virtue, *virtù*. With a violent swing she threw the madras shirt at the wastebasket. It draped itself half in, half out, a short sleeve sticking up pitifully. Not waving but drowning . . . But to go on drowning for twenty-five years?

The window was ajar, and she could hear the sea and her mother's voice down on the front deck answering questions about her husband the eminent educator, the clean-bodied man: How had he written his books? When had he broken with John Dewey's theories? Where had the UNICEF work taken him? Now, little apple-cheeked handmaiden of success, ask me about my husband the eminent odd-job man: how did he quit halfway through graduate school, when had he broken with the drywalling contractor, where had his graveyard shift at the Copy Shop taken him? Phil the Failure, he called himself, with the charming honesty that concealed a hideous smugness that probably but not certainly concealed despair. What was certain was that nobody else in the world knew the depth of Phil's contempt for them, his absolute lack of admiration or sympathy for anything anybody did or was. If that indifference was originally a defense, it had consumed what it had once defended. He was invulnerable, by now. And people were so careful not to hurt him. Finding that she was Dr. Rilow and he was an unemployed drywaller, they assumed it was hard for him; and then when they found that it wasn't, they admired him for being so secure, so unmacho, taking it so easily, handling it so well. Indeed he handled it well, cherished it, his dear failure, his great success at doing what he wanted to do and nothing else. No wonder he was so sweet, so serene, so unstrained. No wonder she had blown up, teaching *Bleak House* last week, at the mooncalf student who couldn't see what was supposed to be wrong with Harold Skimpole. "Don't you see that his behavior is totally irresponsible?" she had demanded in righteous wrath, and the mooncalf had replied with aplomb, "I don't see why *everybody* is supposed to be responsible." It was a kind of Taoist koan, actually. For Taoist wives. It was hard to be married to a man who lived in a perpetual condition of *wu wei* and not to end up totally *wei*, you had to be very careful or you ended up washing the ten thousand shirts.

But then of course Mother had looked after Father's shirts.

The jeans weren't even good for rags, even if they would sell in the Soviet Union for a hundred dollars; she threw them after the shirt, and knocked the wastebasket over. Faintly ashamed, she retrieved them and the shirt and stuffed them into a plastic bag that had been squirreled away in a cranny of the closet. An advantage of Phil's indifference was that he would never come downstairs demanding to know where his wonderful old jeans and madras shirt were. He never got attached to clothes; he wore whatever was provided. "Distrust all occasions that require new clothes." What a prig Thoreau was. Ten to one he meant weddings but hadn't had the guts to say so, let alone get married. Actually Phil liked new clothes, liked to get them for Christmas and birthdays, accepted all presents, cherished none. "Phil is a saint, Mag," his mother had said to her shortly before they were married, and she had agreed, laughing, thinking the exaggeration quite forgivable; but it had not been a burble of mother love. It had been a warning.

She knew that her father had hoped that the marriage wouldn't last. He had never quite said so. By now the matter of her marriage, between her and her mother, was buried miles deep. Between her and her daughter it was an unaskable question. Everybody protecting everybody. It was stupid. It kept her and Gret from saying much to each other. And it wasn't really the right question, the one that needed asking, anyhow. They were married. But there was a question. No one had asked it and she did not know what it was. Possibly, if she found out, her life would change. The headless torso of Apollo would speak: *Du musst dein Leben ändern.* Meanwhile, did she particularly want her life to change? "I will never desert Mr. Micawber," she said under her breath, reaching into yet another cranny of the closet and discovering there yet another plastic bag, which when opened disclosed rust-colored knitted wool: a sweater, which she stared at dumbly till she recognized it as one she had bought on sale for Gret for Christmas several years ago and had utterly forgotten ever since. "Gret! Look here!" she cried, crossing the hall, knocking, opening the door of her daughter's room. "Merry Christmas!"

After explanations, Gret pulled the sweater on. Her dark, thin face emerged from the beautiful color with a serious expression. She looked at the sweater seriously in the mirror. She was very hard to please, preferred to buy her own clothes, and wore the ones she liked till they fell apart. She kept them moderately clean. "Are the sleeves kind of short, a little?" she asked, in the mother tongue.

"Kind of. Probably why it was on sale. It was incredibly cheap, I remember, at the Sheep Tree. Years ago. I liked the color."

"It's neat," Gret said, still judging. She pushed up the sleeves. "Thanks," she said. Her face was a little flushed. She smiled and glanced around at the book lying open on the bed. Something was unsaid, almost said. She did not know how to say it and Mag did not know how to allow her to say it; they both had trouble with their native language. Awkward, intrusive, the mother retreated, saying, "Lunch about one-thirty."

"Need help?"

"Not really. Picnic on the deck. With the interviewer."

"When's she leaving?"

"Before dinner, I hope. It's a good color on you." She went out, closing the door behind her, as she had been taught to do.

Gret took off the orange sweater. It was too hot for the mild day, and she wasn't sure she liked it yet. It would take a while. It would have to sit around a while till she got used to it, and then she would know. She thought she liked it; it felt like she'd worn it before. She put it into a drawer so her mother wouldn't get hurt. Last year when her mother had come into her room at home and stared around, Gret had suddenly realized that the stare wasn't one of disapproval but of pain. Disorder, dirt, disrespect for objects caused her pain, like being shoved or hit. It must be hard for her, living, in general. Knowing that, Gret tried to put stuff away; but it didn't make much difference. She was mostly at college now. Mother went on nagging and ordering and enduring, and Daddy and the boys didn't let it worry them. Just like some goddamn sitcom. Everything about families and people was exactly like some goddamn sitcom. Waiting for David to call, just like a soap opera. Everything the same as it was for everybody else, the same things happening over and over and over, all petty and trivial and stupid, and you couldn't ever get free. It clung to you, held on, pinioned you. Like the dream she used to have of the room with wallpaper that caught and stuck to you, the Velcro dream. She reopened the textbook and read about the nature of gabbro, the origins of slate.

The boys came back from the beach just in time for lunch. They always did. Still. Just as when her milk would spurt and the baby in the next room cried at the exact same moment. Their clomping in to go to the bathroom finally got Phil off the hall floor. He carried out platters to the table on the front porch and talked with whatsername the interviewer, who got quite pink and pleased. Phil looked so thin and short and hairy and vague and middle-aged that they never expected it till whammy! right between the eyes. Wooed and won. Go it, Phil. She looked like an intelligent girl, actually, overserious, and Phil wouldn't hurt her. Wouldn't hurt a fly, would old Phil. St. Philip, bestower of sexual favors. She smiled at them and said, "Come and get it."

Sue Student was being nice to Daddy, talking with him about forest fires or something. Daddy had his little company smile and was being nice to Sue Student. She didn't sound too stupid, actually. She was a vegetarian. "So is Gret," Gran said. "What is it about the U these days? They used to live on raw elk." Why did she always have to disapprove of everything Gret did? She never said stuff like that about the boys. They were scarfing up salami. Mother watched them all loading their plates and making their sandwiches with that brooding hawk expression. Filling her niche. That was the trouble with biology, it was the sitcom. All niches. Mother provides. Better the dark slate levels, the basalt plains. Anything could happen, there.

She was worn out. She went for the wine bottle; food later. She must get by herself for a while, that bit of a nap in the morning hadn't helped. Such a long, long morning, with the drive over from Portland. And talking about old times was a most terrible thing to do. All the lost things, lost chances, all the dead people. The town with no road to it any more. She had had to say ten times, "He's dead now," "No, she's dead." What a strange thing to say, after all! You couldn't *be* dead. You couldn't *be* anything but alive. If you weren't alive, you weren't—you had been. You shouldn't have to say "He's dead now," as if it was just some other way of being, but "He isn't now," or "He was." Keep the past in the past tense. And the present in the present, where it belongs. Because you didn't live on in others, as people said. You changed them, yes. She was entirely different because Amory had lived. But he didn't live on in her, in her memory, or in his books, or anywhere. He had gone. He was gone. Maybe "passed away" wasn't such a whatdyoucallit, after all. At least it was in the passed tense, the past tense, not the present. He had come to her and she had come to him and they had made each other's life what it had been, and then he had gone. Passed away. It wasn't a euphemism, that's what it wasn't. Her mother . . . There was a pause in her thoughts. She drank the wine. Her mother was different, how? She came back to the rock. Of course she was dead, but it did not seem that she had passed away, the way he had. She went back to the table, refilled her glass with the red wine, laid salami, cheese, and green onions on brown bread.

She was beautiful now. In the tight, short, ugly fashions of the sixties, when Mag had first looked at her from any distance and with any judgment, she had looked too big, and for a while after Amory's death and when she had the bone marrow thing she had been gaunt, but now she was extraordinary: the line of the cheek, the long, soft lips, the long-lidded eyes with their fine wrinkle-pleating. What had she said about raw elk? The interviewer hadn't heard and wouldn't understand if she had heard, wouldn't know that she had just been told what Mrs. Amory Inman thought of the institution of which her husband had been the luminary, what indeed she thought, in her increasing aloofness, her oldwomanhood, of most human institutions. Poor little whatsername, trapped in the works and dark machinations of that toughest survivor of the Middle Ages, the university, ground in the mills of assistantships, grants, competitions, examinations, dissertations, all set up to separate the men from the boys and both from the rest of the world, she wouldn't have time for years yet to look up, to look out, to learn that there were such bare, airy places as the place where Rita Inman lived.

"Yes, it is nice, isn't it? We bought it in '55, when things over here were still pretty cheap. We haven't even asked you indoors, how terrible! After lunch you must look round the house. I think I'm going to have a little lie-down, after lunch. Or perhaps you'd like to go down on the beach then—the children will take you walking as far as you'd like, if you like. Mag, Sue says she needs an hour or two more with me. She hasn't asked all . . ." a pause, "the professor's questions yet. I'm afraid I kept wandering off the subject." How sternly beautiful Mag was, her rock-seam mouth, her dark-waterfall hair going silver. Managing everything, as usual, seeing to everything, the good lunch. No, definitely her mother was not dead in the same way Father was dead, or Amory, or Clyde, or Polly, or Jim and Jean; there was something different there. She really must get by herself and think about it.

"Geology." The word came out. Spoken. Mother's ears went up like a cat's, eyebrows flickering, eyes and mouth impassive. Daddy acted like he'd known her decision all along, maybe he had, he couldn't have. Sue Student had to keep asking who was in the Geo department and what you did with geology. She only knew a couple of the professors' names and felt stupid not knowing more. She said, "Oh, you get hired by oil companies, mining companies, all kinds of land-rape companies. Find uranium under Indian reservations." Oh, shut up. Sue Student meant well. Everybody meant well. It spoiled everything. Softened everything. "The grizzled old prospector limps in from twenty years alone in the desert, swearing at her mule," Daddy said, and she laughed, it was funny, Daddy was funny, but she was for a moment, a flash, afraid of him. He was so quick. He knew that this was something important, and did he mean well? He loved her, he liked her, he was like her, but when she wasn't like him did he like it? Mother was saying how geology had been all cut-and-dried when she was in college and how it was all changed now by these new theories. "Plate tectonics isn't exactly new," oh, shut up, shut up. Mother meant well. Sue Student and Mother talked about academic careers in science and got interested comparing, colleaguing.

Sue was at the U but she was younger and only a grad student; Mother was only at a community college but she was older and had a Ph.D. from Berkeley. And Daddy was out of it. And Gran half asleep, and Tom and Sam cleaning up the platters. She said, "It's funny. I was thinking. All of us—the family, I mean—nobody will ever know any of us ever existed. Except for Granddaddy. He's the only real one."

Sue gazed mildly. Daddy nodded in approval. Mother stared, the hawk at bay. Gran said in a curious, distant tone, "Oh I don't think so at all." Tom was throwing bread to a seagull, but Sam, finishing the salami, said, in his mother's voice, "Fame is the spur!" At that, the hawk blinked and stooped to the prey: "Whatever do you mean, Gret? Reality is being a dean of the School of Education?"

"He was important. He has a biography. None of us will."

"Thank goodness," Gran said, getting up. "I do hope you don't mind, if I have just a bit of a lie-down now I'll be much brighter later, I hope."

Everybody moved.

"Boys. You do the dishes. Tom!"

He came. They obeyed. She felt a tremendous, a ridiculous surge, as warm and irresistible as tears or milk, of pride—in them, in herself. They were lovely. Lovely boys. Grumbling, coltish, oafish, gangling, redhanded, they unloaded the table with efficiency and speed, Sam insulting Tom steadily in his half-broken voice, Tom replying on two sweet notes at intervals like a thrush, "Ass-sole. . . . Ass-sole. . . ."

"Who's for a walk on the beach?"

Mag was, the interviewer was, Phil was, Gret surprisingly was.

They crossed Searoad and went single file between the dunes. Down on the beach she looked back to see the front windows and the roof above the dune grass, always remembering the pure delight of seeing it so the first time, the first time ever. To Gret and the boys the beach house was coeval with existence, but to her it was connected with joy. When she was a child they had stayed in other people's beach houses, places in Gearhart and Neskowin, summerhouses of deans and provosts and the rich people who clung to university administrators under the impression that they were intellectuals; or else, as she got older, Dean Inman had taken her and her mother along to his ever more exotic conferences, to

Botswana, Brasilia, Bangkok, until she had rebelled at last. "But they are interesting *places*," her mother had said, deprecating, "you really don't enjoy going?" And she had howled, "I'm sick of feeling like a white giraffe, why can't I ever stay home where people are the same *size?*" And at some indefinite but not long interval after that, they had driven over to look at this house. "What do you think?" her father had asked, standing in the small living room, a smiling sixty-year-old public man, kindly rhetorical. There was no need to ask. They had all three been mad for it from the moment they saw it at the end of the long sand road between the marshes and the sea. "My room, OK?" Mag had said, coming out of the southwest bedroom. She and Phil had had their honeymoon summer there.

She looked across the sand at him. He was walking at the very edge of the water, moving crabwise east when a wave came washing farther in, following the outwash back west, absorbed as a child, slight, stooped, elusive. She veered her way to intersect with his. "Phildog," she said.

"Magdog."

"You know, she was right. What made her say it, do you think?"

"Defending me."

How easily he said it. How easy his assumption. It had not occurred to her.

"Could be. And herself? And me? . . . And then geology! Is she just in love with the course, or is she serious?"

"Never anything but."

"It might be a good major for her. Unless it's all labs now. I don't know, it's just a section of Intro Sci at CC. I'll ask Benjie what geologists do these days. I hope still those little hammers. And khaki shorts."

"That Priestley novel in the bookcase," Phil said, and went on to talk about it, and novelists contemporary with Priestley, and she listened attentively as they walked along the hissing fringes of the continent. If Phil had not quit before the prelims, he would have got much farther in his career than she in hers, because men got farther easier then, of course, but mainly because he was such a natural; he had the right temperament, the necessary indifference and passion of the scholar. He was drawn to early twentieth century English fiction with the perfect combination of detachment and fascination, and could have written a fine study of Priestley, Galsworthy, Bennett, that lot, a book worth a good professorship at a good school. Or worth at least a sense of self-respect. But self-respect wasn't a saint's business, was it? Dean Inman had had plenty of self-respect, and plenty of respect, too. Had she been escaping the various manifestations of respect when she fell for Phil? No. She still missed it, in fact, and supplied it when she could. She had fallen for Phil because she was strong, because of the awful need strength has for weakness. If you're not weak how can I be strong? Years it had taken her, years, until now, to learn that strength, like the lovely boys washing the dishes, like Gret saying that terrible thing at lunch, was what strength needed, craved, rested in. Rested and grew weak in, with the true weakness, the fecundity. Without self-defense. Gret had not been defending Phil, or anybody. Phil had to see it that way. But Gret had been speaking out of the true weakness. Dean Inman wouldn't have understood it, but it wouldn't have worried him; he would have seen that Gret respected him, and that to him would have meant that she respected herself. And Rita? She could not remember what Rita had said, when Gret said that about their not being real. Something not disapproving, but remote. Moving away. Rita was moving away. Like the gulls there ahead of them, always moving away as they advanced towards them, curved wings and watchful, indifferent eyes. Airborne, with hollow bones. She looked back down the sands. Gret and the interviewer were walking slowly, talking, far behind, so that she and Phil kept moving away from them, too. A tongue of the tide ran up the sand between them, crosscurrents drawing lines across it, and hissed softly out again. The horizon was a blue murk, but the sunlight was hot. "Ha!" Phil said, and picked up a fine white sand dollar. He always saw the invaluable treasures, the dollars of no currency; he went on finding Japanese glass netfloats every winter on this beach, years after the Japanese had given up glass floats for plastic, years after anyone else had found one. Some of the floats he found had limpets growing on them. Bearded with moss and in garments green, they had floated for years on the great waves, tiny unburst bubbles, green, translucent earthlets in foam galaxies, moving away, drawing near. "But how much Maupassant is there in *The Old Wives'*

Tale?" she asked. "I mean, that kind of summing-up-women thing?" And Phil, pocketing his sea-paid salary, answered, as her father had answered her questions, and she listened to him and to the sea.

Sue's mother had died of cancer of the womb. Sue had gone home to stay with her before college was out last spring. It had taken her four months to die, and Sue had to talk about it. Gret had to listen. An honor, an imposition, an initiation. From time to time, barely enduring, Gret lifted her head to look out across the grey level of the sea, or up at Breton Head towering closer, or ahead at Mother and Daddy going along like slow sandpipers at the foam-fringe, or down at the damp brown sand and her grotty sneakers making footprints. But she bent her head again to Sue, confining herself. Sue had to tell and she had to listen, to learn all the instruments, the bonds, the knives, the racks and pinions, and how you became part of the torture, complicit with it, and whether in the end the truth, after such efforts to obtain it, would be spoken.

"My father hated the male nurses to touch her," Sue said. "He said it was woman's work, he tried to make them send women nurses in."

She talked about catheters, metastases, transfusions, each word an iron maiden, a toothed vagina. Women's work. "The oncologist said it would get better when he put her on morphine, when her mind would get confused. But it got worse. It was the worst. The last week was the worst thing I will ever go through." She knew what she was saying, and it was tremendous. To be able to say that meant that you need not be afraid again. But it seemed like you had to lose a good deal for that gain.

Gret's escaping gaze passed her mother and father, who had halted at the foot of Breton Head, and followed the breakers on out to where the sea went level. Somebody had told her in high school that if you jumped from a height like Breton Head, hitting the water would be just like hitting rock,

"I didn't mean to go on telling you all that. I'm sorry. I just haven't got through it yet. I have to keep working through it."

"Sure," Gret said.

"Your grandmother is so—she's a beautiful person. And your whole family. You all just seem so real. I really appreciate being here with you."

She stopped walking, and Gret had to stop, too.

"What you said at lunch, about your grandfather being famous."

Gret nodded.

"When I suggested to Professor Nabe about talking to Dean Inman's family, you know, maybe getting some details that weren't just public knowledge, some insights on how his educational theories and his life went together, and his family, and so on—you know what he said? He said, 'But they're all quite unimportant people, aren't they?'"

The two young women walked on side by side.

"That's funny," Gret said, with a grin. She stooped for a black pebble. It was basalt, of course; there was nothing but basalt this whole stretch of the coast, outflow from the great shield volcanoes up the Columbia, or pillow basalts from undersea vents; that's what Mother and Daddy were clambering on now, big, hard pillows from under the sea. The hard sea.

"What did you find?" Sue asked, over-intense about everything, strung out. Gret showed her the dull black pebble, then flipped it at the breakers.

"*Everyone* is important," Sue said. "I learned that this summer."

Was that the truth that the croaking voice had gasped at torture's end? She didn't believe it. Nobody was important. But she couldn't say that. It would sound as cheap, as stupid, as the stupid professor. But the pebble wasn't important, neither was she, neither was Sue. Neither was the sea. Important wasn't the point. Things didn't have rank.

"Want to go on up the Head a ways? There's a sort of path."

Sue consulted her watch. "I don't want to keep your grandmother waiting when she wakes up. I'd better go back. I could listen to her talk forever. She's just amazing." She was going to say, "You're so lucky!" She did.

"Yeah," Gret said. "Some Greek, I think it was some Greek said don't say that to anybody until they're dead." She raised her voice. "Ma! Dad! Yo!" She gestured to them that she and Sue were returning. The small figures on the huge black pillows nodded and waved, and her mother's voice cried something, like a hawk's cry or a gull's, the sea drowning out all consonants, all sense.

Crows cawed and carked over the marshes inland. It was the only sound but the sound of the sea coming in the open window and filling the room and the whole house full as a shell is full of sound that sounds like the sea but is something else, your blood running in your veins, they said, but how could it be that you could hear that in a shell but never in your own ear or your cupped hand? In a coffee cup there was a sound like it, but less, not coming and going like the sea-sound. She had tried it as a child, the hand, the cup, the shell. Caw, cark, caw! Black heavy swoopers, queer. The light like no other on the white ceiling boards. Tongue and groove, tongue in cheek. What had the child said that for, that Amory was the only real one of them? An awful thing to say about reality. The child would have to be very careful, she was so strong. Stronger even than Maggie. Because her father was so weak. Of course that was all backwards, but it was so hard to think the things straight that the words had all backwards. Only she knew that the child would have to be very careful, not to be caught. Cark, ark, caw! the crows cried far over the marshes. What was the sound that kept going on? The wind, it must be the wind across the sagebrush plains. But that was far away. What was it she had wanted to think about when she lay down?

Ether, OR

For the Narrative Americans

Edna

I never go in the Two Blue Moons any more. I thought about that when I was arranging the grocery window today and saw Corrie go in across the street and open up. Never did go into a bar alone in my life. Sook came by for a candy bar and I said that to her, said I wonder if I ought to go have a beer there sometime, see if it tastes different on your own. Sook said Oh Ma you always been on your own. I said I seldom had a moment to myself and four husbands, and she said You know that don't count. Sook's fresh. Breath of fresh air. I saw Needless looking at her with that kind of dog look men get. I was surprised to find it gave me a pang, I don't know what of. I just never saw Needless look that way. What did I expect, Sook is twenty and the man is human. He just always seemed like he did fine on his own. Independent. That's why he's restful. Silvia died years and years and years ago, but I never thought of it before as a long time. I wonder if I have mistaken him. All this time working for him. That would be a strange thing. That was what the pang felt like, like when you know you've made some kind of mistake, been stupid, sewn the seam inside out, left the burner on.

They're all strange, men are. I guess if I understood them I wouldn't find them so interesting. But Toby Walker, of them all he was the strangest. The stranger. I never knew where he was coming from. Roger came out of the desert, Ady came out of the ocean, but Toby came from farther. But he was here when I came. A lovely man, dark all through, dark as forests. I lost my way in him. I loved to lose my way in him. How

I wish it was then, not now! Seems like I can't get lost any more. There's only one way to go. I have to keep plodding along it. I feel like I was walking across Nevada, like the pioneers, carrying a lot of stuff I need, but as I go along I have to keep dropping off things. I had a piano once but it got swamped at a crossing of the Platte. I had a good frypan but it got too heavy and I left it in the Rockies. I had a couple ovaries but they wore out around the time we were in the Carson Sink. I had a good memory but pieces of it keep dropping off, have to leave them scattered around in the sagebrush, on the sand hills. All the kids are still coming along, but I don't have them. I had them, it's not the same as having them. They aren't with me any more, even Archie and Sook. They're all walking along back where I was years ago. I wonder will they get any nearer than I have to the west side of the mountains, the valleys of the orange groves? They're years behind me. They're still in Iowa. They haven't even thought about the Sierras yet. I didn't either till I got here. Now I begin to think I'm a member of the Donner Party.

Thos. Sunn

The way you can't count on Ether is a hindrance sometimes, like when I got up in the dark this morning to catch the minus tide and stepped out the door in my rubber boots and plaid jacket with my clam spade and bucket, and overnight she'd gone inland again. The damn desert and the damn sagebrush. All you could dig up there with your damn spade would be a God damn fossil. Personally I blame it on the Indians. I do not believe that a fully civilised country would allow these kind of irregularities in a town. However as I have lived here since 1949 and could not sell my house and property for chicken feed, I intend to finish up here, like it or not. That should take a few more years, ten or fifteen most likely. Although you can't count on anything these days anywhere let alone a place like this. But I like to look after myself, and I can do it here. There is not so much Government meddling and interference and general hindering in Ether as you would find in the cities. This may be because it isn't usually where the Government thinks it is, though it is, sometimes.

When I first came here I used to take some interest in a woman, but it is my belief that in the long run a man does better not to. A woman is a worse hindrance to a man than anything else, even the Government.

I have read the term "a crusty old bachelor" and would be willing to say that that describes me so long as the crust goes all the way through. I don't like things soft in the center. Softness is no use in this hard world. I am like one of my mother's biscuits.

My mother, Mrs. J. J. Sunn, died in Wichita, KS, in 1944, at the age of 79. She was a fine woman and my experience of women in general does not apply to her in particular.

Since they invented the kind of biscuits that come in a tube which you hit on the edge of the counter and the dough explodes out of it under pressure, that's the kind I buy, and by baking them about one half hour they come out pretty much the way I like them, crust clear through. I used to bake the dough all of a piece, but then discovered that you can break it apart into separate biscuits. I don't hold with reading directions and they are always printed in small, fine print on the damn foil which gets torn when you break open the tube. I use my mother's glasses. They are a good make.

The woman I came here after in 1949 is still here. That was during my brief period of infatuation. Fortunately I can say that she did not get her hooks onto me in the end. Some other men have not been as lucky. She has married or as good as several times and was pregnant and pushing a baby carriage for decades. Sometimes I think everybody under forty in this town is one of Edna's. I had a very narrow escape. I have had a dream about Edna several times. In this dream I am out on the sea fishing for salmon from a small boat, and Edna swims up from the sea waves and tries to climb into the boat. To prevent this I hit her hands with the gutting knife and cut off the fingers, which fall into the water and turn into some kind of little creatures that swim away. I never can tell if they are babies or seals. Then Edna swims after them making a strange noise, and I see that in actuality she is a kind of seal or sea lion, like the big ones in the cave on the south coast, light brown and very large and fat and sleek in the water.

This dream disturbs me, as it is unfair. I am not the kind of man who would do such a thing. It causes me discomfort to remember the strange noise she makes in the dream, when I am in the grocery store and Edna is at the cash register. To make sure she rings it up right and I get the right change, I have to look at her hands opening and shutting the drawers and her fingers working on the keys. What's wrong with women is that you can't count on them. They are not fully civilised.

Roger Hiddenstone

I only come into town sometimes. It's a now and then thing. If the road takes me there, fine, but I don't go hunting for it. I run a two hundred thousand acre cattle ranch, which gives me a good deal to do. I'll look up sometimes and the moon is new that I saw full last night. One summer comes after another like steers through a chute. In the winters, though, sometimes the weeks freeze like the creek water, and things hold still for a while. The air can get still and clear in the winter here in the high desert. I have seen the mountain peaks from Baker and Rainier in the north, Hood and Jefferson, Three-Fingered Jack and the Sisters east of here, on south to Shasta and Lassen, all standing up in the sunlight for eight hundred or a thousand miles. That was when I was flying. From the ground you can't see that much of the ground, though you can see the rest of the universe, nights.

I traded in my two-seater Cessna for a quarterhorse mare, and I generally keep a Ford pickup, though at times I've had a Chevrolet. Any one of them will get me in to town so long as there isn't more than a couple feet of snow on the road. I like to come in now and then and have a Denver omelette at the café for breakfast, and a visit with my wife and son. I have a drink at the Two Blue Moons, and spend the night at the motel. By the next morning I'm ready to go back to the ranch to find out what went wrong while I was gone. It's always something.

Edna was only out to the ranch once while we were married. She spent three weeks. We were so busy in the bed I don't recall much else about it, except the time she tried to learn to ride. I put her on Sally, the cutting horse I traded the Cessna plus fifteen hundred dollars for, a highly reliable horse and more intelligent than most Republicans. But Edna had that mare morally corrupted within ten minutes. I was trying to explain how she'd interpret what you did with your knees, when Edna started yipping and raking her like a bronc rider. They lit out of the yard and went halfway to Ontario at a dead run. I was riding the old roan gelding and only met them coming back. Sally was unrepentant, but Edna was sore and delicate that evening. She claimed all the love had been jolted out of her. I guess that this was true, in the larger sense, since it wasn't long after that that she asked to go back to Ether. I thought she had quit her job at the grocery, but she had only asked for a month off, and she said Needless would want her for the extra business at Christmas. We drove back to town, finding it a little west of where we had left it, in a very pretty location near the Ochoco Mountains, and we had a happy Christmas season in Edna's house with the children.

I don't know whether Archie was begotten there or at the ranch. I'd like to think it was at the ranch so that there would be that in him drawing him to come back some day. I don't know who to leave all this to. Charlie Echeverria is good with the stock, but can't think ahead two days and couldn't deal with the buyers, let alone the corporations. I don't want the corporations profiting from this place. The hands are nice young fellows, but they don't stay put, or want to. Cowboys don't want land. Land owns you. You have to give in to that. I feel sometimes like all the stones on two hundred thousand acres were weighing on me, and my mind's gone to rimrock. And the beasts wandering and calling across all that land. The cows stand with their young calves in the wind that blows March snow like frozen sand across the flats. Their patience is a thing I try to understand.

Gracie Fane

I saw that old rancher on Main Street yesterday, Mr. Hiddenstone, was married to Edna once. He acted like he knew where he was going, but when the street ran out onto the sea cliff he sure did look foolish. Turned round and came back in those high-heel boots, long legs, putting his feet down like a cat the way cowboys do. He's a skinny old man. He went into the Two Blue Moons. Going to try to drink his way back to eastern Oregon, I guess. I don't care if this town is east or west. I don't care if it's anywhere. It never is anywhere anyway. I'm going to leave here and go to Portland, to the Intermountain, the big trucking company, and be a truck driver. I learned to drive when I was five on my grandpa's tractor. When I was ten I started driving my dad's Dodge Ram, and I've driven pickups and delivery vans for Mom and Mr. Needless ever since I got my license. Jase gave me lessons on his eighteen-wheeler last summer. I did real good. I'm a natural. Jase said so. I never got to get out onto the I–5 but only once or twice, though. He kept saying I needed more practice pulling over and parking and shifting up and down. I didn't mind practicing, but then when I got her stopped he'd want to get me into this bed thing he fixed up behind the seats and pull my jeans off, and we had to screw some before he'd go on teaching me anything. My own idea would be to drive a long way and learn a lot and then have some sex and coffee and then drive back a different way, maybe on hills where I'd have to practice braking and stuff. But I guess men have different priorities. Even when I was driving he'd have his arm around my back and be petting my boobs. He has these huge hands can reach right across both boobs at once. It felt good, but it interfered with his concentration teaching me. He would say *Oh baby you're so great* and I would think he meant I was driving great but then he'd start making those sort of groaning noises and I'd have to shift down and find a place to pull out and get in the bed thing again. I used to practice changing gears in my mind when we were screwing and it helped. I could shift him right up and down again. I used to yell *Going eighty!* when I got him really shifted up. *Fuzz on your tail!* And make these siren noises. That's my CB name: Sireen. Jase got his route shifted in August. I made my plans then. I'm driving for the grocery and saving money till I'm seventeen and go to Portland to work for the Intermountain Company. I want to drive the I–5 from Seattle to LA, or get a run to Salt Lake City. Till I can buy my own truck. I got it planned out.

Tobinye Walker

The young people all want to get out of Ether. Young Americans in a small town want to get up and go. And some do, and some come to a time when they stop talking about where they're going to go when they go. They have come to where they are. Their problem, if it's a problem, isn't all that different from mine. We have a window of opportunity; it closes. I used to walk across the years as easy as a child here crosses the street, but I went lame, and had to stop walking. So this is my time, my heyday, my floruit.

When I first knew Edna she said a strange thing to me; we had been talking, I don't remember what about, and she stopped and gazed at me. "You have a look on you like an unborn child," she said. "You look at things like an unborn child." I don't know what I answered, and only later did I wonder how she knew how an unborn child looks, and whether she meant a fetus in the womb or a child that never came to be conceived. Maybe she meant a newborn child. But I think she used the word she meant to use.

When I first stopped by here, before my accident, there was no town, of course, no settlement. Several peoples came through and sometimes encamped for a season, but it was a range without boundary, though it had names. At that time people didn't have the expectation of stability they have now; they knew that so long as a river keeps running it's a river. Nobody but the beavers built dams, then. Ether always covered a lot of territory, and it has retained that property. But its property is not continuous.

The people I used to meet coming through generally said they came down Humbug Creek from the river in the mountains, but Ether itself never has been in the Cascades, to my knowledge. Fairly often you can see them to the west of it, though usually it's west of them, and often west of the Coast Range in the timber or the dairy country, sometimes right on the sea. It has a broken range. It's an unusual place. I'd like to go back to the center to tell about it, but I can't walk any more. I have to do my flourishing here.

J. Needless

People think there are no Californians. Nobody can come from the promise land. You have to be going to it. Die in the desert, grave by the wayside. I come from California, born there, think about it some.

I was born in the Valley of San Arcadio. Orchards. Like a white bay of orange flowers under bare blue-brown mountains. Sunlight like air, like clear water, something you lived in, an element. Our place was a little farmhouse up in the foothills, looking out over the valley. My father was a manager for one of the companies. Oranges flower white, with a sweet, fine scent. Outskirts of Heaven, my mother said once, one morning when she was hanging out the wash. I remember her saying that. We live on the outskirts of Heaven.

She died when I was six and I don't remember a lot but that about her. Now I have come to realise that my wife has been dead so long that I have lost her too. She died when our daughter Corrie was six. Seemed like there was some meaning in it at the time, but if there was I didn't find it.

Ten years ago when Corrie was twenty-one she said she wanted to go to Disneyland for her birthday. With me. Damn if she didn't drag me down there. Spent a good deal to see people dressed up like mice with water on the brain and places made to look like places they weren't. I guess that is the point there. They clean dirt till it is a sanitary substance and spread it out to look like dirt so you don't have to touch dirt. You and Walt are in control there. You can be in any kind of place, space or the ocean or castles in Spain, all sanitary, no dirt. I would have liked it as a boy, when I thought the idea was to run things. Changed my ideas, settled for a grocery.

Corrie wanted to see where I grew up, so we drove over to San Arcadio. It wasn't there, not what I meant by it. Nothing but roofs, houses, streets and houses. Smog so thick it hid the mountains and the sun looked green. God damn, get me out of here, I said, they have changed the color of the sun. Corrie wanted to look for the house but I was serious. Get me out of here, I said, this is the right place but the wrong year. Walt Disney can get rid of the dirt on his property if he likes, but this is going too far. This is my property.

I felt like that. Like I thought it was something I had, but they scraped all the dirt off and underneath was cement and some electronic wiring. I'd as soon not have seen that. People come through here say how can you stand living in a town that doesn't stay in the same place all the time, but have they been to Los Angeles? It's anywhere you want to say it is.

Well, since I don't have California what have I got? A good enough business. Corrie's still here. Good head on her. Talks a lot. Runs that bar like a bar should be run. Runs her husband pretty well too. What do I mean when I say I had a mother, I had a wife? I mean remembering what orange flowers smell like, whiteness, sunlight. I carry that with me. Corinna and Silvia, I carry their names. But what do I have?

What I don't have is right within hand's reach every day. Every day but Sunday. But I can't reach out my hand. Every man in town gave her a child and all I ever gave her was her week's wages. I know she trusts me. That's the trouble. Too late now. Hell, what would she want me in her bed for, the Medicare benefits?

Emma Bodely

Everything is serial killers now. They say everyone is naturally fascinated by a man planning and committing one murder after another without the least reason and not even knowing who he kills personally. There was the man up in the city recently who tortured and tormented three tiny little boys and took photographs of them while he tortured them and of their corpses after he killed them. Authorities are talking now about what they ought to do with these photographs. They could make a lot of money from a book of them. He was apprehended by the police as he lured yet another tiny boy to come with him, as in a nightmare. There were men in California and Texas and I believe Chicago who dismembered and buried innumerably. Then of course it goes back in history to Jack the Ripper who killed poor women and was supposed to be a member of the Royal Family of England, and no doubt before his time there were many other serial killers, many of them members of Royal Families or Emperors and Generals who killed thousands and thousands of people. But in wars they kill people more or less simultaneously, not one by one, so that they are mass murderers, not serial killers, but I'm not sure I see the difference, really. Since for the person being murdered it only happens once.

I should be surprised if we had a serial killer in Ether. Most of the men were soldiers in one of the wars, but they would be mass murderers, unless they had desk jobs. I can't think who here would be a serial killer. No doubt I would be the last to find out. I find being invisible works both ways. Often I don't see as much as I used to when I was visible. Being invisible however I'm less likely to become a serial victim.

It's odd how the natural fascination they talk about doesn't include the serial victims. I suppose it is because I taught young children for thirty-five years, but perhaps I am unnatural, because I think about those three little boys. They were three or four years old. How strange that their whole life was only a few years, like a cat. In their world suddenly instead of their mother there was a man who told them how he was going to hurt them and then did it, so that there was nothing in their life at all but fear and pain. So they died in fear and pain. But all the reporters tell is the nature of the mutilations and how decomposed they were, and that's all about them. They were little boys not men. They are not fascinating. They are just dead. But the serial killer they tell all about over and over and discuss his psychology and how his parents caused him to be so fascinating, and he lives forever, as witness Jack the Ripper and Hitler the Ripper. Everyone around here certainly remembers the name of the man who serially raped and photographed the tortured little boys before he serially murdered them. He was named Westley Dodd but what were their names?

Of course we the people murdered him back. That was what he wanted. He wanted us to murder him. I cannot decide if hanging him was a mass murder or a serial murder. We all did it, like a war, so it is a mass murder, but we each did it, democratically, so I suppose it is serial, too. I would as soon be a serial victim as a serial murderer, but I was not given the choice.

My choices have become less. I never had a great many, as my sexual impulses were not appropriate to my position in life, and no one I fell in love with knew it. I am glad when Ether turns up in a different place as it is kind of like a new choice of where to live, only I didn't have to make it. I am capable only of very small choices. What to eat for breakfast, oatmeal or corn flakes, or perhaps only a piece of fruit? Kiwi fruits were fifteen cents apiece at the grocery and I bought half a dozen. A while ago they were the most exotic thing, from New Zealand I think and a dollar each, and now they raise them all over the Willamette Valley. But then, the Willamette Valley may be quite exotic to a person in New Zealand. I like the way they're cool in your mouth, the same way the flesh of them looks cool, a smooth green you can see into, like jade stone. I still see things like that perfectly clearly. It's only with people that my eyes are more and more transparent, so that I don't always see what they're doing, and so that they can look right through me as if my eyes were air and say, "Hi, Emma, how's life treating you?"

Life's treating me like a serial victim, thank you.

I wonder if she sees me or sees through me. I don't dare look. She is shy and lost in her crystal dreams. If only I could look after her. She needs looking after. A cup of tea. Herbal tea, echinacea maybe, I think her immune system needs strengthening. She is not a practical person. I am a very practical person. Far below her dreams.

Lo still sees me. Of course Lo is a serial killer as far as birds are concerned, and moles, but although it upsets me when the bird's not dead yet it's not the same as the man taking photographs. Mr. Hiddenstone once told me that cats have the instinct to let a mouse or bird stay alive awhile in order to take it to the kittens and train them to hunt, so what seems to be cruelty is thoughtfulness. Now I know that some tom cats kill kittens, and I don't think any tom ever raised kittens and trained them thoughtfully to hunt. The queen cat does that. A tom cat is the Jack the Ripper of the Royal Family. But Lo is neutered, so he might behave like a queen or at least like a kind of uncle if there were kittens around, and bring them his birds to hunt. I don't know. He doesn't mix with other cats much. He stays pretty close to home, keeping an eye on the birds and moles and me. I know that my invisibility is not universal when I wake up in the middle of the night and Lo is sitting on the bed right beside my pillow purring and looking very intently at me. It's a strange thing to do, a little uncanny. His eyes wake me, I think. But it's a good waking, knowing that he can see me, even in the dark.

Edna

All right now, I want an answer. All my life since I was fourteen I have been making my soul. I don't know what else to call it, that's what I called it then, when I was fourteen and came into the possession of my life and the knowledge of my responsibility. Since then I have not had time to find a better name for it. The word responsible means that you have to answer. You can't not answer. You'd might rather not answer, but you have to. When you answer you are making your soul, so that it has a shape to it, and size, and some staying power. I understood that, I came into that knowledge, when I was thirteen and early fourteen, that long winter in the Siskiyous. All right, so ever since then, more or less, I have worked according to that understanding. And I have worked. I have done what came into my hands to do, and I've done it the best I could and with all the mind and strength I had to give to it. There have been jobs, waitressing and clerking, but first of all and always the ordinary work of raising the children and keeping the house so that people can live decently and in health and some degree of peace of mind. Then there is responding to the needs of men. That seems like it should come first. People might say I never thought of anything but answering what men asked, pleasing men and pleasing myself, and goodness knows such questions are a joy to answer if asked by a pleasant man. But in the order of my mind, the children come before the fathers of the children. Maybe I see it that way because I was the eldest daughter and there were four younger than me and my father had gone off. Well, all right then, those are my responsibilities as I see them, those are the questions I have tried always to answer: can people live in this house, and how does a child grow up rightly, and how to be trustworthy.

But now I have my own question. I never asked questions, I was so busy answering them, but am sixty years old this winter and think I should have time for a question. But it's hard to ask. Here it is. It's like all the time I was working keeping house and raising the kids and making love and earning our keep I thought there was going to come a time or there would be some place where all of it all came together. Like it was words I was saying, all my life, all the kinds of work, just a word here and a word there, but finally all the words would make a sentence, and I could read the sentence. I would have made my soul and know what it was for.

But I have made my soul and I don't know what to do with it. Who wants it? I have lived sixty years. All I'll do from now on is the same as what I have done only less of it, while I get weaker and sicker and smaller all the time, shrinking and shrinking around myself, and die. No matter what I did, or made, or know. The words don't mean anything. I ought to talk with Emma about this. She's the only one who doesn't say stuff like, "You're only as old as you think you are," "Oh Edna you'll never be old," rubbish like that. Toby Walker wouldn't talk that way either, but he doesn't say much at all any more. Keeps his sentence to himself. My kids that still live here, Archie and Sook, they don't want to hear anything about it. Nobody young can afford to believe in getting old.

So is all the responsibility you take only useful then, but no use later—disposable? What's the use, then? All the work you did is just gone. It doesn't make anything. But I may be wrong. I hope so, I would like to have more trust in dying. Maybe it's worth while, like some kind of answering, coming into another place. Like I felt that winter in the Siskiyous, walking on the snow road between black firs under all the stars, that I was the same size as the universe, the same *thing* as the universe. And if I kept on walking ahead there was this glory waiting for me. In time I would come into glory. I knew that. So that's what I made my soul for. I made it for glory.

And I have known a good deal of glory. I'm not ungrateful. But it doesn't last. It doesn't come together to make a place where you can live, a house. It's gone and the years go. What's left? Shrinking and forgetting and thinking about aches and acid indigestion and cancers and pulse rates and bunions until the whole world is a room that smells like urine, is that what all the work comes to, is that the end of the babies' kicking legs, the children's eyes, the loving hands, the wild rides, the light on water, the stars over the snow? Somewhere inside it all there has to still be the glory.

Ervin Muth

I have been watching Mr. "Toby" Walker for a good while, checking up
on things, and if I happened to be called upon to I could state with fair
certainty that this "Mr. Walker" is *not an American*. My research has taken
me considerably farther afield than that. But there are these "gray areas"
or some things which many people as a rule are unprepared to accept. It
takes training.

My attention was drawn to these kind of matters in the first
place by scrutinizing the town records on an entirely different subject
of research. Suffice it to say that I was checking the title on the Fane
place at the point in time when Mrs. Osey Jean Fane put the property
into the hands of Ervin Muth Relaty, of which I am proprietor. There
had been a dispute concerning the property line on the east side of the
Fane property in 1939 into which, due to being meticulous concerning
these kind of detailed responsibilities, I checked. To my surprise I was
amazed to discover that the adjoining lot, which had been developed in
1906, had been in the name of Tobinye Walker since that date, 1906! I
naturally assumed at that point in time that this "Tobinye Walker" was
"Mr. Toby Walker's" father and thought little more about the issue until
my researches into another matter, concerning the Essel/Emmer lots, in
the town records indicated that the name "Tobinye Walker" was shown
as purchaser of a livery stable on that site (on Main St. between Rash St.
and Goreman Ave.) in 1880.

While purchasing certain necessaries in the Needless Grocery Store
soon after, I encountered Mr. Walker in person. I remarked in a jocular
vein that I had been meeting his father and grandfather. This was of
course a mere pleasantry. Mr. "Toby" Walker responded in what struck
me as a suspicious fashion. There was some taking aback going on.
Although with laughter. His exact words, to which I can attest, were the
following: "I had no idea that you were capable of travelling in time!"

This was followed by my best efforts to seriously inquire concerning
the persons of his same name which my researches in connection with
my work as a relator had turned up. These were only met with facetious
remarks such as, "I've lived here quite a while, you see," and, "Oh, I

remember when Lewis and Clark came through," a statement in reference to the celebrated explorers of the Oregon Trail, who I ascertained later to have been in Oregon in 1806.

Soon after, Mr. Toby Walker *"walked"* away, thus ending the conversation.

I am convinced by evidence that "Mr. Walker" is an illegal immigrant from a foreign country who has assumed the name of a Founding Father of this fine community, that is to wit the Tobinye Walker who purchased the livery stable in 1880. I have my reasons.

My research shows conclusively that the Lewis and Clark Expedition sent by President Thos. Jefferson did not pass through any of the localities which our fine community of Ether has occupied over the course of its history. Ether never got that far north.

If Ether is to progress to fulfill its destiny as a Destination Resort on the beautiful Oregon Coast and Desert as I visualize it with a complete downtown entertainment center and entrepreneurial business community, including hub motels, RV facilities, and a Theme Park, the kind of thing that is represented by "Mr." Walker will have to go. It is the American way to buy and sell houses and properties continually in the course of moving for the sake of upward mobility and self-improvement. Stagnation is the enemy of the American way. The same person owning the same property since 1906 is unnatural and Unamerican. Ether is an American town and moves all the time. That is its destiny. I can call myself an expert.

Starra Walinow Amethyst

I keep practicing love. I was in love with that French actor Gerard but it's really hard to say his last name. Frenchmen attract me. When I watch *Star Trek The Next Generation* reruns I'm in love with Captain Jean-Luc Picard, but I can't stand Commander Riker. I used to be in love with Heathcliff when I was twelve and Miss Freff gave me *Wuthering Heights* to read. And I was in love with Sting for a while before he got weirder. Sometimes I think I am in love with Lieutenant Worf but that is pretty weird, with all those sort of wrinkles and horns on his forehead, since he's a Klingon, but that's not really what's weird. I mean it's just in the TV that he's an alien. Really he is a human named Michael Dorn. That is so weird to me. I mean I never have seen a real black person except in movies and TV. Everybody in Ether is white. So a black person would actually be an alien here. I thought what it would be like if somebody like that came into like the drug store, really tall, with that dark brown skin and dark eyes and those very soft lips that look like they could get hurt so easily, and asked for something in that really, really deep voice. Like, "Where would I find the aspirin?" And I would show him where the aspirin kind of stuff is. He would be standing beside me in front of the shelf, really big and tall and dark, and I'd feel warmth coming out of him like out of an iron woodstove. He'd say to me in a very low voice, "I don't belong in this town," and I'd say back, "I don't either," and he'd say, "Do you want to come with me?" only really really nicely, not like a come-on but like two prisoners whispering how to get out of prison together. I'd nod, and he'd say, "Back of the gas station, at dusk."

At dusk.

I love that word. Dusk. It sounds like his voice.

Sometimes I feel weird thinking about him like this. I mean because he is actually real. If it was just Worf, that's OK, because Worf is just this alien in some old reruns of a show. But there is actually Michael Dorn. So thinking about him in a sort of story that way makes me uncomfortable sometimes, because it's like I was making him a toy, something I can do anything with, like a doll. That seems like it was unfair to him. And it makes me sort of embarrassed when I think about how he actually has his own life with nothing to do with this dumb girl in some hick town he never heard of. So I try to make up somebody else to make that kind of stories about. But it doesn't work.

I really tried this spring to be in love with Morrie Stromberg, but it didn't work. He's really beautiful-looking. It was when I saw him shooting baskets that I thought maybe I could be in love with him. His legs and arms are long and smooth and he moves smooth and looks kind of like a mountain lion, with a low forehead and short dark blond hair, tawny colored. But all he ever does is hang out with Joe's crowd and talk about sport scores and cars, and once in class he was talking with Joe about me so I could hear, like, "Oh yeah Starra, wow, *she* reads *books*," not really mean, but kind of like I was like an alien from another planet, just totally absolutely strange. Like Worf or Michael Dorn would feel here. Like he meant OK, it's OK to be like that only not here. Somewhere else, OK? As if Ether wasn't already somewhere else. I mean, didn't it use to be the Indians that lived here, and now there aren't any of them either? So who belongs here and where does it belong?

About a month ago Mom told me the reason she left my father. I don't remember anything like that. I don't remember any father. I don't remember anything before Ether. She says we were living in Seattle and they had a store where they sold crystals and oils and New Age stuff, and when she got up one night to go to the bathroom he was in my room holding me. She wanted to tell me everything about how he was holding me and stuff, but I just went, "So, like, he was molesting me." And she went, "Yeah," and I said, "So what did you do?" I thought they would have had a big fight. But she said she didn't say anything, because she was afraid of him. She said, "See, to him it was like he owned me and you. And when I didn't go along with that, he would get real crazy." I think they were into a lot of pot and heavy stuff, she talks about that sometimes. So anyway next day when he went to the store she just took some of the crystals and stuff they kept at home, we still have them, and got some money they kept in a can in the kitchen just like she does here, and got on the bus to Portland with me. Somebody she met there gave us a ride here. I don't remember any of that. It's like I was born here. I asked did he ever try to look for her, and she said she didn't know but if he did he'd have a hard time finding her here. She changed her last name to Amethyst, which is her favorite stone. Walinow was her real name. She says it's Polish.

I don't know what his name was. I don't know what he did. I don't care. It's like nothing happened. I'm never going to belong to anybody.

What I know is this, I am going to love people. They will never know it. But I am going to be a great lover. I know how. I have practiced. It isn't when you belong to somebody or they belong to you or stuff. That's like Chelsey getting married to Tim because she wanted to have the wedding and the husband and a no-wax kitchen floor. She wanted stuff to belong to.

I don't want stuff, but I want practice. Like we live in this shack with no kitchen let alone a no-wax floor, and we cook on a trashburner, with a lot of crystals around, and cat pee from the strays Mom takes in, and Mom does stuff like sweeping out for Myrella's beauty parlor, and gets zits because she eats Hostess Twinkies instead of food. Mom needs to get it together. But I need to give it away.

I thought maybe the way to practice love was to have sex so I had sex with Danny last summer. Mom bought us condoms and made me hold hands with her around a bayberry candle and talk about the Passage Into Womanhood. She wanted Danny to be there too but I talked her out of it. The sex was OK but what I was really trying to do was be in love. It didn't work. Maybe it was the wrong way. He just got used to getting sex and so he kept coming around all fall, going "Hey Starra baby you know you need it." He wouldn't even say that it was him that needed it. If I need it, I can do it a lot better myself than he can. I didn't tell him that. Although I nearly did when he kept not letting me alone after I told him to stop. If he hadn't finally started going with Dana I might would have told him.

I don't know anybody else here I can be in love with. I wish I could practice on Archie but what's the use while there's Gracie Fane? It would just be dumb. I thought about asking Archie's father Mr. Hiddenstone if I could work on his ranch, next time we get near it. I could still come see Mom, and maybe there would be like ranch hands or cowboys. Or Archie would come out sometimes and there wouldn't be Gracie. Or actually there's Mr. Hiddenstone. He looks like Archie. Actually handsomer. But I guess is too old. He has a face like the desert. I noticed his eyes are the same color as Mom's turquoise ring. But I don't know if he needs a cook or anything and I suppose fifteen is too young.

J. Needless

Never have figured out where the Hohovars come from. Somebody said White Russia. That figures. They're all big and tall and heavy with hair so blond it's white and those little blue eyes. They don't look at you. Noses like new potatoes. Women don't talk. Kids don't talk. Men talk like, "Vun case yeast peggets, tree case piggle beet." Never say hello, never say good-bye, never say thanks. But honest. Pay right up in cash. When they come in town they're all dressed head to foot, the women in these long dresses with a lot of fancy stuff around the bottom and sleeves, the little girls just the same as the women, even the babies in the same long stiff skirts, all of them with bonnet things that hide their hair. Even the babies don't look up. Men and boys in long pants and shirt and coat even when it's desert here and a hundred and five in July. Something like those ammish folk on the east coast, I guess. Only the Hohovars have buttons. A lot of buttons. The vest things the women wear have about a thousand buttons. Men's flies the same. Must slow 'em down getting to the action. But everybody says buttons are no problem when they get back to their community. Everything off. Strip naked to go to their church. Tom Sunn swears to it, and Corrie says she used to sneak out there more than once on Sunday with a bunch of other kids to see the Hohovars all going over the hill buck naked, singing in their language. That would be some sight, all those tall, heavy-fleshed, white-skinned, big-ass, big-tit women parading over the hill. Barefoot, too. What the hell they do in church I don't know. Tom says they commit fornication but Tom Sunn don't know shit from a hole in the ground. All talk. Nobody I know has ever been over that hill.

Some Sundays you can hear them singing.

Now religion is a curious thing in America. According to the Christians there is only one of anything. On the contrary there seems to me to be one or more of everything. Even here in Ether we have, that I know of, Baptists of course, Methodists, Church of Christ, Lutheran, Presbyterian, Catholic though no church in town, a Quaker, a lapsed Jew, a witch, the Hohovars, and the gurus or whatever that lot in the grange are. This is not counting most people, who have no religious affiliation except on impulse.

That is a considerable variety for a town this size. What's more, they try out each other's churches, switch around. Maybe the nature of the town makes us restless. Anyhow people in Ether generally live a long time, though not as long as Toby Walker. We have time to try out different things. My daughter Corrie has been a Baptist as a teen-ager, a Methodist while in love with Jim Fry, then had a go at the Lutherans. She was married Methodist but is now the Quaker, having read a book. This may change, as lately she has been talking to the witch, Pearl W. Amethyst, and reading another book, called *Crystals and You.*

Edna says the book is all tosh. But Edna has a harder mind than most.

Edna is my religion, I guess. I was converted years ago.

As for the people in the grange, the guru people, they caused some stir when they arrived ten years ago, or is it twenty now. Maybe it was in the sixties. Seems like they've been there a long time when I think about it. My wife was still alive. Anyhow, that's a case of religion mixed up some way with politics, not that it isn't always.

When they came to Ether they had a hell of a lot of money to throw around, though they didn't throw much my way. Bought the old grange and thirty acres of pasture adjacent. Put a fence right round and God damn if they didn't electrify that fence. I don't mean the little jolt you might run in for steers but a kick would kill an elephant. Remodeled the old grange and built on barns and barracks and even a generator. Everybody inside the fence was to share everything in common with everybody else inside the fence. Though from outside the fence it looked like the guru shared a lot more of it than the rest of 'em. That was the political part. Socialism. The bubonic socialism. Rats carry it and there is no vaccine. I tell you people here were upset. Thought the whole population behind the iron curtain plus all the hippies in California were moving in next Tuesday. Talked about bringing in the National Guard to defend the rights of citizens. Personally I'd of preferred the hippies over the National Guard. Hippies were unarmed. They killed by smell alone, as people said. But at the time there was a siege mentality here. A siege inside the grange, with their electric fence and their socialism, and a siege outside the grange, with their rights of citizens to be white and not foreign and not share anything with anybody.

At first the guru people would come into the town in their orange color T-shirts, doing a little shopping, talking politely. Young people got invited into the grange. They were calling it the osh rom by then. Corrie told me about the altar with the marigolds and the big photograph of Guru Jaya Jaya Jaya. But they weren't really friendly people and they didn't get friendly treatment. Pretty soon they never came into town, just drove in and out the road gate in their orange Buicks. Sometime along in there the Guru Jaya Jaya Jaya was supposed to come from India to visit the osh rom. Never did. Went to South America instead and founded an osh rom for old Nazis, they say. Old Nazis probably have more money to share with him than young Oregonians do. Or maybe he came to find his osh rom and it wasn't where they told him.

It has been kind of depressing to see the T-shirts fade and the Buicks break down. I don't guess there's more than two Buicks and ten, fifteen people left in the osh rom. They still grow garden truck, eggplants, all kinds of peppers, greens, squash, tomatoes, corn, beans, blue and rasp and straw and marion berries, melons. Good quality stuff. Raising crops takes some skill here where the climate will change overnight. They do beautiful irrigation and don't use poisons. Seen them out there picking bugs off the plants by hand. Made a deal with them some years ago to supply my produce counter and have not regretted it. Seems like Ether is meant to be a self-sufficient place. Every time I'd get a routine set up with a supplier in Cottage Grove or Prineville, we'd switch. Have to call up and say sorry, we're on the other side of the mountains again this week, cancel those cantaloupes. Dealing with the guru people is easier. They switch along with us.

What they believe in aside from organic gardening I don't know. Seems like the Guru Jaya Jaya Jaya would take some strenuous believing, but people can put their faith in anything, I guess. Hell, I believe in Edna.

Archie Hiddenstone

Dad got stranded in town again last week. He hung around awhile to see if the range would move back east, finally drove his old Ford over to Eugene and up the McKenzie River highway to get back to the ranch. Said he'd like to stay but Charlie Echeverria would be getting into some kind of trouble if he did. He just doesn't like to stay away from the place more than a night or two. It's hard on him when we turn up way over here on the coast like this.

I know he wishes I'd go back with him. I guess I ought to. I ought to live with him. I could see Mama every time Ether was over there. It isn't that. I ought to get it straight in my mind what I want to do. I ought to go to college. I ought to get out of this town. I ought to get away.

I don't think Gracie ever actually has seen me. I don't do anything she can see. I don't drive a semi.

I ought to learn. If I drove a truck she'd see me. I could come through Ether off the I—5 or down from 84, wherever. Like that shit kept coming here last summer she was so crazy about. Used to come into the Seven-Eleven all the time for Gatorade. Called me Boy. Hey boy gimme the change in quarters. She'd be sitting up in his eighteen-wheeler playing with the gears. She never came in. Never even looked. I used to think maybe she was sitting there with her jeans off. Bareass on that truck seat. I don't know why I thought that. Maybe she was.

I don't want to drive a God damn stinking semi or try to feed a bunch of steers in a God damn desert either or sell God damn Hostess Twinkies to crazy women with purple hair either. I ought to go to college. Learn something. Drive a sports car. A Miata. Am I going to sell Gatorade to shits all my life? I ought to be somewhere that is somewhere.

I dreamed the moon was paper and I lit a match and set fire to it. It flared up just like a newspaper and started dropping down fire on the roofs, scraps of burning. Mama came out of the grocery and said, "That'll take the ocean." Then I woke up. I heard the ocean where the sagebrush hills had been.

I wish I could make Dad proud of me anywhere but the ranch. But that's the only place he lives. He won't ever ask me to come live there. He knows I can't. I ought to.

Edna

Oh how my children tug at my soul just as they tugged at my breasts, so that I want to yell Stop! I'm dry! You drank me dry years ago! Poor sweet stupid Archie. What on earth to do for him. His father found the desert he needed. All Archie's found is a tiny little oasis he's scared to leave.

I dreamed the moon was paper, and Archie came out of the house with a box of matches and tried to set it afire, and I was frightened and ran into the sea.

Ady came out of the sea. There were no tracks on that beach that morning except his, coming up towards me from the breaker line. I keep thinking about the men lately. I keep thinking about Needless. I don't know why. I guess because I never married him. Some of them I wonder why I did, how it came about. There's no reason in it. Who'd ever have thought I'd ever sleep with Tom Sunn? But how could I go on saying no to a need like that? His fly bust every time he saw me across the street. Sleeping with him was like sleeping in a cave. Dark, uncomfortable, echoes, bears farther back in. Bones. But a fire burning. Tom's true soul is that fire burning, but he'll never know it. He starves the fire and smothers it with wet ashes, he makes himself the cave where he sits on cold ground gnawing bones. Women's bones.

But Mollie is a brand snatched from his burning. I miss Mollie. Next time we're over east again I'll go up to Pendleton and see her and the grandbabies. She doesn't come. Never did like the way Ether ranges. She's a stayputter. Says all the moving around would make the children insecure. It didn't make her insecure in any harmful way that I can see. It's her Eric that would disapprove. He's a snob. Prison clerk. What a job. Walk out of a place every night where the others are all locked in, how's that for a ball and chain? Sink you if you ever tried to swim.

Where did Ady swim up from I wonder? Somewhere deep. Once he said he was Greek, once he said he worked on a Australian ship, once he said he had lived on an island in the Philippines where they speak a language nobody else anywhere speaks, once he said he was born in a canoe at sea. It could all have been true. Or not. Maybe Archie should go to sea. Join the Navy or the Coast Guard. But no, he'd drown.

Tad knows he'll never drown. He's Ady's son, he can breathe water. I wonder where Tad is now. That is a tugging too, that not knowing, not knowing where the child is, an aching pull you stop noticing because it never stops. But sometimes it turns you, you find you're facing another direction, like your body was caught by the thorn of a blackberry, by an undertow. The way the moon pulls the tides.

I keep thinking about Archie, I keep thinking about Needless. Ever since I saw him look at Sook. I know what it is, it's that other dream I had. Right after the one with Archie. I dreamed something, it's hard to get hold of, something about being on this long long beach, like I was beached, yes, that's it, I was stranded, and I couldn't move. I was drying up and I couldn't get back to the water. Then I saw somebody walking towards me from way far away down the beach. His tracks in the sand were ahead of him. Each time he stepped in one, in the footprint, it was gone when he lifted his foot. He kept coming straight to me and I knew if he got to me I could get back in the water and be all right. When he got close up I saw it was him. It was Needless. That's an odd dream.

If Archie went to sea he'd drown. He's a drylander, like his father.

Sookie, now, Sook is Toby Walker's daughter. She knows it. She told me, once, I didn't tell her. Sook goes her own way. I don't know if he knows it. I don't think so. She has my eyes and hair. And there were some other possibilities. And I never felt it was the right thing to tell a man unless he asked. Toby didn't ask, because of what he believed about himself. But I knew the night, I knew the moment she was conceived. I felt the child to be leap in me like a fish leaping in the sea, a salmon coming up the river, leaping the rocks and rapids, shining. Toby had told me he couldn't have children—"not with any woman born," he said, with a sorrowful look. He came pretty near telling me where he came from, that night. But I didn't ask. Maybe because of what I believe about myself, that I only have the one life and no range, no freedom to walk in the hidden places.

Anyhow, I told him that that didn't matter, because if I felt like it I could conceive by taking thought. And for all I know that's what happened. I thought Sookie and out she came, red as a salmon, quick and shining. She is the most beautiful child, girl, woman. What does she want to stay here in Ether for? Be an old maid teacher like Emma? Pump gas, give perms, clerk in the grocery? Who'll she meet here? Well, God knows I met enough. I like it, she says, I like not knowing where I'll wake up. She's like me. But still there's the tug, the dry longing. Oh, I guess

I had too many children. I turn this way, that way, like a compass with forty Norths. Yet always going on the same way in the end. Fitting my feet into my footprints that disappear behind me.

It's a long way down from the mountains. My feet hurt.

Tobinye Walker

Man is the animal that binds time, they say. I wonder. We're bound by time, bounded by it. We move from a place to another place, but from a time to another time only in memory and intention, dream and prophecy. Yet time travels us. Uses us as its road, going on never stopping always in one direction. No exits off this freeway.

I say *we* because I am a naturalized citizen. I didn't use to be a citizen at all. Time once was to me what my back yard is to Emma's cat. No fences mattered, no boundaries. But I was forced to stop, to settle, to join. I am an American. I am a castaway. I came to grief.

I admit I've wondered if it's my doing that Ether ranges, doesn't stay put. An effect of my accident. When I lost the power to walk straight, did I impart a twist to the locality? Did it begin to travel because my travelling had ceased? If so, I can't work out the mechanics of it. It's logical, it's neat, yet I don't think it's the fact. Perhaps I'm just dodging my responsibility. But to the best of my memory, ever since Ether was a town it's always been a real American town, a place that isn't where you left it. Even when you live there it isn't where you think it is. It's missing. It's restless. It's off somewhere over the mountains, making up in one dimension what it lacks in another. If it doesn't keep moving the malls will catch it. Nobody's surprised it's gone. The white man's his own burden. And nowhere to lay it down. You can leave town easy enough, but coming back is tricky. You come back to where you left it and there's nothing but the parking lot for the new mall and a giant yellow grinning clown made of balloons. Is that all there was to it? Better not believe it, or that's all you'll ever have: blacktop and cinderblock and a blurred photograph of a little boy smiling. The child was murdered along with many others. There's more to it than that, there is an old glory in it, but it's hard to locate, except by accident. Only Roger Hiddenstone can come back when he wants to, riding his old Ford or his old horse, because Roger owns nothing but the desert and a true heart. And of course wherever Edna is, it is. It's where she lives.

I'll make my prophecy. When Starra and Roger lie in each other's tender arms, she sixteen he sixty, when Gracie and Archie shake his pickup truck to pieces making love on the mattress in the back on the road out to the Hohovars, when Ervin Muth and Thomas Sunn get drunk with the farmers in the ashram and dance and sing and cry all night, when Emma Bodely and Pearl Amethyst gaze long into each other's shining eyes among the cats, among the crystals—that same night Needless the grocer will come at last to Edna. To him she will bear no child but joy. And orange trees will blossom in the streets of Ether.

Half Past Four

A NEW LIFE

Stephen blushed. A fair-skinned man, bald to the crown, he blushed clear pink. He hugged Ann with one arm as she kissed his cheek. "Good to see you, honey," he said, freeing himself, glancing past her, and smiling rather desperately. "Ella just went out. Just ten minutes ago. She had to take some typing over to Bill Hoby. Stay around till she gets back, she'd be real sorry to miss you."

"Sure," Ann said. "Mother's fine, she had this flu, but not as bad as some people. You all been OK?"

"Oh, yeah, sure. You want some coffee? Coke? Come on in." He stood aside and followed her through the small living room crowded with blond furniture to the kitchen where yellow metal slat blinds directed sunlight in molten strips onto the counters.

"Hey, it's hot," Ann said.

"Want some coffee? There's this cinnamon and mocha decaf that Ella and I drink a lot. It sure is. Glad it's Saturday. It's up here somewhere."

"I don't want anything."

"Coke?" He closed the cupboard, opened the refrigerator.

"Oh, sure, OK. Diet if you've got it."

She stood by the counter and watched him get the glass and the ice and the bottle, a plastic half-gallon of cola. She did not want to open doors in this kitchen as if prying, as if entitled, or to change the angle of the slat blinds, as she would have done at home, to shut the hot light out. He fixed her a tall red plastic glass of cola, and she drank off half of it. "Oh, yeah!" she said. "OK!"

"Come on outside."

"No ball game?"

"Been doing some gardening. With Toddie."

Ann had assumed that the boy was with his mother, or rather her imagination had linked him to his mother so that if Ella wasn't here Toddie wasn't here; now she felt betrayed.

Indicating where she should go but making her go first, as when he had brought her through the house, her father ushered her to the back-porch door, and stood aside and followed her as she went past the washer and dryer and the mop bucket and some brooms to the screen door and down the single cement step into the back yard.

He batted the screen door shut with one foot and stood beside her on a brick path, two bricklengths wide, that ran along dividing the flowerbeds under the house wall from the small, shrub-circled lawn. Two small iron chairs painted white, with rust stains where the paint had come off, faced each other across a matching table at one side of the grass plot. Beyond them Toddie crouched, turned away, near a big flowering abelia in the shade of the mirrorplant hedge that enclosed the garden.

Toddie was bigger than she had remembered, as broad-backed as a grown man.

"Hey, Toddie. Here's ah, here's Ann!" Stephen said. His fair, tanned face was still pink. Maybe he wasn't blushing, maybe it was the heat. In the enclosed garden the sunlight glaring from the white house wall burned on the skin like an open fire. Had he been going to say, "your sister"? His voice was loud and jovial. Toddie did not respond in any way.

Ann looked around at the garden. It was an airless, grass-floored room with high green walls and a ceiling of brightness. Beautiful pale-colored poppies swayed by the hose rack, growing in clean, weeded dirt. She looked back at them, away from the stocky figure crouched in the shade across the lawn. She did not want to look at him, and her father had no right to make her be with him and look at him, even if it was superstitious, he should think of protecting the baby, but that was stupid, that was superstitious. "Those are really neat," she said, touching the loose, soft petal of an open poppy. "Terrific colors. This is a nice garden, Daddy. You must have been working hard on it."

"Haven't you ever been out back here?"

She shook her head. She had never even been in the bedrooms. She had been three or four times to this house since Stephen and Ella married. Once for Sunday brunch. Ella had served on trays in the living room, and Toddie had watched TV the whole time. The first time she had been in the house was when Ella was one of Stephen's salesgirls, not his wife. They had stopped by her house for her father to leave off some papers or something. Ann had been in high school, she had stood around in the living room while her father and Ella talked about shoe orders. Knowing that Ella had a retarded child, she had hoped that it wouldn't come into the room but all the same had wanted to see it. When Ella's husband died suddenly of something, Ann's father had said solemnly at the dinner table, "Lucky thing they had that house of theirs paid off," and Ann's mother had said, "Poor thing, with that poor child of theirs, what is it, a mongoloid?" and then they had talked about how mongoloids usually died and it was a mercy. But here he was still alive and Stephen was living in his house.

"I need some shade," Ann said, heading for the iron chairs. "Come and talk with me, Daddy."

He followed her. While she sat down and slipped off her sandals to cool her bare feet in the grass, he stood there. She looked up at him. The curve of his bald forehead shone in the sunlight, open and noble as a high hill standing bare above a crowded subdivision. His face was suburban, crowded with features, chin and long lips and nostrils and fleshy nose and the small, clear, anxious blue eyes. Only the forehead that looked like a big California hill had room. "Oh, Daddy," she said, "how you *been?*"

"Just fine. Just fine," he said, half turned away from her. "The Walnut Creek store is going just great. Walking shoes." He bent to uproot a small dandelion from the short, coarse grass. "Walking shoes outsell running shoes two to one at the Mall. So, you been job hunting? You ever talk to Krim?"

"Oh, yeah, couple weeks ago." Ann yawned. The still heat and the smell of newly turned earth made her sleepy. Everything made her sleepy. Waking up made her sleepy. She yawned again. "Excuse me! He said, oh, he said something might would open up in May."

"Good. Good. Good outfit," Stephen said, looking around the garden, and moving a few steps away. "Good contacts."

"But I'll have to stop working in July because of the baby, so I don't know if it's worth it."

"Get to know people, get started," Stephen said indistinctly. He went to the edge of the lawn nearest the abelia and said in a cheerful, loud voice, "Hey, great work there, Toddie! Hey, look at that! That's my boy. All right!"

A blurred, whitish face under dark hair turned up to him for a moment in shadow.

"Look at that. Diggin' up a storm there. You're a real farmer." Stephen turned and spoke to Ann from shade across the white molten air to her strip of shade: "Toddie's going to put in some more flowers here. Bulbs and stuff for fall."

Ann drank her melted-ice water and got up from the dwarf chair that had already stained her white T-shirt with rust. She came over nearer her father and looked at the strip of upturned earth. The big boy crouched motionless, trowel in hand, head sunk.

"Look, why not sort of round off that corner, see," Stephen said to him, going forward to point. "Dig to here, maybe. Think so?"

The boy nodded and began digging, slowly and forcefully. His hands were white and thick, with very short, wide nails rimmed with black dirt.

"What do you think, maybe dig it up clear over to that rose bush. Space out the bulbs better. Think it'd look good?"

Toddie looked up at him again. Ann looked at the blurred mouth, the dark-haired upper lip. "Yeah, uh-huh," Toddie said, and bent to work again.

"Kind of curve it off there at the rose bush," Stephen said. He glanced round at Ann. His face was relaxed, uncrowded. "This guy's a natural farmer," he said. "Get anything to grow. Teachin' me. Isn't that right, Toddie? Teachin' me!"

"I guess," the low voice said. The head stayed bowed, the thick fingers groped in earth.

Stephen smiled at Ann. "Teachin' me," he said.

"That's neat," she said. The sides of her mouth felt very stiff and her throat ached. "Listen, Daddy, I just looked in to say hi on the way to Permanente, I'm supposed to have a check-up. No, look, I'll just leave this in the kitchen and go out the gate there. It's real good to see you, Daddy."

"Got to go already," he said.

"Yeah, I just wanted to say hi since I was over this way. Say hi to Ella for me. I'm sorry I missed her." She had slipped her sandals back on; she took her empty glass into the kitchen, set it in the sink and ran water into it, came out again to her father standing on the brick path, bald to the sun. She put one foot up on the cement step to refasten the sandal. "My ankles were all swelled up," she said. "Dr. Schell took me off salt. I can't put salt on anything, not even eggs."

"Yeah, they say we should all cut down on salt," Stephen said.

"Yeah, that's right." After a pause Ann said, "Only this is because of being pregnant, that I have high blood pressure and this edema stuff. Unless I'm careful." She looked at her father. He was looking across the lawn.

"You know, Daddy, even if the baby doesn't have a father it can have a grandfather," she said. She laughed, and blushed, feeling the red heat mask her face and tingle in her scalp.

"Yeah, well, sure," he said, "I guess, you know," and if he finished the sentence she did not understand it. "We all got to take care," he said.

"Sure. Well, you take care too, Daddy," she said. She came to him to kiss his cheek. She tasted the faint salt of his sweat on her lips as she went along the brick path to the gate next to the trash cans, and let herself out onto the sidewalk under a purple jacaranda in full flower, and fastened the gate behind her.

UNBREAKING

"My back itches."

Ann reached out the garden fork and lightly raked its clawed tines down her brother's spine.

"Not there. There." He wrapped an arm round himself trying to show her the spot, his thick fingers with dirt-caked nails scrabbling in the air.

She hitched forward and scratched his back vigorously with her own fingertips. "That got it?"

"Uh-huh."

"I want some lemonade."

"Uh-huh," Todd said as she got up, whacking dirt off her bare knees. She had to bend at the knees, not at the waist, to reach them.

The yellow kitchen was hot and close like the inside of a room in a beehive, a cell full of yellow light, smelling of sweet wax, airless. A grub would love it. Ann mixed up instant lemonade, poured it over ice in tall plastic glasses, and carried them out, kicking the screen door shut behind her.

"Here you go, Todd."

He straightened up kneeling and took the glass in his left hand without putting down the trowel in his right. He drank off half the lemonade and then stooped to dig again, still holding the glass.

"Put it down there," Ann said, "by the bush."

He put the glass down carefully on the weedy dirt, and went on digging.

"Hey that's good!" Ann said, sucking at her lemonade, her mouth squirting saliva like a lawn sprinkler. She sat down on the grass with her head in the shade and her legs in the sun, and chewed ice slowly.

"You aren't digging," Todd said after a while.

"Nope."

After a while she told him, "Drink your lemonade. The ice is all melting."

He put down the trowel and picked up the glass. After drinking the lemonade he put the empty glass where it had been before.

"Hey, Ann," he said, not digging, but kneeling there with his bare, thick, pale back to her.

"Hey, Todd."

"Is Daddy coming home at Christmas?"

She tried for a moment to figure this one out. She was too sleepy. "No," she said. "He isn't coming home at all. You know that."

"I thought at Christmas," her brother said, barely audible.

"At Christmas he'll be with his new wife, with Marie. That's where he lives now, that's where his home is, in Riverside."

"I thought he might visit. At Christmas."

"No. He won't do that."

Todd was silent. He picked up the trowel and laid it down again. Ann knew he was unsatisfied but she could not figure out what his problem was and did not want any problems. She got her back against the trunk of the camphor tree and sat feeling the sun on her legs and the prickling grass under them and a sweat-drop trickle down between her breasts and the baby move once softly deep in and over on the left side of the universe.

"Maybe we could ask him to come at Christmas," Todd said.

"Honey," Ann said, "we can't do that. He and Mama got divorced so he could marry Marie. Right? And he'll have Christmas with her now. With Marie. And we'll have our Christmas here like always. Right?" She waited for his nod. She was not sure she got one, but went on anyhow. "If you're missing him a lot, Todd, we can write him and tell him that."

"Maybe we could visit him."

Oh, yeah, dandy. Hi Daddy, here's your moron son and your unwed pregnant daughter on welfare, hi Marie! It struck her funny but not enough to laugh. "We can't," she said. "Hey, look. If you dig over to the end there, in front of the roses, we could put in those canna bulbs Mama got, too. They'd look real good there. They'll be red, big red lilies."

Todd picked up the trowel, and then laid it down again in the same place.

"After Christmas he has to come," he said.

"What for? Why does he have to?"

"For the baby," her brother said, very low and blurry

"Oh," Ann said. "Oh, shit. OK. Well. Listen, Toddie. Look. I'm having the baby, right?"

"After Christmas."

"Right. And it will be mine. Ours. You and Mama are going to help me bring it up. Right? And that's all I need. All I want. All the baby wants. Just you and Mama. All right?" She waited for his nod. "You're going to help me with the baby. Tell me when it cries. Play with it. Like that little girl at school, Sandy, that you help with. OK, Toddie?"

"Yeah. Sure," her brother said in the voice he had sometimes, masculine and matter-of-fact, as if a man spoke through him from somewhere else. He knelt erect, his hands splayed on his bluejeaned thighs, his face and torso in shadow illuminated by the glare of sunlight on the grass. "But he's an older parent," he said.

He's an ex-parent, Ann stopped herself from saying. "Right. So what?"

"Older parents often have Down children."

"Older mothers do. Right. So?"

She looked at Todd's round, heavy face, the sparse mustache at the ends of the upper lip, the dark eyes. He looked away.

"So your baby could be a Down baby," he said.

"Sure, it could. But I'm not an older parent, honey."

"But Daddy is."

"Oh," Ann said, and after a pause, "Right." She hitched herself heavily into the shade, with her bare feet in the fresh dirt Todd had been digging up. "OK, listen, Todd. Daddy is your father. And my father. But *not* the *baby's* father. Right?" No nod. "The baby has a different father. You don't know the baby's father. He doesn't live here. He lives in Davis, where I was. And Daddy is—Daddy isn't anything. He isn't interested. He has a new family. A new wife. Maybe they'll have a baby. They can be older parents. But they can't have this baby. I'm having this baby. It's our baby. It doesn't *have* any father. It doesn't have any *grandfather*. It's got me and Mama and you. Right? You're going to be its uncle. Did you know that? Will you be the baby's Uncle Todd?"

"Yeah," Todd said unhappily. "Sure."

A couple of months ago when she was crying all the time she would have cried, but now the universe inside her surrounded her with distance, through which all emotions travelled so far to reach her that they became quiet and smooth, deep and soft, like the big unbreaking waves out in mid-ocean. Instead of crying she thought about crying, the salty ache. She picked up the three-tined garden fork and reached over, trying to scratch Todd's head with it. He had shifted out of reach.

"Hey kids," their mother said, the screen door banging behind her.

"Hey Ella," Ann said.

"Hi Mama," Todd said, turning away, bending to dig.

"Lemonade in the fridge," Ann said.

"What are you doing? Planting those old bulbs? I dug them up I don't know when, I bet they won't grow now. The cannas ought to. Oh I'm so hot! It's so hot downtown!" She came across the lawn in her high-heeled sandals, pantyhose, yellow cotton shirt dress, silk scarf, makeup, nail polish, sprayed set dyed hair, full secretarial uniform, complete armor. She bent over to kiss the top of her son's head, and kicked the sole of Ann's bare foot with the toe of her sandal. "Dirty children," she said. "Oh! It's so hot! I'm going to have a shower!" She went back across the lawn. The screen door banged. Ann imagined the soft folds released from under the girdle, the makeup sluiced away under warm spraying water running down over her first universe, that soft distance where she lived now, joined.

THE TIGER

Ella had on her yellow sleeveless dress with the black patent belt and black jet costume earrings. She had sprayed her hair. "Who's coming?" Ann asked from the couch.

"I told you yesterday. Stephen Sandies." Ella clipped past on her high wedge-heeled sandals like a circus pony on stilts, leaving a faint wake of hairspray smell and perfume.

"What are you wearing?"

"My yellow dress from the boteek."

"I mean perfume, dummy."

"I can't pronounce it," Ella called from the kitchen.

"Jardins de Bagatelle."

"That's it. The bagatelle part is OK. I used to play bagatelle. But I just pointed and said, 'That one.' I was trying testers at Krim's. Do you like it?"

"Yes. I stole some last night."

"What?"

"Never mind."

Ann raised a leg languidly and looked up along it as if sighting. She spread out her toes fanwise to make sights, closed them together, spread them. "Exercises, exercises, *always do* your *exercises*," she chanted, raising the other leg. "Zhardang, zhardang it all to bagatelle."

"What?"

"Nothing, Ma!"

Ella clipped back into the living room with a vase of red cannas. "I see London, I see France," she observed.

"I'm exercising. When Stephen Sandman comes I'll lie here and do breathing exercises, ha-ah-ha-ah-ha-ah-ha-ah. Who is he?"

"Sandies. He's in Accounting. I asked him to come in for a drink before we go out."

"Go out where?"

"The new Vietnamese place. They only have a beer and wine license."

"Is he nice? Stephen Sandpiper?"

"I don't know him well," Ella said primly. "That is, of course we've known each other at the office slightly for years. He and his wife were divorced a couple of years ago now."

"Ha-ah-ha-ah-ha-ah," Ann said.

Ella stood back from the arrangement of cannas. "Do they look all right?"

"Terrific. What do you want to do about me? Shall I lie here showing my underpants and doing puppy breathing?"

"We'll sit out on the patio, I thought."

"Then the cannas are just for the walk-through."

"And you're very welcome to join us, dear."

"We could impress this guy," Ann said, sitting up and assuming half-lotus position. "I could put on an apron and be the maid. Do we have an apron? One of those little white cap things. I could serve the canapés. Canapé, Mr. Sandpuppy? Canopee, Mr. Sandpoopoo?"

"Oh, hush," her mother said. "You're silly. I hope it'll be warm enough on the patio." She clipped back to the kitchen.

"If you really want to impress him," Ann called, "you'd better hide me."

Ella appeared instantly in the doorway, her mouth drawn in, her small blue eyes burning like the lights on airfields. "I will not listen to you talk that way, Ann!"

"I meant, I'm such a slob, my panties show, I haven't washed my hair, and look at the bottoms of my feet, God."

Ella continued to glare for a moment, then turned and went back into the kitchen. Ann hauled herself out of half-lotus and onto her feet. She came to the kitchen doorway.

"I just thought maybe you'd rather be alone. You know."

"I would like him to meet my daughter," Ella said, fiercely mashing cream cheese.

"I'll get dressed. You smell terrific. He'll die, you know." Ann snuffled around the base of her mother's neck, the creamy, slightly freckled skin in which two soft, round creases appeared when she turned her head, weakly crying, "Don't, don't, it tickles!"

"Vamp," Ann whispered hotly behind her mother's ear.

"Stop!"

Ann went off to the bathroom and showered. Enjoying the sound and the steam and the sluicing of the hot water, she took a long time about it. As she came naked out into the hallway she heard a man's voice and leaped back into the bathroom, pulling the door shut, then reopening it slightly to listen. They had got about as far as the cannas. She slipped out of the bathroom and down the hall to her room. She pulled on bikinis and the T-shirt dress that slithered pleasantly on her skin and embraced her rounded belly in forgiving shapelessness. She blowdried her hair on hot while she teased it with her fingers, put on lipstick and wiped it off, checked in the long mirror, and went sedate and barefoot down the hall, past the cannas, out onto the little flagged terrace.

Stephen Sandies, wearing a cool grey canvas sports coat and white shirt without tie, stood up and gave her a firm handshake. His smile was white but not too. Dark hair greying nicely. Trim, tan, fit, around fifty, stern mouth but not pursy, everything under control. Cool, but not sweating to keep cool. Would do. Good going, Ma, pour on the Zhardang de Big Hotel! Ann winked at her mother, who recrossed her ankles and said, "I forgot the lemonade, dear, if that's what you want? It's in the icebox." Ella was the last person in the Western Industrial Hegemony who said icebox, or canapé, or crossed her legs at the ankles. When Ann returned with a glass of lemonade, Stephen was talking. She sat down in a white webbed chair. Quietly, like a good girl. She sipped. They were on their second margaritas. Stephen's voice was soft, with a kind of burring or slight huskiness in it, very sexy, a kind voice. Drink your lemonade now like a good girl and slope off. Slope off where? The belly telly in the bedroom? Shit. Forget it. Hang on, it's been a nice day. Keep playing tag in Bagatelle Gardens. Can't catch me. What was he saying about his son?

"Well," he said, and fetched a sigh. Fetched it from deep inside, a long haul. He looked up at Ella with the wry, dry grin appropriate to the question, "Do you really want to hear all this?"

She's supposed to say no?

"Yes," Ella said.

"Well, it's a long, dull story, really. Legal battles are dull. Not like Hollywood courtroom scenes. To put it as briefly as possible, when Marie and I separated I was so angry and so . . . bewildered, really, that I agreed to several arrangements too hastily. To put it briefly, I've been forced to the conclusion that she's not fit to bring up my son. So we're into the classic custody battle. I'd rather, frankly, that she didn't even have visiting rights, but I'll compromise if I have to. Judges favor the mother, of course. But I intend to win. And I will. My lawyers are very good. If only the process were faster. It's very painful to me to wait through the delays and procedures. Every day he's with her will have to be undone. It's as if it were a disease for which there is a cure, and I have the cure. But they won't let me have him to begin the cure." Wow. So much conviction, and so quiet. So certain. Ann studied his face briefly sidelong. Handsome, stern, kind, sad, like God. Was he possibly very very very conceited? Was he possibly right?

"Is it—Is she drinking?" Ella hazarded, sounding weak, and setting down her glass.

"Not to the point of alcoholism," Stephen replied in his gently measured way. He looked down into his margarita-slush. "You know,

I don't like to say these things. We were married for eleven years. There were good times."

"Oh, yes," Ella murmured pathetically, squirming with the pain his understatement concealed. But why didn't *he* squirm?

"But," he said. "Well. Far be it from me! God knows. No job, but a credit card—Where my child-support payments go I don't know. Three schools for Todd in two years. Disorder, bohemianism—but if that were all—it isn't that. It's the exposure of my child to immorality."

Ann was terrified. She had not expected this. Debt, dirt, disorder, OK, but immorality—her child would be exposed, exposed to immorality. Naked, soft, helpless, exposed. She would expose it by giving birth to it. By being its mother she would expose it to the dirt, the disorder, the immorality of a woman's life, her life. Its father would come from Riverside with a court order on clean, white paper. It would be taken from her, taken into custody. She would never see it. No visiting rights. No birth rights. It would be stillborn, it would die of immorality even before she could expose it.

Ella's mouth was drawn in, her eyes cast down. Stephen had just said a word to her that explained all. And Ann had not been listening. Had the word been "woman"?

"You see why I can't leave the boy there," Stephen said, and though not squirming he was in pain, no doubt of it, his hand tight on the arm of the chair.

Ella shook her head in agreement.

"And this—woman's friends. All—the same kind. Flaunting it."

Ann saw the monstrous regiment.

Stephen's head moved in tiny, rigid spasms as he spoke. "And the boy alone, in that. With them. Eight years old. A good kid. Straight as an arrow. I can't. I can't stand. To think of him. With them. Learning. That."

Each staccato burst hit Ann like machine-gun fire. She set down her lemonade glass on the flagstone, got carefully to her feet, and slipped away from Margaritaville with a vague smile, bleeding, bleeding evil monthly blood, nine months' worth bleeding from the holes he had shot in her. Behind her, her mother's voice said something consolatory to the man and then was raised, thin and weak, to cry, "Ann?"

"Back in a minute, Mama."

Passing the cannas flaming in twilight, she heard Ella say, "Ann is taking a year off from college. She's five months pregnant." She spoke in a strange tone, warning, boastful. Flaunting.

Ann went on to the bathroom. She had left her old underpants and shorts and T-shirt all over the bathroom when she showered, and he would have come to pee before they left and seen them and then her mother would have too and died. She picked things up. The bullet holes had been closed by her mother's voice. The blood had sublimated and etherealised into tears. She snivelled as she dropped dirty clothes and wet towels into the dirty-clothes hamper, she cried gratefully, she washed her face and opened the bottle of Jardins de Bagatelle, the perfume of the mother tiger, and put it on her hands and on her face where she could smell it.

LIVING IN YINLAND

Duffy slung on her knapsack and went out, saying over her shoulder, "Back around seven."

Her motorcycle revving and roaring off left silence behind. The Sunday paper was all over the living room. Nobody had got up till after noon.

"God, you know," Ella said, dropping the comics, "we get our periods exactly the same time now, within a day?"

"Hey, yeah? I've heard of that. That's kind of neat."

"Yeah, only I was beginning to stop having periods most of the time. Oh well. Tit for tat, as they say." Ella snorted. "I want some more coffee." She got up and shuffled off to the kitchen. "You want some?" she called.

"Not now."

Ella shuffled back in. She wore pink feather mules with low heels that flopped off if she lifted her foot.

"Those are really frivolous, El. I mean seriously frivolous."

"Duffy ordered them for me from some mail order catalogue." Ella sat down on the couch again, set her coffee cup on the table, and lifted one leg to look at the slipper. "She thought they'd suit me. Actually it's kind of like the things Stephen used to buy me sometimes. Mistakes."

"Like the stuff you make at school and then your parents have to use them."

"Like women buying men ties, it really is true. I love paisley and Stephen hated it, he thought paisley looked like bugs, those curvy sort of shapes, you know, and I didn't realise it and I always bought him these beautiful paisley ties."

"Isn't it weird how . . ."

"How what?"

"I don't know, how we don't get through to each other, you know, only we sort of do, only not where we thought we were. I mean, like you're *wearing* those. Well, and like both of us thinking the other one would like disapprove, and all that stuff you went through psyching yourself up to call me about selling Mother's house. Everything backwards. But it works. Sometimes."

"Yeah," Ella said. "Sometimes." She had put both pink-feathered feet up on the edge of the coffee table, and gazed at them, her small, bright, light-blue eyes stern, judgmental. Her half-sister Ann, a much larger woman fifteen years younger, sat on the floor amidst the comics and classifieds and coffee cups, wearing purple sweatpants and a red sweatshirt with an expressionless yellow circle-face on it labelled, "Have A Day."

"Mom used that chicken ashtray I made in fourth grade till she died," Ella said.

"Even after she quit smoking. El, did you like my dad?"

Ella gazed at her feet. "Yeah," she said. "I liked him. You know, I didn't ever remember a whole lot about my own father. I was only six when he got killed and he'd been overseas a year. I don't think I even cried except because Mom cried. So I wasn't comparing, or anything. I guess what I didn't like when Mom and Bill married was I missed her and me being together. Like this, you know, slopping around. Women slopping around. That's partly why I like it with Duffy. Only Duffy's more, well, it has to do with sex, not gender, I guess. With Duffy it's not so easy, you have to watch it. With Mom it was so easy. With you it's easy."

"Too easy, sort of?"

"I don't know. Maybe. I like it, though. Anyhow. I wasn't ever jealous of Bill or anything. He was a sweet guy. I guess in fact I had a crush on him for a while. Trying to compete with Mom. Practicing . . ."

Ella's smile, which was infrequent, curved her long, thin lips into a charming half-circle.

"I got a crush on everybody. My math teacher. The bus driver. The paper boy. God, I used to get up in the dark and wait at the window to see the paper boy."

"Always men?"

Ella nodded. "They hadn't invented women yet, then," she said.

Ann stretched out flat on the floor and raised first one purple leg, pointing her toes at the ceiling, then the other.

"What were you when you got married? Nineteen?" she asked.

"Nineteen. Young. Younger than, Christ, fresh eggs. But you know, I wasn't really dumb. I mean Stephen was a really good guy, I mean a prince. You probably only remember him after he was drinking."

"I remember your wedding."

"Oh Christ yes, when you were flower girl."

"And that little fart son of Aunt Marie's was ring bearer, and we got into a fight."

"Oh God yes, and Marie started crying and saying she never thought to have people in the *family* who were *minorities*, and Mom got mad and said why not call Bill a spick straight out then, and Marie did, she started yelling, 'A spick then! A spick then!' And she had hysterics, and Bill's brother the vet got her squiffed in the vestry. No wonder things went wrong with a start like that. But I did want to say about Steve, he was a really, really bright, lovely guy. See, I can't say that to Duffy. It would just hurt her for no reason. She isn't very secure. But sometimes I need to say it, to be fair to him, and to myself. Because it was so unfair what being alcoholic did to him. And you know, I had to finally just get out and run. And for me that was OK, it's worked out fine. But I think of how he started out and how he ended up, and it, I don't know, it isn't fair."

"You ever hear from him any more?"

Ella shook her head. "I've been thinking the last year or so he's probably dead," she said in the same quiet voice. "He was down so far. But I won't ever know."

"Was he the only guy you went with seriously?"

Ella nodded one nod.

After a while, looking at her pink-feathered feet, she said, "Sex with a drunk is not the biggest turn-on. I don't guess anybody but Duffy could of got through to me, maybe." She blushed, a delicate but vivid pink appearing suddenly in her rather sallow cheeks and fading slowly. "Duffy's a very kind person," she said.

"I like her," Ann said.

Ella sighed. She slid her feet out of the feathered mules, letting them drop to the floor, and curled herself up on the couch. "What is this, true confession time?" she said. "I was wanting to ask you how come you didn't want to stay with the baby's father, was he a jerk or something."

"Oh God."

"I'm sorry."

"No. It's just embarrassing to say. Todd's seventeen. Eighteen by now, I guess. One of my Computer Programming students." Ann sat up and bowed her head down to her knees, stretching tension out of her back and hiding her face, then sat up straight; she was smiling.

"Does he know?"

"Nope."

"Did you think about an abortion at all?"

"Oh, yeah. But see. It was me that was careless. So I wondered, why was I careless? And I wanted to quit teaching anyhow. And get out of Riverside. I want to stay around the Bay here and get work. Temping to start with, till I find what I want. I can always find a job, that's no problem for me. I want to get into programming eventually, and maybe consulting. I can have the baby and then go back part time. And I want to live alone with the baby and kind of take my time. Because I kept sort of rushing into everything, you know? But what I think is I'm a maternal type, actually, more than a wife type or a lover type."

"Could take some finding out," Ella said.

"Well, that's why I want to sort of slow down. But I'll tell you my long-range plans. I'll find this executive, fifty, fifty up, maybe sixty up, and marry him. Mommy marries Daddy, see?" She bowed her head to her knees again and came up smiling.

"Dumb, dumb, dumb," Ella said. "Dumb shit sister. You can leave the baby here on your honeymoon."

"With Auntie Ella."

"And Uncle Duffy. Christ. I haven't seen Duffy with a baby."

"Is Duffy her real name?"

"She'd kill me if she knew I told you. Marie."

"Cross my heart."

They unfolded and refolded various sections of the paper, leafed slowly. Ann looked at pictures of resorts in the Northern Coast Range, read advertisements from travel agencies, fly to Hawaii, cruise Alaska.

"What ever happened to that little fart son of Aunt Marie's, anyhow?"

"Wayne. He got some degree in Business Administration at UCLA."

"It figures."

"What are you? Pisces?"

"I think so."

"It says this is a good day for you to make long-range plans, and look out for an important Scorpio. That's your sugar daddy, I guess."

"No, what's November, is that Scorpio?"

"Yeah. Till the twenty-fourth, it says."

"OK, that's this long-range plan in here. I'll look out for it. . . ."

After a pause Ella, reading, said, "Seventeen."

"*All* right," Ann said, reading.

MIRRORING

The lower edge of the lawn above the riverbank was planted in red cannas. Beyond that intense color the river was gunbarrel blue. Both the red line and the blue reflected in Stephen's mirror-finish sun glasses, moving up and down across the surface and seeming to change the expression of his face incomprehensibly. Todd looked away from this display with an irritable turn of the head. Stephen asked at once, "What's wrong?"

"I wish you didn't wear mirror shades."

"See yourself reflected in them?" Smiling, Stephen slowly took the glasses off. "Is that so bad?"

"What I see is all these colors running across your face like some robot in the movies. Mirror shades are like aggressive, you know? Black dudes coming on cool. Hank Williams Junior."

"If you're behind them, they're defensive. Soft-bodied animal hiding. Protective mimicry. I bought them for this trip." Stephen's face without the glasses did look soft, not doughy or rubbery but soft-finished like stone or wood long used, worn down to fineness. All the lines that etched his face were fine, and the cut of lip and nostril and eyelid was delicate but blurred by that softening, that abrasion of years. Todd looked down at his own big, smooth hands and knees and thighs with a sense of self-consciousness that sharpened to discomfort. He looked back at Stephen's hands holding the sun glasses.

"No, you're right," Stephen said, "they're aggressive." He was holding them so that the curved, insectile planes reflected his own face and behind it the white facade of the hotel against the dark mountain. "I see you—you don't see me. . . . But I want to look at you all the time. And with these on, I can do just that. And you don't have to see as much of me."

"I like seeing you," Todd said, but Stephen was fitting the glasses back across his face.

"Now I can be contemplating the river, for all *they* know, while all the time inside here I'm actually staring, staring, staring at you, trying to get my fill. . . . I don't believe you. I can't believe you. That you came. That you wanted to come. That you wanted to give me this incredible gift. I have to wear these when I look at you. You are nineteen years old. I could go blind. You don't have to say anything. Letting me say these things is your gift to me. Part of your gift to me." When he wore the mirroring glasses his voice was smoother, softer, deflecting answers.

Todd said doggedly, "The giving goes the other way too. Mostly, in fact."

"No, no, no," Stephen murmured. "Nothing. Nothing."

"All this?" Todd looked around at the red cannas, the white hotel, the dark ridges, the river.

"All this," Stephen repeated. "Plus Miz Gertrude and Miz Alice B. My God, those women follow us like reflections in a funnyhouse. Don't look!"

Todd was already looking over his shoulder to see the two women coming up the path between the lawns from the river. The old one was in the lead and the young one a good ways behind her, carrying fishing poles. Seeing him turn, the old one held up a couple of good-sized trout and called out something ending with "breakfast!"

Todd nodded and made a V for Victory sign.

"They catch fish," Stephen murmured. "They beach whales. They play five-card stud. They fell giant sequoias. They deploy missiles. They gut bears. Only please God let them stay busy and leave us alone! A fish-waving bull dyke is more than I can cope with just now. Tell me that they're going away."

"They're going away."

"Good. Good." The curved black surfaces turned again, canna-red flashing across them. "They'll have vacated the rowboat we were hoping for, presumably. Shall we go on the river?"

"Sure." Todd stood up.

"Do you want to, Tadziu?"

Todd nodded.

"You do whatever I ask or suggest. You should do what *you* like. Your pleasure is my pleasure."

"Let's go."

"Let's go," Stephen repeated, smiling, standing up.

On the lazy water of the lake above the dam, Todd shipped the oars and slid down to lie with his back against the seat.

Behind him Stephen's husky voice sang in a whisper, "*Dans les jardins de mon père . . .*" and then, after a silence, spoke softly aloud:

> "*Ame, te souvient-il, au fond du paradis,*
> *De la gare d'Auteuil, et des trains de jadis?*"

"No assignments on spring break," Todd said.

"No one could translate it in any case."

Todd felt Stephen's finger like a feather caress the outer rim of his left ear, once.

It was completely silent on the water. On his lips Todd tasted the salt of his sweat from rowing. Behind him Stephen sitting in the prow made no sound, said nothing.

"One of them left a fly box under the seat here," Todd said, looking down at it.

"Under no circumstances take it to them. I'll turn it in at the hotel desk. Or drop it overboard. It's the excuse they've been waiting for. It's a plant. Oh how kind of you we've just been dying to talk to you and your father and I'm Alice B and this is Gertie and isn't this place just bully for all us boys? It's called the dyke bursting."

Todd laughed. Again the feather touch went round his ear, and he laughed again, repressing a shudder of pleasure.

All he could see as he half lay in the boat was colorless sky and one long sunlit ridge.

"You know," he said, "I think actually you've got them wrong. The girl was talking last night to that girl Marie that cooks, you know? On the terrace, when I went out to smoke a joint, last night late, you know. And she was telling her she came here with her mother, because her brother died, and her mother had been nursing him, or something, like he was sick for a long time or like brain damaged or something. So when he died she wanted to bring her mother up here for a rest and like a change. So actually they'd be mother and daughter. I looked in the registration book when I came in and it said Ella Sanderson and Ann Sanderson."

The silence behind him continued. He tipped his head back and back till he could see Stephen's face upside down, the black sun glasses mirroring the sky.

"Does it matter?" Stephen's voice said, terribly melancholy.

"No."

Todd lifted his head and looked across the colorless water at the colorless sky beyond where the ridges narrowed in the dam.

"It doesn't matter at all," he said.

"I could sink the boat now," the sorrowful, tender voice behind him said. "Like a stone."

"OK."

"You understand . . . ?"

"Sure. This is the center. Like which is water and which is sky. So sinking's flying. It doesn't matter. At the center. Go on."

After a long time Todd sat back up on the seat, reset the oars, and began rowing in long, quiet strokes away from the lip of the dam. He did not look around.

EARTHWORKS

Ann's father had recently made a pond from a spring below the ranch house, and after lunch they walked down to see it. Horses grazed on the high, bare, golden hill on the far side of the water. From the rainy-season highwater line the banks were bare and muddy down to the summer level, making a reddish rim. A rowboat, looking oversized, was pulled up beside the tiny dock. They sat on the dock, in bathing suits, dangling their feet in the tepid water. They were too full of food and wine to want to swim yet. Although the baby did not yet crawl and was sound asleep anyhow, the knowledge that he was sleeping with water a foot or two away on either side of him was a dim unease in Ann's mind, making her look round at him quite frequently and keep one hand touching the flannel blanket he lay on. To hide her overprotectiveness or to excuse it from herself, each time she looked round at the baby she readjusted the cotton shirt which she had taken off and tented up over him to protect his head from the sun.

"Now," said her father, "I want to know about your life. The place you live. The woman you live with. Start there."

"Ground floor of an old house in San Pablo. Two bedrooms, and a walk-in closet for Toddie's room. Old Japanese couple have the upstairs. The neighborhood's a little rough but there's a lot of nice people, and our block is OK. OK? Then Marie. She's gay, but we're not living together. It's actually Toddie she was interested in."

"Jesus!"

"I mean, she wanted to help parent a baby." Ann broke into a laugh that was both genuine and nervous. "She does computer programming and counselling, so she works at home a lot. It works out really well for care-sharing. The way it works out with her and me, we each have a wife."

"Great," Stephen said.

"I mean, you know, a person you can count on to sort of take over if you can't. And do the shitwork, and you know."

"Not my experience of wives," her father said. "So you've given up on men, then."

"No. Like I said, Marie and I aren't together. She has lesbian friends, a lot of my friends are straight, but just now, I don't know, I'm just not into that a whole lot. I will again, you know. It's not like I'm bitter or anything. I wanted to have the baby. I just want to be with him mainly at this point. The job's weird hours, but that means when I'm out Marie's there, and mostly when he's awake, I'm there. So it's real good now. And later it'll change. . . ."

As she spoke she felt in her father, sitting a foot or two from her, a physical resistance, a great impatience; she felt it physically as a high, hard, slanting blade, like the blade of a bulldozer. The owner of the land had the right to clear it, to clear out this underbrush of odd jobs, half-couplings, rented closets, hiding places, makeshifts. The blade advanced.

"Since Penny and I divorced I've done a lot of stock-taking. Sitting right here. Or riding Dolly over there around the ranch." Her father was looking across the pond at the high hill as he spoke, watching the grazing mare and colt and the white gelding. "Thinking about both my marriages. Especially about the first one, strangely enough. I began to see that I didn't ever work through the whole thing before I married Penny. I never really handled the pain your mother caused me. I denied it. Macho, tough guy—real men don't feel pain. You can keep up that crap for years. But it finally catches up with you. And then you realise all you've done is save your shit to drown in. So I've been doing the work I should have done ten, twelve years ago. And some of it's almost too late. I have to face the fact that I wasted a lot of those years, wasted a marriage. Started it and ended it in all the unfinished business from the first marriage. Well, OK. Win one, lose one. What I'm doing now is establishing priorities. What's important. What comes first. And doing that, I've been able to see what my mistake, my one real mistake, was. You know what it was?"

He looked at her so keenly with his clear, light-blue eyes that she flinched. He waited, smiling slightly, alert.

"Divorcing Mama, I guess," she said, looking down and swallowing the words because she knew they were wrong. He did not speak, and she looked back at him. He was still smiling, and she thought what a handsome man he was, looking like a Roman general now with his short-cropped hair and silver-blue eyes, long lips and eagle nose, but wearing a Plains Indian beaded talisman on a rawhide cord about his neck. He was very deeply tanned. On his ranch in summer he wore nothing but shorts and thong sandals, or went naked.

"That was no mistake," he said. "That was one of the right things I did. And buying this place. I had to move *on*. And Ella isn't willing, isn't able to go on, to act, move, develop. Her strength is in staying put. God, what strength! But it's all in that. So the shit piles up around her, and she never clears it away. Hell, she builds walls of it! Fecal fortifications. Defending her from, God forbid, change. From, God forbid, freedom . . . I had to break out of her fortress. I was suffocating. Buried alive. I tried to take her with me. She wouldn't come. Wouldn't move. Ella never had any use for freedom, her own or anybody else's. And I was so desperate for it by then that I'd take it on any terms. So that's where I made my mistake."

She felt remiss at still not understanding what his mistake had been, but he said nothing, and she was obliged to admit it: "I guess I don't know what mistake," she said, feeling as she said it that it must have something to do with her, and oppressed by the feeling. She glanced over her shoulder at the sleeping baby.

"Leaving you," her father said quietly. "Not putting up a fight for custody."

She knew that this was very important to him and ought to be so to her, but all she felt was that she was being crowded, pushed along by the slanting, uprooting blade, and she looked back again at the baby and moved the shirttail unnecessarily to shade his legs.

"A little late to think about that, she thinks," her father's voice said gently.

"Oh, I don't know. Anyhow we got to see each other every summer," she said, blushing red.

The blade moved forward, levelling and making clear. "I needed freedom in order to go on living, and I saw you as part of the jail. Part of Ella. I *literally* didn't separate you from her—you see? She didn't allow that possibility even as an idea. You were her, you were her motherhood, and she was the Great Mother. She had you built right into the walls. And I bought that. Maybe if you'd been a boy I'd have seen what was going on sooner. I'd have felt my part in you, my claim—my right to get you out of the shitfort, the earthworks. *My* right to assert *your* right to freedom. You see? But I didn't see it. I didn't look. I just got loose and left you as hostage. It's taken me twelve years to be able to admit that. I want you to know that I do admit it now."

Ann picked a foxtail from the corner of the baby's blanket by her hip. "Yeah, well," she said. "I guess it worked out OK, anyhow, you know, Mom and me, and anyhow Penny didn't want some teen-age stepdaughter around all the time."

"If I'd fought for you and won custody—and if I'd fought I'd have won—what Penny wanted or didn't want would have been a matter of supreme indifference. I probably wouldn't have married her. One mistake leads to the next one. You'd have lived here. All your summers here. Gone to a good school. And a four-year college, maybe an Eastern school, Smith or Vassar. And you wouldn't be living with a lesbian in San Pablo, working nights for a phone company. I'm not blaming you, I'm blaming myself. I can't believe how true to form Ella is, how unchangingly unchanging—how she dug you in, walled you into the same dirt, the same futureless trap. What kind of future does your life spell for your kid, Ann?"

But I was really lucky to get the job, Ann thought, but what's neat is that for a while things aren't changing all the time, but you haven't even seen Mom for ten years so how do you know? All these thoughts were mere shadows and underbrush, among which her mind hopped like a rabbit.

"Well," she said, "things are really OK the way they worked out," and, unable to control her increasing anxiety about Toddie, she turned away from her father and knelt above the sleeping baby, pretending that he had waked up. "All right then! Up you come! Hey baby bunny boy.

Hey you sleepy bunny." The baby's head wobbled, his eyes looked in different directions, and as soon as she settled him on her lap he fell fast asleep again. His small, warm, neat weight gave her substance. She stirred the lake with her toes and said, "You shouldn't worry about it, Daddy. I'm really happy. I just wish you were, if you aren't."

"You're happy," he said, with one glance of his light eyes, the almost scornfully accurate touch she remembered, that reversed the poles.

"Yes, I am," she said. "But there's one thing I wanted to tell you about."

While she summoned up words, Stephen said, with satisfaction in his acuteness, "I thought so. The father's back in the picture."

"No," Ann said vaguely, not heeding. "Well, see, they think at the clinic that Toddie had some brain damage, probably at birth. That's why he's slow developing in some ways. We noticed it pretty soon. They can't tell how much yet, and they think it isn't real severe. But they know there's some impairment." She drew her fingertip very lightly around the tiny pink curve of the baby's ear. "So. That's taken some, you know, thinking. Getting used to. It's not as big a deal as I thought. But it is, in some ways."

"What are you doing about it?"

"There isn't anything to do. Now. Sort of wait and see. And watch. He's only five months. They noticed a—"

"What are you doing about correcting it?"

"There isn't anything like that to do."

"You're just going to take this?"

She was silent.

"Ann, this is my grandson."

She nodded.

"Don't cut me out. You may be angry at the father, but don't take it out on men, don't join the castraters, for God's sake! Let me help. Let me get some competent doctors, let's get some light on this. Don't dig down into a hole with all these fears and old wives' tales, and smother the kid with them. I don't accept this. Not on the word of some midwife at this women's clinic that botched the kid's birth! My God, Ann! You can't take this out on *him!* There are things that can be done!"

"I've taken him to Permanente," Ann said.

"Shit! Permanente! You need first-class doctors, specialists, neurologists—Bill can give us some recommendations. I'll get onto it when we go back to the house. I'll call him. My God. This is what I meant! This is it. This is what I left you in—the mud—My God! how could you sit here all day with him and me and *not tell me?*"

"It isn't your fault, Daddy."

"Yes," he said, "it is. Exactly. If I—"

She interrupted. "It's the way he is. And there's a best way for him to be, like anybody. And that's what we can do, is find that. So please don't talk shit about 'correcting.' Look, I'd like to have a swim now, I think. Will you hold him?"

She saw that he was startled, even frightened, but he said nothing. She carefully transferred the rosy, sweaty, silky baby onto his thin thighs covered with sparse sun-bleached hairs. She saw his large, fine hand cup the small head. She got up then and went three steps to the end of the little dock and stood on the weather-gnawed grey planks. The water was shallow, and she did not dive but splashed down in, her feet tangling for a moment in slimy weeds. She swam. Ten or fifteen yards out she turned, floated awhile, trod water to look back at the dock. Stephen sat motionless in the flood of sunlight, his head bowed over the baby, whom she could not even see in the shadow of her father's body.   ·

THE PHOTOGRAPH

As she was scrubbing out the kitchen sink, where she had let bleaching powder stand to whiten the old rust stains, Ella saw that the girl from the complex was talking with Stephen. She rinsed out the sink, got her dark glasses from the kitchen oddments drawer, polished them a bit with the dishtowel, put them on, and went out into the back yard.

Stephen was weeding the vegetable plot by the fence, and the girl was standing on the other side of the fence, just her head and shoulders showing. She had her baby in one of those kangaroo things that mashed it up against its mother's front. It was asleep, nothing visible but the tiny sleek head like a kitten's back. Stephen was working, his head bent down as usual, and didn't seem to be paying attention to the girl, but just as she came out, before the screen door banged, Ella heard him say, "Green beans."

The girl looked up and said, "Oh, hi, Mrs. Hoby!" in a bright voice. Stephen kept his head bent down at his weeding.

Ella came over to the laundry roundabout and felt the clothes she had hung out earlier in the afternoon. Stephen's T-shirts and her yellow wash dress were dry already, but Stephen's jeans were still damp, as she had expected; feeling them was nothing but an excuse for coming out.

"You sure have a nice garden," the girl said.

The complex of eight apartments they had built next door ten years ago had nothing but cement and garages behind it where the Pannis's garden with the big jacaranda had been. There was no place for a child to play there. But before the baby was old enough the girl would have moved on, the welfare-and-food-stamp people never stayed, the men with no jobs and the girls with no husbands, playing their big radio-tape machines loud and smoking dope at night in those hot little apartments.

"Stephen and I know each other from the store," the girl said. "He carried my groceries home for me last week. That was a nice thing to do. I had the baby, and my arms were just about falling off."

Stephen laughed his "huh-huh," not looking up.

"Have you lived here for a long time?" the girl asked. Ella was rehanging the jeans, for something to do. She answered after she had got the seams matched. "My brother has lived here all his life. This is his house."

"It is? That's neat," the girl said. "All his *life*? That's amazing! How old are you, Stephen?"

Ella thought he would not answer, and it might serve the girl right, but after a considerable pause he said, "Four. Forty-four."

"Forty-four years right here? That's wonderful. It's a nice house, too."

"It was," Ella said. "It was all single-family houses when we were children here." She spoke dryly, but she had to admit that the girl did not mean to patronise, and was pleasant, the way she talked right to Stephen instead of across him the way most people did, or else they shouted at him as if he were deaf, which he was only slightly, in the right ear.

Stephen stood up, dusted off his knees carefully, and went across the grass and into the house, hooking the screen door shut behind him with his foot.

Ella had sat down on the small cement base of the laundry round-about to pull at a dandelion clump in the grass. It had been there for years, always coming back. You had to get every single piece of root of a dandelion, and the roots went under the cement.

"Did I hurt his feelings?" the girl asked, shifting the baby in its carrier.

"No," Ella said. "He's probably getting a photograph to show you. Of the house."

"I really like him," the girl said. Her voice was low and a little husky, with a break in it, like some children's voices. What they used to call a whiskey voice, only childlike. The poor thing was not much more than a child. Babies having babies, they had said on the television.

"Have you always lived here too, Mrs. Hoby?"

Ella worked at the dandelion root, loosening it, then took off her sun glasses and looked round at the girl. "My husband and I ran a resort hotel," she said. "Up in the redwood country, on a river. A very old place, built in the eighteen eighties, quite well known. We owned it for twenty-seven years. When my husband passed away I ran it for two more years. Then when my mother passed away and left the house to Stephen, I decided to retire and come live here with him. He has never lived with strangers. He's fifty-four, not forty-four. Numbers confuse him sometimes."

The girl listened intently. "Did you have to sell the resort? Do you still own it?"

"I sold it," Ella said.

"What was it like?"

"A big country hotel, up north. Twenty-six rooms. High ceilings. A terraced dining room over the river. We had to modernise the kitchens and the plumbing entirely when we bought it. There used to be places like that. Elegant. Before the motels. People came for a week, or a month. Some people, families and single people, came every summer or fall for years. They made their reservation for the next year before they left. We offered fishing, good trout fishing, and horseback riding, and mountain walks. It was called The Old River Inn. It's mentioned in several books.

The present owners call it a 'bed and breakfast.'" Ella dug her fingers in under the dandelion root, sinewy there in its dirt darkness, and pried. It broke. She should have got the weeder or the garden fork.

"What an amazing kind of thing to do," the girl said, "running a place like that." Ella could have told her that they had never had a vacation themselves for a quarter of a century and that the hotel had worn her out and finally killed Bill and eaten up their lives for nothing, mortgaged and remortgaged and the payments from the bed and breakfast people not even enough to live on here, but because there was a break or a catch in the girl's voice that sounded as if she saw the forest ridges and the Inn on its lawns above the river as Ella saw it, as the old, noble, beautiful, remote thing, she said only, "It was hard work," but smiled a little as she said it.

Stephen came out of the house and straight across the grass, glancing up once at the girl and then down again at the picture he held. It was the framed photograph of Mama and Papa on the porch of the house, the year they bought it, and Ella in her pinafore dress sitting on the top front step, and Baby Stephen sitting in the pram. The girl took it and looked at it for quite a time.

"That's Mama. That's Papa. That's Ella. That's me, the baby," he said, and laughed quietly, "huh-huh!"

The girl laughed too and sniffled and wiped her nose and her eyes quite openly. "Look how little all the trees are!" she said. "You've been doing a lot of gardening since they took that picture, I guess." She handed it carefully back across the fence to Stephen. "Thank you for showing it to me," she said, and her little whiskey voice was so sad that Ella turned her head away and scraped her nails in the dirt trying to seize the broken root, in vain, till the girl had gone, because there was nothing to say to her but what she knew already.

THE STORY

Ann sat erect in the white-painted iron chair on the little flagged terrace behind the house. She wore white, and was barefoot. The old abelia bushes behind her, above the terrace, were in full flower. Her child sat among scattered plastic toys on the edge of the terrace where it met the lawn, near her. Ella looked at them from the kitchen window, through the yellow metal blinds that were slanted to send the hot afternoon light upward to the ceiling, making the low room glow like the wax of a lighted beeswax candle. Todd moved the toys about, but she could not see a pattern in the way he moved or placed them; they did not seem to relate to each other. He did not talk when he picked up one or another. There was no story being told. He dropped an animal figure and picked up a broken-off dandelion flower, dropped it. Only from time to time he made a humming or droning noise, loud enough that Ella could hear it pretty clearly, a rhythmic, nasal sound, "Anh-hanh, anh-hanh, hanh . . ." When he was making this music of his he swayed or rocked a little and his face, half hidden by thick glasses, brightened and relaxed. He was a pretty child.

His mother, Ann, was very beautiful there in the sunlight, her pale skin shining with sweat, her dark hair loose and bright against the shadow and the small, pale, creamy flowers of the abelia. Had she given promise of such beauty? Ella had thought her rather plain as a child, but then she had held herself back from the child, not looking for her beauty, knowing that if she found it all it meant was losing it, since Stephen and Marie came West so seldom, and after the divorce Marie never wanted to send the child alone. Three or four years would pass when she never saw Ann. And a grandchild's life goes by so fast, faster than a child's.

Stephen had been a pretty child, now! People had stopped her to admire him in his little blue and white suit in the pram, or when he was walking and held her hand and walked with her down to the old Cash and Carry Market. His blue eyes were so bright and clear, and his fair hair curled all over his head. And that innocent look some little boys have, that trusting look, he had kept that so long, right into his teens, really. And how Stephen had told stories when he was this child's age! From morning till night there had been some tale going, till it drove her crazy sometimes, Stephen babbling softly away at table, anywhere, telling his unending saga about the Wood Dog and what was it?—the Puncha. The Puncha, and other characters he had made up out of his head. They didn't have the TV then, or the bright plastic toys, soldiers and tanks and monsters. While they lived up on the ranch, Stephen had had no playmates at all, unless Shirley brought her girls over for the day. So he told his endless adventures, which Ella could never understand, playing with a toy car or two and bits of mill ends for blocks, or an old spool, wooden the way spools were, and wooden clothespins, and the little husky monotone voice: "So they went up there rrrrrm, rrrrrm, rrrrrm, and they were waiting there, so they went along there, rrrrrm, rrrrrm, so then the road stopped and they fell off, they fell down, down, down, help help where's Puncha?" And so on and on like that, even in his bed at night.

"Stephen?"

"Yes Mama!"

"Hush now and go to sleep!"

"I *am* asleep, Mama!" Virtuous indignation. She hid her laugh. She tiptoed to the door, and in a minute the little voice would begin to whisper again: "So then they said Let's go to the, to the lake. So there was this boat on the lake and so then Wood Dog started sinking, crash, splash, help help where's Puncha? Here I am Wood Dog. . . ." Then at last a small yawn. Then silence.

Where did all that go? What happened to it? The funny little boy making everything in the world into his story, he never would have understood any story about a telephone company executive recently married for the third time whose only child by his first marriage was sitting now in the white chair watching her only child by no marriage rock back and forth restlessly and endlessly, droning his music of one nasal syllable.

"Ann," Ella said, lifting the slatted blind, "diet cola or lemonade?"

"Lemonade, Grandmother."

What became of it? she asked again, getting the ice out of the refrigerator, getting the glasses down from the cupboard. Why didn't the story make sense? Such hope she had had for Stephen, so sure he would do something noble. Not a word people used, and of course it was silly to expect a happy ending. Would it have been better to be like poor young Ann, who had no hope or pride beyond the most austere realism—"He won't be fully self-sufficient, but his dependence level can be reduced a good deal. . . ." Was it better, more honest, to tell only very short stories, like that? Were all the others mere lies, romances?

She put the two tall tumblers and the plastic cup on a tray, filled them with ice and lemonade, then clicked her tongue at herself in disgust, took the ice out of Todd's cup, and refilled it with plain lemonade. She put four animal crackers in a row on the tray and carried it out, batting the screen door shut behind her with her foot. Ann stood up and took the tray from her and set it down on the wobbly iron table, its curlicues clogged solid with years of repainting with white enamel, but still rusting through in spots.

"Can someone have the cookies?" Ella inquired softly.

"Oh, yes," Ann said. "Oh, very much yes, Todd. Look what's here. Look what Grandmother brought you!"

The thick little glasses peered round. The child got up and came to the table.

"Grandmother will give you a cookie, Todd," the young mother said, clear and serious.

The child stood still.

Ella picked up an animal cracker. "Here you are, sweetie," she said. "It's a tiger, I do believe. Here comes the tiger, walking to you." She walked the cracker across the tray, hopped it over the edge of the tray, and walked it onto the table's edge. She was not sure the four-year-old was watching.

"Take it, Todd," the mother said.

Slowly the child raised his open hand towards the table.

"Hop!" Ella said, hopping the tiger into the hand.

Todd looked at the tiger and then at his mother.

"Eat it, Todd. It's very good."

The child stood still, the cracker lying on his palm. He looked at it again. "Hop," he said.

"That's right! It went Hop! right to Toddie!" Ella said. Tears came into her eyes. She walked the next cracker across the tray. "This one is a pig. It can go Hop! too, Toddie. Do you want it to go Hop?"

"Hop!" the child said.

It was better than no story at all.

"Hop!" said the great-grandmother.

Record of First Publication

About the Author

Ursula K. Le Guin is one of the finest writers of our time. Her books have attracted millions of devoted readers and won many awards, including the National Book Award, the Hugo and Nebula Awards and a Newbury Honor. Among her novels, *The Left Hand of Darkness*, *The Dispossessed* and the six books of Earthsea have attainged undisputed classic status; and her recent series, the Annals of the Western Shore, has wond her the PEN Center USA Children's literature award and the Nebula Award for best novel. She lives in Portland, Oregon.